Unseen Unsung

Hilary Custance Green has a passion for both music and language. Her first novel, *A Small Rain*, explored the consolations of poetry and music in times of grief, sickness and joy. *Unseen Unsung* also reaches for music to shore up sanity against the random arrows of the world.

After taking a degree in Fine Arts and Music, Hilary went to St Martin's in London to study Sculpture. For twenty years she practised sculpture, married and brought up two children. She then studied cognitive psychology with the Open University and followed this with a PhD at Cambridge. She finds scientific writing and fiction benefit from being bedfellows. Her novels celebrate the small kindnesses that allow us to survive the larger troubles of this world.

First published in 2008
Threadgold Press

ISBN 978-0-9560127-0-8
Copyright © Hilary Custance Green 2008

A CIP catalogue for this book is available from the British Library

Cover design by Anthony Furness
Typeset by Anthony Furness

Printed and bound by CPI Antony Rowe, Eastbourne

Threadgold Press, PO Box 1138, Cambridge CB21 4WB
threadgoldpress@waitrose.com
www.unseen-unsung.com

Unseen Unsung

Hilary Custance Green

Threadgold Press

Acknowledgements

Two people, Sian Miller and Paul Beck, travelled with me chapter by chapter as I wrote *Unseen Unsung*. To their honesty and insight I owe this book's existence.

For guidance in the early stages thanks go to fellow members of writewords.org.uk and Bernie Ross. Thanks for help with understanding the life of an opera singer go to Gini Wray, Catharine Hancock and Olivia Ray. My thanks also go to Sarah Peters who stopped me from making foolish errors (any errors left are mine). Kevin Symonds always found answers to my queries. Mark Boulton gave me a significant name.

To the readers of drafts, Eleanor and Amy Green, Anthony, Emma and Mathilda Furness, Jenifer Roberts, Lis Hill, Hedwig Gockel, Karalyn Patterson, Tricia Stileman, Alan Blackwell and Helen Arnold thanks are due for suggestions and encouragement. Cornerstones Literary Consultants gave me invaluable critical feedback.

I am deeply indebted to Anthony Furness for leading me with skill and patience through the intricacies of getting into print.

My husband, Edwin's, unfailing grace in the face of repeated questions, and his ability to see the funny side of events made the whole enterprise possible.

1

London: Luca

Luca stopped shouting, not because someone had moved the weight off his chest but because his voice had been stolen; snatched out of his mouth and silenced before it reached his ears. Or perhaps it was the other way round, perhaps his ears ...? Not deaf, surely not deaf?

He lay rigid, ears aching, willing himself to hear the feathers rustling in his pillow. Nothing. He tried to touch his ears. Nothing moved. Then faintly, through the walls, came voices singing.

Not deaf then.

Thick, dry air pressed down on his face. Something heavier than a duvet lay on his chest. He took a breath and held it, listening again. No singing this time, but in the distance familiar sirens wailed. He concentrated on his fingertips; under them lay something familiar. The ridge of seam on his jeans? Between one heartbeat and the next, he was awake, his body shaking and all sound obliterated by the drumming in his chest.

The voices again; not singing, but crying. 'Mama? Dad? Mama? Dad?' Then, nearby, the screeching of furniture dragged across a bare floor. Luca opened his mouth to call out, but could only cough. Dusty grit filled his throat. He spat and retched, suddenly furious. He had never planned to be this uncomfortable. Someone had got it wrong.

Opening and closing his eyes, he found only darkness and with it the smell of old earth. Underneath him lay wood or – he scratched with his fingertips – tough carpet perhaps? A solid object lay across his chest pinning his arms to his side. He lifted his head, suddenly the weight of a cannonball, to wipe his mouth on his shoulder and groaned. Far away an animal gnawed at his ankle, the pain travelling in sudden snatches through his limbs.

The distant whimper began again. 'Mama? Dad?'

Pushing his chest against the weight that lay on it, he filled his lungs and bellowed: 'Is anyone there?' Silence. Into its emptiness crept the notion that he had made a fool of himself. In more moderate tones he called out, 'Hello! Can I help?' A burning sensation shot from ear to hairline as he tried to move his head.

'Da-ad?'

'No, sorry, I'm Luca – Luke.' Silence. He raised his voice a notch. 'My name's Luke. I'm stuck. Can you move at all?'

'Ssh! Don't speak so loudly! Yes I can move a bit; I'm frightened of things falling.'

Luke listened, distracted by the strange timbre of the acoustics, both clanging and flat. Things falling? Not speak loudly? What kind of room was this that failed to resonate normally? At least the voice sounded like an adult, not the child he'd been imagining. Would she be strong enough to release him?

Her muted shout came again. 'Hello? Luke? Say something and I'll try and find you.' She added, as if needing reassurance, 'It *is* dark isn't it?'

'Yes, *totally*!'

'Oh!' Several seconds passed. 'Can't you see *anything*?'

'No. Can you?'

Another pause. She laughed softly, disconcertingly. 'No, I can't see a thing either. Keep talking. I can't come fast because of the glass.'

He was silent, dragging his mind from the pleasing quality of her laughter to the confusing statement about glass. 'Glass? What do you mean?'

'Well . . . it's all over the floor – the glass from the windows. I don't want to cut myself. At least things seem to have stopped falling now.'

'What happened to the windows?'

After a moment, her voice came again, hesitating between a shout and a whisper. 'Don't you know? I suppose they broke when the explosions came.'

Explosions? He reached into his memory but, like the sky meeting the sea, nothing emerged. 'Where *are* we?' His voice pitched a shade higher than he expected.

'I'm not sure. The waiting area has gone.'

The echo of her voice reminded Luke of the tomato packing warehouse where he worked. What did she mean, *waiting*? 'What waiting area? I mean what was it in?'

'Don't you remember? The post office.'

'No . . . Yes. I'm not sure. I think I may have been asleep or . . .

What post office?'

He twisted his neck to orient himself to the sounds of her approach then gasped at the pinching pain in his forehead.

She called out, 'Keep talking so I know I'm heading the right way.'

Luke took a breath and the dust caught again at his throat. He hesitated. 'I don't really like to, the dust is a problem for me.'

'What's that? The *dust* is hurting you?'

'No, just my vocal cords.' He was astonished to hear another spurt of laughter.

'Sorry . . . I don't mean to be rude. I wouldn't worry about your cords. I'd settle for getting out alive.' He flushed in the dark; people never understand about a singer's throat. His mind flipped to a smoky pub and a girl – Penny, or was it Pam – lighting a cigarette and blowing smoke in his face. With this image, his mind drifted out of the present.

A startled cry from the girl jerked him back. Luke called out, 'Are you all right? Did you hurt yourself? I'm sorry I can't come and help; I'm stuck – tied down, I think.

'I'm all right, but I can't get through this way.' He felt a moment's impatience. She went on, 'I think I've just . . . I think there's a person here . . . I think it's a dead person.'

A dead person? He didn't really know where to start. The sum of his experience brought inappropriate images to mind: limp birds hanging from the cat's jaws, the body of Christ on the banner of his local church. 'Is the person warm?'

'Not really.'

'Then there's probably nothing you can do to help – Oh God. It's not your . . . it's not someone you know, is it?'

'What? No. No it's not my Mama or Dad.' She sounded strangely certain.

'I should leave it then. Can you find another way through? I may not be much use, but we can talk until . . . ' Until what? He had been in an explosion, or so she said, and he – they – needed rescuing. He listened for sounds suggesting rescue; he could hear only the girl's soft scrabbling. Far away, in another world, machinery hummed and groaned. Here were only brief noises: metal on metal creaks, the whoosh of sand emptying from a cup. And sensations: inhaling air like flour, the cold rap on his knuckles as

7

he knocked at the barrier on his chest.

'Luke?'

The girl sounded much nearer now. He tried to give the exploded structure a mental image, but he could not remember the building in the first place. If you had no rooms, how could the spaces fit together? What if this space was the only one, in the middle of a gigantic heap of rubble? Which post office? What if his voice was affected? He began to sing quietly. His voice sounded as it always had. Calmed by this reconnection with himself, he lifted the volume gradually, concentrating on the sounds, trying to work within the constraint of the burden on his chest.

The girl called out again. 'What's that?'

He had forgotten about her. 'Uh...oh I was just singing – from an opera.'

'Which opera?'

'Il Corsaro.'

'Verdi?'

Amazement silenced him. Most people had never even heard of the opera. Unable to resist, he said, as if he were having a social conversation, 'Yes. I'm singing chorus and cover for Corrado at Buxton.'

She did not respond. Luke felt a wave of unaccustomed misery. She had not been impressed. She might never find a way through to him. He might never sing at Buxton. Tears leaked out of his eyes; warm pools spilling down and cooling as they ran into his ears. He needed to blow his nose. This was totally absurd. He never cried, even on stage: especially not on stage.

The girl's voice, wavery now, came through again. 'Oh no! There's something in the way *here* as well.' He could hear grunting. '*And* I can't shift it. I'll have to try another way, though I suppose there may not be a way through. Please sing again, I liked that.'

In sudden excitement, Luke called out, 'Stop! Stay still! Now speak again. I heard you clearly just then, which way were you facing?'

'I don't know. I was feeling all round when I spoke.'

'OK, feel all round again, but slowly and keep talking.'

'I am...moving...round in...a...'

'That's it! Now go forward.'

Time became unhinged in the dark; her approach went into invisible slow motion. As she sounded closer, they spoke less and less, proximity brought with it both expectation and embarrassment. Thumps and clicks marked her physical passage as she shuffled and crept towards him; little gasps and whimpers her state of mind. Now that she was, so to speak, in the same space, Luke began to feel unsettled. Anticipating a ten-year-old from the early cries, and then a grown woman from her voice and her reactions, his natural reflexes dithered. Her voice implied maturity; a slight imperfection edging a warm tone, like the hint of roughness in good honey. Voices mattered; he could not understand his friends whose choice of girls seemed to be made entirely on appearance. There had been one girl at school with a voice that you wanted to pour out of a jug. He used to hover in the corridor outside her classroom just to hear her say, "Hi Kelly, got'ny gum?".

This girl was quite close now; he could hear the uneven whisper of her breathing, and the tremble in her voice. 'Luke? It is Luke isn't it? Are you under here?' With the use of his name, the atmosphere changed.

Lying in the thick dark, waiting to be touched, his identity wavered between man and child. Heat washed through his body; words spilled out. 'I don't know where I am, I can't move my hands much, I can't reach my face. I don't *know* what's around me.'

'Nearly there, sorry to be slow, but there's glass and all sorts and there's not really a floor or much overhead space just here.' She chuckled, 'I suppose you can't even scratch your nose.'

Reaching his side, she changed character again. 'I'm right next to you now and I'm going to touch you.' Something brushed his neck and then, with a pleasing certainty her hand moved over his head. She stopped.

'You're wet! It could be water, but it might be blood, of course. Does it hurt?'

'No ...' he replied uncertainly. He genuinely didn't know what he was feeling, as if the dark were in his mind as well as outside. With her hands on his face and in his hair, he felt part of a different kind of encounter, one in which he would normally be in control.

Reinforcing this sensation, she said, 'Your hair! It's ... like a

9

seal, all thick and silky. I touched a seal once. Is it all right if I feel over it very gently? Just say if it hurts.'

'Sure. No, it doesn't hurt. I don't seem to feel things the way I usually do. I can't remember where I was or anything. That's nice.' He sighed with pleasure. Her hands were immensely reassuring, and the overstrung feel in his body began to drift off.

Her fingers stopped their movements. 'I think this is blood on the back of your head.'

'Are you sure?'

'Mmm, blood, especially as it clots, feels different from water. It tastes metallic too.'

'Are you a nurse? Or,' (remembering his sister shouting at him for being sexist) 'a doctor?'

'No such luck, I'm afraid. Do you think perhaps you've been unconscious? Maybe you should try and remember facts, like ... I don't know, dates, birthdays. Go ahead. Talk to me while I try and feel this thing lying on top of you.'

'Well, I'm Luca Danford, but everyone calls me Luke – except Mum and my sisters sometimes ...'

'What do they call you?'

He snorted. 'Topo, after some Italian mouse in a Tom and Jerry cartoon ... Mum's family is Italian.'

She laughed. 'My aunt let me watch Tom and Jerry on television when I was little. Go on.'

'Well, what shall I tell you? I'm twenty-eight and ... I'm a singer and ... I've got two sisters, Claudia and Barbara. My dad drives fruit and veg. around Europe ... Birthdays? OK mine's ... Ouch!'

'Sorry! I think we'd better try and move *you* not the things you are stuck under. It could be a doorframe and there's a lumpy metal thing on this side holding it up – one of those things you keep papers in, perhaps? It doesn't feel very ... I don't think it would be a good idea to try and shift it. Is there any room around your legs?'

'Not much, there's something hard close to my right knee. I can move my hands up and down though. Do you think that's a wall I can feel?'

'Maybe. I'm trying to decide whether to push you into the space the other side or pull you into this one.' She sounded reassuringly practical, but his stomach clenched.

'I'd rather be pulled, do you think you can?'

'I can try, anyway.' Crouching behind his head, with her face beside his because of the shortage of headroom, she took hold of him under the shoulders and heaved. A screech of metal on metal and Luke's gasp of pain made her stop immediately. The superstructure creaked and resettled while his body froze helplessly beneath it. Instinctively, the girl scrambled out of reach and he lay rigid for many dragging seconds. Heat spurted between his legs; he had wet himself. As the roaring in his ears subsided he heard panting noises then a scraping sound. She was coming back. He began to breathe again.

Something hard shoved up against his right arm. She gasped, 'I'm going to push ... this thing ... in beside you, in case ... There, that should hold it.' She crept closer, her breathing still ragged, and crouched on his other side. After a while she said firmly. 'Let's just talk, shall we? Until we're rescued, I mean.'

'Ye-es!' An irresistible tremor defied all his years of voice training.

'Do you really not remember any of today?'

'Yes of course I do ... at least ... is it Wednesday? No, no of course not, I saw Claudia just as she came off duty on Wednesday, and that's not today.' He stopped, bewildered by his mind's recalcitrance. It had never before disobeyed his command to state the day and date.

He felt a hand on his sleeve. 'Who's Claudia?'

'My sister – my oldest sister. I wish she were here now; she's just qualified as a doctor. Why can't I remember the day?'

'Don't worry. Shall I tell you?'

'No, let me work it out. I *must* know ... Tell me your name?'

She was silent a moment. Then he heard her soft chuckle. 'It's a funny name – Heloise.'

'Heloise?' He laughed too, 'as in ... Abelard?'

'That's right! How did you know?' Even in the dark he could hear her pleasure.

In fact, the name brought a comforting image to mind of his grandmother sitting on the side of his bed. He smiled to himself.

She repeated, 'How did you know?'

'Oh sorry. My Nonna told me about them when I was little. She used to tell the best stories. She always said it was a shame

11

Verdi hadn't chosen Heloise and Abelard for an opera, because he'd have had a splendid time with all that medieval passion and the church getting their knick ... getting into such a quandary. Though I don't suppose the censors would ever have passed it. When she was little, my Nonna was allowed to read saints' stories during mass. That one was her favourite.'

'Nonna?'

'Yes, my Granny, but she was Italian, so we called her Nonna.'

'Nobody told me the story. I found it in a book when I was little. Mama was very cross when I told her, she said it was not a 'nice' story at all.'

'Then why did they call you Heloise?'

He heard her funny little gasp then she said slowly, 'I don't know ... I've often wondered, but they wouldn't say. They're ... um ... especially religious. They're ...' She stopped abruptly.

Luke could almost hear her wondering if they were still alive and remembering the forlorn "Mama, Dad?" tried to think of something to say. She might have lost both her parents. He still gulped when he thought of his grandmother's death. 'Heloise, how old are you?'

She didn't answer immediately and the whisper when it emerged sounded embarrassed. 'I'm twenty-five, but I ...' She stopped again.

Twenty-five? Surely not. Luke struggled once more to create an image of this girl beside him. Was she fibbing about her age? There was something out of sync. She came over like a difficult score, with strange rhythms and transitions. What if his own perceptions were jumbled?

'Maybe your parents have been rescued.'

'Maybe, but I haven't heard anyone else since ... since it happened. People must have died like that person I touched.'

Luke wanted to reach out to her, but only his head moved. 'Heloise?' (He *did* like her name running softly over his tongue). 'I think you'd better fill me in. I don't really understand what happened. My head feels weird, sort of loose inside, like sand trickling down in one of those egg timers.'

'Really? I'd better check again just to make sure it's not still bleeding somewhere. Just a minute while I see if there is enough room to sit then I can use both hands.' He was aware of her limbs rearranging themselves close to his shoulder. With a little outward breath she settled her knee against his neck. Absurdly, this bony contact gave him a sense of protection. He took a deep breath and snuggled gratefully against her. Realising how childish he felt himself, he wondered if perhaps she was as old as she said. Maybe it was the darkness breeding this dependence and uncertainty.

Heloise took hold of his head, and turned it gently so that his cheek lay in her right hand; she moved the fingers of her left hand methodically over every reachable part of his scalp. Then she turned his head into her left palm and repeated the investigation with her right hand. So peaceful and caressing was her touch that, with the edges of his mouth nestled against the ball of her thumb, he had to stop himself turning to kiss her hand.

She gave a satisfied sigh. 'No, I think it is mostly *dried* blood right at the back, though I think you've got a cut on your forehead too. I can feel something on my palm.' She put his head down on the floor again. And very delicately ran her fingers over his hairline and down to his eyebrows. He gasped as her fingers encountered the area over his right temple. 'Sorry. There's definitely a wound of some kind there. At least it's stopped bleeding now. It may have bled quite a lot in all these hours.'

'Hours! What do you mean?'

'We've been here for hours.'

'But...How do you know?'

'Well ... ' she answered, triumph glowing in her voice, 'I've got a speaking watch. Listen...' A soft female voice intoned "six, thirty-four". 'That's six hours after the bangs'.

'Jesus, that's weird.'

'Well it was a present. And you shouldn't swear.'

He choked down a laugh. 'No, really, I'm impressed. Does it do jokes, too? Or better still, water divination? I'm thirsty.'

A little huffiness, delightful to Luke, entered her voice. 'My father went to a lot of trouble to find it for me and it does the date.' A male voice this time "Ten, June, nineteen ninety nine".'

'Wow! The tenth? It feels like the ninth, are you sure about that?'

'I think you may have a bit of amnesia. It's definitely the tenth.'

The thought silenced him. He had this unreasonable feeling that if he could see, he would remember. Only now, when moving could be measured in millimetres and thoughts vanished down a foggy hole, did he begin to have a concept of the power he had lost. Twelve hours ago he could have made sense of this encounter. Now he couldn't even remember the date.

'You're right about the water, though, Luke. We'll die without that.'

'Die?' He asked, as if the idea had never crossed his mind. 'Please tell me what happened.'

'Well it's Thursday – Thursday evening now, I suppose. It happened soon after midday, in this big post office in Pimlico somewhere. We came in a taxi over Vauxhall Bridge, but I think it's near Victoria Tube Station. You know it?' Luke tried to remember. It must be close to the gym where he worked part-time. 'We had just sent off an application for my passport. They had this special area with its own windows just for passport applications. Are you applying for a passport too? Are you going abroad?'

Puzzlement filled his voice. 'Ye … es, but I often go abroad. My Uncle lives in Rome and …', but it wasn't that. A singing competition? Surely his current passport was still valid. Had he needed stamps? But there were post offices close to home. '… I don't understand.' He rolled his head in frustration, and felt a sympathetic press from her knee.

'There were quite a lot of other people there. I'm not sure why no one else is here now. I suppose when the first bang happened, everybody ran away.'

'Even your mother and father?'

'I don't know. The first bang was quite loud. People started running around, shouting. I was scared, so I just sat still. Dad said to sit still. Then there was a much bigger noise, the biggest I've ever heard. So you couldn't hear anything at all for a long time afterwards. Things started moving and we started falling. I just curled up small. The sofa thing I'd been sitting on rolled on top of me and I could feel things hitting it, but it must have protected me, because I'm not hurt at all. I stayed there for ages. It sounds stupid but I thought someone would come and rescue me, and things did go on and on bumping and crunching for ages; I felt safer underneath. I tried calling Mama and Dad sometimes.

Then I couldn't get out from the sofa thing because it was wedged against something else. Then I found I could move me and the sofa together.' She laughed. 'I was like a giant snail. After a bit of crawling with it on top, I suddenly found I could push up one end. I was so tired by the time I crawled out that ...' she chuckled again, 'I just fell asleep.'

Luke listened peacefully. An endearing quality infused her narrative, as if Heloise found her own actions a source of fun. 'When I woke up it was after 4 o'clock, and it was dead silent. Even the funny clinking noises that had started after I got out of the sofa had gone.'

'What about when it actually happened, didn't you hear anybody shouting or anything?'

'No I ... but there must have been people making all sorts of noise ...' she gasped and her hand closed on his arm. 'Do you think perhaps I was deaf at first? I can't remember any sound until just before I slept. It was all moving, like swimming without water. Mama and Dad might have been there and I wouldn't have heard them.'

'But ...' He realised that the sudden death of her parents by flying glass might be no more acceptable to her than a slow one beside her. Luke felt completely detached from the events she related. His mind was very clear on the subject, it had no memory of such happenings, and therefore he had not been part of them.

A faint thumping sounded in the distance. Neither spoke as they stretched their hearing, vainly trying to interpret this rhythmic thud into rescue noises.

'Heloise, I think we ought to try and attract attention. Did you shout at all after you woke up?'

'No. I ... I'm afraid I had a little cry.'

'I know,' he said 'it's a good thing you did. I heard you and realized that I wasn't dreaming. Let's shout.'

A ragged chorus of hellos left their throats to be damped and swallowed by their chaotic surroundings. Heloise sighed. 'Maybe we didn't shout loud enough.'

He grimaced in the dark, his throat begging for water. 'I can probably make more noise singing than shouting.'

'You sing then and I'll shout.' He tried to draw air into his lungs, but of course there was this bloody great thing on his chest.

As if sensing his efforts she said, 'I don't suppose you can breathe properly, can you?'

'I'll be fine once I get going. I'll warm up with a bit of Corsaro, then I'll belt out ... oh ... something people will recognise. How about *La donna é mobile*?

She tried to laugh. 'Why not, I'd like that. Wait a minute, we ought to listen properly to the silence first.' They listened, trying not to breathe, for about thirty seconds. Random clinks and grating noises occurred, but no regular sounds and nothing that could be construed as rescue noises. Suddenly sober, she whispered, 'This is it, isn't it? We're going to die ... There's too much brick and concrete between us and the rescuers; they can't hear us. We'll die like people in an earthquake.' Unwilling to allow these thoughts in, Luke started to hum gently, searching for the right key. She went on, 'Humans are *so* stupid; I thought I wouldn't mind dying. But I do mind and I don't want glass and dust and thirst with my death.' He could hear the tears in her throat, and he gripped at the cloth of his jeans in frustration. If his hands had been free he could have dug a way out for both of them. As he took a breath to argue against her pessimism, an upsurge of power flooded with the air into his lungs.

With quite deliberate tenderness, he sang from Corsaro, '*Oh, così tetre immagini dal tuo pensier discaccia ... (Oh, cast these darkest imaginings from out of your thoughts ...)*'

2

Lambeth: St Thomas'

Luke turned his face into the warm flannel. 'Water! Ah, that's good...*so good*. Heloise?'

'Luca? Hello? I'm just going to wash your face.'

Luke opened his eyes. The darkness had lifted a little. A face leaned over him. 'Heloise?'

'Hello Luca, I'm Janet. How are you feeling?' The woman spoke in a middle-of-the-night voice. It was not Heloise's voice. Luke looked around. Lights blinked and electrical noises whirred. Perhaps he was in someone's kitchen, or perhaps the little robot machine that visited him after Heloise left had come back. He looked at the woman above him. 'Heloise?' he whispered.

'It's late, Luca, there's no one here except me at the moment. Is there anything you want? I'm here to look after you.'

'Heloise. I want Heloise.' He pulled at the sheet, trying to get up. 'Where is she?'

The sunshine floated in before his dreams had quite floated out. Luke opened his eyes, and seeing nothing, shut them again. Travelling as much as he did, he had discovered that in order to see, he had to remember first where he expected to be. What his brain relayed to him made him open his eyes again in a hurry. An unfamiliar woman in uniform stood by his bed calmly looking down at him.

'Good morning Luca. Are you feeling better?' Seeing his astonished face she added, 'You're in hospital.'

In hospital! So some of the jumbled images inhabiting his mind might just be true. Somewhere within, bubbling up through these images, lay an undercurrent of excitement.

The nurse leant over to engage his attention. 'Would you like something to drink?'

'Please.' A straw appeared in his mouth. After a couple of sips the world swung out of view again as his eyelids dropped. He wanted to say thank you because of the water, because someone had taken the thing off his chest and because the terrible cramping in his back and legs had stopped; but the words refused to assemble on his tongue and the darkness poured in again.

Luke opened his eyes and looked round carefully. Pale, empty walls beamed down on him. Everything glowed yellow, grey or white; he rather liked that. He lifted his hand and found a clear plastic tube attached to his wrist. Yet he didn't feel ill and nothing hurt. Then he tried turning his head, and found it fixed. In rising anxiety he brought his hand up to his face, half expecting to meet an obstruction. There was none. Tender lumpy skin met his hands, then a bandage. Perhaps he was scarred for life, no more leading tenor roles. The sun reached in and the walls grew too bright. Luke allowed his weighted eyelids to drop.

After a moment he tried lifting them again. To his surprise one of his sisters was sitting beside his bed. 'Barbara?' he whispered.

'Luke!' she sounded astonished.

'Drink?' He croaked, and Barbara, with shaking fingers, held a straw to his mouth. He drank gratefully. He was just going to tell her that now he had a scar she would be able to practice her much-vaunted beautician skills on him, when his eyelids started their automatic closing game and his mind slid away, like a wave retreating down a beach.

When he next opened his eyes, Barbara's soft chin had turned into the familiar, bristly jowls of his father. His father was snoring. He shut his eyes. It's like a revolving door, he thought, wondering who would come next. The snoring persisted. 'Dad?' He was astonished at the feeble noise he made, and at the weakness of his voice a cascade of fears tumbled through his mind: hospitals, anaesthetics, damaged vocal cords.

'Dad!' he called more urgently. His father's mouth shut abruptly

'Blimey Luke! You made me jump.'

Luke found himself smiling. It was so like his father to be taken by surprise even by someone stuck in a hospital bed.

'Were you expecting someone else?'

'Blimey Luke!' he repeated. 'You can make jokes? You all right?'

'Yes . . . I think so . . . I just don't understand . . . how did I get here?'

Gordon Danford stared uncertainly at his son. 'You mean, like, in the ambulance?'

'Yes but ... how did I get into the ambulance?'

'You were rescued. They dug you out and you were still alive.' Gordon's eyes filled and he coughed firmly. 'I must get Maria. Don't go to sleep again, please just stay awake a little moment while I fetch Mum.'

'Wait ... I don't mean to go to sleep ... just tell me which bits are real.'

'What do you mean?'

Luke was about to try and explain his confusion when yet another strange woman loomed over him. 'Glad to see you awake, young man. How are you feeling?'

'Sort of odd. Are you a doctor?'

'Yes, I'm Dr Lee. In what way odd?'

'Well,' he said cautiously, 'I've had a lot of funny dreams and I'm not sure what's happened to me.'

'What's the last thing you remember that you're sure about?'

'Well that's the problem, I remember talking to Claudia ... at home ... about Corsaro. I think that was Wednesday ... but then I remember being in this building with Heloise. She said it was Thursday. There'd been an explosion.' Luke looked towards his father. 'Was there *really* an explosion?'

Gordon opened his mouth, but it was the doctor who responded. 'That's right. What else?'

He reached out to the doctor. 'Heloise? Is she all right? I *must* see her.'

Doctor Lee glanced at his father's blank face. 'We'll look in a minute, just tell me what you remember about the explosion.'

'I *can't* remember though,' he said, his voice rising like a child's. 'Heloise said I was in a post office doing something about a passport, but I don't need a passport. Heloise will explain, can I talk to her?'

'Who is Heloise? Was she with you?'

'Yes, she found me. She ... Isn't she here with me?'

'She's not in this ward. Casualties were admitted to a number of hospitals, so we may not be able to track her down straight away. It's important that you remember as much as possible by yourself; you see you've had an operation on your head. You had a small haemorrhage, just under the surface of the bone. We've relieved this, and there should be no permanent damage, but it may take your brain a little while to recover from the insult.'

Luke's father, hovering beside the doctor, interrupted; 'Please, can I go and tell Maria that Luke's awake?'

'Of course, but just one visitor at a time, please.'

Maria sat down in the plastic chair by the bed and looked at her son. He was fast asleep, just as he had been yesterday and the day before and the day before that, as she sat through the hours. Yet Barbara had spoken to him and Claudia had seen him stir and mutter. Now here was Gordon claiming that he had made a joke only a few minutes before. Why did he lie so still? Maria folded her hands with a sigh and settled to watch. After a while, she leant over and picked up her son's hand. She studied it with the same amazement as she had felt at his birth. Then, as she had done many times before, she leant over and kissed the bit of his forehead between the stitches.

The dark lashes stirred, then lifted. He looked up at her in surprise. 'Mum?'

Her turn. 'Topo. Hello darling.'

'Oh Mum!' He sighed as if bringing her news of the most unforgivable misdemeanour that needed her, and only her, absolution.

She stroked back his hair and saw tears starting to trickle out. 'It's going to be all right. You'll see Luke. You're going to be fine.'

'And my voice?'

'Don't worry, Claudia told them not to use ... that ... whatever it is that's bad for it. You don't need to worry about anything, Topo.'

She watched him look up from her face to the room as if he had just realised the world was still out there. Then his hand clutched hers urgently. 'Mum, just explain what happened. No one will tell me and I keep falling asleep. How did I get here?'

'They dug you out Luke. A robot found you and told them you were still alive, so they went on digging until they got to you. We were there. We saw you come out. You mustn't worry about anything. The Doctors say you're going to be fine. Even Claudia says you're going to be fine.'

He plucked at the sheet, puzzled. 'A robot? You mean that bit *wasn't* a dream?'

Luke shut his eyes again, this time on purpose. His mind retreated to that moment when the little machine suddenly arrived, blinking at him out of the endless dark. He lay in his cocoon of pain and it seemed no more than a miraculous distraction; a construct of his desperate imagination. The thing buzzed as it moved with an electrical whine and threw out several pencil beams of light, which criss-crossed like a laser show. Then the buzzing ceased and the fine pencils merged into a single, wider beam and swept over him to and fro like a giant paintbrush. He shut his eyes against the glare and lay soothed by the stroking light. As the beam left his face and began to light his prison, his heart jerked at the stag leaping over his head. Then the beam passed on and he remembered that he lay in a broken building. His brain translated the stag into the ragged end of a snapped concrete pier, with bent metal rods, poised about four feet above his face. He could summon only a detached interest in these giant spillikins. He wondered what the little Dalek made of them. He wanted to ask it to fetch water. He tried to speak to it but no sound came out. It went on surveying the area for perhaps ten minutes while he twisted his head to follow the tiny searchlight beams. Finally it buzzed further and further off until he could no longer see or hear it. Sadness engulfed him, as it had when Heloise had left.

Luke hurriedly opened his eyes. 'Did I fall asleep again? Mum?' His hands moved restlessly over the covers.

'You had your eyes shut, that's all. What is it, Luca?

'Mum, have they found Heloise?'

'Heloise? Dad said something about an Heloise. Who is she?'

'She was there in the . . . in the building with me. She . . . we talked and she looked after me.' Seeing her blank face, he became more urgent, pulling at her sleeve. 'They must have found her. She wasn't hurt; she was fine. Mum, where is she?'

'Hey Luca, calm down. She'll be somewhere. It's all a bit confusing at the moment. People got taken to lots of different hospitals. Lots of people got out. I'm sure we'll find her.'

'Mum, please go and look for her, find out where she is.'

'It's all right. Wherever she is now I'm sure they'll look after her. You'll find her.'

'But, Mum, she might still be in there.'

'I don't think so, Luca. They've found all the missing people.

It's six days since it happened. They've not found anyone ... anyone alive since that third day when they found you and the two others.'

Luke stared at her in disbelief. 'Six days?' he whispered. 'You mean I was talking to Heloise *days* ago? I thought it was yesterday.'

'You've been really sick, Luca. They did this operation on your head, and you didn't wake up for two days. You've been sleeping plenty.' Seeing his troubled eyes, she went on, 'Maybe you need to sleep again now?'

'Mum, please, please find Heloise. Tell them to go *on* looking if you can't find her. Tell them to look again in the post office.'

'Sure, Topo. Close your eyes now, there's a good boy.'

Maria put the hand she was holding back on his chest. It clung to hers for a moment, but his eyes went vague and the eyelids drooped. She bent to stroke the hair back from his poor, broken forehead – her beautiful boy with great black spiders of stitches crawling over his face. But alive, able to talk and think. Her mind began its familiar search for consolations. The usual buffers against misfortune: risotto marinara, a CD, a new jacket, did not seem adequate for his present troubles. She sighed and looked for inspiration at the family photograph she had put on Luke's bedside locker. They were all there: Gordon looking at the floor and Maria, herself, looking at Luca, Claudia uncharacteristically cheerful and Barbara, posing as usual, in a funny green dress. Still, it showed Luca centre-stage, tall and glowing, so different from the bruised, yellow-faced creature beside her now. Barbara! She looked at her watch and heaved herself to her feet, a hopeful gleam brightening her eyes. She knew that Barbara, waiting outside in the corridor, had brought her faithful giant of a boyfriend along for company. Lewis was a fireman. If anyone could help Luca find his missing girl, a fireman might.

Maria leant over the bed. Even with his eyes closed and the confusion of stitches, she could detect the signs of unhappiness. She said quietly, 'Topo, don't you worry, Barbara is coming to see you now and we'll get Lewis to track down your Heloise...'

His eyes flickered open. Half-smiling he said, 'Good idea, Mum,' before the lids dropped again.

Rewarded, Maria picked up her bag and, finding her address

book, scribbled Heloise on it. Just Heloise? It wasn't much to go on. She should have asked for more information, but his eyes were closed again and she was not one to rake over trouble. Never mind, there weren't going to be too many Heloise's out there.

It seemed to Luke that whenever he woke up some doctor or nurse would appear to offer him tea (which made him feel sick) or attach or detach another bag of liquid. On top of that they wanted him to count dots, wiggle his toes or look into a torch beam. After that they wanted him to count backwards and play games for children. It didn't matter how often he did these things, they came back and asked him to do them again.

Worse still, they never came to tell him about Heloise. Finally, eight days after the explosion, a doctor released Luke from the head brace and he was allowed to sit up and eat his first proper meal. As he finished a man appeared. He ducked to avoid the stand with Luke's drip, sat down in the visitor's chair and introduced himself.

'Sergeant Conway. I understand you reported meeting a girl in the Cardon Street site. We have not so far traced this individual; perhaps you can help us with more details. Just tell me everything you can remember about her.'

It took Luke a moment to realise that he was talking about the post office explosion. *Everything* about her? He started hesitantly. 'Well...I heard her first...I thought she was a child...she was crying, and she said her parents had been with her, but she couldn't find them.'

'So we are talking about a family group of three people? No other brothers or sisters.'

'No...no...just her, and she wasn't a child, she was twenty-five years old.'

'OK, a middle aged couple and a twenty-five year old woman. Names?'

'Well, her name was Heloise...'

The pencil paused. 'Spelt?'

'H.. E.. L.. O.. I.. S.. E..' This was becoming surreal.

'What?'

'H..E..L..'

'No, Heloise *what*?'

'...I don't know, I never thought to ask. We were together. I thought we would be found...or we would die together. *I didn't ask!*'

The policeman raised his eyes from the notebook to the damaged young man in the bed. He paused, taking in the tubes snaking at knee level and the sachet swinging inches from his head. He refocused on his notes. 'No, no of course not,' he said soothingly. 'Just tell me what you *do* remember. Anything about her appearance? Her hair? What she was wearing?'

Luke gazed at him in disbelief. 'It was dark for chrissake... real, total dark. I couldn't see a single thing. *I don't know what she looked like!* Oh! Hang on a moment, she did say she had fair hair...and I think it was quite long, because it fell on my face sometimes.'

The policeman, picking his words, asked, 'If you were close together for some time, were you able to tell what kind of clothes she was wearing for instance?'

'No. No, of course not. My hands were trapped. She could touch me, but I had this thing on my chest. *I couldn't touch her!*' Luke tried to pull open the drawer of his locker. 'There's a photo in here somewhere, one the robot took of me as I lay there trapped.'

The policeman nodded. 'Yes, of course, I saw that.'

Luke lay back again. 'Are they still searching? She's got to be somewhere.'

'I'm afraid the search stopped four days ago.' Seeing Luke's open-mouthed dismay, he added, 'Everyone reported missing has been traced.'

'But I've reported Heloise missing, and she has *not* been traced.'

The policeman stared at Luke while unbuttoning his jacket. 'Most missing people are reported by relatives, usually by more than one relative. If no one has missed this young woman and her parents, except you, then...there is likely to be a different explanation for her disappearance. You say this woman was uninjured. We think that your friend may have been taken to another hospital and discharged herself. There were a hundred and fifteen people treated, you know, and there are still around thirty in hospital. All the dead have been identified and no one of the name Heloise is registered among the dead, so that must be good news.'

'But what if her only relatives are her parents, and what if they died in the building too? What if she's still under there? She must be rescued. She wasn't injured at all, she must have survived.'

The policeman shivered. On his way to interview Luke, he had driven past the Cardon street site. There were bulldozers now shovelling up the remains. He shut his notebook. 'Perhaps she never went into hospital, we think some of the people who got out that first day, before the gas scare, just went home. We're still trying to trace those people.'

Luke stared, unseeing, at the white rail that ended his bed. 'She was with me for a long, long time, longer than a day. They told me that everyone pulled out of the building after they realised that gas was involved, was taken to hospital. Anyway, if she got out, she would have waited for me. What about her parents? She seemed to think they were dead.'

His visitor perked up. 'There were definitely no couples among the dead, that's for sure, though whether all those in hospital will...' He scratched his head, brushing the drip carrier as he did so. He jumped up. 'Are you sure this Heloise was with you? You're not remembering her from another time, or anything?' He watched Luke shake his head. He restored the notebook to his pocket. 'I think I'll just take the information you've given me and see if we can get any matches...'

'Hey, wait just a minute!' Luke reached out towards the man's trousers, but they swayed just out of touching distance. ' I can't remember a thing about this explosion. The only things I know are things Heloise told me. She must have been there or I wouldn't have ever known I was in a post office.'

'Well you've had a bang on the head, stands to reason you might be a bit muddled in your mind about things.'

'But I'm not! I can remember everything perfectly...' As Luke's voice rose, Sergeant Conway slid towards the door. 'I remember clearly from when I woke up and heard Heloise for the first time, to when...to when...I must have fallen asleep and she must have gone off to try and get help.'

The door handle twitched under the man's fingers. He turned and muttered, 'I'll do my best, mate, honest I will.' And he was gone.

3

St Thomas': Angela and Kes

The grey floor tiles swung up towards him and the grip on his arm suddenly tightened.

'Enough?' The nursing assistant helped Luke to stumble back down the ward on his new crutches. He reconnected Luke's drip, muttered, 'Not bad,' and moved on to his next charge.

Luke climbed stiffly onto his bed, located now in a teeming ward, and sank against his pillows. A nurse trundled a commode chair up to his bed, swung the curtains smartly into place, looked at Luke in a perplexed way and went into reverse. She muttered, 'Sorry, wrong one,' and was off again. A volunteer with a trolley offered him a newspaper. The moment she left, the curtains swung round him again and the brisk voice of Dr Penter, the neurologist, congratulated him on his release from the side ward. Once more Luke counted fingers in the air, located pencils held on either side of his nose, crossed out stars on pieces of paper and bisected horizontal lines.

Dr Penter got up to go. Luke dropped back onto his pillows and watched the loop of metal reappear above his head as the curtains swished open once again. Did nothing ever stay still in a hospital? He felt as if someone had exchanged all his muscles for tissue paper and then taken his insides for a spin at Brands Hatch. At least he had got rid of all the attachments except the drip. If only his head would work properly. Every now and again some part of his mind seemed to dive sideways. A spot of turbulence in the brain? A neural air pocket perhaps? Whatever it was, although it righted itself instantly, he felt each time that he hovered on the edge of a thousand foot drop. He pressed his hands to his eyes, thinking almost fondly of his old, lonely room.

With eyes closed, music instantly invaded his head. Reaching out to the box on his locker, he rummaged through the tapes Barbara had brought in and watched the clock. The neurological ward had strict visiting hours, but today, at last, his friends would be allowed to visit. Dave. More than anyone he needed Dave – the nearest thing he had to a brother. Luke turned too sharply towards the windows and his head groaned at him. He lay still. As soon as he could get out of this place Dave would help him find Heloise.

On the dot of 4 pm the entrance darkened and within seconds the ward resounded with all the jumbled languages of London; each visitor carrying enough produce to supply a market stall. He spotted two fellow singers, Angela and Kes. No Dave.

Angela approached the bed, glancing all around like an uneasy gazelle. She leaned to kiss his cheek with nervous precision, her eyes straying to the nearby areas of healing flesh. The stitches had come out only the day before and his forehead had a raw, patchy look to it. 'Luke,' she whispered, her eyes bulging with sympathy, 'you poor baby.'

Kes perched himself on the far end of the bed and stared around in frank curiosity. He gazed at the patterns etched across Luke's face. 'You auditioning for Phantom next?' Seeing Luke glance around he asked, 'What's the matter?'

'Is Dave coming?'

'He's in Cardiff, remember?'

'Damn!' Luke had not remembered.

'You want him to look for this girl?'

'Yes, Heloise. How d'you know?'

Kes shrugged, but Angela took Luke's hand, 'Claudia said when I rang this morning.'

'What else did she say? That I've lost my marbles, that I'm hallucinating over Heloise?' Intercepting the anxious glance darting from Angela to Kes, he went on, 'It's OK. I know what Claudia thinks, but she's wrong. Heloise is flesh and blood. I felt her breath on my face. I heard ... anyway she's out there somewhere.'

'But Luke ...'

'Leave it Ange.' Kes spread his hands out as if conducting a diminuendo. 'We know damn all about this, but if there's something you want us to do, Luke, just say.' He prowled round the bed, reached up and squeezed the drip sachet. 'Hey, what's this thing for? Have a feel of that, Ange, it's really weird.'

'Kes, leave my drip alone, I'm joined to it, idiot.' Luke shaded his eyes with his free hand. His brain buzzed, beginning to feel too big for its bony casing. '

Kes abandoned the drip and reached for the carrier bag at

Angela's feet. 'Have you given Luke the tapes yet?'

Angela released Luke's hand. 'Oh,' she dived into her handbag, 'we made these tapes of the old Carreras Corsaro for you. Barbara said you only had a tape recorder in here. I thought you'd want to rehearse ...' The shout of laughter from Kes and Luke's blank look stopped her. 'What's up? Your Mum said your voice was fine.' She looked from one to the other, her eyes wide. 'You'll still be doing the Stockholm performance, won't you?'

'Dumbo! How can he rehearse in this place? No piano? No quiet?' Kes ran his voice over a quick arpeggio, ignoring the heads turned suddenly towards him. He grinned. 'Acoustics not ideal either.'

Luke's smile was half-hearted. 'Sure, I'll be doing Stockholm, presuming they ever let me out of here. I'm just taking a break from training while old Gulli's on holiday.'

Angela continued to frown. 'You should practise, you know. Especially after the anaesthetics and the dust and all that. You should go on training whether Gulli's here or not.'

Kes rolled his eyes. He also trained with the same unforgiving voice coach. 'Lighten up, Ange. The guy's had a near death experience. He works hard enough the rest of the year.'

Luke looked at his friends' faces and closed his eyes for a moment. There were soft vibrations in his head from the notes that Kes had sung. The most tedious music call would have been bliss to him at this moment. If he had still been in the side ward, they could have sung together. Even the idea revived him for a moment.

He smiled. 'The men in white coats would definitely turn up if I let rip with my voice in here, but thanks for the tapes.' He turned to his locker to extract the tape recorder. A clatter louder than the usual sound of plastic chair hitting metal bed leg made him jerk up again. 'Kes! For chrissake, those are my crutches. And that's someone else's locker.' Luke's voice rose above the hubbub of surrounding visitors. 'Oh god, can you take Kes away before he wrecks the place.' He put his hands over his face.

Angela grabbed Kes by the arm. 'Stop that now! Give Luke a break.' She picked up her bag and gave Luke another careful peck. 'I'll come again in a day or so. I won't bring Kes next time. Bless!'

Luke clutched her hand. 'No, wait a minute, where's Dave? I need him. I need him to help me find Heloise. Why didn't he come?'

Kes raised an eyebrow. 'Head not working yet, Luke? I told you, Dave's in Cardiff. I had a call yesterday. He's wowing the judges; he's made it to the next round – jammy bugger. Mike's already out, he thinks Dave has an advantage because he's technically black.'

'Kes!' Angela turned shocked eyes on him.

Head tilted, Kes considered the idea. 'I'd say having a black grandparent was about thirty percent advantage to seventy percent disadvantage, myself.' He turned to doodle experimentally on the white-board behind Luke's bed. 'It really pisses me off this black/white thing. I mean – it's so inexact. You know what I mean? Dave is much the same urban beige as me, but his Grandma's Jamaican, so he's called 'black'. Luke here is coffee coloured (apart from the new pink bits), but his mum's Italian so he's called 'white'. It makes no sense.' His tone changed to one of dreamy admiration. 'Imagine, though, Dave – Cardiff Singer of the World!' With yet another switch of tone, he turned to the exhausted figure in the bed. 'You want a sleuth, Luke? I know a bloke in the private eye business. I'll send him along, if you like. Bye now.'

Within minutes of their departure Luke fell into a shattered sleep. Twenty-four hours after achieving freedoms that had seemed all he asked of life, he felt as though someone had unplugged him and was letting him drain away.

Barbara, dropping in on her way home from work, found her brother back in a single room again and fast asleep. She picked over the photocopied papers on the chair beside him. They offered counselling, compensation claims and various aids to surviving a disaster. She frowned. According to Claudia, Luke had seen a new consultant – a psychiatrist. They seemed to think, just because *they* couldn't find this wretched girl, that *Luke* was sick. Inside the hospital they had no idea of the chaos out there in the real world. More than a hundred people had been treated after the explosion, but a whole load of other people had just got out and gone home. There were thirty or forty people still in hospitals all over London and a lot more had been discharged. The only thing

29

they seemed sure about was that twenty-three people had died. She and Lewis had spent an hour on the newly published list.

'Barbara? Was I asleep? I didn't know you'd arrived. Did Lewis find anything?'

'I'm sorry Luke. It is still a mystery. They say there's no Heloise on the survivors list – though we know this is incomplete – and she's not on the list of those who died; we've looked at it every which way. None of them were called Heloise or anything remotely similar. Lewis tried to get a peek at the lists of people reported as missing, too, but the police wouldn't release them. Apparently these include people who've been missing for years. They did at least confirm that all those newly reported missing, except for your girl, have been accounted for. Lewis will go on checking; I told him you were quite sure she was with you. The doctors are most likely wrong.'

Luke grimaced. 'They think I am making it up, don't they?'

Barbara looked at her brother. He had no need to dream up girls; he spent enough time brushing them off. If he said there was a girl in that building with him, then there had been. The doctors had got it wrong.

She grinned. 'They don't know what to think. Remember, they only started to doubt you when nobody could find her. They're making up answers to fit what they think are the facts. It's the best they can do. Don't fret, Luke, we'll keep on looking. She's out there somewhere. Lewis has sent an internal email round the Fire Service, let's see what they come up with.'

Luke pulled himself up and sat on the side of the bed. 'I'm so sick of being stuck here, Ba. I must get out. I'll find her. I *know* she's real; she did things for me, she . . . I can't explain. People don't just vanish.'

'Well you can start your own investigation tomorrow morning, Luke. There's a man here who was with his wife and child in the Cardon Street post office. They've gone home, but he is still in Ward J10 – orthopaedics. I just popped in to tell you. I've got a couple of clients first thing, then I'll come in and take you to see him.'

Luke wriggled off the bed and, balancing shakily, wrapped his arms round his sister. 'You're a star. I can start *doing* something at last. And look at this! Here, hold my drip.' He grabbed his crutches and struggled across to the window. 'Watch! I'll be down at the gym next week.'

'Does it hurt, Luke?'

'Well, the outside of my ankle, where the skin was so messed up, hurts more than the inside now. I guess the bone is healing, but the skin grafts and the stretched bits still give me grief. Pretty, isn't it?'

Barbara smiled confidently. 'I'll work on the scars when they finish with you, especially your face. Shame about that, but it's sort of dramatic.' Barbara tilted her head and raised her brows, looking at her brother first with the eye of a beautician, then with the eye of a woman. The inspection at an end, she nodded. 'It's OK. You'll just look sexier than before.'

He grinned. 'Good old Ba! I'll be in your parlour as soon as they release me.' Then seeing Barbara gathering her bits, he struggled back to his bed. 'Ring Mum and tell her to bring me some dates and ... and real cheese, tonight, will you? The food here is so bloody *English* – tea with everything.

4

St Thomas': Louise

Brother and sister paused at the centre of the hospital's internal crossroads, one in a wheelchair, the other pushing, their heads tilted at the same angle. Passers-by skirted them glancing with admiration followed by compassion, even shock, as they took in the tramlines on Luke's face, the exposed areas of scalp and the flowers glowing in his hands. The pair listened, both faces alert yet self-absorbed.

'What is it, Luca?'

'Shh!' Luke turned his head slowly from left to right. 'It's breathing – the building, I mean. It's . . . digesting.' He looked down at the flowers he held. 'What do you call these?'

'Anemone de Caen.'

The flowers Barbara had bought to give to Mr Braithwaite trembled in Luke's lap. He felt dazed by the scarlet, magenta, and royal blue petals around their black centres. He sniffed their greenhouse smell. He inhaled the mixed smells of food, soaps and stationery, drunk on the familiarity and variety after the confined body odours of the ward. He made Barbara linger outside the hairdressers in the hospital mall, so that he could breathe in the damp, perfumed air as it was pumped out. He felt like a dried out sponge refilling to its proper size.

Radiators along corridors murmured rhythmically to him as he approached and passed by, lifts whined and the whole building turned over with a subdued throbbing; he felt as though he were gliding through the innards of a sleeping dragon. This was how a building should feel: warm, buzzing, an entity. Lying, ten days ago (if it really was ten days ago), in that scrap heap of a post office, this was what he had missed – this living quality. In that chaos Heloise, curled up beside him, had talked about the lack of defining edges, about having no real floor, no markers of up and down. For him, unable to feel his surroundings, it was the uncoordinated sounds that gave it away as a non-building. Do all buildings, he wondered, have an individual resonance, an identity?

Luke reached up to touch his sister's hand. 'Wait a minute

longer, Ba.'

He continued his exploration of the air, his head moving in a slow arc, like a snail with antennae tasting the atmosphere. He stopped suddenly. 'Hey, I smell burgers. God, I could murder some junk food.'

Barbara laughed, ruffling her brother's short hair. 'Luke, this guy, Mr Braithwaite, is expecting you, don't you want to see him?'

'Sure, but I bet he can't help.'

'Hey, none of that. *Chi la dura la vince*, you persevere you'll win. Positive action, that's what you need. Lewis and I are ...' she stopped, '... are buying a washing machine.'

'Uh? Did I miss a line?' Luke leant back to see his sister's face and found it slightly flushed. 'What's the deal with a washing machine?' There was no immediate answer, so he added jokingly, 'You getting married or something?' Barbara hesitated again. 'Great heavens! You are? Why on earth didn't you tell me?' He turned to her, his eyes bright with laughter. 'You can't think I'm going to have a relapse because my sister's getting hitched.'

'I didn't mean to tell you yet. We've only just decided and .. . I wanted it to be the new news when you got home. You don't mind?

'Of course not. I like Lewis.'

'Good.' She leant down over the wheelchair to kiss the top of her brother's head. 'Got to get you up and running again first, anyway.'

Her face, hidden from Luke, registered both relief and a residual uncertainty. This boy, with a mind so akin to hers that she had wandered in and out of it all her life, had recently pulled a shutter down. It was all guesswork now. Her childhood co-conspirator didn't want to play any more. Adult life stretched ahead a chilly and more serious prospect than she had imagined. She shook away the thought, released the brake and set the wheelchair in motion.

Fifteen minutes of unaccustomed wheelchair pushing began testing Barbara's arms. Luke had grown silent. With some relief she negotiated the doors into Mr Braithwaite's ward, had a short argument with the sister on duty about out-of-hours visiting, and entered the ward.

Half way down in one of the bays Bill Braithwaite lay beneath what looked like a gantry; his skin a patchwork of scarlet and white and his expression set with pain. Luke, faced with a complete stranger, found his recent vitality draining away. He drooped in his wheelchair and let Barbara do the introductions.

Bill, roused from his stupor, spoke to Luke in a friendly voice, but with no spark of recognition, 'What's your damage?'

Luke lifted a vague hand. 'Oh a bump on the head, this stuff on my face and a broken ankle. I should be home by the end of next week. How about you?'

'I think I'm in for a bit longer than that. I got a concrete pier tangled up with my hip and they are having trouble separating it all out.' He sighed, then brightened. 'Rather me than my girls at any rate.'

'Your girls?'

Bill's forehead smoothed for a moment into a real smile. 'Yes, neither my wife nor my little girl was hurt much at all. It's easier this way round.'

Barbara, had disappeared to get a vase for the flowers. The air seemed to slacken between the two men. The heat inside the ward raised a fine beading of sweat on Luke's face. Fingering the healing scars on his forehead, he said abruptly, 'You don't remember seeing me there, do you? I mean before it happened. You see, I can't remember anything about it.'

'Good thing too, if you ask me. I wish I could forget most of it. No, sorry, I don't remember seeing you. Then watching Luke's face, he added, 'Maybe the others will – my wife and daughter, I mean.'

'I'd like to forget it all too, but I need to remember it first, if you see what I mean.' Bill shrugged , then grimaced. Luke tried again, 'It's just that it's a bit unsettling having this hole in your life. I just wondered if you could tell what happened.'

Bill, who had already told his story to various authorities and had satisfied the curiosity of family and friends, looked towards the window on the far side of the ward. He turned back and asked a trifle wearily, 'How old are you, son?'

'Twenty-eight.'

'When you get to my age you'll have one or two more holes in your mind and you won't care that much about them.'

Barbara reappeared at that moment. Both men looked up and watched as she carried the flowers with their frilly black faces and glowing petals and put the vase down carefully on the tiled window ledge. She stroked a petal into place, murmured something soothing to the flowers, shifted them to look their best from Bill's viewpoint and finally turned and beamed at Bill and Luke.

The two men relaxed a notch. Bill turned to her. 'Your brother says he wants to hear my version of events. I don't reckon that's going to be much help, do you?'

Barbara smiled warmly at him. 'Well, the doctors say that the more Luke is taken over it, the more likely he is to recall that time. Perhaps you could tell him about the place and how it looked *before* the explosion, it would take a weight off his…our minds.'

'Oh, *before* the explosion, OK, if that's what you want.' He paused again, smiled at some private thought, and started. 'We'd gone into the post office to send Carol's passport to be renewed. I'd left it a bit late as we were going on this holiday in a couple of weeks – we would have set off the day after tomorrow.' Barbara made a sympathetic noise. 'Anyway, Carol had just gone over to the desk…'

Luke interrupted: 'Why a post office? Can you really renew passports in them?'

'I'm not sure you can in most of them but Cardon Street's the biggest in West London.' Bill sighed. 'I think they started after that mess-up over passports a few years back? Well Cardon Street must have been one of the first to be used for passport applications. They made over this whole area just for dealing with them in a hurry. So you go in through the main post office door, then through the swing doors on your left to what used to be part of Woolworths before they moved. It's quite plushy with lots of seats and desks for filling out forms and the photo booth. You had to take a ticket and wait your turn.' He paused, eyes on some distant image. 'We'd have been all right in the main part of the post office, Luke, because they reckon now that gas leaked into a disused arm of the Victorian sewer underneath the car park. Well the car park is right under the old Woolworths and not under the main section. Most of the people who died or got trapped were in the passport bit.'

Luke shook his head. 'Why can't I remember?'

'Shall I go on, or is it no good?'

'Please. Yes please go on.'

'Well, Carol went up to the cashier – or whatever she calls herself, when her number was called, and I wandered over to look at some posters. That's how we all got separated. There were two bangs. The first was smaller – though it seemed big enough at the time. I guess the first bang broke through from the old sewer into the gas main itself. I just started towards Carol and Louise, when the second...'

Brother and sister spoke simultaneously. 'What?' 'Who!'

'The second explosion.'

'No, the names you just said...say them again, please?'

'Carol – my wife and Louise – my daughter. What's the matter?'

A sticky dryness swelled Luke's throat. Bubbles of prayers rose within him: please let this be her, please, please, please let her be alive, please let this be my Heloise. Nothing came out of his mouth, and it was Barbara who asked, 'Your daughter, Louise, did she say anything about helping someone? When was she rescued? Is she all right now?'

Bill looked from one intense face to the other. 'She's fine. What do you mean about helping someone? They found Louise in the middle of that night. I think she was with another woman, not Carol though. I was in the operating theatre by then. Luckily they got me out of the building quite quickly or I don't suppose I'd be here now. It was the first thing they told me when I came to.' His voice wobbled but he went on. 'Louise just had a few cuts, I think. Oh yes, and she lost her shoes, but she's fine ...' He looked at Luke. 'You look like you've seen the Angel Gabriel, son, what's up?'

'How old is ...Louise? Luke whispered.

Bill's face lit up. 'Now, there's a coincidence! Guess what? It's her sixteenth birthday today.' His eyes filled. He lifted his uninjured hand in the air and closed the thumb and forefinger to an invisible gap. 'She came that close to never seeing sixteen – that close. But she made it. We all did.'

Barbara's face fell, but Luke's shone. Several pieces of the jigsaw seemed to him to have fallen into place. 'I knew it! She was fibbing about her age. She told me she was twenty-five. The little ...'

'What are you on about? When did she tell you she was twenty-five? Louise wouldn't do a thing like that. When have you met her?'

'It's all right,' Barbara spoke soothingly; frowning down Luke's exuberance, 'While Luke was stuck in that place, unable to move, a girl came and ... talked to him for a bit. All he could remember was that her name was Heloise. He thinks she said she was twenty-five. But you could have been confused, couldn't you Luke? And Heloise is very close to Louise when you say them out loud.'

Luke, about to refute this, caught his sister's eye and shut his mouth. There were some parts of the encounter that he was absolutely certain about, and that was one of them. Still, Ba usually knew what she was up to and just now she was signalling to keep quiet. He mumbled, 'Sure.'

Bill looked from brother to sister, astounded. 'You met my little Louise in that ... that dungeon, and she never told me a thing about it? She said she spent the night with a woman. I'm sure they were rescued together. I don't understand, she wouldn't *not* tell us about meeting you, would she?'

Luke reviewing some of his less certain, but more intimate, memories of the encounter, thought there might have been good reason for Louise's reticence. Fifteen years old! If she had expanded her age, could she have developed her name too?

By now it was apparent that Bill was not only baffled by their disclosures but also exhausted and in pain. Seeing the nurse advancing, Barbara hastily poured more oil, 'Don't worry, Bill, we've probably got it all wrong. It would help us a lot, though, if you could get your wife and daughter to pop in and see Luke when they come this evening. I'll write his ward number down here. I tell you what, we'll give Louise a sixteenth birthday present.' She fished in her bag. 'There, that's a voucher for a free make-over for her in the salon where I work.'

Claudia, her small, intense face lit up in anticipation, marched towards Luke's ward. Unlike the rest of the family she had begun to doubt Heloise's existence. Her medical training had raised spectres of brain damage and hallucinations. Since Luke was her particular property to love, scold and protect, it would have been her task to tell him Heloise was imaginary. Now it looked at though this girl had turned up after all.

She found Luke back in his original side ward. He sat fully dressed in the chair next to his bed. A bit of the old shine had returned at last to his smile.

'When are you expecting her, Luke?'

'In the next hour or so. Bill, her father, said he'd ask her and her mother to visit us on their way out. It should be before 8.30, but it's her sixteenth birthday, so she'll want to see her Dad.'

Claudia frowned. 'Sixteenth, I thought ... Luke, what *is* this? You've been talking about a woman; fifteen is a child.'

He flushed. 'Sixteen. It's so silly, Claudia. When she told me her age in that ghastly place, I just knew she was fibbing. She said she was twenty-five, but when I first heard her she was crying for her mum and dad. You don't know how good she was to me, sitting beside me for hours on end, when she could have been searching for a way out. We talked about ... well everything. I wouldn't have wanted to bother with staying alive after a while if it hadn't been for her. You wait, she has a voice to die for, and her laugh ... You wait.'

'But sixteen, Luke? You can't have fallen for someone ten years younger than you?'

'It's not like that. I haven't *fallen*, I just need to see her again. Anyway, I didn't exactly plan the meeting, did I?'

More than an hour passed before a head with tufty brown hair and owl-sized eyes popped unannounced round the door, then vanished again. A voice with a distinct South London twang rang out in the corridor: 'Mum, I think he's in here.'

A quick glance at Luke's blank face showed Claudia that, whoever this girl was, she was not the owner of the voice that he had been dreaming about. She moved swiftly to his side and put a hand on his shoulder, finding it rigid under her fingers.

Two almost identical figures, both small and with the kind of bones that poked their way through clothing, arrived, hand in hand, through the door. They instantly overwhelmed Claudia (thinking she was Barbara), with thanks for Louise's birthday makeover gift, before turning to Luke.

Louise said, 'Mr Danford?'

'Call me Luke.'

'OK, Luke, Dad said you thought you might have talked to me after the explosion, but I guess it must have been someone else.'

Carol added, 'It definitely wasn't Lou.'

'No, it wasn't me.'

'No,' Luke whispered, 'it wasn't you.' He held one hand flat against his chest as if to keep his heart from rocking. He had been expecting a drama in which he had all the best lines, and here he was in some comedy act without any lines at all. In the same way that they shared genes, Carol and Louise shared their conversations, so that it was difficult to know which one to answer.

'It wasn't us but,' Louise's eyes glinted in excitement, 'we did see you, didn't we Mum?'

'Yes, in the post office, before the bangs.' Carol chimed in.

'You had your picture in the paper on the day you were being rescued, and Mum said "That's the guy we saw ...".'

Carol took over. 'Then when Bill told us about you just now, Louise said, "I bet that's the guy who was rescued last, the one we saw", and she was right, you are.' Luke stared in confusion at the two utterly unrecognisable women. Both faces were sparkling as if they still held delightful secrets. He needed to ask them about it all, but a stone seemed to be lying on his tongue.

Claudia, equally staggered, let go of Luke. Then, as if she feared they might run away, she gathered the two women and sat them down on Luke's bed. Reverting to her role as a doctor, she interrogated them politely. Luke continued to sit, lips parted and breathing shallow, in front of them. As they both answered all Claudia's questions, sometimes simultaneously, but mostly in alternate half sentences, the comedy routine sensation grew stronger with every minute. Looking from one to the other as they tossed the questions back and forth, Luke began to feel like an umpire at a tennis match.

They had seen him, not in the passport area but in the main post office, on their way in. What's more he had been talking to a girl. They had noticed him because (at this point the recital fell into blushes and giggles) they thought that he and this girl must both be film stars. Also, Luke was looking at this girl in a way that ... well ... It was like something out of a film.

Claudia, seeing Luke's eyes widen, asked, 'A girl? What did she look like? Where was Luke talking to her?'

'Well,' Carol answered, 'you were near the doors to the passport area and we had to push past you to get in, didn't we Lou?'

'Yes, but you didn't notice us, because of this girl. Is it true you can't remember anything?'

Luke nodded.

Carol took up the story. 'I wish you could, Mr Dan … Luke. She really was special. You seemed to know her.'

'You did really. We watched you – I hope you don't mind – through the glass doors. We honestly thought, didn't we Mum, that you were film stars.'

'That's right. Lou would have asked for your autograph only we didn't know your names.'

'Then you both came through into the Passport section and went into the photo booth.'

'Tell me about her, please?'

His sudden intensity sobered the women, who, still speaking alternately, painted a picture of the young woman.

'Well, she had this fair hair, almost white, it was …'

'Ash-blonde.'

'That's right. It wasn't dyed, though.'

'Definitely not. It was loose, quite long …'

'Well, shoulder length really, but beautifully cut. She had real quality about her, you know …'

'Clothes – designer gear it looked, and the figure to carry it off. Not skinny, though. Just about right.'

'And that bracelet, don't you remember, Mum?'

'We honestly thought she was in films, didn't we, Lou.'

Luke held up a hand to stop the flood. 'Her voice, did you hear her speak? What was that like?'

Carol looked at her daughter and then answered hesitantly, 'I don't remember really, except that I didn't think she was English. I mean everything I heard was perfect, but just not completely English. What do you think, Lou?'

'I dunno. She sounded English to me. Maybe she was American?'

Eventually they ran out of phrases and Luke was left with this image of perfection that he had been witnessed talking to and who had left not the tiniest imprint on his memory. While Carol and Louise, just passing by, had observed, discussed and remembered the encounter in unnerving detail. Singular the mother and daughter might be, but their candid recital was without guile, therefore it must be true. So, had he just bumped into this miracle girl inside the post office? It sounded as though he knew her better than that, yet his memory was fine up to the day before the explosion and it contained no paragon such as they had described. So she must have been a stranger. Had he gone there just to meet her? Biggest question of all, where was she now?

He asked unnecessarily, 'If you saw her again, would you recognise her?' The women nodded in unison. Then, after an exchange of addresses and promises to help him in his search, they left. Claudia and Luke stared helplessly at each other.

'This girl, Luke, the one Carol and Louise saw, could she ... do you think this is Heloise?'

'No,' he muttered, head bent. He began slowly to unbutton his shirt.

Claudia took over the undressing as though he were eight not twenty-eight. 'I'm sorry, Topo. What makes you so certain? I mean ... if you can't remember her anyway ...'

'I'm certain that Heloise ...' He stopped. The girl he had talked to in those interminable hours under that building had not been worldly. In fact, she had markedly lacked any of the sophistication implied by Carol and Louise's description. It wasn't this that made him certain though. It was an inner conviction that when he first talked to Heloise, she was somebody entirely new in his life. Given his memory loss, this was not going to sound convincing. He shut his eyes.

'Well, when she crawled up to me in the dark – and I *definitely* remember that bit – she knew nothing about me. She'd been with her parents, before it happened. I mean, if she'd just been talking to me, she'd have recognised my name. *She* remembered everything from before the explosion. *She* told me about it. I don't have any memory of it except hers, not a single drumbeat.'

Claudia watched astonished. 'Luke, don't take on so. This new girl, if we can find her, she might be able to help. At least there are witnesses to her existence.'

'Whereas you only have my word that Heloise exists, is that it?'

Claudia put out a hand but he shrugged it off. 'No Luke, I

41

didn't mean that.' She helped him back into bed just as a nurse appeared with an offer of a night-time drink.

Claudia fiddled with the window blinds until the nurse left then turned to her brother. 'Luca, listen. I desperately want you to be right about Heloise and to find her again. I mostly believe what you tell me, but I cannot ignore my training, which tells me that it's possible – just possible – for the brain, after injury, to be deceived about its perceptions. What I meant when I talked about witnesses was that, now we have a description from other people who do remember the explosion, we have some hope of finding this new girl and she may, in turn, help you to find Heloise. That's the problem with Heloise; getting a start. If you're the only person to have met her, and you don't remember anything about her, we can't make a start.' Claudia put her arms around her brother. 'I'm sorry this girl tonight wasn't Heloise, Topo, but we have a thread to follow now. There's a chance of making the next step. It's a better position than yesterday.' Claudia pulled the sheet up and bent over to kiss her brother goodnight. She whispered, 'I know you think there's something special about her voice, but just don't forget that *you* are the person with a voice to dream about.'

5
Catford: Maria

Luke's mother, her dark hair pinned up neatly, stood in the narrow hallway of her Catford home buttoning up her jacket. On the radiator shelf at her side lay the round metal casing of a portable CD player. She lifted it and weighed it in her hand. On the free CD that came with it, she read: Anniversary Album, 1979–1999, Sony celebrates 20 years. Luca would love the machine, Maria knew; with this she could make her son happy. Every extra hour's sewing needed to afford this latest gadget had given her pleasure, accompanied as it was by the certainty of his delight.

By working late to make another half dozen dresses and rompers for well-heeled infants, she had felt she could contribute to Luke's recovery. She had finished them in time to despatch them with Gordon on one of his long haul trips from Bromley down to the toe of Italy. They would travel, these tiny garments, with their embroidered butterflies rustling in tissue paper, sliding softly against each other in a box in the cab of Gordon's lorry. This way Gordon could feel that he too was actively helping his son. He would give the box to her Uncle at Ciampino, outside Rome, who would hand them to her cousin.

Maria imagined Clara's softly uttered, '*Bella! Bellissima!*' as she pulled out the apricot dress and watched the blue butterflies unfold: the first person to touch the pure cotton since it had left her own hands. Clara's shop in the Piazza Navona sold mostly to tourists, so Maria lived in constant hope of spotting one of her miniature creations back in the West End – not that she spent much time in the West End. Still it might happen one day.

Smiling, Maria replaced the CD player in its box and the box in the slippery plastic cover. The whole package slotted neatly into her handbag. Letting out a puff of satisfaction, she opened her front door, picked up the empty sports bag at her feet and set off for the bus stop. She eyed the watery mid-morning sun and sent it silent instructions to get itself up to temperature before she picked up Luke. He was being transferred from St Thomas to the new hospital at Lewisham, so that he could start his physiotherapy as an in-patient and finish it after being discharged. Maria climbed into the bus for the short run from Catford to Lewisham. She'd have to change there for a bus to Westminster Bridge. They'd have a taxi for the journey back to the new hospital at Lewisham, because of Luke's leg.

The CD player weighed like a gold ingot, dragging at her shoulder; a pleasing ache really, a reminder of the pleasure she would give Luke. According to Claudia, he was in a bad way about the Louise girl not being Heloise after all. Still, he had never been difficult to console; he loved receiving presents. Maria smiled, remembering a four-year-old Luke in the centre of a crowd of relatives. It must have been around Easter, because the children were begging for sweets during Lent. Luke's namesake, uncle Luca, had handed the boy a small bag of sweet wrappers. It had been intended as a joke, even a torment, but Luke, his face glowing with delight, had picked up the pieces of coloured cellophane and silver paper one by one, beaming and saying '*grazie, grazie*'. Standing within the circle of doting grown-ups, he had chosen a colour through which to look at each of them.

'*Giallo*, yellow, for Aunty Laura, like the sun? *Rosso*, red for Uncle, *come il vino* , like the wine.' They had laughed and Luke had known, even then, that his audience belonged to him. They adored him, all of them, even Claudia and Barbara, though he undoubtedly stole their limelight from the day of his birth. Maria shook her head in puzzlement at the thought of her eldest daughter, Claudia: so hardworking, so determined, so ... uncomfortable?

Frowning now, Maria looked up as the bus sat stranded outside the white, curved bulk of the Lewisham Theatre. The icing sugar detail always made her feel as though the Alhambra had come to town. She'd been in and out of the great glass doors, or the small stage door at the back, so many times with Luke, it felt like personal property. Oliver in 1986, was it? Joseph in 89. Dave and Luke had both starred in that.

Maria shifted the heavy bag onto her other shoulder, and prepared to change buses. A young man, who looked faintly familiar, followed her onto the 36 bus and hung on a strap near to her seat. Unable to place him, Maria found herself watching his profile. There was something odd about him, his skin perhaps? It was almost transparent; one of those skins underneath which you can almost see the blood moving. Just at the moment though, he seemed to have no blood at all, his face showed eggshell white under the fair hair. She looked away and then back, puzzled by her own fascination.

His expression too, with the eyes artificially wide open as though someone were wrenching his hair backwards, reminded her of the people waiting outside the exploded post office. So many people with faces just like that sitting or pacing about in that cleared out shop in Cardon Street. She, too, must have looked like that.

With a crowd of about sixty relatives, they had waited hour after hour as the rescue teams searched. Hoping every second to get a phone call from Luke to say he had forgotten to tell them he'd gone to a gig in Glasgow, or something; yet knowing from that first phone call, two hours after the explosion, that he was in there somewhere. Lewisham Theatre had rung wanting to know why Luke had failed to turn up to rehearse, why his mobile was not answering. Where was he? Maria, standing in his bedroom, looking at his leather coat, his shaving kit and his new trainers, had known he had not gone far. As they waited, people had appeared, at intervals, from nowhere with coffee and sandwiches but never (or almost never) with any news.

She stole another glance at the man. As well as the widened eyes, his lips were parted, so that the shallow breaths could come and go with minimal effort. Disturbed, Maria dragged her eyes away from the fragile face above her and stared out of the bus window. Camberwell's red and white striped Art College unrolled beside her, but all she could see, in imagination, was the facade of the windowless post office as she and Gordon waited for news. Ten days, only ten days ago. Listening was the most forceful activity those waiting could engage in. They all listened passionately to the unfamiliar noises and the strained silences. The strangeness lived with her still; the hum of generators at night, the clotting of people and lights, the happy enthusiasm of the sniffer dogs and the sudden excitement of a possible find, then the disintegration of the group when it turned out to be nothing. Neither she nor Gordon had slept more than odd minutes from that first phone call onwards. At times it seemed to Maria as if that missing sleep had never been restored. She turned her eyes from the bus

45

windows; the disturbing young man still stood beside her, rocking with the bus.

It would be fine when Luca came home again and she could ...well she could feed him up for a start. He, like the young man she had been watching, was becoming too hard-edged, too adult. She sighed. There was nothing she could do about this missing girl, this Heloise. Claudia was afraid that the girl might not be real anyway, might simply be in Luke's mind. Surely it would be better for the girl to be unreal rather than dead. Better for the girl, better for him.

Barbara was doing fine, though: encouraging Lewis to look for this Heloise, finding other people for Luke to talk to, getting engaged. Maria smiled. That was one good thing to come out of this mayhem, the young people making decisions at last. Lewis was the right man for Barbara. Maria felt she had known this for nearly two, patient years. Twenty-nine for heaven's sake! Claudia was over thirty and it didn't look as though she would ever get round to marriage – too busy, too keen on her freedom. Now she was a doctor as well; what man would want to marry someone that clever?

The bus jerked on its way and the woman beside her squeezed past and into the aisle. Maria moved into the window seat and the young man she had gazed at earlier collapsed into the seat beside her. He's no older than Luke, she thought. Now, all she could see were his hands. These were very slight, with the same thin skin as his face, and they trembled. The handwriting on the envelope he held dithered so much that only the word SCOTLAND was readable. He started flicking one corner up and down with his thumb. Maria had to resist the temptation to put her own hand on his to still the trembling.

She was not surprised when he, like her, got off at the hospital. She followed him up to the entrance, where he suddenly turned to face her.

'Excuse me, do you know if there's a postbox inside?'

Seen full on at last, his face gave her a small jolt. No wonder he seemed familiar. He *had* actually been one of the waiting relatives outside the post office. She touched his arm and pointed out the pillar box almost directly behind him. He suddenly recognised her, gave her a quick, tight smile and followed her into the hospital.

They went different ways. If he has come to the hospital, thought Maria, then his relative must have been pulled out alive. Unless, of course... her memory produced a Morning News headline – *25th Victim* , and she wondered. Her concern for the young man dissipated as she approached Luke's ward. It was a happy day today and nothing was going to spoil it.

Luke, fully dressed, lay on his bed. It was two days since Louise Braithwaite had turned out not to be Heloise. He had got used to that now. He had only believed that she might be for a moment and then only because he thought (as he still thought) that Heloise had been fibbing about her age. This other girl, though, the blonde one he was supposed to have met before the explosion; he couldn't fit her into the picture at all. He closed his eyes. If this were a part in an opera, then he would think his way into it, filling out all the details, until he believed in them. That was all acting needed – believing. It seemed to work for him at any rate. Why couldn't he simply believe in this girl? Perhaps the problem was that she didn't have a name. He tried thinking of her as Heloise, but his mind refused. This new girl needed a glamorous film star name to go with her hair and designer clothes – Gloria perhaps. He would call her Gloria and imagine talking to her in the pre-explosion building.

The trouble was that he had no memory of the building either, no whisper in his mind of entering or leaving such a structure. Not even of walking down Cardon Street recently. Even though he had spent forty-eight hours inside the building's broken guts, he had neither touched nor seen his prison. He corrected himself, remembering the little robot with its toy beams lighting the jagged mess above his head, yet that memory was more like a computer game than reality. Perhaps the whole world was lying to him; perhaps he had never been in this explosion at all? Perhaps it was a road accident; perhaps he was still unconscious? Perhaps it was all a dream – not Heloise, he begged, please not Heloise. Teetering on the edge of sleep, he consulted her.

'Not Gloria,' Heloise said, 'I think she should be called Brigitte.'
'No. Too sixties.'
'What about Violetta?'

'No, Violetta should be dark.'

'I thought men preferred blondes.'

'You do have some daft old-fashioned ideas. What colour's your hair, Heloise?'

'Oh…I don't know…sort of fairish. It was blonde when I was little. Will you sing again.'

He laughed, recognising by now her inclination to slither out of personal questions. Why did she evade him so much? In his frustration Luke shifted, causing astonishing momentary pain in his ankle. For a groaning moment he lost track of his mind.

'Luke? Luke, speak to me. Where does it hurt?'

The pain ebbed and he returned to his strange world. 'It's my ankle, and there's nothing you can do about that. God, I shall be glad when we get out.'

'But Luke…?'

It was his turn to be evasive. 'Shall I sing again? You choose. You seem to know a lot of opera.

'All right, but I've never actually seen an opera.'

He was confused yet again. She had recognised Corsaro, a really obscure opera, such as only a dedicated Verdi lover would know. 'What d'you mean? You've never been to an opera? How come you're familiar with early Verdi then?'

She gave another of her little gasps so reminiscent of a child caught with its hand in the sweet tin. 'I…well…we don't live near enough to an Opera House. My parents don't really approve of Opera. It's my secret *vice*.' The word "vice" uttered in her rich voice, with such breathless horror, made him splutter. 'My cousin lets me listen,' she finished.

Luke was baffled, even indignant; opera was his whole life. 'What on earth's wrong with opera? My Nonna used to sing me the tunes as a lullaby. I don't want to be rude, but your parents sound way out of date.

She laughed. 'Yes, a bit. But it's more to do with religion. They're very strict.'

'You mean like Jehovah's Witnesses?'

'Oh no, no they're quite different. They … would you sing some more. Please.'

Luke flushed in the dark; her parents might now be dead.

'What would you like then? No, I know, *who* would you like

48

to be? Choose a heroine, from the Verdi/Puccini repertoire and I'll sing to you. Would you like that?'

'Oh please, yes please. I want to be all of them.' Her voice fluctuated in childish excitement. 'I want to be Gilda, and Violetta and Luisa Miller and Mimi ...'

'Hey, steady on, one at a time; I like to get in character. Who's your favourite, who do you dream of singing?'

'I don't know, they are all so different, so much more exciting than I am, they all move freely about the world. I don't know, you choose.'

'All right, let's start simple. You can be Mimi ...' He hesitated remembering that Mimi's life was doomed. Then brushing this away, went on, 'Just imagine you're a poor seamstress ...'

She interrupted, chuckling, 'That's more or less what I am; I work with threads and wools.'

'No! Just like my mother.' Luke thrust this thought of his mother quickly aside, 'OK, so you're a seamstress and your only light, your candle, has gone out and you can't see to work.'

'I'd manage in the dark.'

'Don't be difficult, you can't sew in the dark. Anyway, Mimi has been trying to meet the students in the flat below for some time. So she comes for a light and then she drops her keys. You – Mimi, and I – Rodolfo are both feeling around in the dark for this key, but Rodolfo has other ideas. You ask if I am *really* looking and I answer – *Cerco (I am looking)*.' He sang the two notes and they hung in the strange air. He whispered, 'Put your hand on my cheek.' Heloise's fingers tentatively brushed his cheek, then moved down and rested on his neck. With his voice slowly building in richness and tone, he sang, '*Che gelida manina ... (What a cold little hand ...)*.'

Heloise's fingers lay on his throat, light, warm and trembling with the vibrations of his voice. For a moment he nearly choked, feeling them as yet another fetter. Her fingers shifted and Luke knew himself safe, almost released. He sang on, finishing, '*Now tell me who you are.*'

As he ended the aria he closed his eyes, half expecting her to sing Mimi's answer, but she started shaking his shoulder. 'Luke, Luke, wake up now.'

He opened his eyes. Heloise had gone; light poured over him.

For a moment he didn't understand. He looked round the ward and up into the face of the nurse beside his bed. She had a handful of papers that he was to take with him to the next hospital and yet another package of leaflets about the services available to survivors of the disaster. A huge wash of disappointment flushed through him. Then he saw his mother walking across the ward and beaming, and he struggled not to weep his relief.

'Hello, Luca, you look surprised. Remember we're going to the other hospital today – in a taxi. The sun is out.'

'Mum! Oh Mum, it's so good you're here. I fell asleep . . . at least I think I was asleep.' He paused uncertainly. 'I'm not sure if I was dreaming . . . or . . . perhaps just remembering. It made sense . . . well it wasn't nonsense, anyway.' He rubbed his face and swung his legs down to sit up. 'Sorry, Mum, I'm talking rubbish. Come on, let's get out of this place.'

'OK, Luca. But look at what I have for you.' She withdrew the plastic wrapped packet from her handbag and watched his eyes widen as he recognised the shop name. Satisfaction filled her as he tore excitedly at the wrapping.

'Mum! Oh Mum! Is this the new, shock-proof one?'

'Yes. I looked at the mini ones, but they said not for opera.'

'No, no. This is perfect.'

Luke slid on his bottom until he was near his locker and fumbled awkwardly inside, eventually finding the CD Dave had sent. Then, with the earplugs in, Luke pressed a button. After a moment he looked up at his mother, his eyes sparkling with delight, his thumb raised in triumph. A minute later he removed one earplug and put it to his mother's ear and watched her. Both sat on the side of the bed for several minutes, one earplug apiece and their faces alight with pleasure.

Twenty minutes later they both stood, turned like sunflowers towards the light, just outside the main entrance of the hospital. To Maria's astonishment the young man from the bus reappeared. He, too, must have been picking something up. He carried a large white plastic bag and looked, if anything, paler than before. At the sight of them, he pressed his lips in a half smile of recognition. Maria, remembering how much of the journey from Lewisham they had shared, said, 'We have a taxi coming to take us back to Lewisham, do you want to share?' The young man shook his head, and walked off, shoulders hunched, to the bus stop.

It was only in the taxi that Maria mentioned to Luke that the young man had had relatives in the post office too.

6

Cairngorms: Nina

By ten o'clock the mist had cleared off Ben Macdhui and when Nina Binyon opened her front door the grey-blue immensity of the hills seemed to come in and expand her tiny living room. Hearing the post van from Tomintoul chugging up the hill, she thought, without any particular hope, that maybe she would get a letter today. The van stopped and a prickle of excitement lifted her spirits. Receiving post was still as thrilling now as it had been during dull boarding school days. Not that there was any comparison between those smelly brick corridors and these birch covered Scottish hills. Nina reached out and patted the grey stone windowsill of her cottage affectionately. Funny that the mind should leap back twenty years like that on the wings of one small thought. It was just the idea of someone wanting so positively to communicate, that they had lifted a hand and laboriously (in these computer days) scored pen across paper, that appealed.

Still standing in the doorway, she watched John Drew stomp up her short path. Of course, if she did have any post it would be printed, signature and all, not handwritten. Even the placing in envelopes would have been the work of machines these days.

In fact there were two hand-addressed letters to Miss N. Binyon; both with the same unfamiliar handwriting. She held them unopened as she chatted to John, waiting for him to go, so that she could open them in private. Confusion crept up on her. It is one thing, she discovered, to dream of letters from an unexpected source, it is less comfortable to receive them. Why two from the same person? Surprised to find her hands a trifle shaky, she opened one, and drew out the single sheet.

Dear Nina B., (only the children, as far as she could recall, had ever called her that) *As I feared when I first wrote to you, Dan never recovered from his injuries. I'm afraid he died early this morning...*

She turned the page over to look at the signature, but couldn't decipher it. Then she compared the two envelopes. The one she had opened was postmarked the 8th July, the other the 25th June.

She carried both envelopes and the letter into the kitchen and sat down heavily at the table. Her hands, now suddenly thick and rough, struggled to open the envelope with the earlier postmark. Looking up to take a steadying breath, she spotted her knitting on the dresser. Taking up the fine steel needle she slipped it inside the flap, ripped open the seal and pulled out four sheets of paper. She read:

Dear Nina B., please don't mind me calling you this. I can't think of you by another name. I hope you remember me, Morris, Ruth's cousin. I am writing because I don't know who to turn to for help and you were very kind to me as well as Ruth when we were both little and you looked after us. It is about Ruth that I am writing. Well, actually, it is about Dan and Martha. You must have heard about the terrible explosion at the Cardon Street post office in London on June the 9th, well they were in the building. They were going to apply to get Ruth a passport, because she had won a holiday with the Blind Association. Ruth is fine, not even scratched, but Martha was killed instantly ...

Martha dead? Nina pushed the sheets of paper away from her and clutched the edge of the table. For fifteen years she had imagined hearing this news. Like the letters, though, the actuality failed to match the dream. Her soul refused to give the expected yell of triumph. Nina picked up the letter again.

... The worst part is that Dan is alive, but very badly injured. The doctors have been very frank with us; they are doing everything they can but think his recovery is unlikely.

Nina, I don't know what to do about Ruth. I have been living with her since it happened, but I think she needs a woman. She is brilliant in the house, and she gets around very well, but she can't live alone. When she went on that training course in York they suggested that she should train with a Guide Dog, but you know what Dan and Martha were like; they wouldn't hear of it. They only sent her on the course because social services were getting to be a nuisance. It would take a long time to train a dog with her and I don't know if I can cope that long ...

Ruth in trouble? Responsibility, laid aside so reluctantly fifteen years ago, shifted back onto Nina's shoulders.

... It will probably seem unimportant to you, but I desperately want to go ahead with our joint exhibition (I don't suppose you

even know about this, but the Grosjean Gallery will be showing our weaving next month), not just for my sake, but because Ruth will need to make her own living now and to have something to live for too. She has gone all quiet, and it worries me. She sits with Dan all day. Thank God she can't see his face, or anything around her. The hospital is full of fearsome injuries. Sorry, I don't mean to sound so cowardly. I have thought of my parents, but they are in Hong Kong at the moment, and you will remember (since it was you who had to look after me when I fell off the garage roof that summer), just how much use they are in a crisis.

Sorry Nina, I'm rambling a bit now, I really am at my wits end. If Dan dies it will get even more complicated. I know things went wrong between you and Martha, but she was some kind of relative to you wasn't she? So presumably you are related to Ruth. I don't know of any other relatives. I know that it's about fifteen years since you left, but I can't think who else to turn to. Dear Nina B. could you possibly come and look after Ruth until we can get something sorted?

Love from Morris (Gardiner)

Nina put the letter down on the table. Her eyes lifted to the blue hills framed by the tiny window and seemed to freeze there. She felt like something out of a painting, something stalled forever in just that second of time. Inside her brain, cells fired; outside neither her hands nor her feet moved in obedience. It was not her heart that was pole-axed, but her wits. For Martha she felt, at best, dislike; for Dan, pity. She had excised any other emotion for them years ago. Fifteen years ago. Their death was the fulfilment of a wicked wish. Ruth was now . . . she counted carefully, she must be nearly thirty years old? And Morris? Such a spiky, skinny child, with his fair complexion and his riveting grey eyes – a grown man? Her vision of Ruth and Morris refused to move forward into this new reality.

Nina sat on. Eventually, growling at herself in exasperation, she struggled to her feet and put the kettle on the hotplate. She was spooning a ration of tea leaves into the pot when it occurred to her that she had never read the second letter – apart, that is, from the first line telling of Dan's death. The table seemed to be littered with paper and in the end she had to spread the sheets out like playing cards to find it. She read:-

Dear Nina B., As I feared when I first wrote to you, Dan never recovered from his injuries. I'm afraid he died early this morning. The hospital rang to tell me. I am going in soon to say goodbye and pick up his things. I was going to write again anyway because life has got, if possible, even more complicated. Last Thursday Ruth had a fall, she seemed fine afterwards, just a few bruises, but by the next morning she was running a temperature. I took her to the doctor that evening and I'm afraid she has been admitted to hospital with suspected pneumonia.

She is in the new hospital in Lewisham so at least it is round the corner. She seems quite comfortable but a bit out of it. Dear Nina B. I don't know if you got my first letter and I wouldn't bother you again if I could think of another solution, but please could you come and help us. Could you ring me on my mobile number (see above). Love Morris.

Nina glanced at the address and the strange-looking number. Once again she felt paralysed by all that Morris's request would mean for her. She finished making the tea, then carried her cup out and sat on the old bench overlooking the vegetable patch. The cup rattled on its saucer and she put it down carefully beside her.

In front of her rows of pale green shoots, some feathery, some spiky, pushed through the earth; the broad beans and early potatoes looked ready to crop; the winter cabbages needed grubbing up, though there were still a couple of edible ones left. Back in the kitchen, she remembered, were two bags full of knitting, one with a jumper for the peripatetic designer who gave her occasional work, the other with some regular Arran knitting for the tourist shop in Aviemore. Each required hours more work, perhaps as many as twelve or even eighteen.

Yet, four hundred miles away, Ruth and Morris needed her badly. Nina corrected herself. Morris needed her, but what did Ruth think? Perhaps she, like Martha and Dan, wanted nothing to do with her. Not one word had she heard since the day she had been told to pack her bags fifteen years ago. For three years after that she had sent Ruth cards and gifts at birthdays and Christmas. Had Ruth ever received them?

Nina emptied her cold tea onto the grass and went into the kitchen to refill her cup. Looking around the kitchen, which was also her workroom, she felt tears pushing from within. It was absurd to love furniture, but the neat shelves, so carefully built to her specifications by Hugo and Geoff, filled with her wools and patterns, were her life now. Almost as if she had filled the gap left by Ruth's absence with a thousand strands of coloured wool, she felt that if she abandoned her workroom now she might unravel. She pulled out the drawer in the table to see what other orders were waiting to be filled. The account book stared up at her and another shadow crossed her mind – money.

Here, in the back of beyond, she could live on the tiny sums she earned; knitting piece-work in the winter and helping out in the local nurseries Spring to Autumn. All she owned was this cottage and a tiny sum saved in a fixed bond. There was no money to speak of in the bank. She shivered, and walked quickly to shut the front door as if the bailiffs were that moment approaching. Nothing, but nothing, would make her part with the cottage. It was the only thing in the whole wide world that was actually hers. She laughed, suddenly feeling stronger. With the idea of the cottage she had at last found her bedrock; something solid that was not going to change. Even if the rest of her universe rocked, the cottage would remain here and would remain hers.

She stood up and walked into her bedroom as another thought occurred. Perhaps Ruth could come to her. As she squeezed into her shoebox of a bedroom, Nina's common sense chipped in. In all honesty, 'cottage' was rather a grand term for her three and a half rooms. Two people could only share such a space on the most intimate of footings, and if one of them were blind . . . Perhaps Hugo and Geoff could build another room?

Irritated to find herself daydreaming when she had big decisions to make, Nina got out a pad and pencil and jotted down Morris's number. She pulled on her boots and jacket and tramped towards the village shop two miles down the road.

Behind the counter Mrs Caymen asked her standard question, 'Long distance or local?' as she turned the phone round and pushed it across the counter to Nina.

'Oh long distance, definitely long distance. It's a funny number. I suppose it's one of those mobile thingummies.'

'Oh Miss Binyon, you don't want to ring one of them, that's pounds not pennies for every minute. Bert said I must charge three times as much per minute for those numbers, only I keep forgetting.

I tell you what, when Bert rings our boy on one of them, he makes him ring back. Why don't you do that?'

Nina stared helplessly at the ancient dial telephone on the counter. Perhaps she should go to Hugo's instead. She had to speak to Morris and yet she had only three pounds in her purse. She stared at Mrs Caymen's concerned face. 'All right. I'll do just that.' She picked up the receiver and dialled. 'Morris, is that you? It's Nina Binyon here. Can you ring me back on this number...'

Moments later, he came through. 'Nina B.? I can't believe it. Thank goodness you're there. I was afraid...I didn't know if...if you were still in the same place. Please say you'll come.'

'Morris, dear child, you sound exactly as you did fifteen years ago. Are you sure you've grown up?'

'Yes, I have, truly I have. It's just hearing your voice again in the nick of time. Can you come?'

'Listen Morris, I only got your letters this morning – both of them. I haven't yet had time to work out what I can do. Let's deal with the practical things first. Is there somewhere for me to live?'

'Well of course, you would live with Ruth. I mean there's the whole Blackheath house now with just Ruth rattling around in it. That's where I'm ringing from now. I thought of moving in permanently but . . . well, I have my own place and there's things . . . I think Ruth really needs a woman, anyway.'

'All right, there's somewhere for me to live, anyway. The other problem, Morris dear, is that I have no money that I can get hold of. My small saving is in a closed account, I can't get at it until 2004. I don't think I even have enough to get a coach ticket to London at the moment. I need so little to live on here that I only work when I have to. I could probably borrow the fare from friends of mine, but how would I pay them back and what would I live on in London?'

'Yes, that's a bit tricky at the moment, Nina. Dan gave me power of attorney, while he was alive, but now that he's dead it all has to wait for the solicitors to sort out the will – you know, probate. The trouble is Ruth has no money or bank account or anything. You know what Dan and Martha were like. In fact you probably know better than I do. I'm seeing the solicitor this afternoon and I'm hoping she's going to be able to make some kind of interim allowance from the estate for Ruth. One thing to be thankful for is that Dan had actually made a will in Ruth's favour. With Ruth being blind, I reckon the solicitor will look kindly on giving her some money to cover the cost of live-in care. If we get that, could you somehow manage? Will you come? Please?'

'I expect I'll manage, so long as there's *some* money. Morris, tell me honestly, does Ruth want me to come?'

'Yes, oh yes. Well of *course* she does.'

'Morris, be truthful, dear.'

'I am. She was funny at first when I suggested it. But it turns out that they never told her why you had left. She actually thought you were dead at one point. I've explained things to her, as best I can. You'll explain it better when you come. But she really does want you, Nina, she's so lonely at the moment. Will you really come?'

'Yes Morris, I'll come. But you must sort out some money. I don't suppose London has got any cheaper ... Morris, dear, are you all right?'

'I'm fine ... I'm fine ... I'm just so relieved and ... Well, you know what I felt about Martha, but it was awful seeing Dan at the end ... I'm just so glad you're coming. I'll get the money sorted, truly I will. Can you ring me this evening?'

Nina thought quickly. She could use the public box if it was working but it was another mile on at the end of the village. She could still hear Morris through the handset, sniffing and blowing his nose. 'Yes, I'll phone back around 5.30. Will that be all right?'

She set off back up the hill, the list of things to be done unrolling its fearsome length in her mind's eye. One of the biggest problems was the coach fare. Her tin of current money at home had exactly £12.40 in it, her bank account approximately £20. There was another £30 due but it might not come for a week or two. She turned round and headed back into the village towards the house of her closest friends. Might as well get things done now as later. I've burned all my boats anyway, she thought. She made her way down the single village street until she came to Geoff and Hugo's house. To her great relief Hugo was in – on his own. His shoulder was by far the softer of the two.

Two days later Nina heaved her borrowed suitcase into the hold and climbed up into the coach. She took her last gulp of warm, Scottish morning air knowing that by nightfall the pollution thickened substance of London would be drifting in and out of her lungs She waved miserably at Geoff and made shooing gestures to stop him waiting any longer and then settled down with her thoughts and her knitting for the ten-hour journey South. Once more expectation failed to marry actuality; coming home to Ruth now felt like leaving home.

7

Lewisham Hospital: Morris

Putting on the paper face mask, Morris entered the ultra-modern hospital cubicle with a cheery, 'Good morning, Ruth.'

He got no reply. He opened the blinds and turned to look at his cousin. She lay still and unresponsive, but her eyes were open. For a moment sweat rose on his skin. He drew closer. 'Ruth? Are you ...'

'Morris?' It was a thread of a voice, barely audible through the oxygen mask over her mouth and nose. He sat beside her, stroking her hand. He had planned to tell her that Nina would be coming soon, but the right words failed to materialise and he left it for later. Instead he talked about their work.

'I've been to the gallery, Ruth. There are two rooms, the bigger one is a good height, perfect for your bed-spread sized pieces and there's a space between two long windows which should look great for the one with the blue pipes. I really thought you'd lost it when you started that one.' The limp hand in his twitched and the shadow of a grin came and went on Ruth's lips. Relieved, his hand tightened. 'It's going to look fabulous. You've got to get better, Ruth, you've got experience people's reaction to what you've made, and see it in a proper setting.'

In another part of the same hospital Luke stood at one end of an empty corridor. The floors, walls and ceiling gleamed with soft greys. Even the photos on the walls, great stretching seascapes, were black and white. At head height small lights glowed in a succession of niches, giving the passage a strangely monastic feel. Elsewhere in the hospital determinedly cheerful colours had been added to the architect's purist vision. Here he had obviously had his way. On the whole Luke approved of brighter colours; just now, however, this quiet empty space filled him with relief. If it hadn't been for the crutches he'd have danced all the way down.

He'd been in this new hospital for three days now. Each day he ranged further afield, asking, searching, throwing himself into the physiotherapy, pushing his way back into the life stream. His body ached to be free of constraints. He glanced up the corridor, gripped his crutches and started moving in rhythmical hops, letting the soft *chock chock, chock chock* of his sticks create their own timing. His body swayed a little more with each move. Pleased with the sensation he looked about for an audience and flushed to find a nurse, on silent rubber-soled shoes, only a few feet from him. She smiled.

He grinned back. 'Just practising.'

'Sure. You'll be on stage soon.'

'I will too.' He answered with such quiet conviction that the nurse, passing by, gave his face a searching look.

After she had gone he felt a moment's dizziness. If he had still been fooling around he might have fallen. He froze until his feet regained solid contact with the floor and then took a surreptitious look behind. The nurse had already turned off the long corridor. Proceeding a little more cautiously he arrived at the row of lifts that would take him up to Ward 808. Were there really more than eight floors in this spaceship of a hospital?

An empty lift; more space to himself. He got inside and pressed the button for floor 8. At the sight of the closing doors some gremlin of terror seized Luke from within. High-pitched whimpers pushed their way out of his throat. He dropped his crutches and scrabbled at the door's invisible seam. He slumped like a winded boxer against the metal casing, beating the walls, and ignoring the buttons that might have stopped his ascent. The lift swooped to a halt in less than ten seconds. As he struggled to suppress the noises he was making, the door opened, and he was exposed gulping like a landed fish. Luke shuffled upright and pulled himself off the walls. A couple about to enter the lift gave him uncertain looks. The man half lifted a hand towards him, thought better of it, and held the door open to let Luke out. He brushed past them and leaned, shaking, against the windows opposite the lift door. Like an animal meeting an electric fence for the first time, he had no idea what had happened to him. With trembling knees, he struggled merely to remain upright. Sweat poured off him and the crutches slithered about in his hands. He needed to sort his breathing out. He needed to sit down. He needed a pee.

People walked past, catching the lift with no more than a passing glance at the wet, white face by the window. This was a hospital, after all. He turned to look outwards, leaning his head against the cool glass. Eventually his heart slowed and he moved on.

Off his feet at last, in the sanctuary of the Gents, he sat, his arms across his knees, his head on his arms. What had happened back there in the lift? It was all right in here even with the door locked. In fact it was so good; it was going to be difficult ever to leave, especially with the prospect of the lift back down. He had been in other lifts in the other hospital; big rattly, cranky lifts; lifts that ought to have been scary. He had been in them on a bed, in a wheelchair, on crutches. He wiped his face, blowing his nose on handfuls of toilet paper. This lift ... he shuddered ... this lift was a state-of-the-art vehicle; silky smooth, well lit, perfectly sealed. Sealed ... dead ... empty ... impossible to get out of ... soundless.

It was nearly twelve o'clock. He'd have to get back to his ward soon. He gritted his teeth and started to get up. Ten minutes he'd been in there. After splashing water generously over himself, he stared at a stranger's face in the mirror, with dark, water-flattened hair and grimly visible scars. He made his way onwards to Ward 808. According to Lewis (through the internal fireman's network), there was a woman there who had been the last person, apart from himself, to be rescued from the building.

Luke entered the security box outside ward 808. Like some science fiction fantasy, a hidden camera checked him and then a buzz, announcing his face to be acceptable, heralded the automatic opening of the second set of doors. He was used to this system now. Inside the ward he was quickly lost; a series of closed mini-wards with glass portholes, spread out north, south and east. After wandering and peering down two arms of the ward, he spotted a group of nurses clustered around a sort of bar.

The nurse he approached shook her head at his request. 'Ruth Gardiner? Not unless you're a relative. I'm sorry, but Ruth isn't well enough to receive visitors. Anyway, it's one at a time and she has a relative with her already.'

Luke, seeing his almighty journey about to become pointless, looked at the nurse in some desperation. 'I just need to speak to her – only for a moment. We were both in the Cardon Street explosion you see.'

The nurse looked puzzled. 'Kay, did Ruth come in off Cardon Street? I thought she was new here last week.'

'That's right, she's got a chest infection. She's not an injury case.'

Luke wondered suddenly whether he had overestimated Lewis's detective abilities. 'This relative,' he asked, 'could I just have a few words with her?'

'Him,' the nurse corrected. 'I don't see why not.' She turned to the other nurse, 'Are you going down to fourteen, Kay, could you give twelve a knock and see if he is still with her. Thanks.' With that she turned away to get on with her work.

Luke, deflated, slid down onto an upholstered bench. He shut his eyes and leant his wet head back against the wall.

'Hallo. Did you want to see me?'

He opened his eyes quickly to see a face close to his own. The eyes, grey with charcoal edges to the irises, were startling. Luke remembered the agitated man outside the other hospital, refusing to share their taxi. He hitched himself quickly to his feet. 'Yes, I was hoping to speak to Ruth Gardiner. She *was* in the Cardon Street post office, wasn't she?'

'That's right. Who are you? If you don't mind me asking?'

'Sorry, Luca Danford – Luke. I was there too.'

'Ah yes. I'm Morris.' He put a warm hand briefly on top of Luke's where it held the crutch. 'You want to talk to her about it? I wish you could but it might be difficult, she won't talk about it, even to me. And just at the moment she is too sick to talk to anyone. I have to wear one of these each time I go in.' He gestured to the face mask dangling from one hand

Luke landed sharply on the bench again.

Morris hovered over him. 'Are you all right? Can I do anything?'

The concern in Morris's expression threatened to destabilize Luke. Tears pricked at his eyes. He shook his head. 'I just needed to ask Ruth if she saw or talked to a girl called Heloise, or if she has ever seen me.' Luke saw Morris's brows twitch together and he hurried on. 'You see, the problem is, I can't remember anything until after the explosion. All I know is what Heloise told me, but I can't find her.'

Morris looked at him uncertainly then touching Luke lightly on the shoulder, sat down beside him. After a moment he spoke. 'I'd better explain. I'm afraid Ruth wouldn't have been able to see you, or this girl. Ruth is blind.'

Luke stared at the floor blinking hard. Morris went on, 'She is very, very sick at the moment. Nothing to do with the explosion – at least I don't think so. She has pneumonia. I sit there but she hardly ever speaks to me, and I'm the closest relative she has. Just at the moment I can't ask anything of her that might set her back. Perhaps when she's better ...'

Luke was silent. What could he say? He could hardly curse the poor woman for being blind and sick. He'd better get back to his ward or he would miss lunch. And there was still the lift problem lurking.

Morris spoke again. 'Do you want to see her even if she won't talk? You can look through the little window, then you won't have to put on one of these thingies,' he lifted the mask. 'As you were both in the post office before the explosion, perhaps *you* will recognise *her*.'

Reluctantly following Morris, he arrived at a small window. A woman lay fast asleep, a clear mask hiding her mouth and nose. Dark shoulder length hair lay lank and untidy over the pillow. She appeared to be a complete stranger; yet another blank wall. He stared in frustration at the pale face behind the ugly mask. Forgetting Morris, he released one hand from his crutches and beat his fist lightly on the glass before resting his forehead on his fist. Why couldn't Lewis, if he was so brilliant, have found out about her blindness as well? Why had he sent Luke on this stupid trek through this nightmare of a hospital?

He jumped when Morris spoke. 'Have you seen her before?'

'No. No, I don't recognise her. She's not ... I hope she gets well soon. I'd better go or I'll miss lunch. Thanks for your help. Perhaps ... if you could ask her ... No, I suppose if she couldn't see that would be silly. Bye.' He turned away abruptly and set off. Morris followed him to the security door, and pressed a business card on him.

' – In case you ever want to get in touch. Please do come and talk to Ruth when she's better.'

Fifteen minutes later Luke was still standing outside the lift doors, swearing quietly. Six flights of stairs on crutches in his current state of weariness would take forever. He was *not* scared of lifts. It had just been a one-off. Perhaps the stairs wouldn't be so bad.

Suddenly Morris was beside him again. 'You OK?'

He flushed. 'I...I was trying to make up my mind about taking the stairs – for the exercise.'

Morris lifted his brows, giving Luke the full impact of his strange eyes. 'Are you mad? It's eight flights. Lift for me.' He pressed the button, then looking at Luke's face again, he said more gently, 'Come on, come with me.'

Another couple appeared at that moment, the lift doors opened and Luke levered himself off the wall and followed Morris in. It was all right. The acoustics in the lift were different because of the presence of other people. Nevertheless, he was breathing fast when he got out on the second floor. To his surprise Morris got out too.

'I'll come this way for a change. I like to see new corners of the Starship Enterprise. Where do you hang out?'

Luke chuckled, buoyant now that he had survived the lift. 'Well I've been promoted from the headcase ward in St Thomas' to the broken bones one here in Lewisham.' He turned his head so that Morris could see the operation scars. 'This 90s haircut is where they dipped into my brain. It still works, most of the time – the brain, I mean. I should be going home tomorrow. I'm down the end of this corridor with all the eye-level illuminations.'

They moved slowly down the long gallery together. On either side the recessed miniature lights glowed.

'Do you think the lights are doing something?' Morris wondered aloud, 'I mean are they attached to a computer or is it just the architect dreaming of submarines?'

'Search me. This is my pad. I'm over there.' They both looked through the double glass security doors into Luke's ward. Luke's bed was the first one beyond the doors. He jerked upright. 'Hey!' The exclamation was at the sight of two women with their heads in his bedside locker. The women looked up and spotted him at that moment.

'Looks like you've got a reception committee, I'll be on my way.'

'It's only my sisters. I wonder what's up. Oh bye, Morris, and thanks for the help.'

'Well, I wasn't much use, was I? But do ... keep in touch. Maybe Ruth will be able to help when's she's better. You've got my card? Good. See you.' His hand brushed Luke's shoulder and he disappeared before Luke could take him in and introduce him to Claudia and Barbara.

Claudia, busy disembowelling Luke's locker, looked sharply at him as he collapsed onto his bed. 'Luke you look all in. Who was that with you?'

Luke sighed. 'Oh he was a relative of a woman who was in the post office – the last one out but me. And no, she doesn't recognise me. I didn't even speak to her. She's blind and she's very sick.' Seeing Barbara staring at Morris's retreating back, he asked. 'What is it Ba?'

'Nothing, I was just curious about your friend. Not exactly a hunk, but dishy all the same. Something about the eyes, but I bet he's gay. You're coming home, Luke. They don't want you any more, they want the bed instead.'

'But ...' He stopped. For the last twenty minutes he had been concentrating on the moment when he would be able to lie down and let go of all the thousand muscles that seemed to be involved in keeping him upright these days. Home? Coming home? A need so overwhelming for his own nest gaped in front of him. For the third time that day his throat started to swell.

He rolled over and spoke aggressively to Barbara. 'What do you mean, gay? You can't possibly know, you didn't even speak to him.'

She lifted her brows. 'Trust me. When a guy looks too good to be true ... Hey, aren't you pleased – about coming home, I mean.'

'Sure.' He gulped and closed his eyes. 'Just beam me up.' He opened them again and sitting up, turned to Claudia. 'Are you certain? Don't I have to do any more of those tests for nutters? I told them the wrong date this morning, I thought they'd have me back in the Neuro ward in a flash.'

Claudia pushed him back on the bed. 'Lie still, we've nearly done. No, they don't want to see you for tests for another four days. The skin grafts on your ankle are healing well. You saw the physio this morning and she gave you your exercise regime, and they want your bed now. So you can go home and come in to out-patients on Tuesday morning. I've got my car and Mum's making a celebration lunch. Dad's on a long haul, but he might be back Saturday. Hey Topo! What's up now?'

'Nothing! Nothing! I just can't wait, that's all.' He turned and buried his head in the pillow.

Claudia shook her head and continued to pack Luke's wash-bag and slippers into a rucksack. Barbara patted Luke's shoulders. 'Nearly home, Topo. Think of Mum's mushroom risotto and forget the rest. You're just tired. What would you like most in the world.'

Luke jerked his head up. 'To find Heloise.'

His sisters exchanged glances.

On the bus, Morris sat staring out of the window, absently zipping his jacket up and down. He should have talked more to Luke, persuaded him to explain what it felt like under the rubble. That might have given him some insight into Ruth's state of mind. She seemed determined not to let him, or anyone else, into that memory. Surely she ought to talk through these things to get better but she had refused to go to the Survivors' meetings or meet either the priest or the counsellor who had offered to visit her. And just now, when he tried to tell her about Luke and his memory problems, she had gone crazy, weeping, coughing and choking as if this reminder of the explosion had unhinged her. Nurses had barged in and hustled him out. It had been a stroke of luck that Luke had left so slowly; at least he knew where to find him in the hospital now.

8

Catford & Hackney: Dave

His mind still loose with sleep, Luke listened to the traffic outside his bedroom window for a clue about the time of day. He stretched and his skin moved sweetly against the familiar sheets, meeting the comfort of ridges and nubbles on a mattress that had kept his body company for twenty or more years. He wasn't exactly awake, yet his drifting mind knew he was home again: in control again. No tubes. No catheter. No need to get up; Mum would give him leeway for a few days. Traffic? It sounded fairly heavy, end of the morning rush hour perhaps? From inside the house a faint stop-start humming reached his ears – his mother's sewing machine. He rolled over and opened one eye at his bedside clock. Twelve o'clock? In disbelief, he groped for his watch. Yes, twelve. No wonder he felt different. In hospital it had been six o'clock waking day after day with incessant night-time comings and goings. No wonder he had felt ill in there. He sniffed the air. If he went to the bathroom to alert his mother then perhaps the smell of coffee ... and with the thought the first brain-teasing whiffs of caffeine trickled under his door. Bliss!

He snuggled back into his pit half-minded to sleep on. Then, as he realised that he was now free to think and believe what he damned well liked, his mind defied him and flickered into full wakefulness. Flinging back the duvet, he leapt upright, steadying himself for a moment on the wardrobe. The dizzy fit passed. The mirror startled him a bit. He had seen himself in enough hospital mirrors, but somehow had expected his own mirror to return his old face. He put one hand up to cover his damaged brow. The face that gazed back at him remained strange, even his hand looked unfamiliar. He touched his face with experimental tenderness as if his hand belonged to someone else. He closed his eyes to stop the usual images taking over, but quickly opened them again as his body made a disobedient lurch. He studied his eyes. An old childhood game: he shifted the lamp trying to get the light on his eyes direct enough to squeeze the pupils into a tight ball and reveal the tiny gold-brown streaks against the darker liquorice background.

Achieving this and relieved that something fundamental remained as before, he refocused on the whole face again. Perhaps the scars would change how people treated to him.

Tiring of this self-inquisition, he pulled a face, opened his door and shouted downstairs. 'Mum, I'm up.' This meant that he would find fresh coffee waiting as soon as he was dressed. He walked over to the window and pulled the curtain back. He stood looking out, relieved that the close-packed 1950s terrace with its peeling discordant paintwork remained as it always had. Reassured, he headed for the bathroom. His new jeans, the ones he had bought shortly before the explosion, told him what had changed. They hung loosely on his hips. He had another dizzy moment later when he leant down to put on his shoes, but decided to ignore it. He was free for the first time since ... well presumably the explosion on June the ninth, but as far as he was concerned since his conversation with Claudia the night before that. Four weeks of chaos and incarceration of one sort or another.

All over. Time now to get fit again, get his voice back up to speed and find Heloise, because she *was* real, and she *wasn't* on the list of the dead and he was *not* off his trolley. Now he could go and search for himself and no one could stop him. Dave would help him. Dave had rung from Cardiff last night to say that he was out of the singing competition and would wrap things up and be back to see Luke in a couple of days. Two *more* days! Luke found himself blinking; he really needed Dave now. He would fill the time until he arrived with making plans. His best theory was that Heloise had another first name, the way dad's sister was Rose Caroline, but everyone called her Caro. Maybe Heloise had been rescued but had muddled her memory and told a different story about her time in the building. He would find her and then ... Never in the whole of his effortless life had Luke felt such an ardent desire, such implacable determination to achieve something. It made auditioning for Don José for the Guildhall look like child's play. Then there was this other girl, who didn't sound half bad, but was definitely not Heloise. If he found her, she might explain what he was doing in the post office in the first place.

Before going down to breakfast, he ran his voice over a five-minute exercise. Gulli, his voice tutor, would be back in another week and he would not regard all-out war, never mind a mere forty-eight hours of imprisonment in a blown-up building, as an excuse for a sagging voice. The voice was a bit rough, but he'd missed the Corvale festival now and he had plenty of time before Stockholm. At least Gulli had worked him mercilessly before the ...Before the what? It was difficult to give a name to an event you had somehow failed to experience. In fact in his head he mostly referred to it as before and after Heloise.

Luke deliberately abandoned his crutches and limped down the stairs; there were no wide, empty spaces or gigantic staircases here, no slippery surfaces either. With help from a radiator here and a shelf there, he reached the kitchen. The humming of the sewing machine ceased. Maria appeared and conjured warm rolls and a steaming mug of coffee onto the table. Fresh bread! Real coffee! The steam from the roll rose as he tore it open, the butter sat taut on the white bed then relaxed into a yellow pool. For a heady moment, as the first swig of coffee rose from taste bud to brain cell, Luke thought nothing else in life mattered a scrap.

A few mouthfuls in and he began to curse Dave for being so far away still. This seemed more unfair than the scars or the broken ankle. He had pleaded with him on the phone last night, but nothing would reduce the red tape or make Cardiff instantly five miles from London.

Towards the end of his first coffee another siren voice murmured in his ear, drowning his mother's gentle chatter. Heloise came back to haunt him; he could not have dreamt up that voice. Its soft vibrations still buzzed in his head. Even if the most ghastly outcome were true; if, say, they had bulldozed her to death, they would have found something by now. Every brick and nail of that building, according to Lewis, was being passed through a sieve. There were people who didn't believe it was gas in the old sewers that had killed their child or their father: the conspiracy theorists were merrily spinning stories out of the ether, the Gas Board were blaming the Local Council and the National Car Parks who'd had space under the building were blaming the Gas Board . . . Then there was always the IRA, the Red Army or the guy behind the Nairobi bomb – Bin Laden. The IRA seemed most likely, they had targeted London often before, but the possibilities seemed to be endless. Anyway, a lot of people needed answers. Perhaps he should go to the place where they were collecting the debris?

'Luke? What is it?'

'Sorry, Mum, nothing. Is there more coffee?'

He sighed then smiled at his mother's look of concentration as she refilled his mug. She picked up a pile of newspaper cuttings collected by Claudia and handed them to him with a disapproving snort. He grinned at her, they were both too easy-going to resist Claudia's instructions, but united in their feeling that she gave them just a few too many.

He settled on the sofa in the front room to make a show of reading through the cuttings. Claudia had actually saved him hours of tedious searching and he allowed his irritation to pass into mild gratitude. He soon tired of the newspaper print and looked round for diversions but his new CD player was upstairs and his mother's machine, whirring familiarly from the back room, made a sufficiently soothing backdrop.

At least he didn't have to go out to work yet. Money was a bit short, but they'd kept his part-time job at the gym and he would be back there in a couple of weeks. Anyway, he'd chalked up a lot of credit by being nearly dead. So much credit in fact that Dad had given him a couple of hundred quid *not* to go back to working nights at Nine Elms market, heaving crates of tomatoes out of lorries. That wouldn't go far, but the last few weeks had been cheap if nothing else. He didn't feel up to nightlife, besides his last girlfriend had gone back to Australia.

He must have dozed because he didn't hear the doorbell only his mother's exclamation of pleasure: 'Dave!'

He heaved himself onto his feet and stumbled dizzily, hands on both walls, along the hall to the front door to fall into Dave's waiting bear hug.

'Luke, what a sight! You been wrestling with aliens in my absence? Can't have that, boyo.'

'God, you disappear for a couple of weeks and turn into a Welshman without so much as asking me.'

'The Welsh suit me. I shall emigrate or become adopted or whatever.'

'You can't, unless you learn their language.'

'Hmmm, yes, a serious drawback that.' Dave dropped into song, *'I'm reviewing the situation ... I think I'd better think it out again.'* He stood on the doorstep, his hands on Luke's shoulders, scanning the altered face. Dropping back into speech as he pushed Luke into the house: 'I can't stand here or I'll fall asleep, I spent the night sorting stuff, I had to see people first thing this morning, then up the M4 and I'm knackered.'

'Sorry, I didn't mean ... I've got stuff I need to tell you.'

'I know.' Dave thrust him back onto the sofa. 'I'll come again tomorrow. I just dropped in to make sure you weren't a ghost. I need to sleep now to the point of no contest. If I could grab a coffee, Maria, just to get me home ...'

'Of course.' Maria looked at her son's face. 'Dave, you could stay here, Barbara's with Lewis and you could have her bed. In fact it's the spare bed. I mean she's been with Lewis for a year now. They're getting married, you know.'

'Great stuff! Stirring things happen when I go away. Kind of you, but I need to get home before the post starts climbing back out of the letterbox.'

Dave tilted his head to consider Luke, slumped now on the sofa, then turned and followed Maria into the kitchen. 'Maria, would you lend me Luke? He needs to talk and I need to drive to Hackney without falling asleep, and pick up some food on the way. I'll look after him and bring him back in one piece.'

She nodded slowly. 'Yes, that would make him happy. He's all right now, I mean he won't get sick again, now, I don't suppose. He does get a bit dizzy, but then they've been inside his brain, so it's not surprising really. Hang on Dave, there's no need to shop. I'll pop a few bits in a bag.'

'You're a saint, Maria. I really will look after him. You don't need to worry at all.'

She shook her head. 'I'm not worrying; you're both grown men. Don't smile at me like that. Luke leads his own life now, it's just that ... well it's all taking some getting used to. He only came home yesterday. He's not supposed to be alone or go out without someone for a few days.'

'Fear not. I will guard him like a baby. He'll be fine, you'll see. He has more bounce than Zebedee and in a year's time the big opera houses will be queuing up for him. The scars won't do any harm, Maria.'

She smiled. 'I know, I know. We're just feeling a bit jittery at the moment, though it doesn't look as though it was terrorists after all. But it's this Heloise thing. Has he told you?'

'Not much. I think that's what he's aching to offload.'

Maria, with the fridge door open, turned an anxious face to Dave, 'Well this Heloise business has changed him.' She shrugged. 'This girl is just...nowhere. You'll help, won't you?'

He gave her a quick hug and leaned down to pick up the generously filled bag. 'I'll do what I can.'

Maria's frown faded, soothed by the deep voice and large presence. Who would have thought that undernourished little Dave would grow up into such a reassuringly solid animal? She collected Luke plus his crutches and his new CD player and helped to stuff them into Dave's decrepit Fiesta.

Dave whistled in a gratifying way at the sight of the CD player. 'Jesus, I've had dreams about this baby. They spoil you, Luke.'

'Mmm, it was no fun at the time, but there are some compensations for tangling with death.'

Dave flicked him a glance. 'You're going to tell me about it.' He drove for a while and then turned into the parking area of a vast supermarket. 'Sit tight, Luke. I won't be a mo. Your Mum is among the Chosen, but I think we need some low-life brain food. You allowed alcohol? A six pack? Two?' Twenty minutes later they stood at the bottom of the endless flights of stairs to Dave's flat and looked up.

His own eyelids barely defying gravity, Dave watched as Luke's dark lashes drooped and lay still and the voice, which had run almost continuously for the last two hours, eased into silence. Seeing him motionless at last, in the dusty late afternoon sunlight, Dave was able to examine the ugly lumps of skin bunched around the darker dots where the stitches had been. After a year or two, he thought, this pattern will reverse; the dots will become orderly bleached freckles on the biscuit-coloured skin. The face had mislaid some of its old appeal; a characteristic softness had melted off the bones, leaving sharp angles, like bird's wings, under the skin. No doubt women would still swoon over it.

Dave, now almost drowning under the approaching wave of sleep, hung on for another few minutes. Finally Luke gave a great hiccuping sigh, like a child that has been crying. Dave eased off his and Luke's shoes, picked up his mobile and went quietly onto the landing outside his tiny flat.

'Maria? It's me, Dave. Luke's fast asleep. No, he's fine, just talked himself to sleep. I must get some kip myself. OK, if I bring him back tomorrow? We've still got some talking to do . . . don't you worry, he'll be fine . . . Bye.'

Dave returned silently. Although a bright July sun was still battling its way through the London smog, he switched on the small light over the cooker. Then he surveyed his room; the only bed sagged under Luke's body. He had a choice between the floor and the broken armchair he had been sitting in all afternoon. There was barely enough floor space for a child, never mind a body of his dimensions. He took his unopened travel bag and set it as a footrest at the end of the battered chair then, bending his limbs into an S shape he finally let go. As sleep rolled in, his mind wandered among the experiences of the last few days: the warmth of the send-off from Cardiff and the promised work offers; the battle with sleep on the M4; the difficulty of getting Luke up the five flights of concrete steps to his flat, and the incredible jumble of information, eased by the beer, that spilled out of Luke.

Luke's story poured in relentless flow: Heloise, and how she crept up on Luke, what she said to him, what she did for him and how she had then slipped into nowhere; the unremembered explosion; the robot; Carol, Louise and the blonde film star girl; Barbara and Lewis getting married; Claudia thinking he was hallucinating; Ange and Kes; even hospital details – bath hoists, commodes, stitch removals, endless tests like children's games, and all of these different events melded by the heat of Luke's confusion. It was not a conversation. Dave, head to one side, listened meditatively, as though to a complex piece of music. He had said very little.

Six hours later, the two men still slept, Dave motionless, Luke twitching and murmuring. The miniature flickers of his limbs giving only the barest indication of the upheavals in his dreams. Why had the kitchen at home grown so very small and dark. Was that Mum in the corner – or perhaps Heloise? Why couldn't he see properly, only – how did it go? – *through a glass darkly?* Yes, that was it.

'Heloise, can you reach the light?'

'Luke, there's no light here. Are you awake?'

'Yes. Yes of course there's no light here. We've had an explosion. You told me. I think I was dreaming. What is it, are you crying? Please don't. Put your face close. There,' he mustered a weak laugh, 'I'm drinking your tears.'

The tears fell faster. 'Luke, I've got to do something awful. I've got to leave you. While you were ... asleep I heard some sounds in the distance. I may be imagining things, but I *have* to go and find out. I couldn't leave you without saying anything, but it's our only chance. Please, please forgive me ... Are you listening, Luke?'

'Yes.'

'I'm going now.'

'Yes.'

A quick, soft bumping of her lips on his, her fingers in his hair, a small scrabbling noise – then nothing.

Heart lurching, he tried to reach after her but a jingling and whooshing filled his ears. A light shower pattered his face. Tiny hands, babies' hands were brushing his cheeks, his nose, his lips; he opened his eyes and looked round in alarm – Dave's room. Grey dark, not black dark; the rising thud in his chest steadied. The white ceiling soared at a comfortable distance above his head. Now something was tickling his neck – a feather. He patted himself, finding several feathers on his face and half a dozen tiny silvery coins on his chest. Eventually his wandering hands located a plastic beaker behind his head. He glanced around in perplexity. Dave lay zonked out on the old chair. Why did he keep a collection of feathers and five pence coins in a cup by his bed, for heaven's sakes? Luke looked over at the awkwardly sprawled limbs and the heavy close-cropped head just visible in the weak light coming from the cooker. This light turned the one ear he could see, scarlet. No wonder, thought Luke after all he'd poured into it. There was something odd though, why had the room darkened so early? He peered at his watch in disbelief – midnight, surely not? He sat up suddenly.

'Dave, sorry, I didn't mean to wake you. I have to ring Mum. She'll be frantic!'

'Relax, I rang hours ago.'

'Phew, thanks. Don't you want your bed?'

'That's all right; I'm good at chairs or floors. You should remember.'

Luke grinned. 'I do. Thank God you're back, Dave.'

Luke, now fully awake, reached up to switch on the anglepoise above the bed. He smiled affectionately across the room at his friend. With a couple of beers, two hours of solid conversation and an extra sleep he felt, in spite of disturbing dreams, like Atlas having handed the world he had been bearing to a stronger man. The stronger man looked like he was dropping off again. Luke's eyes wandered over the room. Dave had never succumbed to prevailing tastes. Whereas Luke had obediently passed through every peer-driven childhood and adolescent fad: Walkmans, Doc Martens, Gameboys, posters of rock bands and girls, girls, girls, Dave had maintained his own idiosyncratic route, doing precisely what he actually felt like doing, regardless of contemporary crazes. His room had the spoils of happy afternoons at car boot sales. Luke lifted his head to contemplate some of his favourites. He remembered Dave's especial delight in finding half a dozen paintings of peonies; great blowsy flowers brushed in with the softest of watercolour strokes. At the time, Luke had been aghast, later he decided that the very sweetness of the images in Dave's masculine quarters were an ironic statement. Later still he came to see each one as a thing of beauty. Talking through the night once, Dave, in a rare expansive moment, had explained that when singing, just occasionally, he felt like one of those peonies; some conjunction of the sounds in his throat meeting the air then lifting, rounding and spreading in his chest, matched the soft structure of the flower.

Luke stroked a feather to and fro across his lips and then across his scarred forehead – very comforting. The lingering terror from his dream began to ease. A giant sigh shuddered through him.

'Luke?'

'Oh hi Dave, you awake again?'

'Yup. Treat my feathers with respect, they're not meant for washing your face.'

'They're very soothing. Whose are they.'

'I dunno. None of my friends are feathered.'

Luke chuckled. 'I've missed you.'

'I'm sorry I went.'

'Liar! You did good, right? Nearly Cardiff Singer of the

World?'

Dave smiled sleepily, 'Well – third round.'

'Yeesh! I'd better get my skates on.'

'Next one in two years. What'll you be? Thirty? Ideal for a tenor. You could win, Luke, if you put your mind to it.'

'Sure, sure.'

'What's the matter?'

'I don't know. I just feel a bit sidetracked by all this business.' Luke's hand wandered up to his jagged forehead. 'Until this happened, all I thought about was singing: Stockholm and the Buxton Opera, and now ...'

'And girls, and Glyndebourne chorus and girls again. Don't laugh, you're a liability.' Dave heaved himself to his feet and crossed the room to his kitchen corner. 'Well, it may be one a.m. but I'm famished.' He shoved pasta into one saucepan and sauce into another.

Luke hauled himself off the bed, crossed the room to the tiny plastic table and propped himself on a stool. With his customary swiftness, Dave threw ingredients – both Maria's and his own from store – into saucepans. Luke, reacting to the familiar smells of Dave's cooking, felt quivers of his old self stirring like blood returning to a cramped limb. He would have opened his arms to this self, but the formless image of Heloise stood between now and then, blocking the way.

'Dave? Had I just met someone before you left? I mean a girl?'

'I don't know, Luke. I've tried to think, but my head's on the woolly side. I left for Cardiff a whole week before the explosion, you know. There was no girl then – unless you were keeping quiet.'

'No, I'd have told you. I always do. Anyway, you get them next. I've never worked that out.'

Dave grunted. 'I just stand under the tree and wait for the fruit to fall.'

'Lazy bugger!'

Dave produced a bass chuckle. 'There was no girl when I left. Mind you, I'd say you were actively searching. Which makes it pretty likely that there was one by the end of the week.' He put a plate of steaming tagliatelle in front of Luke, gathered a pencil and an old envelope and sat down with his own plate of food. 'OK let's get practical. What have you done so far? Police, Fire service, adverts? Papers? Actually papers are not such a good idea, you've got your career to think about.'

'Fuck my career.'

Dave raised a sceptical eyebrow, but said nothing. They ate. Pushing the empty plates aside, he tried again. 'OK, let's gather together the info we do have. What do we know for sure? Little things.' He started writing, repeating the 'facts' as Luke threw them out. 'So, she lives with mother and father, cried for them like a child but says she's twenty-five. Hang on Luke, what's your best guess about her age?'

'I don't *know*. There's no making sense of it. She wasn't at all savvy. Like, I don't think she'd ever kissed a man before – that makes her a kid, I suppose ... '

'Luke, you kissed this girl, that you'd just met, that you'd never even seen, when you were in danger of your life? In what circumstances would you have to be *not* to kiss a girl?'

'Dave, it wasn't like that. We were together for hours, we thought we would die; you do funny things when time looks like running out on you. She kissed like a ... a novice, but she touched me like ... I can't explain; it was as if I'd always known her. I've been waiting for her voice and hands all along. She might even have been older than me, it didn't matter. She made my head stop hurting, just by stroking it, she looked after me. Her voice was not a child's. I don't *know*, Dave.' Luke looked down at his empty plate, blinking. 'Perhaps I just dreamt the kissing bit.'

'Never mind, we'll leave her age; let's move on to what you do know.' As Luke ran through the scraps of information he could be sure of, Dave scribbled on. ' ... She is just about to get her first passport. Her hands are amazing and her voice is the sweetest, most exciting ... like a cross between Cleo Laine and Kathleen Ferrier ... Steady on, Luke, this is beginning to sound like fantasy.' A sound made Dave look up in time to see Luke's beautiful mouth harden into an angry line. 'For Chrissake, Luke. I didn't mean anything, just that she sounds like every man's dream.' Getting nothing more than a bleak stare, he put a hand out and shook Luke by the shoulder. 'Don't go cold on me, boyo; I've come to help. I mean practical help. If she's out there, we'll find her.'

'She *is* out there. I *know*. If *you* think I'm mad, I really will go mad. Oh God ... I sometimes wonder. Is there another beer?'

Treading more carefully, Dave continued to write his list. 'Just a thought, Luke, you know you have a feeling she was ... fibbing about her age? Could she possibly have given you a false ... I mean an imaginary, name as well?'

9

Richmond: Sylvie

Back home the next day, Luke resumed his trawl through the newspaper cuttings from the comfort of the sofa. The ringing phone made a welcome interruption, and he reached out lazily for it.

'Hello, Luke, it's Carol.'

He sat up sharply. 'Carol? . . . ' He sank back again, 'Oh yes – Mrs Braithwaite, sorry – Carol . . . Well that's very kind of you, but I can't make it on Wednesday. If this other girl does come, you'll recognise her, won't you? A photo of me? Sure, there's one on my website . . . Oh, I'll see if Mum has one to post, it might get there.' Luke copied the address he was given. Then searched out an old publicity folder for photos.

He could have accepted Carol's invitation to the survivors' meeting; his social life was about as busy as a hive in winter. Yet Carol and Louise made him want to laugh, and the other people who would be attending would surely be in a crying state. Luke wanted explanations not emotions. He didn't feel sad, he felt frustrated. Of course, someone else there might recognise him – perhaps next time. Still arguing with himself, Luke sank back. His mobile rang, Lewis this time. He had tracked down a girl. She was fair, twenty-five years old, and she had died in the Cardon Street disaster. Her name was Sylvie van Claes and she had lived at home with her parents and he had their phone number.

'But what am I supposed to do with that?'

'Ring them, find out more about her.'

'Lewis, for chrissake, this Sylvie, she's dead, isn't she?'

'Yes, but Luke, don't you want to know?'

'Sure, I want to know, but Heloise is NOT dead.' Luke, moved the phone from one ear to the other. 'You still there, Lewis? Sorry man, I didn't mean to bellow. It's just . . . '

'Luke, ring them. They want to talk to anyone who might have been there. You never know, this girl was twenty-five and fair-haired. It's not much, but it's the best fit so far.'

' . . . OK, OK, I'll ring them. *Leave no stone unturned*. I know

... Yup, Yup, I know. And thanks.'

The distance from the back of the bus to the ground seemed to have stretched since he got on. Luke waited for his jarred ankle to settle, wishing he had brought even one crutch with him. Blinking in the sudden glare, he felt in his jacket pocket for his sunglasses. Not there. He patted all his pockets, perplexed. His mother? But his jacket had been with him in his room since he came in last night, unless ... perhaps he had left it in the kitchen after talking to Barbara ... He shaded his eyes, frowning, then shrugged as he opened the A to Z and checked his route.

The first two streets he walked down seemed to be composed entirely of glass shops and metallic cars. The August sun, a sheet of white fire today, bounced straight off these surfaces and into his defenceless eyes. The whereabouts of the missing sunglasses and the niggling worry that his memory might not be working properly distracted him from his route. He stopped to lean against a lamppost and re-orientate himself. When he looked up again a familiar sliding sensation made him stand quite still for a moment until his feet and head remembered which way was up and which down. Claudia had assured him that the after effects of the anaesthetic and the surgery could go on for some time and would eventually wear off. Most of the time he believed her. Just sometimes he wondered if the surgeons had let the knife slip and made a few little cuts into his brain, like his mother preparing pastry for the oven. Perhaps some of the essential connections had been severed. Perhaps they would heal again, like the wounds on his face and ankle.

He moved on. The next street was cooler, greener. Finally he turned into Rosemary Road and almost laughed. It was like something out of Walt Disney. The front gardens spilled over with bushes in contrasting colours: red-leaved cotinus with a froth of pink flowers, jostled with the yellow-splashed leaves of eleagnus and weeping silver-leaved pears; Pampas grass rose out of a bed of soft pink pebbles, and blue gums trembled above pink flecked ground cover. Plain green was clearly unfashionable in these parts. Cheered by this so human attitude to nature and by the way these colours absorbed the hammering sun, Luke looked at the individual front doors, searching for number 26. Number 26 turned out to be the maverick. For every other house in the avenue, you would have needed a painter's guide to name the colours. Number 26 was an uncompromising red, white and green; sparkling white paint, green window boxes and red geraniums. The Italian side of Luke had no quarrel with this celebration of the positive, but his unshaded eyes baulked at the contrasts.

He pressed the bell then glanced at his watch realising, as he heard the elaborate chimes ring out, that he was nearly ten minutes early. The man who opened the door was sniffing and blowing his nose on a large handkerchief. He held an unopened envelope in his hand and he stared at Luke as though he were the last person on earth he had expected to find at his front door. Luke waited, perplexed, for the mopping to finish, so as to offer his hand. 'I'm Luca. Luca Danford. I rang about the Cardon Street explosion ... you remember?'

The man shook himself and after one further look at the envelope he held and a final blowing of the nose waved Luke through and in.

It was only at this moment, as Luke ducked his head into the doorway, stepped onto the deep plush of the hall and looked into the red-rimmed eyes of Sylvie's father that he understood that he had taken part in a real tragedy. He put out a hand to steady himself on the wall. His head, which had failed him so often in the past few days, stopped swimming and came into sharp focus, it was his body that now wanted to slip sideways. Fear such as he had not felt all these weeks since he had lain under the debris, now welled up from belly to chest. Perversely, the fear was greater because it was not just himself he had to worry about. He was all right. Heloise was all right (he still felt sure about that, she had not been in any pain). It was what had happened to the others that he suddenly comprehended. Numbers had passed through his brain without lodging anywhere, as he lay in the hospital bed pinned down by tubes and absorbed by his own small, stupid confusions: one hundred and eighty injured, twenty three dead. He'd read the newspapers, looked at photos of the devastation. He'd talked to Carol and Louise and seen Bill Braithwaite in real pain. Yet this was still someone else's drama and he had not dropped a heartbeat for those dead or injured. He had cared only for details, descriptions of hair, ages, names that might possibly match one person – Heloise. Now he gaped weakly in the face of genuine loss.

Sylvie's father, Peter, seeing the young man looking faint, and aware of the vivid half-healed gash he could see in the shaved area on the back of his head, put out a steadying hand. He took Luke's elbow and guided him into a chair in the nearby sitting room.

'I'm sorry. You find us overwhelmed this morning. A letter has come for our daughter from a friend in Netherlands. You think it is all done, then a letter arrives and there is someone else you must ring and explain to them that this terrible thing has happened.' Even as he spoke, with that clean, minutely accented English that the Dutch manage so well, Luke could see the tears threatening again. 'There will be no finish of these shocks; we cannot go back to before it happened.' He shook his head. 'Next week is her birthday.'

Luke opened his mouth and shut it again as a small woman, with the same pink-rimmed eyes joined them. Peter introduced her: 'This is my wife, Gulda.' She shook Luke's hand then perched on the white sofa opposite his chair.

Luke tried again, 'I'm sorry, I'm Luca Danford, I…I shouldn't have come so soon after…I'm sorry.'

The woman spoke on a sigh. 'It is already four weeks, but when we wake up each morning it is still yesterday. I don't think it will be different in another week, another year. I shall bring some tea. Peter will tell you about Sylvie and Helga.' On the last word she whisked herself out of the room, as if in flight from her own courage. She was too fast for Luke, for whom the drinking of a cup of tea was an ordeal. He sat, mouth agape at the introduction of yet another person – Helga.

Luke found his mind now working on two planes, one noted, in a relatively detached way that Sylvie's mother, like her husband, also had that faint, tidy Dutch accent. Heloise had not sounded like either of them in accent or in the very individual timbre of her voice. Luke knew now that he should not have come, that he had never met Sylvie, that he had nothing of comfort to say to Peter or his wife. And who was Helga? No one had ever mentioned her before. The other part of his mind quivered in the here and now. Aware that the fragile state in which Peter, his wife and Luke himself currently lived might collapse at a single word. Any one of them could dissolve, could decide to stop playing the social game. Luke looked down and realised he had on his old grey trainers. They seemed to grow enormous, while Peter on the sofa opposite diminished with Alice-like suddenness. He felt large, out of place and dirty in this pristine and oh-so-empty house.

Peter looked at the envelope in his hands again, then in anticipation at Luke's face. After a moment he prodded; 'Did you say on the telephone that you talked to our ... to Sylvie after the explosion?'

Luke floundered, scrabbling for some social toehold. 'The phone call. Yes. I'm afraid I ... you may have thought from what I said that I ... that it was Syl ...,' seeing the man opposite flinch, he corrected himself, 'that it was your daughter that I spoke to. The girl I spoke to was called Heloise. I'm sorry, I shouldn't have troubled you. It is just that Heloise has not been found and I ... I'm trying to discover what happened to her. I wondered ...' he touched the scar on his face, 'if S ... if your daughter was ever called Heloise or ... or had a friend ... you said something about Helga ...' his voice drifted to nothing as the Peter stared at him in bewilderment.

'You did not speak to ... Sylvie then?'

'No, no I don't think I did.' He pressed both hands on his face for a moment. 'I'm so sorry, I didn't mean to confuse things for you.'

Peter smiled suddenly, coming back into focus. 'It's better so. It's better that she died quickly when the explosion happened. I was afraid she had lived in that horror: that she had suffered beyond the moment. Excuse me a minute.' He left hurriedly by the same door as his wife. Luca sat quite still staring at his grubby trainers and then at the white sofa. He tried not to listen to the offstage voices; the high-pitched whimpers, the darker murmurs. He hoped they would forget the tea. He wished he had the courage to get up and leave. Who was Helga?

After a few minutes they both returned, smiling and bearing a tray of tea.

Gulda poured, Peter handed him a cup. 'You asked about Helga – Sylvie's cousin. She was on the other side of the road. She had cuts from the glass but, thank God, she is well. She has returned now to Copenhagen.' Seeing Luke's frown, he added, 'She

84

works for the travelling company there.' Peter stood up abruptly. 'We have pictures of our daughter, would you like to see them?' He didn't wait for an answer. Album after album appeared. Sylvie looked unreal; someone proud parents would have invented in an ideal world. She was the Heloise he had imagined: built small but not bony, with long, fair hair and honey-coloured skin. Even flat on the plasticized page, something of her personality radiated over the viewer. Luke had the strange impression, probably due to the generosity of images and the speed of her transition from baby to woman, of an old freeze-frame movie. He quickly ran dry of superlatives. Sylvie's mother and father appeared content that he should just gaze. This was, after all, the only part that was left, this endless shining two-dimensional Sylvie.

Luke struggled to get his mind round an appalling concept, that for these two friendly people, all that mattered in the world now resided between the covers of a dozen photograph albums. The Sylvie that remained to them could never be hugged again, never heard to speak or laugh. To Luke, for whom touch and sound far outweighed vision, their tiny remnant of Sylvie's life seemed painful beyond imagining. It would be like watching life through a permanently closed window. This could easily have been him – with Mum and Dad looking through the albums. If he had died, at least Claudia and Barbara would be there as a focus on the future. Peter and Gulda had lost even that, there were clearly no brothers or sisters. What were they going to live on when they had shown these to everyone they knew? They would have to start all over again. Luke made the first consciously altruistic resolution of his life. He decided that he would come back each year to go through these albums, to give Sylvie's parents another reason to open them. He could see that it didn't matter *who* looked at them, only that *someone* did.

When he got up to go, his tea heroically half drunk, they begged him to visit again, he could only say 'of course'. They had been so warm, so kind, so interested in him. With new-found insight he realised that he represented for them a living thread tied to their lost daughter. They had asked him about his career and were flatteringly interested in his prospects as a singer. In their heightened emotional states empathy seemed to increase faster than normal. By some unjustified leaps and bounds, he had become their might-have-been son-in-law, they his surrogate for Heloise's parents. Luke remembered feeling unkindly towards Heloise's parents, who had incomprehensibly disapproved of opera. He could get fond of Peter and Gulda.

He walked out into the dazzling light of the street, waving back at them in their darkened doorway. At the end of the street the soft shrubs became sparse and the harder more commercial contrasts of working London filled his vision again. As he walked, the sense of having left half his bodyweight behind in that desolate house increased, almost as if the hot sun were sucking the juice out of him.

Needing to rehydrate and also to neutralise the lingering taste of tea, Luke stumbled into a coffee bar. Perched on a stool, he tried to make some sense of it all. He had not found Heloise, in fact he had added yet another missing person to that delicate area of his thinking which seemed to feel so much. It was getting crowded in there and he was making no progress. His mind seemed capable of framing only the simplest of statements: Sylvie is not Heloise, I could have fallen for Sylvie, but I have already fallen for Heloise, Sylvie and Heloise are both unavailable. And now Helga?

Thinking that he might like to talk to Helga, Sylvie's parents had pressed an email address on him as he left. What was he supposed to say to her? What if he passed Heloise in the street? She wouldn't recognise him or he her. Only her voice, he would recognise that anywhere. He shut his eyes, hummed a few bars from Bohème, then got out his mobile.

'Dave, where are you ... no wonder there's such a racket! No, she wasn't Heloise. She was beautiful though. Her parents are in a terrible state. I wish I hadn't gone. The photos though ... they showed me photos from when she was a baby. There was a moment when I thought I remembered her ... but I just know she wasn't Heloise ... She had blonde almost white hair; looked stunning. Legs to die for ... Oh god! I shouldn't have said that ... What? The girl I'm supposed to have met before the explosion? Oh! I didn't think ... I was looking for Heloise ... No, I'm still here. I'm thinking. I wonder if they'd lend me a photo. Dave, I've got to go, I need to think this one through.'

Sylvie as the other girl, the one Carol and Louise had seen him talking to? Why not? Why hadn't he thought of that for himself?

But to go back and ask for a photo...he couldn't do that to them. Perhaps the newspapers ...? Now he would definitely have to attend one of the fortnightly Survivors's Meetings that Carol and Louise kept inviting him to. Luke leant his face on his hand over the empty cup of coffee.

10
Lewisham Hospital: Ruth, Morris & Nina

'A letter?' Luke took it from the nurse in some surprise. He had come in to the hospital for his last physiotherapy session. Anyone who might possibly write to him would surely write to his home.

'Yes, a nice young man came here yesterday and asked me to give it to you specially.'

Opening it Luke discovered that it wasn't a letter after all, just some junk mail about an exhibition. He was about to drop it in the bin, when he realised that it did have some handwriting on it. Underneath the printed invitation to a Private View for an Exhibition of Fine Art Weaving by Morris and Ruth Gardiner, Morris had scrawled across the bottom: "Luke, please come – Morris". Weaving? Morris Gardiner? Surely he had been the guy with Ruth Gardiner, and Ruth was the blind woman who had been rescued just before him? What kind of weaving could this Ruth do, if she couldn't see? Luke lifted his arm to flick the card in the nearest bin; then he paused. Although this woman couldn't possibly help him, since she had been unable to see, if he didn't talk to her, he would always wonder. Still dithering, he looked down at the card again, it said, "Admit two". Maybe Mum would enjoy it, weaving was a bit like sewing after all. He pushed it into his jacket pocket.

Up on the eighth floor of the hospital Morris stood looking down at Ruth. She lay on her side, the tears slowly trickling out and down her pillow. She didn't sob or wipe her eyes, in fact the only signs of life were the minimal rasping breaths released from her open mouth. He approached, trying to speak encouragingly. 'Ruth, Sweetie, what is it?' She didn't move, so he picked up one limp hand and sat on the bed. 'Come on, talk to me. The nurses say you've been like this all day.'

'Morris?'

'Yes, it's me. Tell me what's the matter.'

'I thought it would be easier than this to die.'

Morris had to lean close to pick up the blurred words. 'You're not going to die, Ruth. You're going to get better, you're going to

88

come home.'

Between breaths she said, 'I want to go now. Mama and Dad have gone. Nobody needs me.'

'Hey, Ruth, don't talk like that. You know I need you.' Morris stroked the wet hair away from her face. The tears streamed on. 'Ruth, I think it's being ill that makes you feel like this – and being sad about Dan and Martha.'

Ruth turned her face towards him at last. 'I'm so tired, Morris. Whenever I shut my eyes ... I can hear Dad groaning. Mama said dying would be easy ... like going to sleep. Life would be better ... on the other side – in heaven. If only Dad had not made ... such noises before he died. You don't even believe in heaven, do you?'

'Oh Ruth, it doesn't matter what I think. He's all right now, he's not in pain any more.'

'I can still hear him ... all night.'

'Ruth, Sweetie, you should have told me.' Morris leant down and lifted the passive body into his arms. After a moment she pulled her mask away and turned to cling to him. He held her tight. 'I hear Dan's groans too, sometimes. It's only natural. You must put another sound there instead. What would you like to be hearing? What would drown out poor Dan's voice?'

Her tears kept coming. 'Nothing, nothing!'

'Shh, Ruth, listen, listen a minute. It will get better. I'm going to help you. You'd better put your mask back on; come on, deep breaths, that's my girl.' Morris pushed a tissue into her hand and helped her replace the mask. 'Ssh, Ruth, I've got an idea, just hold on a while longer. It's going to be all right.' He rocked her in his arms, alternately rubbing and patting her back as if she were a sick child. 'What is this thing you're wearing. Where does ... did Martha get your clothes. Oh Ruth, it's not fair, you've never been given a chance to grow up like other women. You must get better. We'll work together. We'll amaze the world with our weaving. We'll do things with wool that no one has ever thought of.'

When Ruth lay quiet and semi-conscious again, Morris left. He had meant to tell her that Nina would be arriving tomorrow, but he had flunked it for the third day running. He'd had a whole week between speaking to Nina and her arrival. He still felt unsure of Ruth's reaction to the nanny who had disappeared without explanation when she was fifteen and in Ruth's current state he was unwilling to give her any unsettling news. Now he had to get on with preparing and mounting the work for their exhibition.

He caught the bus to Greenwich. The whole point of putting the weaving on show would be the wider publicity gained for Ruth's work. His own, he could sell through ordinary shops. There was a steady profit now, the sticky years almost forgotten, but Ruth's work was in a different league. She did these strange three-dimensional hangings that made buyers and visitors gasp in wonder as they entered his studio. This had made Ruth happy enough, but the shops didn't buy her work; too much power radiated from each piece to make it something you would hang over the mantelpiece of an ordinary home.

Morris, opening the front door of his house, glanced up at one of her pieces hanging in the hall. Between the delicate lines of the pattern, clusters of autumnal scarlets made him feel warm every time he entered the house. Six months ago Martha, making a rare visit to his studio, had looked briefly at this vibrant piece of work while it lay nearly finished on the loom.

With pride quickening his voice Morris explained: 'Ruth did that, isn't...'

'Ruth? What on earth for? Who would want such a thing?'

'Martha, it's beautiful!'

'Don't exaggerate, Morris. This – thing –– is too big, the colours are loud and I can't see it being of any use to anyone. If that's how Ruth spends her time here, she might as well stay at home.'

Morris, lying through his clenched teeth, had assured Martha that Ruth in fact spent most of her time in useful labour: winding bobbins, preparing warp threads, sorting the different gauges of wool, dressing the looms etc. That same evening he had gone through all the photos of his and Ruth's work, selecting ones the buyers had exclaimed over. The next day he had asked a professional photographer in and, turning his sitting room and staircase into a studio, had hung Ruth's pieces up as best he could. Many of them were too big for his Victorian terrace walls, but he managed.

Two weeks later, with the newly created folio in his arms and burning zeal in his heart he had started going round the fine art galleries. He expected to march for days and spend hours arguing the case for weaving versus painting. His second try had been the

Grosjean in Knightsbridge, who had fairly snatched the folio out of his hands. The exhibition arranged so long ago, would open in a couple of weeks now; too late to impress Martha and Dan. He now regretted his decision to keep it a secret from them until the private view, grinding his teeth every time he remembered this. Dan had never even seen his daughter's amazing achievements.

Morris returned to the hospital just before the end of visiting hour that night. He put into Ruth's hand a miniature compact disc player. He put the earplugs into her ears and put her finger on the play button. As the first bright trumpets of Don Carlos filtered into Ruth head, her eyebrows lifted in wonder and her strange unseeing eyes grew enormous.

'Where's the machine?' she whispered.

'In your hand, Sweetie.'

She held her hands up, the disc player between her palms. 'It's a miracle. Oh Morris, Morris, can it stay with me for a while.'

'Ruth, it's a present. It's your very own. I'm afraid it's nothing special; you won't get the best sounds from treble and bass. It takes CDs; not tapes, I've brought in the Don Carlos, some Handel arias and the Verdi choruses. I don't have many CDs, I thought you would like these ones best.'

Having taught her hands to work the player and left some spare batteries, Morris barely had time to mention that Nina would be coming to see her the next day. When he did, Ruth simply said, 'Nina? Nina B?' in a mildly curious voice. So he left it at that.

Ruth pushed her fingers under the pillow. Her hand closed over the warm metal disc that had lain under her cheek all night and even sneaked into her dreams. Just touching it seemed to ease the breath into her sore lungs. Morris had called this magical source of pleasure a CD player, though it was totally unlike the box he had installed a few years ago in his workshop. In her mind's eye it looked like a minuscule flying saucer and, like something unexpected from outer space, it had altered her whole perspective. When Morris had taken her hand, put the cool metal into it and then taken her other hand to show her fingers which buttons to press, she had already decided to let go; to stop making the pointless effort of waking up yet again to remember her father's agony, her mother's non-existence and the other complex memories that seemed to grow more not less painful with the passing time. How could the voices and instruments coming out of this strange metal sandwich make such a difference to her mind?

All that morning Ruth lay peacefully listening, her breathing a little less shallow than before; a smile, new to the hospital staff, curving her lips. She ate a few mouthfuls of lunch by herself. The nurses, who had struggled to interact with this remote, unseeing woman, responded to the smiles, bringing the lilies on her shelf close enough for her to touch and smell, reporting the rain outside (the first for three weeks) trying to reconnect her to the sensations of real life again. Even her sleep seemed to change in quality and she looked more like a child and less like a restless scarecrow.

Ruth woke in the late afternoon. Hearing a movement, she lifted her oxygen mask. 'Morris?'

'No dear, it's me, Nina.'

'Nina B? Is that really you?'

'Yes, dear.'

'I'm so glad you've come home.' She let the mask drop again.

Nina shut her eyes for a millisecond. Air – no something more medicinal – oxygen, seemed at last to find a route through crowded pathways into her lungs. Oxygen, like the stuff pumping through the tube into Ruth's mouth and nose. She moved a strand of Ruth's hair from under the mask and murmured, 'Yes, Ruth, I've come home.'

There was silence. Ruth's eyes had closed again, such a non-event of a reunion. For the first time in a week Nina found that she had nothing to do but sit and watch. In the compass of eight days she had gone from sleeping on her mother's worn linen to lying wakeful on Dan and Martha's clinging polyester sheets; she had breathed in the sharp air of the Cairngorms and the limp dust of London. Oddest, most difficult alteration of all, she had exchanged the solid weight of her steel kettle, always warm on its hotplate, for an insubstantial plastic one with its electrified tray. Safety kettle? Compared to her fat steel friend, this flimsy green affair was like a high-sided lorry in a wind. London was no longer home.

As the light faded, Nina sat on in the darkness, thoughts skittering randomly across her mind. Would Morris succeed in getting some money from the solicitors? How could people breathe in London? Would Hugo remember to check the mousetrap?

Nina had spent the last fourteen years, turning three and a half derelict stone rooms into somewhere a body could just about live. All that time she had been aching for her missing nursling, dreaming of the summons to return to her and calling her life in the hills temporary. Her dream had come true yet nothing felt quite right. Her place of exile had become her refuge, London a war zone. Beside her lay Ruth, her face still that of the child she had yearned for but now overlaid with a stranger's twenty-nine years. Even more difficult to digest, Ruth had acquired an independent skill. She could not only weave but also do it well enough to have her work exhibited. Or was that just Morris being kind?

On this thought her mind closed down temporarily until Ruth's voice woke her.

'Nurse?'

'What is it, love?'

Nina took the restless hand and lifted it up to her forty-five year old face. Ruth had last traced her features when Nina had been only thirty.

'Nina B? Is it you? I thought I was dreaming. You know they died – Mama and Dad? Morris will explain.' Ruth paused for a few more mouthfuls of oxygen. 'I'm glad you've come. I don't know what to do next.'

'That's easy, dear. You just concentrate on getting well. Morris and I will sort out everything.'

Ruth produced a sudden chuckle. 'Oh Nina I feel little again with you here. I have to learn to do things for myself. I'm grown up, you know.'

'Yes ... yes, but you're sick, my dear. So you can be little for a while longer. Time to grow up when you're well again. I'm so glad to see you grown up. I was afraid that they would keep you too close to home for safety.'

'Well, they did. I might never have left the house at all, if it hadn't been for Morris. He employs me. He taught me to weave. Ask him.' Ruth ran out of breath and had to replace the mask.

Nina opened then closed her mouth. She needed to ask what they had told Ruth when she left. What had happened to Ruth. Had Martha gone ahead with her grim plan? If she had, did Ruth know what had been done to her? Morris might know, but he had only been seventeen at the time. He'd never argued with Martha, or asked awkward questions. Most of his childhood, when not at boarding school or on rare visits to his parents abroad, had been spent with Martha, Dan and Nina. He painted when given the chance but mostly mastered the art of blending himself with the scenery.

A little later Ruth spoke again. 'You will go to our exhibition won't you, Nina?'

11

Vauxhall Social Centre: Survivors' Meeting

Fourteen bodies, nudging each other like yachts in a harbour, filled the floor of a small, functional room. The vicar, backed into a corner, had hitched himself up onto the work surface. From here he began to address the jumble of limbs and minds, talking them through a whole body relaxation exercise. This was familiar territory to Luke, such sessions having been part of his singing training, but the environment and the different shapes and states of health of the participants made the experience more surreal than usual.

Luke, with many of the instincts of a cat, soon found himself on the borderlands of sleep. Only the twitching of Louise, lying next to him, and the heavy breathing of her father, Bill, kept him from crossing the frontier. He concentrated on the regular rise and fall of his chest and began to feel at last that sense of separation of mind and body, the uncoupling of thought from the solid weight of limbs, which signified release. To maintain the floating sensation, it was necessary to remain unfocused. To allow the stray thoughts that sneaked into his grey cells to pass on, neither welcomed nor shunned, just treated as ships in the night. They rolled up: Heloise, his own disfigured face, Barbara's wedding, his unpaid mobile bill, his coach's recent reappearance and comments on his voice and a thousand other miniature twitchings of his neurons. He gave them a wave of recognition, let them pass on their way and let the soft brushing of air through his nostrils hold the centre of his being. A small groan from Bill still encased in plaster and for whom the floor, in spite of thin mats, must be agonising, alerted Luke to a change in the Vicar's text.

'...you have been through a life changing experience. We have come together not to dwell on this experience nor even to try and understand why it should happen to each one of us, but simply to hold hands. You all feel a little bit different from others in the world now, but you do have each other and you have God. You are not alone. Together you will find that the pain and confusion you now feel can be allowed, very gently, to slip into the past

– not forgotten, not ignored, just accepted as one of the bricks in the wall of life; a life that each one of you must continue to build. There is no going back, no starting from the bottom; life is about adding not subtraction. Each of these bricks...'

As the vicar talked on, Luke's mind reconnected reluctantly with his stiffening limbs and the photo of Sylvie weighing in his jacket pocket. In the flurry of greeting and Louise and Carol's instant capture of him, he had not yet had a chance to show the photo to anyone. His sense of urgency had faded now; doubts surrounded this whole survivors' meeting enterprise.

Luke tuned in to the vicar again. 'A couple of you have talked to me about the cause of the explosion. For some of you the fact that there appears to have been no foul play, that no one wanted to harm you that, like a volcanic eruption, it just happened because several factors coincided, has helped. It feels better to you that, due to wear and tear, gas leaked into a Victorian sewage system not designed for that purpose. On the other hand, some of you find it less comfortable being a victim of blind chance than of malevolent intent. You feel that if there were some group or person behind this atrocity, some figurehead with a label such as the IRA or Bin Laden, you will have someone distant from yourself to blame, somewhere to send the anger and hurt that you are feeling...'

Anger? Victim? Luke tested the words, but they didn't fit. No one he knew wished him ill. The hatred of strangers was not a concept that had ever troubled his mind. His minimal awareness of the greater world was limited to self-relevant news. The burning of La Fenice opera house in Venice had troubled him for as much as ten minutes; mostly because it had affected all the staff at Music College and put Gulli, his coach into such an unpleasant mood. On the whole though, stuff happened to other people in other places and did not concern him. Now that the world beyond his family and work had reached out and grabbed him, he still felt only a negligible interest; the event was beyond recall by him or anyone. Only the maddening disappearance of Heloise really constituted a step too far. This punch in his mind left him forever poking in the mental debris convinced that the missing hours and explanations about Heloise must be forthcoming.

He looked around. One of the others had recognised him from

before the explosion; that much he had established. He recognised no one. If someone recognised Sylvie too, what would that prove? No more than that a beautiful girl that he had been chatting to had been killed. Where did that take him, or anyone?

Tea break. The invincible duo took him over and demanded the photo. In high pitched excitement they confirmed her identity: 'It *is* her!'

'Definitely her! Look at the hair.'

'Isn't she a dream?'

'The poor girl's dead, Lou.'

'I know, poor Luke. You must be so sad. Except you can't remember her, can you?'

'No.'

Luke listened to their exclamations with the image of the Peter and Gulda, their white sofa and their innumerable photograph albums glowing in his mind. Should he tell Sylvie's parents that he had met someone who had seen her there? How would they cope with the bouncing enthusiasm of Carol and Louise? He recovered the photo and looked around to see if there was a way out of the continued inquisition.

A quiet woman rescued him. She, too, remembered seeing him in the doorway of passport area. 'Hello, it's Luca, isn't it? Carol tells me you have no memory of the explosion including beforehand. Is that right?'

'Well, I can remember bits from when I was stuck. I can remember this robot thing, and that was real, but nothing from beforehand, or the actual explosion. In some ways, I suppose, I am lucky.'

'My husband has the same problem. He finds it supremely frustrating.' Luke looked round. 'No, he's not here. He ... won't be able to leave hospital for a while yet.' Luke made a sympathetic noise. 'He wasn't well before the explosion, so this has complicated things. But, tell me, is it right that you're a singer? Opera?'

'Yes.' He smiled, safe territory fanned out before him.

'My name is Judith Grosvenor; we're huge opera fans. They said, in that article about you in the paper the day you were rescued, that you had won the Caledonia prize while still at college, and were expected to become an international star.'

Luke said easily, 'Well, you know – newspapers, they have to say something.'

'Indeed, but there seemed to be a lot to back this story up. I'm so glad you got out and have recovered. How's your voice? Was it affected?'

'Well it seems to be OK, I haven't had to do anything very testing yet. I'll be singing a full opera in Stockholm in six weeks, so I should find out then. My coach was not as rude as I expected when he came back from holiday, so I guess I've been lucky there as well. If only I could remember things ...'

'Don't! Please don't worry about what has gone, just accept a little gap, don't let it distract you.'

'No but, there's something important. I spent hours and hours under that building with a girl. Now I can't find her and no one seems to have come across her and I have so few clues. Her name was Heloise.' He looked into Judith's kindly but unsurprised face.

'Yes, I know, Carol and Louise were telling me all about it. You don't think she could be something your mind made up for you, to keep you alive?'

Luke sagged and shook his head. The vicar then summoned them round in a circle and invited them, in particular Luke and a dried-out man, to share anything that they had on their minds: a large invitation. Luke, gesturing the other man to go first, looked at his surroundings in disbelief. The survivors meeting seemed to be taking place in a cross between a kindergarten and a canteen. Several low plastic tables and little classroom chairs had been spread out again after the relaxation exercise. High and low cupboards lined the walls, and there was even a sink and a gas water heater but no cooker; a kettle and mugs but no obvious fridge. Cramped incongruously into one corner stood a piano. The urge to go and finger the keys built up inside him.

The dried-out man laboured to explain that it should have been him and not his friend Carl who should have died. Everyone joined in to reassure him of his error. Luke passed round his photo of Sylvie. Three more people, apart from Carol, Louise and Judith seemed variously certain or almost sure that they had seen her. Only Judith had seen Luke *inside* the passport area, just before the actual bangs. Feeling suddenly protective and unwilling to expose his memory of Heloise to this avidly solicitous crowd,

Luke fell silent.

Carol, eyes bulging with excitement, pressed, 'Luke, tell them about Heloise.'

He opened and shut his mouth. The vicar put his head on one side. 'Perhaps you would rather leave that for another meeting, Luke? We could finish with some songs.'

'Luke's a singer,' Judith suggested. 'Oh, I'm sorry, Luke, perhaps you'd rather not ...'

With the sweetest possible smile Luke rose, crossed the room to the piano and opened the lid. 'I'm a little rusty, but I'll sing any time. I'm not so hot on the piano, any pianists?' There were no volunteers. Luke dropped onto the stool and ran his fingers over a quick arpeggio.

'Amazing, it's in tune.'

The vicar puffed with satisfaction. 'Yes Mrs Henson does all her lessons here, so we look after it for her.'

Luke cast a quick eye round the assembled group and seeing the vicar with a jolly tune in mind, launched quickly into a popular Handel song – *Did you not hear my Lady go down to the garden singing* – knowing it to be a gentle warm-up for his voice. Relief flooded his limbs along with the oxygen filling his lungs. He had not sung to anyone, except a critical Gulli, since Heloise lay, with her head on his shoulder in the mess of the Cardon Street building. In spite of the cramped room, the sensation of walking out of doors, of free air surrounding him at last, lifted his spirits. He turned to the scattered applause at the end.

'Was that a bit loud? It always takes a while to adjust to the acoustics of a small room.'

'It was beautiful,' breathed Judith. 'Please go on.'

'I can only accompany myself with a few pieces.'

'Can you do *Amazing Grace*?' begged Louise.

He hesitated, requesting *Amazing Grace* was the equivalent to asking a pianist to play chopsticks, but lying was not one of Luke's accomplishments. Years as a choirboy and concerts at drama school had made such songs part of his bloodstream. He cast an apologetic look at Judith and thrilled most of the survivors, and the vicar, with a powerful rendering of the song. When he finished, before anyone else could make a suggestion, Judith asked for the piece that had won him the Caledonian competition.

Without explanation he launched into the aria *Questa o quella* from Rigoletto.

'Very jolly,' commented the vicar. Luke's startled gaze met Judith's amused eyes. He didn't have the heart to explain that the song outlined the profligate Duke of Mantua's view that all cats are alike in the dark.

After the inevitable *We Shall Overcome*, the vicar blessed them and sent them on their way. Outside the church hall, Luke turned down a lift, veered away from the convenient tube station (he might get dizzy on the escalators) and moved happily towards the bus stop. Waiting in the damp London night, he let the feel of release take over his whole body. Waves of tension melted quietly off him, just like after a good workout. How he had missed this sensation of warm, used muscles. Feelings like this had been a daily occurrence before the explosion, no wonder he had felt odd since then.

His checked his mobile and found a text from Dave saying he would be in The Merlin in New Cross if Luke wanted to meet up. Twenty minutes later, beer in hand, he dropped with a sigh onto a bench next to Dave.

'She was the girl I talked to before the explosion, Sylvie, I mean. They recognised her and another woman remembered me. Now that I know, why can I *still* not remember?'

'I guess it's the difference between a live performance and a recording. How did it all go? I mean the vicar and all the other survivors?'

'It was OK actually. We did a relaxation exercise; the vicar talked pretty good sense for a vicar. I felt fine till we got to the confessions bit. I was just beginning to get claustrophobic when someone asked for a song. It got quite cheery after that.'

'I bet, but what did you sing? You could hardly wow them with the Toreador's song.'

'Believe it or not, I sang *Amazing Grace* – with the correct words and a straight face.'

'Luke, you're a saint. Wish I'd heard that. Did they weep?'

'I think so, I had my back to them, but I could hear it when I stopped. I also sang that 'very jolly' song from Rigoletto about how all women are much the same ...'

'"Very jolly"?'

'Vicar's description, not mine.'

'You subversive devil, were you taking the mickey out of the poor fellow all evening?'

'Not at all, I behaved perfectly ... Dave, I feel more like my old self. I'm starting at the gym again tomorrow. I can sit behind the desk for a week, then back to normal ... Oh I forgot to tell you, when I spoke to Guy at the gym, he said that Jason and Vicky, who work in the canteen, had seen me leave on the morning of the explosion with a blonde and a dark girl. I didn't believe him when he told me, but that must be Sylvie and this Helga girl. D'you think I should try and meet up with Helga?'

'Mmm.' Dave watched the guileless face beside him. For a few minutes, as the old Luke bubbled through the scarred surface, he had forgotten how vulnerable his friend had become. Luke's question returned the atmosphere to the danger zone. Would Helga prove to be another dead end or would she continue the healing process? Would she help to rebuild Luke's confidence? Perhaps she could substitute for the missing Heloise. If only Luke didn't rely on him to supply the right answers.

Curious at Dave's silence, Luke raised his brows and tilted back his head. Dave laughed out and gave him a light punch. 'Stop it, Luke, you look like a puppy waiting by the front door. Why not? – see Helga, I mean. She can only add information – help fill the picture. That's what you want, isn't it?'

Later, on the bus to Catford, Luke digested two facts: he had independent confirmation of his presence in the post office in the hours before the explosion and he had talked to Sylvie van Claes before she died. How could he not remember if he had really been there? Why should Judith, a complete stranger, be more convincing than his co-workers at the gym, who had seen him leave work with the two girls? Dr Penter had said that those missing hours might well come back to him; they felt as unreal as ever. What next? Should he contact Helga? By the time he reached home he had a plan.

A couple of days later over breakfast he finalised the idea. 'Mum, I've decided to go to Stockholm a day earlier than I'd planned. I spoke to Sylvie's parents again last night. They've talked to this girl Helga – you remember, she was Sylvie's friend, but didn't go in to the post office. She's working in Copenhagen at the moment, so I can take a bus and a ferry from Stockholm, stay overnight and get back the next day.'

'That's a lot of travel, Luke, just before you have the rehearsal.'

'I like travel, Mum; it'll be relaxing. I need to see this girl, she could fill in the only bit that's still missing, from when I left the gym until those people saw me in the post office just before the explosion.'

Maria opened her mouth to mention the time under the building with the non-existent Heloise, but seeing Luke's face alight with hope she smiled. 'Fine, Topo. Have you got enough money for the ticket?'

12

Mayfair Street: Grosjean Gallery

Light filtered in a deadpan way through the muslin blinds, giving the high, white interior a churchlike quality. Into this cavern, colour spilled; great torrents of it cascading down the walls. The texture of the colours defied analysis; they were thick, yet translucent, warm yet precise. Each of these artworks was woven and the main, though not the only, ingredient was wool. Yet not the faintest whiff of domesticity clung to them. In scale and brilliance this dazzling outpouring reminded Nina of the jewelled glass of the Sainte Chapelle in Paris.

She wandered, her usual smart trot reduced to dazed meander, and stared in silence. Any connections between the materials woven into these great panels and the soft skeins with which she constructed her practical garments seemed entirely absent. She was glad now she had listened to Morris and left her knitting at home, though it felt odd to be empty-handed.

'Morris, I really don't know what to say. They're gigantic pictures, aren't they? They don't feel woollen at all. More like abstract oil paintings.'

'See why I wanted you to wait for the exhibition to see them? Aren't they just stunning? You proud?'

'Proud? I'm flabbergasted. Are these really Ruth's?'

'Yup. She ...'

'But did Ruth really do these herself? I mean, did she decide on the design or did you ...'

'She chose the colours, dreamt up the designs and wove the fabric. I helped to dress the loom, that's all. I don't do work like this. Mine are in the next room, through here. The Grosjean knew who would pull in the crowds.'

Nina smiled, suddenly. 'I'm proud of you both, Morris. You've done great things for her. How did you get away with it?'

'Oh, when she turned twenty-one, I suggested to Martha that Ruth could be gainfully employed sorting and looking after my workshop. I could see she was bored; well she had less freedom than a ten year old. Dan and Martha were used to me and they confused familiarity with security. I corrupted Ruth shamelessly, introduced her to wicked music – opera no less.' Nina chuckled. 'I got out audio books from the library for her; she'd not read a book from the day you left.' At the look on Nina's face, Morris plunged on. 'She taught herself Braille, you know. We kept it all in my workshop. After a year or so she really started reading. Mind you, I'm not sure she really understands the facts of life even now. I wanted to pay her for her work, but of course Martha insisted on taking the money; I don't think Ruth ever saw a penny. From the beginning, though, she was doing her own stuff. She claims she can tell some of the colours apart by touch. It's true that some of the earth dyes change the texture of the wool, but I couldn't do it. Her work is completely original.'

Morris marched towards a soaring strip of colour that reminded Nina of scaffolding seen at midnight under lamplight. 'Take this tall hanging here, I'd never have dared put a vertical design on something only eighteen inches wide. And she's wicked with colours. Most people go all oatmeal and naïf as soon as they touch a loom, they have a notion of weaving as some kind of 'natural' expression of simple rural living. Ruth has this passion for colour that's much closer to reality. I mean look at Peruvian cloth – not that Ruth can, of course. But she remembers colours; she cares about the difference between poppy and tomato red. She asked me the other day if the star of light on her design was more like midday sun on a wing-mirror or the morning sun on the shaving mirror in the small bathroom at Blackheath. God knows how she can remember such things. She knows exactly what she is doing, better than if she could see it. This, the stuff we're looking at, it's the inside of her mind, her imagination out here for us to see. These are works of art. And do you know what?' Morris growled unexpectedly. 'Martha took one look at these and thought they were useless. Dan never even saw them. I want to savage that woman whenever I think about that. I cannot understand how my uncle ever came to marry her in the first place.'

'Oh Morris.' Nina laughed into the flushed face above her. 'You haven't changed much. Nothing comes out of your mouth for a month; then suddenly you boil over. I do understand how you feel. Ruth, though, she's changed so much. I don't really know her any more.'

'Part of her is still a child, that should be familiar to you. The other? I don't know, Nina. She's lost. Sometimes I'm so afraid she'll never work again. I don't know what went on when she was stuck under that building, but something did. Or maybe it was afterwards in those hours with Dan dying. She won't talk about it – no, I mustn't start on that now. We're here to celebrate. Let's open the Champagne. The world and his wife will be arriving any minute.'

'I've never had Champagne before.'

'Nina, you're amazing. You'd better start living. When Ruth gets home, I want your entire life story.' He turned to wrestle with the Champagne, and missed the flush that swept over Nina's face. He poured the frothing liquid into two tiny glasses. 'There's got to be some sense behind all these weird things in my child-hood. Oops! Here, get that down you and feel the flutter. You know the press were here at midday? They were pretty excited and I had a hard time persuading them that Ruth couldn't even be visited. She's going to be famous, you know. You'll have to turn into a dragon of a bodyguard; she won't like being pestered by strangers.'

Luke and Maria reached the Grosjean Gallery midway through the preview party. Luke, having had an altercation with a rowing machine, was back on crutches temporarily. The rooms were heaving with noisy, drinking people, only a few of them even looking up at the walls. The two wandered in a dazed way from weaving to weaving. Between the dainty, handkerchief-sized garments with their delicate hues that flowed from Maria's machine, and these swathes of fierce textured colours, lay an unbridgeable gulf.

'Luke, I thought you said it was a sewing exhibition.'

'Yeah, well, sewing/weaving, I thought there'd be *some* connection. Looks like I was wrong. Great stuff though. Like the scale, it'd look brilliant on a stage. I wonder if this guy, Morris, has ever thought of doing stage design.'

'These big ones are by the woman – a blind woman, it says here. The little ones in the next room are by the man.'

'Jesus, you wouldn't think someone who couldn't see, could get it so together, would you? There's something stimulating about them, they make you feel bigger. What d'you think, Mum?'

Maria, perplexity wrinkling her forehead, looked up at her son. 'I think they do the opposite to me. I feel a bit like a mouse waking up in a jungle. Everything seems a bit ... well ... oversized?'

Luke grinned, then looked about again. 'Ah, there's Morris in the corner. He's the guy who invited me.' Luke freed a hand from his crutches to wave and to his surprise Morris pushed his way through the crowd, his strange eyes alight with Champagne and success.

He beamed at Luke and Maria. 'You came! I'm so pleased.'

'Hi, Morris. Yes, I thought my mother would be interested, she does fancy sewing – for babies.' He laughed. 'I thought this would be her kind of thing, but the scale's a bit different, isn't it Mum?'

Morris smiled at Maria. 'That's all it is really – scale. I mean all cloth is woven. You may use a tiny needle and push it between minute parallel threads of white cotton; we use a shuttle and chuck it to and fro between thick parallel lines of string or wool. Same thing really.' He winked at Luke, while Maria gazed unconvinced at one of Ruth's works: a bamboo grove of colours and lines.

Luke looked round. 'Morris, is your cousin here tonight? I'd still like to talk to her sometime.'

'She's not out of hospital yet, I'm afraid. And,' he shook his head, 'to be honest, she won't talk about that time at all.' He scanned the crowd. 'Her old nurse has come to look after her; she might be able to help. She's under the lights over there, with a bun.' He pointed to a weather-beaten woman in her late forties, then laughed. 'Come, I'll introduce you. Poor Nina, she's looks as though she's been dumped in the Monkey House, she's been living in the wilds of Scotland for years.'

Two hours later Morris, his slight body still vibrating with excitement, draped an arm round Nina's comfortable shoulders.

'Wow! Thank God that is over. I'm exhausted. How about you? This must be pretty weird for you.'

'No, I'm fine. My head feels a bit odd though. Will that be the Champagne?'

'Yup. You may have a bit of a head in the morning, but it was worth it. The management say we're free to go. We'll take a taxi – at Ruth's expense.'

'Don't be foolish, we haven't got money to throw away.'

'Ruth has. Look at those red dots on that hanging there and the three up the far end. Do you know what that means? They're sold; she's made three – no four – and a half thousand on those hangings tonight.'

'Morris!' Nina patted her bun, pushing the hairpins more firmly in as if the shock might loosen them. She stared in disbelief at the bedspread-sized piece of work above her. It felt like a slice of sea that had been picked up and flung against the wall: the soft fluidity in the detail at odds with the weight of the major features – rocks within a stormy wave.

Morris hugged her. 'Nina, what shocks you most: Ruth making money or people spending so much on something to hang on their walls?'

'Everything. It is just so far outside my world I don't…Morris, dear, I hope you made a lot of money too.'

'I'm not in Ruth's league – more domestic really, but I did well.'

'I liked the three you called *Listening to Birdsong*.'

'Good, they're my favourites. I just refused to sell them. Perhaps I'll keep them in Ruth's house in Blackheath then you can enjoy them every day.'

'But Morris, are you thinking I'm going to stay here forever? I came down to help, I can't stay … my house … I did wonder if Ruth could come back with me, but now, seeing this … I don't think.'

Morris, took the trembling arm and tucked it firmly into his. 'It's much too soon for big questions like this. Let's get that taxi. On the way back to Blackheath you're going to explain things to me. Starting with the real reason why you disappeared to Scotland. I can't help if I don't understand what the row was about, can I?'

In the leathery dark of the taxi with lights blinking all around, Nina sat waiting to make contact with the sealed container in her mind. The story Morris had requested had never once been spoken out loud, only bound tighter and tighter into an explosive ball in her mind. Someone had once described to Nina the fierce concentration of matter that made a star turn into a black hole of unimaginable density; her mind contained such a black hole. In this hole thoughts churned in on themselves.

Morris shifted to look at Nina. 'Start with the day you left.'

'But that's the end of the story.'

'Where's the beginning?'

'I think that it started a year before I left ... but sometimes I think I'm wrong and that it goes even further back, but I must be imagining that. Surely Martha would not harm her own child just to punish me?'

'I wouldn't ... no of course not. For heaven's sake Nina, what have you been blaming yourself for over the years?'

'Oh dear, I had forgotten just how acute you are Morris. Well, I'd better start from the things I am sure about. I think it begins with Ruth becoming a woman – you know, starting her periods. She was thirteen and Martha sort of clamped down on her. She seemed to think this child, *her* child, was going to become a loose woman overnight. She started to dress her in oversize ugly dresses, restricted what I read to her – mostly children's stories anyway. She barely allowed her to leave the house. We were permitted to go to concerts still, but I got into trouble one day because after we went to a Murray Perahia piano recital, Ruth told Martha about her conversation with the man who sat beside her. He was in his seventies, I'll swear, though Ruth didn't know that, of course. That was the last concert she attended.' Nina stopped and turned towards Morris in the half-light of the taxi. 'Morris?'

'Mmm?'

'Have you ever wondered if Martha was mad?'

'I've known it for the last ten years. Back then I just thought 'that's Martha' and accepted it. There's not much you can do as a child, without paying the price.'

'Yes, well I know too now; I was daft not to realize it then. My mother had a mental illness – agoraphobia – but compared with Martha, she was completely normal. Anyway, after Ruth's fourteenth birthday Martha sat me down one day to explain that her daughter was in danger. First because she was blind – fair enough; second because she carried this lethal gene that had made her blind – all right; third because she was so innocent, not having been able to go out into the world like ordinary children – well, yes and no, that was partly Martha's fault. Anyway, there I am nodding away, it was always easier to agree with Martha when she started

108

lecturing, then she began on this weird theme: the blindness is a message from God, Ruth has tainted genes and they must never be passed on. Martha goes on about these genes and God's message and I'm still foolishly nodding away; there's so little you can say when God gets into the act. Then she concludes, as though there's no other answer, that she must obey God's directive and have Ruth sterilised!'

Morris clutched at the handle as the taxi jerked forward. 'The hag! The rotten hag! Poor Ruth, did she do it? Surely no doctor would ever have agreed.'

'I still don't know. I really did fight. At first I was so sick I couldn't think properly. Then I asked about the doctor, but she'd already got someone to agree. She wasn't asking for my approval; I was, apparently, the last person she would consult on such a subject.'

'Poor Nina! What about Dan? Did you talk to him.'

'I tried, but she sort of guarded him, and anyway he always did what she asked. She sounded so reasonable too, so convinced.'

'Couldn't you have gone to someone? The Social Services? I don't know?'

'I tried that too. It was the most humiliating thing. I rang the NSPCC when I thought Martha was out. I tried to explain and I could hear that they only half believed me. They said no doctor would agree to it. The awful thing was, that Martha came back and heard me. She took the phone and talked to them, told them lies and they believed everything she said. It was amazing; she said that she was very sorry for me, but that I had had an abortion fifteen years ago and become sterile and was obsessed with this idea; she told them that her beloved daughter was simply having an investigation, having been referred by her doctor to a specialist because of pains in her ovaries. Indeed, the investigation would ensure that she was able to have a full reproductive life. Martha invited them to come and visit if they felt in any doubt. She was superb – and terrifying. It was all lies. *I* told the truth, but they believed *her*.'

Nina hugged her handbag to try and control her shuddering.

Morris put a comforting arm around her. 'I can't believe she'd go through with anything so evil. I wish I'd known. Not that a seventeen-year-old schoolboy can do much, though I might have managed an uproar. Jesus, I can't get my head around this. Did you say anything to Ruth at the time?'

'I never saw her again. Martha had me on a train with a one-way ticket to Scotland that night. She knew my parents had left me a property there. I don't know if she realised that it didn't even have a roof. She employed me, so she dismissed me. She put my remaining wages in my bank account, that's the last I heard. I wrote on and off for three years, but I never heard a thing – until your letter.'

'Great heavens, I thought Martha was related to you. My letters must have come as an awful shock.'

'Well, I was a bit shaken. But you're right, she is related, sort of, she's my mother's eldest cousin's daughter; she married Dan when I was sixteen, she was twenty-four then. I only met her a couple of times. It was when Ruth started going blind she got in touch. I'd just finished training as a nanny, and my Mum had just died, so I was thrilled to get my first job so quickly. I must admit, though, I found Martha pretty scary even then; she had such an unfair advantage over the rest of us, always having God on her side. I felt glad when you wrote about how Martha died. It seemed so appropriate. Almost as if her God had struck her down and you don't need to tell me that's a silly way to think.'

'Well, I never bought the God package anyway, but I know what you mean. So, what are you going to tell Ruth? She'll never have babies, that's a really big deal for a woman, isn't it?'

'I don't know what to tell her. We haven't spoken about why I left, but I get the feeling that there's a closed door between us. At first she seemed glad to see me, sort of relieved and pleased to be a child again, but she seems to be slipping away as she gets better. All she cares about is the music you gave her. I don't know where to start. I can hardly ask her if she's been sterilised, can I?'

'No, I suppose not – at least not yet. I can talk to her about most things.' Morris paused, listened to his memory and qualified his statement. 'I suppose we mostly talk about things to do with our work or music. She works really hard, you know. Those hangings represent countless hours of weaving. I've got to think about this. We can't set her back just as she is getting better.' He let his eyes lose focus among the lights around the stationary taxi and spoke almost to himself. 'I had to know about this, but I wanted her to taste the triumph of this evening and now when I tell her, I'll be thinking…' He turned to Nina, his recent euphoria drained out of his voice. 'Will she never get a square deal out of life?'

'I'm not sure anyone does, Morris.'

A half-laugh escaped him. 'No, you're right. We can't change the past anyway.' He spoke with determined vigour, 'OK. Let's give her a simplified version of your bust up with Martha. We could say that Martha sent you away because you wouldn't agree to restricting Ruth's life or something? I'll think. What about scars? If she had the operation, she'll have scars.'

Nina pulled a handkerchief out of her sleeve. 'She does. I had to help her change her nightie, and there are scars. Oh Morris, I'm so ashamed.'

'Ashamed? Nina, don't be absurd. Martha was a bulldozer. If she was determined, there is nothing you could have done.'

'I still think it's my fault. If it's done there's no going back, is there?'

'I wouldn't know. I imagine not. But just remember the fantastic reactions tonight. We must be pleased for what she can do. Maybe she wouldn't have wanted babies at all. I mean she has never shown any interest in men. Perhaps she's inclined the other way, you never know.'

'Yes, I am trying to be positive; nothing else will help her now. I don't think she is…I mean I don't think she prefers women. I could be wrong of course, but she was always keen on the prince in fairy stories.' Nina gave her nose a final blow. 'Morris, who was that very taking young man with the scars and crutches who wanted me to get him an interview with Ruth, not a journalist, surely?'

'Good God no! I don't know what he does, but he was in the Cardon Street nightmare and he's lost his memory. I think he just wants to talk to anyone else who was there. Definitely a prince.' Morris sighed.

Nina tucked away her handkerchief and spoke tentatively. 'Morris, do you mind my asking, do you prefer…men?'

'Yup, bullseye! Who's acute now? But I am quite, *quite* sure Luke prefers girls, so no dice, as they say. You're not shocked?

'My closest friends in Scotland are Hugo and Geoff. I miss them every day.'

13
Copenhagen & Stockholm: Helga & *I Lombardi*

Even though the damp air threatened further rain, Luke sat down at an outside table. He ordered a coffee. Any of these women walking across the square could be Helga. A faint tingle of excitement stirred him. This was, in effect, a blind date. Alien buildings surrounded him; Copenhagen's planners had a penchant for large areas of colour from pleasing yellow brick to less agreeable blue or ochre paint. Luke inhaled; a novel foreign-city smell hovered in the air. Sitting at leisure, watching a fountain, waiting to spend a whole afternoon and evening with a girl – these passive activities spelt out holiday to him. Being alone, also meant being free, of family, responsibility and endless, kindly questions.

'Luke?'

'Helga?'

Not a typical Scandinavian: dark curls framed a neat face with big, hopeful eyes. Did she look familiar?

'Yes, I'm Helga. You do look a bit different with the scars.' Her eyes widened in embarrassment. 'But it looks fine. You look fine.' She even sounded familiar.

'I feel fine. Have a seat. Do you want coffee?'

'Yes. You must try the cake here, Luke – Luca?'

'Luke.'

'Luke. It's good and you are thin – but you are fine.' As her eyes widened again, Luke laughed.

They ordered coffee and cakes. The cakes brought on a frivolous mood as they battled with cream squelching out of fragile pastry. For the next twenty minutes they managed to pretend that they were a young, carefree chance-met couple. Luke talked about his journey and the fat landlady in his guesthouse. Helga talked about her work translating travel brochures. They continued to find the cakes, the other coffee-drinkers, the people crossing the square even the predatory pigeons amusing.

A man with a porter's trolley unloaded a barrel and the sudden clang made them both jump. Helga giggled. 'I do that now, all the time. You do it too?'

'No. Yes, perhaps I do. But that's crazy; I don't remember the explosion, so why should I react to bangs?'

Helga picked up flakes of pastry on her fingers. 'I wish I didn't remember. I get frightened every night, thinking I'm going to dream about it again. Do you have dreams about it, Luke?'

Luke signalled to the waiter. 'Mmm. Sometimes.'

'I'm very lonely in the night.'

Luke turned, somewhat startled, then saw her blush as she heard what she had said. He smiled but said quickly: 'Shall we go someplace. Show me the town, you must see some interesting stuff in these guide books you translate.'

'Well the Tivoli gardens are very beautiful. Don't you want me to tell you about Sylvie?'

'Yes, of course, you can tell me on the way. How do we get there?'

'We walk.'

'Good.' He could stroll beside her and listen, without being exposed to her too speaking eyes. Wandering on, Luke relaxed further, even, as his arm brushed against hers, feeling a small prickle of excitement. Helga had a certain awkward charm; in the hours ahead anything might happen.

'OK, Helga, tell me from when we met at the gym.'

'Well, we saw you putting away the mats after the aerobics class and Sylvie ... ' she took a sharp breath and began to pleat the edge of her cardigan. This story had one ghastly inevitable ending. 'Sylvie said *I bet he could tell us* – she meant tell us where to go for this record she wished to buy for me. So she – Sylvie is not shy, you understand – she spoke to you and then we all went there together. You talked a lot to Sylvie; I know she felt happy then. She had been apart from her boyfriend for a month. I keep telling myself that it's good, if she was going to die, that she had that time with you first.'

Intrigued, Luke turned to Helga, but she kept her head lowered. He pushed his fingers through his hair. 'I'm sure I enjoyed being with her too, only I can't remember.'

'Can you remember me?'

'Not really, but ... I'm not absolutely certain. It's as if part of my brain recognises you and the other part says I am being foolish. In fact,' Luke laughed, 'it's a bit mixed up in there.'

She laughed too. 'I will try and help with the unmixing...the sorting.'

She seemed very sweet. 'OK, and then?'

Serious again, she continued. 'We arrived at the GoldenDisc place and Sylvie looks across the road and says *a post office, I can get my photo done after all. You go and start looking for the record, I won't be long.* Then, Luke, you say why don't we come and help with the photo. You're joking; she knows you will make her laugh. She tries to forbid you, but you follow her across the road. I stay there by the GoldenDisc, but I'm looking at the post office. When the explosion happens, the glass window behind me blows out. That's why I have glass in the back of my legs.'

Helga twisted and pulled up her trousers to reveal some familiar looking tram lines on the back of her calves. She pulled up her sleeve to show some more on the back of her forearm.

Luke took the wrist and peered sympathetically at the damage, then said lightly, 'You poor thing.' He patted the punctured skin and let her hand go again. She remained silent. He prompted: 'Did the explosion happen as soon as Sylvie went in there?'

'No, you were both in there a long time. I went into a chemist. Then I came out and waited by the record store. I thought perhaps you had gone away together and left me, I nearly came over to find you. Then came the bangs – so loud, *so loud*, bigger than any noise, bigger than thunder or guns. Such a big mess, too, Luke. All dust everywhere, so you couldn't see. Just lumps of building and glass, glass, glass. Then I kept hoping that you and Sylvie *had* gone somewhere without me. If you had...' Her face puckered.

'We wouldn't have done that.'

'But,' Helga turned away as her she lost control of her mouth, and wailed, 'if you had done that Sylvie would be alive now.'

Luke put his arm round her. The story she related still felt to him like a story about other people. Her small shuddering frame felt real enough under his hands, though. He concentrated on soothing her; restoring her to the rather charmingly self-conscious person she had been during their time in the café. By the time they reached the gardens, her uncontrolled weeping had ceased. She snuggled against his shoulder, slightly diverted by telling him about the astonishing kindness of the English policeman who had helped her.

Luke let go of her as they wandered into the gardens, but at the first resurgence of tears he put his arm round her again. In the garden they sat on a bench close together, talking about Sylvie's parents. Luke attempted the hopeless task of convincing Helga that she could not be to blame for their unhappiness. They barely looked at the damp green trees and elaborate flowerbeds.

Later Helga took him to the harbour area where all the inhabitants of Copenhagen seemed to be out enjoying themselves. They wandered, talking less intensely now, by the waterside. They had a meal, drinking the light Danish beer. It was 9 o'clock, they had been together for six hours. They had talked about Sylvie for much of the time but as the beer went down they talked increasingly of themselves. Leaving the restaurant to wander again by the waterside, knowing that they had very little more time together, Luke sensed a recklessness in his companion as well as in himself. The intensity of their shared past, even though Luke remembered so little of it, had accelerated their intimacy. This and a kind of holiday irresponsibility, alcohol fuelled, now took over. Luke leant against the low harbour wall and teased her. 'Why didn't you come into the post office with us?'

She dropped her head. 'I told you, Luke. You and Sylvie . . . you seemed so together and I . . . I wanted it to be me. It seemed unfair.'

He slid his arms around her and pulled her close. It all seemed very straightforward. 'Well I'm here now.' He kissed her lazily, comfortably, not really minding if this was all or the beginning of something more. She responded almost with relief, as though she had feared not arriving at this point. As Luke's hands began to explore he encountered very little resistance. They moved on to a less exposed spot and Luke thought with anticipated comfort, I'm going to get laid tonight. Thank God, another first since the explosion. This is what I need, this is back to normal. There's nothing wrong with me. Be healing for us both, he rationalised.

Somewhere between this thought and the moment when Helga, out of breath, said that the bus to her suburb would be going soon, did he want to . . . see her flat, his mind and body began to fall out. Sure he *wanted*, but not exactly this. Wouldn't this do for the time being though? Perhaps. Perhaps not. Oh come on, this is a willing girl, be good for both of you. A newly acquired sense of responsibility nudged him. Yes, but after? This is a fragile girl, who might need more than just a night's consolation and anyway, who are you kidding? You want to find Heloise, you know she's out there. Going with Helga is just a distraction, it just proves that you believe them, believe she's dead, believe you imagined her, whatever. Christ! I just want to get laid, what's the big deal?

Luke lifted his head to accept the invitation. The anxious eyes stared up at him, he paused and the moment passed. 'You're very kind Helga, of course I'd love to come home with you, but I've got to catch a plane early, I'll be rehearsing straight after lunch tomorrow. I'll take you to your bus stop. Anyway,' he said, searching for consoling words 'I'm not sure this will make anything better. I live a long way away, I couldn't...'

'Just for tonight, Luke? I have such bad dreams.'

He could hardly say, but I have such good dreams with someone else. Helga's urgent hands held none of the magic that had been in Heloise's lightest touch. Still battling with himself, he took her to the bus stop, where they kissed feverishly until the bus arrived and where, to his own surprise, he waved her goodbye before walking back to his hotel. He arrived there cold, dissatisfied and worried by his decision.

'Dave? You still awake? I know it's after twelve, but I need to talk.'

'OK, I'm still up. How did it go with the girl ... what's her name?'

'Helga. Fine, well better than that ... but I didn't really feel like the sequel.'

'Fool, you should make hay ... well, there's a first time for everything. Anyway, did she tell you anything useful?'

'Yes, she really does know about me and Sylvie.'

'Brilliant, one mystery down, one to go. Tell me.'

Luke, looked round his room and then at the phone in his hand. 'Is there someone with you, Dave? I keep hearing noises, am I interrupting something?'

'Yup, there is – and no, you're not.'

'Who?'

'Just a bloke I met, you don't know him.'

'What's his name?'

Dave sighed audibly. 'John.'

Luke lifted the phone from his ear in surprise, as a saxophone sounded at the other end, then laughed. 'Dave, is that neighbour of yours away? You can't get away with a gig after midnight, can you?'

'She went into a home months ago, but this isn't a gig. Come on Luke tell me what the lovely Helga told you.'

'Well, she filled in my movements between leaving the gym and going into the post office in Cardon Street. Sylvie wanted passport photos, and I went along for the ride. If I knew about the photo-booth, I must have known there was a post office there, mustn't I?'

'I guess so. Go on.'

'Well, Helga says that Sylvie and I were going great guns. I can believe that; when I saw the photos of her at her parents I thought she was someone I could fall for. Mind you, even talking about her to Helga, I still can't actually remember Sylvie as a real person at all. Anyway, we all walked to the post office and Sylvie went in and apparently I followed her because we were still talking. So you see, I was there just by chance. I wasn't doing anything.'

'Except pursuing skirt, of course. Nothing new there.'

'You saw the photo, Dave, anyone would've fallen for her.'

'Sure. Why did Helga stay outside?'

'My fault, apparently. It took a while to get her to tell me. It was only when I suggested that she had taken against me, that she ...are you there Dave?'

'Just a minute, Luke. I'll ring you back. John wants to get going. Ring you in a couple of ticks.'

It was a good ten minutes later, when Dave rang back. Curiosity distracted Luke momentarily from his story. 'What were you doing talking to a strange bloke at one am.'

'Nothing new. I often talk to blokes, strange or otherwise, all night – most frequently you.'

'I suppose.'

'So, why was Helga not in the post office and why was this your fault? If it was, you probably saved her life.'

'Hmm, she thinks so too. Apparently, she felt pissed off because I preferred Sylvie. She didn't come into the post office but decided to sulk in the chemist opposite. Being dumb, I followed

poor Sylvie into the post office. Now, because we two have survived, Helga wonders if destiny isn't sending us a message. The
trouble is I'm not getting the same message. So I left Helga moping
and I'm no nearer to finding Heloise. In fact, I came all this way
for nothing'

'Hey Luke, what's with all this sighing, it's still progress. And
you don't have to sleep with every woman who fancies you; you'd
be flat out for the rest of your life. You're a singer – remember?
Get into role. Lombardi, isn't it? From now on you're Oronte, the
very confused son of an Eastern potentate. That should give you
plenty to worry about. Where are you performing?'

'Royal Swedish Opera, for two nights – one 'invitation only'
– and then four more in Drottningholm Palace Theatre, on an
island.'

'Sounds a ball. First international opera house! Wish I could
come. I'm for bed now. Go to sleep, Luke, and dream about
wowing the critics.'

'Dave, thank God you're still there.'

The bus lurched suddenly and Luke woke up. Heavy city buildings, all glass and concrete, reared up around him. He shut his
eyes again waiting for his lagging memory to explain his current
whereabouts; the airport bus to Stockholm. He drowsed again.
What would his soprano, a French girl, be like? He had yet to meet
Michelle and they only had six days of rehearsal between now and
the first night – yikes! Luke's eyes flew open on this thought. For
a moment his memory wobbled as pine-clad banks with nestling
villas and beaches and swung into view. Montecarlo? No, it was
definitely Stockholm. Of course Sweden was mostly sea. Even so,
it felt inside out with the sea in the centre and skyscrapers at the
edge of the city.

Perhaps this Michelle had been at the Versailles Masterclass
two years ago. If so, she had not made a lasting impression. Still,
it would be good to sing opposite a soprano other than Angela. As
a fellow student, friend and the finest soprano on his postgraduate
course, Angela had inevitably partnered him for years. She had
also auditioned for the part in Sweden, been short-listed, but not
chosen. A cause of much angst, resulting in wearisome weeping
sessions, now happily dried out as she had been selected for the

English Verdi Festival tour the following year. Of course Angela had the virtues of familiarity and reliability, not to mention perfect pitch, an immense range and a great deal of controlled power. Yet her voice left him vaguely dissatisfied. For him, each performance had an element of skydiving about it. He expected – gloried in – moments of free fall, when his voice pleased itself, then took an almost equal pleasure in regaining control of the sounds and landing softly, without fuss. Angela sang with her parachute always open, always in perfect control, always correctly and carefully paced. He positively wanted a little more danger in his partnerships. Most importantly, he didn't want to find himself paired with her for the rest of his career.

Arriving at his hotel, Luke attempted to unpack, but with his hands full of T-shirts he stood quite still to puzzle over the last forty-eight hours. He dropped the clothing back into his suitcase and lay on the bed to think. Heloise, Helga, Sylvie, Heloise, Helga. Someone had put him on a roundabout with these unconnected characters, doomed to circle forever never quite catching up with any of them. That was silly, he had at least caught up with Helga. He looked at his watch; this time yesterday, he had been sitting in a café in Kongens Nytorv in Copenhagen, watching Helga talk.

Why had he turned her down? Had he changed that much? Age? The doctors tinkering with his brain? Or the memory of Heloise snuggled at his shoulder in the painful dark, her mesmerising voice holding him back from oblivion? What if he never found her? He was hardly going to abstain from sex for the rest of his life. He should have gone home with Helga.

His mind continued to turn like a hamster on a wheel as he lay half asleep, half unpacked. Why could he not remember Sylvie if he had met her *before* the explosion. Why had Dave been talking to someone in the middle of the night when he phoned?

Somewhere along the stream of his thoughts Luke fell asleep, with the result that he arrived late for the first rehearsal. He found himself the subject of some uncomfortable curiosity. Lars Diener, the director, looked him rather too firmly in the eye. 'I have had words with Anton – your teacher, Mr Gulli. He tells me the voice works very well, but the psychology has been in a small trouble. We have your alternative, what you call your cover, Pieter, here. When the mind is not well, you will tell us and Pieter will manage, yes?'

'No. I mean yes, of course. But I'm fine, never better.'

The soprano, Michelle, turned out to be melon shaped, with twinkling eyes that disappeared when she laughed; her voice, on the other hand, bubbled and swept through the music like molten silver. Relief filled Luke; this combination suited him fine. A sense of humour and considerable acting powers supplemented Michelle's voice and by the end of the first rehearsal a familiar buzz of commitment and power filtered through him.

They rehearsed from three o'clock in the afternoon until nine thirty and then broke for a visit by the press and a meal. Lars gave bemused journalists a potted version of the story. 'In Lombardy there is a patricide in error and the criminal hides in the Holy Land. Then the daughter of the Lombards, Giselda,' he turned and shot out a finger at Michelle, 'is stolen by the Tyrant of Antioch.' He waved towards another singer. 'The Lombards go on a Crusade to rescue her and behave very bad with rapeings and killings. In Antioch, the Tyrant, a Muslim, has a son, Oronte.' Lars suddenly turned and pointed to Luke, 'and a wife, Sofia,' he pointed again. 'Sofia is secretly a Christian. The son loves the prisoner, Giselda, and is religiously confused.'

'Aren't we all?' muttered a journalist.

Luke caught Michelle's eye and she spluttered. By the time Lars had finished his tale in which all the main characters change either religious or political loyalty at some time in the opera before, in most cases, dying, the journalists were almost cross-eyed with bewilderment and stirring restlessly.

They had come hungry for new celebrities. As a vaunted European enterprise, featuring the stars of the future in their first appearance in a major opera house, they expected some good copy. Naturally, they majored on Luke's recent experience, photographed his newly marred face, and encouraged him to talk about the missing Heloise until Lars, carefully orchestrating the interview, intervened. Heloise featured in the press the next day as his "guardian angel", thus sidestepping the question of her existence in the real world. One enthusiast insisted on a shot of the back of Luke's head. The growing hair had still not hidden the jagged line where some metallic spar had ripped through his skin and under which the surgeons' neater work was concealed.

Later in the bar Luke, juggling a mixture of Italian, English and

French and surrounded by singers, many of whom he knew, sat with his body comfortably cushioned by Michelle as she perched on the adjacent stool and knew himself momentarily happy again. As if during the last six weeks he had been in the hands of some erratic wind, unable to get his feet onto the ground for more than a few moments at a time. Now, here he was, grounded, back to base. Doing the right thing with the right people. He remembered to ring Claudia that night knowing that she would understand and be pleased for him.

During the next three days, progress with the opera went smoothly. Lars ceased to ask Pieter to attend every rehearsal with Luke. On the fourth they had a slow technical with lights and some difficult scenery. Everyone felt exposed and uncomfortable after the intimacy of the rehearsal room. Luke, owing to some vigorous dancing in the early hours of the previous day, stumbled over a couch on stage. His weak ankle turned and the doctor attending the group insisted on strapping and the return of the crutch. Luke, his eye on Lars, sang faultlessly, leaning unashamedly on the accommodating Michelle to minimise the use of the crutch. On the fifth night, a Friday, they had a dress rehearsal, with press preview. This would only be their second run-through with the full orchestra. Most of the cast, already gagging with nerves, paled further when Michelle, taking a quick peek, said that every country in Europe had sent critics, as far as she could see. Luke, for whom performance nerves amounted to a pleasurable adrenalin rush, grinned with delight.

Oronte, making his first appearance in the second act, has to launch straight into an anguished love song. Luke seemed to have been born with a heart-wrenching ache in his voice; he made the most of it. The previously noisy listeners hushed to silence. By the end of his aria, his bright, lyrical tone lifting confidently out into the auditorium, Luke had laid out the critics. Enjoying every minute, he took them, shook them then set them gently back on their feet again and they made much of him. Michelle gave him an enveloping hug as he left the stage. He only appeared in two further scenes. In the first he is wandering in exile, having abandoned friends and country, he rediscovers Giselda and she chooses to flee into exile with him, so he offers to convert to her religion. This scene went relatively smoothly, apart from Michelle tripping over a rock and arriving rather more comprehensively in his arms than anticipated. He tried to disguise this with an unscripted passionate embrace, but the two of them struggled with laughter and afterwards heard that Lars was not amused.

In his next scene, Oronte, arriving on stage with Giselda, is already dying of his wounds. Sobered by their natural involvement in the story, the two trailed on stage and sang their desperation at their approaching separation. At the climax of the scene as Luke lay dying in Michelle's arms, three cracking explosions vibrated through the opera house. Luke's voice shut off instantly leaving the audience to assume that he had died. Michelle covered the gap by sobbing audibly. The ensuing trio of the act became a duet between Michelle and the attendant hermit, while Luke lay, his throat completely closed up, a shaking sweating wreck, centre stage, until the curtain dropped. Fireworks continued to pop away in the distance, none as loud as the first couple of bangs. Michelle and the baritone, one kindly the other maddened, hauled him off stage at the end.

Unfortunately, although Oronte is technically dead, he still has to sing in the last act. The aria is sung offstage to indicate that it comes from heaven. Pieter, summoned, stood in the wings trembling and humming desperately. One of the backstage men produced a bottle of water and Luke, a crumpled heap on the floor, drank this slowly, taking very little notice of the bustle around him. As Giselda came to the end of her aria – the cue for his entry from heaven, Luke finally looked up and saw Pieter's face. Unprepared, not warmed up, the sweat visible on his forehead, the boy looked resolute but deeply unhappy. Luke smiled up at him and held up his hand. Pieter pulled him to his feet; Luke opened his lungs and sang from heaven.

Lars, always a fierce taskmaster, treated them to an exacting post mortem after the dress rehearsal. His scathing comments on Luke's levity (the passionate embrace in act two), his unprofessional behaviour and feebleness of mind (a few fireworks for heaven's sake!) and finally his cruelty in snatching Pieter's chance to shine, poured out in a fluent stream of almost correct English. The other performers received some moderate praise and many suggestions for improvements.

'Now,' Lars concluded, facing the shattered singers, 'it seems that the press are so insufficient-educated that they remain unaware of the large, shocking errors in the performance. They have talked – in their so big ignorance – of a new Domingo. Hah! It is the Bergonzi voice you have.' He laughed suddenly. 'Luke, your errors are compensated by the voice. We will not be frightening Pieter again. Tell your inward psychology that a firework is a firework is a firework. No more this fainting on stage, huh? Ever.'

'Never!' Luke managed to keep his trembling legs upright as Lars stalked off into the wings, then he dropped to the floor, giggling insanely.

Miles of dark forest unrolled beside Luke all the way back to the airport. Such vastness and impenetrability didn't bear thinking about, yet this was all that was on offer as an alternative to the thoughts on the jogging circuit in his mind. Heloise shut in that dark hole both metaphorically and possibly for real, lived at present only in his head. Luke tried to concentrate on the world outside the coach window – clumps of fir trees edged with the pale shafts of birch. Why had he turned down Helga for heaven's sake? He looked up again – more fir trees. Dave seemed to be chatting with John (and possibly Dick and Harry) and not missing him at all. He blinked, but the fir trees continued. Hidden manholes lay in wait for him now; lifts, the Underground, fireworks. He frowned, more fir trees, some birches, a farm then fir trees again. Still, he had mostly chorus work between now and Christmas: Buxton and Glyndebourne Touring Company. It should be relaxing. Of course there was the Deepwater Festival in October; televised master classes with performances of scenes in the Birne Theatre to follow – nothing too heavy really. He should still be able to search in between. The bus paused at a crossroads.

There was talk of hiring him to alternate with a world-renowned tenor in Rigoletto in Rome the following May. He'd get three out of the ten nights, because the other guy had engagements elsewhere. If that came off he'd be made. Against the other's power and reputation he could set almost a half metre difference in height and the ability to act. He'd had to invent an agent in Italy when they phoned. Still, his cousin Carlo had been a sort of unofficial agent for years. Carlo had already placed Angela in one of the touring Verdi Festival operas. Perhaps Dave, too, could be persuaded out of England now that he was making waves. Who had Dave been talking to the other night? He shook himself and looked up. In the distance, the low buildings of Stockholm South airport broke through the sea of fir trees.

14
Blackheath: Ruth

Ruth, home at last, made a circuit of her bedroom touching surfaces and objects: the shells on the dressing table; the little teddy
that she had been given by Morris's mother on a holiday in Cornwall; the bookcase full of prayer books, saints' lives and fairy stories, unread since Nina had left; a vase with dried grasses, a high-
backed wooden chair. Nina followed her round the room.

'What happened to your dolls?'

'Mama gave them to the hospital when you went away.'

'All of them? But you loved them!'

Ruth sighed. 'Dolls are for children. I'm grown up now.'

Nina sat heavily on the bed. 'Do you miss them? You used to
play such games with them.' Ruth continued her rediscovery tour,
saying nothing. Nina recalled her slipping away from Martha's
questions, with just that same air of concentration. Nina watched
her, seeing, in the sharp sunlight falling through the window the
grown woman with the first lines on her face and yet also the child
she remembered. Suddenly she smiled, 'Your dolls had such long
funny names.'

Nina sat on the bed looking at the bleak tin wastebasket now
occupying the crib's space. 'The tiny doll with the blue dress, what
was her name?'

'Susannatheelder.'

Nina chuckled. 'That's right. I remember, you wouldn't listen
when Martha told you the name was incorrect. Poor Susannatheelder had to live in the cellar until you agreed to call her plain
Susan. You remember your soft doll HildaColumbaHeloise?'

Ruth's fingers, moving across the wall, had just begun to tour
the rippled edge of a frame round a lacklustre St Francis. They
stopped.

'She used to lie in that crib you had in the corner with Dan-
ielSebastian...or was it DanielLuke?'

'I don't remember.'

'Anyway, I thought of her the other night. I met a young man
at your weaving exhibition looking for someone called Heloise;

such a personable young man, with such speaking eyes.' Ruth, who had started coughing, crossed over to the bed to sit. Nina rubbed her back for a while. 'He got caught in Cardon Street too, you know. They've had to put stitches across his face, and he's on crutches, but he seems fine except that he can't remember things properly, because they operated on his brain. He's looking for this girl he met while he was stuck there. He does so want to talk to anyone who was there and I just wondered...?

'Nina, no! I've told Morris already. I don't want to meet anyone from that time. I didn't talk to anyone. I can't help him. I just want to forget. I want to come home and get used to being here without Mama and Dad.'

'Of course, dear, you just concentrate on getting better. I know it must be strange without Dan and Martha.' Nina straightened the rumpled bedspread. 'Do you miss her?' As soon as she had spoken, she shut her mouth tight, wishing to recall the words, fearing Ruth would withdraw again.

To her surprise, after considering a while, Ruth spoke. 'Well, it doesn't feel right in the house yet. I don't know if that's 'missing her'. I do miss Dad, which is odd, because he was out at work so much of the time. I liked it best when he came home. Of course, in the last few years I spent most days in the studio in Greenwich with Morris.' She stopped, head up. Then ran her hand over the bedspread. 'My weaving! I can have my weaving in the house now, can't I? We can put it on the walls like Morris does. Morris said ...Morris thinks that Dad would have liked my weaving. People must like it if they spend so much money on it, mustn't they?'

Nina pulled the grown-up body impulsively into her arms, whispering into her ear, 'Everyone loves your weaving. It is beautiful, splendid, astonishing ... I can't believe my little girl has become a great artist.'

For a moment Ruth snuggled against her and giggled. 'Mama would not want me to be an artist.' Even as she spoke, the laugh died out of her face. She drew away from Nina. 'I don't know what I feel. I think I'm just going to walk down the garden, maybe that will feel right.'

'Just a moment,' Nina blew her nose and pushed her hanky back into her sleeve, 'let me find you a cardigan. You're supposed to try and keep an even temperature. Here we are, feel this, it's a dark blue woolly, do you think it's yours?'

Ruth put out her hand and felt around the collar until she reached a wooden button. 'Yes, that's mine. I'll be plenty warm in that.'

'Has Morris put Martha's clothes away somewhere else? Everything I've found seems to be yours. Only I don't want to keep asking.'

'He said he'd put Dad and Mama's clothes in the trunk under the bed in his old room. I'll sort them some day, but I don't feel like it now.'

'No, of course not dear, it's just difficult to know . . . but if they're all yours, I needn't keep asking.' Nina looked uncertainly at the bear-size tweed coat hanging in the hall. Ruth was tall, but the coat would swamp her widthways. Had Ruth not been bought any clothes of her own? Everything she had worn so far appeared to be something Martha had discarded years ago. Martha had been twice Ruth's size.

Nina watched Ruth drift into the garden and didn't follow, guessing that she needed to rediscover something by herself. Ruth wandered up to a flowering shrub, touched the leaves, lifted a white flower to her nose and stood quite still for almost a minute. Then she moved familiarly on, like a host at a party, touching, (even talking perhaps) to shrubs and trees. She seemed to be shaking hands with old friends. She turned behind the beech tree and disappeared from sight.

Well, thought Nina returning to the kitchen, the garden was always more of a home to Ruth than the house. Inside the house, Martha would censor her every move, always exasperated by Ruth's blunderings, forever imposing pointless tasks: polishing already shining silver, refolding folded tea towels, washing clean cutlery. She always had reasons for these endeavours, and by connections that Nina and Ruth accepted at the time (without making sense of them), the reasons were religious. Martha said that polishing meant directing your energy towards maintaining God's gifts to man. This energy, she implied, might otherwise get dissipated in useless activity. Nina had never dared to point out that butter dishes, candlesticks and sweet bowls, not to mention cigarette holders and snuff boxes, were probably not uses for which God had intended the gift of silver.

Nina, extracting supermarket vegetables from the fridge and chopping them with a wince of disapproval, marvelled at her own blindness. How could Martha's madness have seemed so normal then? Her own mother had, from one day to the next, decided that she could no longer leave the house. Nina, aged ten, had revelled in the responsibility of shopping for her. Her mother had been cheerful, sweet-tempered and grateful for any service. According to the doctors, though, she had been mad. Whereas Martha, running the local Sunday School, maintaining the Overseas Church Association letter, looking after her blind child, lying to Social Services, sterilising her own daughter and, with her cold and vengeful God, terrifying everyone who came in contact with her, had been deemed sane.

This conundrum, along with the memory of her last battle with Martha, made Nina long for her Scottish nest. London seemed to revive old confusions and present new ones. Ruth, grown up, detached, so unlike the cuddly fourteen-year-old Nina had been forced to leave behind, made her feel emotionally redundant.

Nina put the salad on the kitchen table and trotted back to the French windows in the sitting room to check, as she had day after day during Ruth's childhood, that her charge was playing happily. Ruth wandered back into view and stood at one end of the old bench near the three birch trees. For a moment Nina could imagine her a child again playing with Morris, when he was sent home from boarding school with the whooping cough. The boy all wrapped up and lying on the bench, the girl, her dark hair under a white woollen hat, capering about at his direction and making pictures on the ground with sticks and leaves; looking totally at home in the green space, though she lived entirely in her own darkness by then. Strange that Martha never stopped these games, as she did the indoor ones. Martha, on her rare visits to the garden, stared past these leaf and twig paintings as if she did not see them. Perhaps she didn't.

Nina's face creased into a smile; at least the image of Ruth in the garden reminded her of the child she had cared for though all those years. That child had scrambled into her lap whenever she could, clung to her, whispered in her ear while the two of them colluded to keep their friendship hidden from Martha's censorious eyes. The smile faded. The Ruth she had rediscovered in the hospital kept the world at a safe distance, slipped out of conversations by falling asleep and now – home at last – by simply walking away.

Nina went up to her room to collect a writing pad. She came and sat near the French windows as she wrote to Hugo who was keeping an eye on her cottage.

Yes, please do cut the cauliflowers and eat them, and anything else you can find, there might be some raspberries by now. If you could open the front door for half an hour while you're round there, it would help to stop that smell accumulating again.

Ruth came home from hospital today and is now definitely on the mend. I think it will be some time before she can manage on her own, so I imagine it will be a while before I see the hills, or you, again. She is very different from the child I once described to you – though of course that could be due to her recent ghastly experiences. She won't talk about either her time trapped in the building after the explosion or about Dan's death. I'm sure she would be happier if she did. She won't even meet up with the charming young man who so desperately wanted to speak to her about it all. I am trying to be patient. Perhaps she will confide more in me as she recovers, though I fear I maybe too old and set in my ways to understand this world she lives in now with computers and mobiles everywhere you go. They talk out loud on the buses. I find myself disapproving of so much – very aging.

You asked about the explosion. Well in spite of terrorism fears, the explosion itself was, apparently, caused by a coincidence – the crumbling of an unused Victorian passage and the build up of methane in a nearby sewage pipe. This got blocked at one end during renovations. How the methane was ignited remains a mystery. Nobody, according to the various authorities, could have foreseen the catastrophic consequences – but they would say that, wouldn't they. Whatever the cause, there are many lives, besides Ruth's, that will never be the same again.

Nina looked up to see Ruth settle on the old bench, her back to the house.

If Geoff is going up the hill, could you ask him to set the mousetrap again. Don't worry if you go, I know you don't like the beastly things…

Nina glanced up. Ruth's shoulders were shaking. She put down her pad and grasped the door handle, then stood still.

Ruth ran her fingers cautiously along the wooden seat of the old bench. She moved to the middle and folded her hands. Coming back home again, reaching out and touching the world she had known before the explosion hadn't reconnected her with that time. Nor had it lifted the burden she carried. She hung her head. Mama would say that she had allowed the Devil to tempt her. Why oh why hadn't she died in that fearsome upside-down building? Why hadn't she died of pneumonia? She had sinned and stayed alive. Mama had prayed every day, yet she had been killed. Dad had always done as he was told and yet he had groaned his way slowly to death. Perhaps Morris was right; God was just an idea. Some people needed a God to make sense of the world and others thought it even more nonsensical to imagine any Being in charge of such random events. The tears dripped onto her hands; she didn't trouble to wipe them.

Who could she talk to? She had told Dan everything, holding his one unbandaged hand and speaking over his mutterings and groans; if he heard, he didn't reply. How many weeks had passed since she had crawled through the debris to the voices? Eight? Ten? Time didn't matter; voices mattered. Different men had such different kinds of voices. There were the strange plastic-coated men who had pulled her out of the broken building, then given her unimaginably sweet water. They had quick, solid voices: 'We've got you now.' 'You're going to be fine.' 'Lift your arm.' 'Hold my hand.' 'Tell me your name.' Others had slower voices, 'I'm going to give you something to make you feel comfier; you'll feel a little scratch.' Then Dad's voice in hospital, not sounding like Dad, but stretched with pain. Later, after the pneumonia started, Morris's familiar voice saying that a young man wanted to speak to her about the explosion, a beautiful man who'd been injured there. Then later still the voice of the tenor on the CD Morris gave her, Luis Lima. He had a voice that made her feel tall and light. Were men beautiful? Perhaps Luis Lima would be beautiful. Ruth shuddered; no one could make her talk about that time. If only she had died with the coughing.

She hadn't died. For a moment sitting on the bench, she dreamt that it had not happened – any of it. In a moment Mama's voice would break into the birdsong and garden rustles, calling her to lunch. Why didn't the thought make her feel happy again? Surely, *surely* it would be better to go back to before the explosion.

Ruth wriggled until she could feel the hardness of the garden seat through her clothes. Sensation or sound, these were the routes off the spinning turntable of her mind. Sometimes nowadays when the turning slowed, images flooded in. So many new ones had crowded in since the explosions; the exquisite delight of water, Dad's unendurable whimpers, the touch and sound of so many strangers.

Ruth unfolded her hands and flinched as a leaf, released from the tree above into the still air, came spinning silently down and landed on one of them. She held the leaf between her fingers, feeling the surface and the insubstantiality of it – a thin, tired leaf. Ruth sniffed the air. Autumn so soon? She felt her watch – September 17. She'd spent the summer in hospital; a whole season chopped out of her life. She would be twenty-nine before she would feel the heat of the midsummer sun again. She lifted her face, greedy for what remained of its heat, and resolved to spend the next few weeks in the garden.

Nina opened the front door to Morris. 'She's in the garden, she's been crying again. I can tell.'

'She's grieving. It's natural. They say children love their parents even when they're cruel. Of course she's not a child, but since you left she's only really talked to Martha, Dan or me. And, apart from the month with the blind institute, she's only ever been to the studio and back. That's it. The events and the people in the last few weeks must have blown her mind. It's amazing she's coping at all.'

'I just wish she'd talk to me. This morning she said something about having sinned, but when I asked her how, she just smiled and walked away.'

'It's Martha and all those damned stories. Poor Ruth, her imagination is totally unhindered by reality. It's just a potent brew of fairy stories, lurid events from saints' lives, the limited literature that I've been able to get for her in Braille and operatic libretti.' Morris laughed. 'Think of it Nina. It makes for wonderfully creative weaving, but it's surprising that she is sane at all. I'm going to try and persuade her to come to the studio this afternoon.'

Nina raised her brows. 'You'll be lucky. I'll fetch her in, shall I?' She opened the back door and called: 'Ruth, Morris is here and lunch is ready.'

'Oh Nina, I'm so sorry; I've been no help at all. I'm coming.'

'That's all right, dear, you're convalescing. You're supposed to take it very gently for a couple of weeks.'

Morris walked out and put an arm round Ruth's shoulders. 'Hi Sweetie, how are you feeling now you're out in the big wide world again?'

'Fine, fine. I missed the summer, didn't I?'

'Well, if you count rain throughout August as summer, yup, you missed it. September's been better so far. What's that? A leaf? Do you want make a leaf picture again?'

Ruth smiled, but shook her head and moved indoors.

As they came to the end of lunch, Morris asked casually, 'Do you fancy coming back to the studio with me this afternoon? The piece you were working on is beginning to gather dust.' Once more Ruth simply shook her head without answering. Morris persisted, 'I didn't walk; I brought the car. You could just pop in and then come back home again.'

'I'm going to sit in the garden again this afternoon.'

Morris glanced at Nina, but she just smiled and shook her head philosophically.

'OK, Sweetie, whatever, it's early days yet. One more thing, you know you said you'd like to go to an opera now that Ma ... now that there's no one to stop you?'

Ruth turned towards him, her sightless eyes fixed on him intently. 'Yes?'

"Well, it's not exactly an opera, but the nearest thing to it – Verdi's Requiem. We've been sent tickets because it's being done as a memorial for the victims and survivors of the Cardon Street disaster.'

'Yes, oh yes please!' Ruth, like a little child, clapped her hands in excitement. Morris, grinning widely, sighed with relief.

15

City of London: Requiem

Luke, following directions, went through a door and gazed un-happily at his surroundings. He stood in a small room with a heavy brown and gold-swirled carpet. Much of this lay hidden beneath tiny tables and substantial padded armchairs. Floor to ceiling curtains, with yet more gold swirls, covered one wall and pairs of dim lights with frilly shades the other three. None of the other singers had yet arrived.

He passed a hand over his face and spoke out loud, 'I can't warm up in here.'

On cue, like a genie out of a bottle, a woman popped through a hidden door on the other side of the room. She grasped his arm. 'Follow me.'

The genie turned out to be the headmaster's wife, who showed Luke into an empty classroom. Standing among the school tables and chairs, he breathed deeply and let his shoulders drop. He'd rehearsed in so many classrooms in both childhood and through singing engagements during the college years, that the smell of used wood and the special timbre of a room furnished with hard objects, steadied him.

Tonight he would show them – all of them: Gulli and Claudia, the selectors for this memorial concert, the doctors and his friends and anyone else who looked sideways at him, that he had not lost his marbles. Yes, he still believed Heloise existed. Never mind their arguments and evidence, their lists and medical explanations, he alone had actually been there under those lumps of concrete and mangled steel rods. Heloise had been there too.

He let his voice swell and fill the bare room, and heard with satisfaction the fullness of the tone, knowing that he had regained not just his former power, but also something new as well. His body no longer distracted him as he sang. He no longer found himself, as it were, balancing too many crates in his arms or trying to steer and tune the radio at the same time. Now, when he opened his throat, the soles of his feet and the skin on his scalp breathed and sang with him. A few years ago such moments of internal resonance had come perhaps once in each performance; now he confidently awaited them each time he filled his lungs.

Luke smiled at the empty chairs. Even Gulli, sour old Gulli had said in surprise, 'The tessitura – it improves – you are arriving.' Before hastily back-tracking, 'There is still a distance to travel. You should not have done the Lombardi, but you are ready now for Puccini, Gianni Schicchi, perhaps, Bohème soon, later Verdi – Macduff would be good.'

Never had his teacher sounded so positive. Luke, lungs warm, mind momentarily uncluttered, yearned now to be out there in front of the orchestra, to test himself in this ancient chapel, with its famously tender acoustics. All morning in rehearsal he had listened impatiently to the sound, hearing it harden and clash against the stone floor. Tonight it would be different, with eight hundred bodies now pouring into their seats, there would be warmth in the air, a cushion to absorb the vibration; the physical presence of flesh and clothing would mop up the sounds that tried to bounce back from the ground.

Luke ran a hand through his hair and fingered his scars. He winced remembering the soprano, whose flickering glances at his damaged face all through the rehearsal had irritated him. Even her singing had shown signs of distracted phrasing. He felt like shouting at her, sing, goddam you, it's only a few stitches. He picked up his score and joined the other soloists in the side chapel. The rumble from the audience faded then turned to applause as the conductor took the rostrum. Luke moved into place behind the mezzo and the soloists filed into the great chapel. The audience, hemmed in by high white walls like dark water between two giant liners, rippled and sighed. Wooden doors in the soaring timber wall at the far end closed heavily. Luke stood with the vast orchestra spread out behind him, and behind them row upon row of blue-robed chorus. He exchanged glances with the conductor then lifted his eyes and let them lose focus as he gazed at the far wall above the sea of heads. He made no attempt to seek out familiar faces. He would sing for everyone and for himself and no one could stop him singing for Heloise alive, dead or imaginary. He smiled.

In the fourth row of the audience Claudia sat with the other medical personnel. She leant forward, trying to read Luke's expression. Barbara, Lewis and Maria, half way down the 200-foot length of the London Chapel of St Margaret, sat on the edges of their seats. A couple of rows behind them, Peter and Gulda, Sylvie's parents, sat, heads down, absorbed in the programme notes. Three rows from the rear of the chapel Morris and Ruth, hand-in-hand, squeezed into their seats. Nina had not qualified for a ticket.

Several hundred miles away, between the steep green slopes of an Austrian alp north of the Brenner Pass, Gordon sat in the cab of his twenty-ton pantechnicon adjusting the radio to the World Service. He waited confidently to hear his son sing.

Claudia rolled up her programme and turned it over and over in her hands as she waited. She caught the flickering smile that passed over Luke's face and involuntarily smiled herself. Her gaze remained riveted to the fragile string of single figures: soprano, mezzo, conductor, tenor and baritone, as they stood on the podium, hung between the mass of people behind her and the purposeful orchestra behind them. She, too, glanced briefly at the conductor and then fixed her eyes on the tenor.

With the first muted chords of the Verdi Requiem the hairs lifted gently at the back of Claudia's head. The chorus – the whole of humanity – sang in a whisper at first. Their humming filled the corridor of air above her head, as they begged for eternal rest. The voices rose and fell and rose again. Claudia, soothed by these universal intercessions, let her breath out. Luke dropped his eyes to the conductor, opened his chest and lifted his head. His voice rang out clear above this cushion of sound, *'Kyrie eleison . . . ' Lord, have mercy.*

Tears bulged out of Claudia's eyes and slipped down her cheeks. She stayed quite still. Surely no God could resist a plea as beautiful as that? A soft rustle in the audience indicated that others, like her, had unwound in the atmosphere. The audience, all relatives of the dead or injured survivors of the post office explosion, or members of the rescue and medical teams involved in the aftermath, had found a voice at last for the grief howling inside them.

Claudia looked gratefully at the orchestra, the chorus and the soloists, all professionals performing for free. Three experienced tenors had offered to sing, not counting Luke. He had only offered and auditioned at her insistence and been picked without the selectors being aware of his role in the explosion. In fact when they had found out, the organisers, far from being pleased, had been inclined to drop him, for fear, they explained, of an emotional reaction. Only the interventions of Gulli and other senior staff at the Guildhall on his behalf had made them abide by their selection. With her tears Claudia sensed some of the weight of responsibility – to Luke, to the grieving relatives, even to the wretched board of selectors – slipping from her shoulders.

At the back of the Chapel, Ruth, still wobbly and pale since being released from hospital, sat with her head tipped back. She appeared to be gazing at the roof beams as the sounds wrapped around her. Morris wondered if he had been crazy to accept the invitation, Ruth still seemed fragile physically and had so little experience of crowds, but surely nothing could more certainly revive her than listening to Verdi on her first live music outing in years? With seats so far back the soloists were stick-men in the distance, but Morris had been to concerts in this chapel before; he knew the acoustics of old and listened confidently. The programme lay unread in his lap. Having no expectation of seeing a familiar name, it did not occur to him that the young tenor might be someone he had met. He, too, sat with tears dropping unchecked into his lap.

Rarely can an orchestra, soloists and a choir have had such malleable listeners. Every person in the chapel travelled obediently through sadness, anger and pity to redemption. With the final chords a damp, eased atmosphere, a compound of grief and the dizzying aftermath of the music, spread through the audience, as if sea creatures had been breathing gently into the chapel. The applause, tentative at first seemed to gain hold and then be unable to stop. No one wanted this to be the end. No one wanted to go back into the ordinary world, leaving the companionship of the only other people who genuinely shared their trauma.

Ruth sat on, apparently in a trance, then she gripped Morris's arm.

'I've remembered!'

'What?'

'What the music feels like. You remember, on my tenth birthday, when I couldn't see even the light any more?'

'Mmm.'

'Your parents came and took us down to Polperro, and Mama couldn't come because she was sick?'

'Ye...es?'

'Well, in the sea I couldn't bump into anything except water. Water is never sharp. It's strong and sometimes hard, but always ...' Ruth sighed, 'I don't know how you'd say it – bone-friendly? Music is the same. It can make your skin funny, it can be burning and icy like water, but once it reaches your bones it's loving. Like being stroked inside. Are you crying Morris? Doesn't it make you feel happier?'

'Ruth, you're a miracle. Yes, I've been crying. Music – well music like this – does something different to me, it makes everything fall apart in my chest. For me what they're singing about matters as much as the sound. Next time I'll try feeling with my bones as well.'

'Is everyone going?'

'Yes, but we'll wait. It's mayhem and you'd get squashed.'

'I don't mind being squashed. I like feeling people round me. It's so different from how it used to be.'

Back in the Blackheath house, Ruth, colour in her cheeks at last, held Nina's hands, excited and truly happy. Morris remembered her looking like that when she finished her first weaving. Perhaps now their lives could get back on track, perhaps now she would come back to the studio.

Gordon eased his great monster back into the traffic, his cheeks raised in a luminous, amazed smile. That voice coming out of the radio so powerfully – that was his son. Gordon gave the Almighty a familiar nod. He felt on good terms with God now. Only four months ago he had been wringing his hands and alternately cursing and praying as the rescue teams started shaking their heads. After that he had sat beside the comatose and battered body of his son in a state of permanent argument with whoever (mostly God) could have any responsibility for this appalling act of desecration. Since then he had had to put up with Claudia scaring them to death with her talk of permanent brain damage, saying that a psychiatrist would do more good than God. Then there was Maria weeping over her sewing machine and Barbara occupying the front room, searching telephone directories with that boy-friend of hers. Well, they should have had faith. He had just been listening to his son, surely the most lyrical tenor in all Europe – in the world perhaps.

16

Greenwich: Morris's Studio

Morris watched as Ruth ran her fingers along one of the many wooden struts of the loom; a monster of a loom that sat like a great spider occupying two thirds of his larger basement room. She moved her body in closer until she had reconnected with its complex, logical structure. She spoke without lifting her head. 'I'll be fine now, Morris. You can go and get on.'

'Don't you want to open and sort the supplies? There's a lot of new stuff.'

'In a bit. I think I need to arrive properly, I mean, I need to believe I'm here again. I have this feeling all the time that this is not my real life.' Her hand moved onwards seeking something, then reached up towards the great reed that traversed the whole width of the loom; she stilled as the metal edge came under her fingers. 'This is what I need; to find these solid parts all in their expected places. Perhaps I'll be able to put myself together again then. I feel a bit like Humpty Dumpty at this moment.' She chuckled.

This seemed to Morris like the first time in weeks he had heard her laugh out loud. Both relieved and yet perversely on the edge of tears, he tried to laugh too. 'I hope you don't mean Humpty Dumpty, he was beyond repair and you look pretty much mended to me. I'll be in my room if you want me. I've enough orders to keep me at it for the next six months.'

He circled the loom and passed through a glass door into a second room, facing out onto his hillside Greenwich garden. A smaller loom occupied about a third of the space. Over the last two years, he had worked almost exclusively on this table loom or one of the frames stacked against the wall. Meanwhile Ruth became more and more inventive as the scale of her work continued to grow, so that she needed the big loom most of the time. Today was a bit like going back nearly ten years to when Ruth had first come to help him. She had felt her way round then, fingering every surface and object, chirruping at all the strange new textures. Later, like uncorked lemonade, she had begun to bubble over with questions. Now, as he watched through the glass, he could see it all over again: Ruth, like a child at the seashore, moving from object to object, touching, putting them to her lips, murmuring in wonder.

Morris wandered over to stare out of the garden doors. Gold-splashed ivy, dripping with rain, ran up one side of the garden completely hiding the old fence. A wren skittered among the leaf debris at the bottom of the fence. Then nothing moved at all for a long minute. He found himself no longer looking out but listening, because all sounds of movement from Ruth's room had ceased. He turned to look through the glass door again. She sat motionless at the loom. Perhaps music would help. He looked through his records then opened the door into Ruth's area. She looked to be in some distant dream.

After a moment she lifted her head, suddenly alert. 'Is that you, Morris? I didn't hear you.'

'You were dreaming. I know that expression. I hope it was a grand design in your mind. Or don't you feel like working yet? Do you want some music?'

'Morris? When can we go to an opera, a real opera? Mama can't stop me now, can she?'

'She can't stop you doing anything now, Sweetie.'

'No, I suppose not. She's in my head though. Somehow I feel worse now about doing the things she didn't like, than I did when she was alive. All I had to do then was believe either you or her. It's the other way round now. I have to positively reject her opinion and she isn't there to defend it. That feels unfair.'

'Ruth, listen to me. Your mother was a bit different from most other people. When you decide to do something she would disapprove of you can reckon that most of the rest of the world would be in favour of it. Ask Nina, if you feel unsure about anything. Anyway, I'm certainly going to take you to the opera. Are you going to finish this?' Morris patted the warp threads on the loom so that they vibrated under Ruth's fingers, 'or have you got something different in your head after all this time?'

'I'll finish this. I've got ideas but I don't mind letting them grow for a bit.'

Relief caused Morris to close his eyes. After searching in his mind for a reward, he went on as coolly as possible, 'That package of yarn you ordered from New Zealand came a week ago. I've got a few minutes to help you sort it. Shall I open it?'

'How exciting! No, let me. You know I love opening parcels.'

Morris, grinning, heaved the box onto the narrow workbench that ran across the end of the room and stood to one side. With barely a hesitation, Ruth circled the gigantic loom, her hands touching the frame here, the outer wall there, until she reached the bench. Her fingers made a reconnaissance of the box and then, with a certainty that was pleasing to watch, she reached down the scissors from their hook above the workbench, opened them and used the blade to score through the parcel tape on the box. Lifting out the heavy skeins of wool one by one, her head tilted as if, like a safe-breaker, she were listening to the messages relayed by her fingers, she laid the thirty long loops side by side on the bench. Then began what Morris thought of as the colour dance. She fingered each one again and again, moving one from the middle to near the end, and one from the end a little further in. He watched, mesmerised. He knew not to help, if she could sort them herself she would be able to find them again.

'Morris, are you still there? I want to go yellow to orange to red, then purples, blues and greens.'

'You're doing well. You've made three groups: browns and reds in one; yellows greens and some blues in another and the other blues with all the pinks and purples in the third. For some reason you've got three creams in this last pile too.'

She dropped her hands into the third pile, her fingers nibbling first one skein and then another. 'Is this one of the creams ... and this?'

'Yes, you've got them. I'll talk you through until they're in the right order now, shall I?' He spoke slowly and her hands lifted and replaced the skeins in a dancing motion.

'Have a feel, Morris, they're really thick and bouncy compared to the Herdwick wools. It's guaranteed back and shoulder fleece.'

'Mmm, yes, they're a trifle thick for my canvases. I'm an alpaca or silk man, really. You're going to need some new labels. There are shades here that are not in your existing spectrum.'

'Wonderful!' Ruth reached up for her label-punching machine. 'OK talk me through them.'

'Well, there are three yellows there.' Ruth touched a skein on her left. 'That's a deep buttercup, perhaps a shade deeper than the

Merino wool you have already, but not far off.' Ruth, holding the wool in her left hand reached up to the series of homemade cardboard pigeonholes above her workbench and fingered the plastic stick-on labels made with the old Dymo letter punch kit. Then she popped the skein into the appropriate hole and put a hand on the next one, 'What about this?'

'That's tricky. It's stronger than primrose.' Morris cast his mind back to eight year old Ruth and the coloured things she might recall before her world went dark. 'Do you remember the colour of the hedge outside your home in autumn? A sort of soft pale yellow, with a bit of bite in it?'

'Mmm, I think I can picture it?' She started to punch out a label letter by letter onto the sticky backed plastic strip. 'Can you fit another box in between the primrose and the buttercup?'

'Yup. Ruth, you know you've got your own money now? We could get you a Braille computer. You could print out sticky labels on it, and do all your orders as well.'

'Yes, I suppose so. I'm not quite ready for more changes, but I like the idea.'

They continued to work quietly through the colours. Morris stretching his imagination and memory to describe colours that Ruth would remember, Ruth trying to recover the equilibrium that belonged to her life in Morris's studio. This pacing of the colours, as Morris termed it, was a game they had played since Ruth first started to go blind. The only place out of Martha's hearing, yet within bounds, was the bottom of the garden. Whole holidays were spent there making 'garden pictures', really embryo tapestries, using anything they could find. In better weather Nina might be in relaxed attendance, but they frequently had the place to themselves.

One year, when he'd contracted whooping cough, he'd been sent home from boarding school to Martha to convalesce. It was November and Martha, finding the constant coughing unbearable, allowed a chair to be taken down the garden. Morris, wrapped like an Eskimo, lay in the chair grandly directing operations. He was fourteen and Ruth eleven. Although she was by then completely blind, she moved around the garden with the certainty of a fish through water. Morris would first direct her to clear a space on the grass and edge it with sticks: his empty canvas. Next came the painting, 'I want the pale washy leaves from under Guinevere's tree in the top corner. Yes, those, lots and lots. Pale, pale, pale. Further to your right, OK. Now some of the crispy, brown ones from under the hazel. They're a muddy colour but it looks good. Put them underneath the pale ones. I didn't mean a curve. No, no don't change it, I like it, now it's there.'

Coughing apart, these coloured November afternoons came nearer to bliss for Morris than any other part of his disrupted childhood. The little sprite, Ruth, bobbing about at his command and occasionally disobeying him with great flair, soothed some of the prickles he kept permanently raised the rest of the time. In spite of her blindness, her rigid mother and her distant father, Ruth laughed. She laughed when she tumbled over a tree-root, when she dropped her bread and jam onto the grass and put her hand on it, when she put her coat on upside down. Social embarrassment was unknown to her. Morris wished he could carry her, like a talisman, tucked into his pocket throughout life. Her chuckles, like some magic nostrum, would absorb all the painful remarks that he seemed to attract.

He had almost achieved this. Ruth was his; the genie in his studio, and anyway he had other defences now. In the last few weeks though, Ruth's chuckle had become muted, as if in those hours under the rubble or in the bleak wire and tube filled days of Dan's slow dying, it had been packed away like a childish thing and adult consciousness had taken its place.

Eventually all the skeins had been named and placed and Morris reluctantly got to his feet. 'I'll leave you to it then. Shall I open the partition?'

'No. No thanks.'

Morris returned to his studio and the smaller loom. He moved mechanically hoping the familiar clacking of the pedals as he wove would trip a switch in Ruth's brain. He recognised the thinness of the path he was trying to negotiate. Ruth could not be handled as you would an ordinary person. Like a deer she might take fright at hazards hidden to others, or she might move gracefully and speedily forward into territory that the average person would not dream of investigating. That she remained deeply troubled from her recent experience was unquestionable, but the crux of her unhappiness remained hidden from him. It had seemed, back there in the hospital, as she sobbed in his arms, that Dan's excruciating last days had burned such an indelible mark on her that she might never be whole again. Yet, he now felt reasonably sure that something else lay beneath this pain. Something she would not share. He guessed that it might well be something she had no need to worry about, some legacy of Martha's twisted logic. Morris thrust the shuttle too hard between the warp threads and it overshot his pattern boundary. How could he dispel her distress unless he knew what had created it? And then there was Nina. She was not really happy away from Scotland and something seemed to be holding her apart from Ruth.

Two days ago, he had dropped in to the big house in Greenwich, to see what had come of a clothes-shopping expedition: one grey skirt, for heaven's sake, and a pair of yellow pyjamas spotted with teddy bears. Ruth and Nina had joined his laughter but he sensed a fundamental discomfort about the whole outing.

'Well but Morris, the adult pyjamas cost *thirty-five* pounds, and they looked...unsuitable. Martha would have had a fit.'

'Nina listen, first, Ruth has just earned several thousand pounds. She could have bought a dozen silk jimjams without noticing the cost. Second, Martha had this idea of keeping Ruth as a child – she'll be twenty-nine next year, for heaven's sake!' He put a hand on Ruth's shoulder and she turned her quiet listening face towards him. 'Don't you want silk pyjamas, Sweetie?'

'I did like stroking them but they slipped away from my fingers; I would have felt undressed.' Ruth giggled like a child. Nina, smiled tautly.

'And the grey skirt?'

'But Morris, that cost forty pounds. I like the feel of it and it is lined. Mama would like it.'

Morris caught his breath, then paused and spoke carefully. 'Ruth, it's a nice skirt, but it's so plain. You need something jollier now. You don't have to live in brown, grey and navy blue any more.'

Two shocked faces turned to him. He left the house, thinking hard.

17
Ireland: Melanie

Water slithered under the ferry in an oily brown swell. Luke shivered and turned from the rail. People were still trailing up the gangway, but Angela and Kes had gone below decks into the fug. They were the only two of the old student gang coming with him to Ireland. Dave would not be coming to the Deepwater Festival this year. He pulled his jacket collar up. Below would be warmer but...It would be dim, unnervingly mobile and smelling of diesel. Below would also be full of people. Some of them people who had last seen him before the scars; people who would ask, or glance, frown and *not* ask what he'd been up to.

He looked over the rail again. Fishguard squatted below. Arbitrary yellow, red and white lines marked out the acres of empty tarmac. The rain made them gleam, standing out from their grey ground like some abstract painting – far too clean to drive over. Like some arena for rollerblade displays. Half a mile to the right, a line of heavy lorries, silent and also strangely clean lined up for another ferry going south to Jersey, not a route his father often travelled. Anyway there was no sign of Gordon's familiar orange cab.

A clump of people drifted from the customs house onto the gangway. Following them came a girl with a pushbike, her raincape the same blinding yellow as the lines on the tarmac. A heavy rucksack bulged under the cape. Her hair, ragged and wet around her neck fell in a blonde mop, paler than the cape but somehow blending with it. A neat completeness about her outline appealed to him. She turned her damp face up to scan the ferry and tilted her head as she spotted Luke staring down. Not an unattractive face, thought Luke. As she disappeared, his memory tweaked – another singer? She must be coming to Deepwater too.

Half an hour into the journey Luke made up his mind to go below and find the others. If only ships didn't clang so. They have too much metal in them, he decided. The metal always fighting its way out from under layers of dimpled white paint; everywhere streaks of rust leaking from joints and edges and no doubt salt invisibly eating its way in. Keeping the rust in check must, he supposed, be like painting the Forth Bridge, on and on and then start again. The other trouble with metal is the echo it gives out at the slightest touch; like living inside a kettle.

He clattered down a gangway and paused at one of the doors into a closed deck. It opened in his face and the girl in the yellow cape shoved through. Her face lit up. 'Hey Luca, I thought it was you. You going in?'

'I prefer it outside. It's Melanie, isn't it? Mezzo. And Bruce. Is Bruce here?'

He remembered Melanie as soon as she spoke, a low round voice, a bees-in-lavender voice. Bruce, on the other hand, in spite of a full-toned baritone singing voice, had a sloppy, slurpy speaking voice, as if some of his syllables were always dripping over the edges. Perhaps he was out of the picture and Melanie a free agent now.

'He'll come later; he's got an audition – Stowe. He should get in tomorrow evening.'

'Impressive!'

'Mmm, I'm green. But I've got Glyndebourne chorus next year, so I'm not complaining. Someone said you were getting lead roles.'

'Provincial mostly, but I've got a Rigoletto next June in Rome. I'm nearly twenty-nine, for heaven's sake, I'm ready.'

'Wow! The Duke to an Italian audience! I forgot, you're half Italian aren't you?'

'Yup. But there won't be many Italians in the Baths of Caracalla in August, it'll be wall to wall Brits and Germans.'

'I suppose. I'm still impressed.' She grinned up at him. 'We took bets last year about who in the group would get the first major role. You came out top, so at least our judgment was OK.'

'Thanks. You remember Dave – bass? He's auditioning for Welsh National Opera, that's why he's not here. I'd put some money on him, if I were you. What are you doing for the masterclass?'

'What do you think? Mozart of course – Dorabella.' Luke looked puzzled. 'And yes you're right, it's high for a mezzo, but I've been developing my range; I can reach the notes. My teacher is so devoid of imagination – Mozart for ever . . . and ever – it sucks. You've got Anton Gulli, haven't you? I know he's tough, but at least he has vision beyond Mozart. What are you doing?'

'Gulli's a sadist. Repertoire's not my problem. It's Italian romantic – full stop. Aida last act, our heroic traitor – Radames.'

'At least you look the part, especially with those new scars. The last Radames I saw looked like he'd faint at the sight of a sword.'

'Dorabella's good.' He said quickly, 'Lavinia's doing the masterclass, isn't she? She's Mozart to the core. You'll get the best out of her. What's Bruce doing?'

'Britten, Sid, you know, from Albert Herring. Why is Gulli a sadist?'

'Oh, he uh … he never lets up. He kicked my ass for not practising after I … after my accident. Kes and Ange are here. Shall we go and find them.'

Avoiding Melanie's querying glance, he set off into the bowels of the ferry.

Melanie did not come to the pub that night. Luke, reaching in vain for his usual party spirit drank several pints rather quickly. Then, still feeling disconnected from his companions, wandered off to the Gents. Finishing there, he walked towards the Pool room instead of returning to his friends and leant heavily against the doorframe. The quiet smack and thud of the balls making their way across the green baize soothed his buzzing head; four pints seemed to knock him sideways these days. After the first glance, none of the locals took any notice of him; no doubt they accepted Festival tourists as a necessary evil. A small bearded man to Luke's right, began quietly preparing a pipe. Eventually he lit it and a vile-smelling stench invaded the room. Luke left hurriedly, catching a smirk from one of the codgers at the table. He lingered near the bar, still unwilling to rejoin the noisy gang at his table. As he came within earshot he heard a complaining voice, 'Well, he used to be good for a laugh, what's bitten him?'

'Luke? Didn't you know?' Angela, swelling with importance, launched into the saga. This was her legitimate cue; Luke had begged her not to bring up the explosion or tell anyone about it, unless they actually asked. He had had a wearisome re-run of Angela's infatuation, as he saw it, over the last three months.

She had passionately hoped to cure him of his 'delusion' about Heloise. Preferably by filling the void herself. She had mistaken Luke's apathy for some kind of acquiescence, resulting in weepy interviews, which sapped his resolve. He looked at the rest of the group round the table; Kes was absent, rehearsing; the Italian girl was silent and had a passing resemblance to a potato. The prettier soprano was attached, entwined even, with her boyfriend, who was one of the Festival administrators. Luke quite liked the two baritones, Joshua and Darren, and the little Russian mezzo, Anna, but he wished Melanie had not stayed behind at the hostel. He hesitated in the shadows. Angela was in mid-drama. Re-joining them would be hard work.

Luke stepped back a few paces, and slipped his coat and scarf off the hook then, already half out of the door, he called out, 'Ange, I've got an early session tomorrow. See you at Galovko's masterclass. 'Night!' He almost fell out of the door and attempted to stride down the street. His legs, he found, had developed a disobediently rubbery gait. Still, the hostel was only half a mile away.

He really did need to rehearse for the master class. He drew a breath. '*La fatal pietra sovra me si chiuse (the fatal stone has closed over me)*'. The slow repeated notes vibrated – diaphragm – chest chamber – head. The ground steadied beneath his feet. '*Ecco la tomba mia. Del di la luce piu non vedro ... (This is my tomb. Never again shall I see the light of day...).*' What cruel urge had made Gulli choose this piece for his masterclass aria? To test him? Gulli had not been sympathetic about the fireworks fiasco in Stockholm. '*Non rivedro piu Aida. (Never again shall I see Aida.)*' Luke stopped to lean against a lamppost. Never again see Heloise? Well of course he never had *seen* her. The idea of 'never', once so remote, had crept over the horizon in the last month and now hovered distant, but permanently visible. Never see Heloise?

He shook himself; nearly fell over, and wandered on listening to the notes swelling in his throat and passing freely into the night. '*Aida, ove sei tu? (Aida, where are you?)*'. The air chilled his lungs as he pulled it in. He leant against a lamppost and discovered that if he put his hands over his mouth he could warm the air before he drew the breath. He managed several phrases stopping between each one to warm the air. *Not* bad he told himself out loud – *lovely tessitura, Mr Danford*. He paused by yet another lamppost to take in air for his climax. A nearby window opened. 'Will you take your noise where its wanted, young man. It's after ten o'clock and the babies are sleeping.'

He slid into the hostel, silent and unsteady; staggered up one set of stairs and tried to open his door, but his key would not go into the hole. He stood for a moment, before realising that he was only on the first floor. He went up yet another set of stairs. He could hear a funny noise as he turned down his corridor, a sort of swishing whimpering sound, like somebody sweeping a floor with a squeaky broom. Melanie, stood half way down the corridor, rattling her doorknob, kicking the door with her slippered foot and swearing. Luke paused, trying to make sense of this. Each kick forced out a small squeak like an aggressive kitten.

Luke interrupted, 'Hi.'

'Oh God no! Luke!' She pulled a pyjama sleeve over her scarlet face.

'You OK?'

'Fine.'

Luke laughed. 'Sure. I believe you.' He leant against the wall watching her, 'What's the problem, key not working?'

Melanie gave the door a final kick, looked at Luke's casual, but settled pose and slumped to the ground. Tears cascaded down already wet, pink cheeks. Fascinating, thought Luke, like a fountain. Confused by this excess, he suggested, 'Perhaps you're on the wrong floor. I tried the wrong floor first.'

Melanie, stared wildly at him. 'Wrong floor? I haven't got a key.'

'Ah.' Luke looked up and down the empty corridor. 'Don't cry. Get another.' Seeing this effort achieving no more success than his last, and finding the floor too far away, Luke slid down beside her.

'Tell me again.'

Once more the tears spurted; she leant against Luke, wailing, 'I'm locked out. I'm so stupid. I just went to the phone, because my mobile won't work here and I absolutely *had* to make a call, and I made it, and it was awful and I didn't think I had locked the door, but now I can't open it and there's no one in the reception place and I just want to go to bed and cry.'

Luke, having difficulty assembling this information, put his arms around her and simply patted what lay under his hands. Her hot damp face against his neck felt cosy after the cold outside. Her breath against his skin tickled, but not unpleasantly. Under his fingers her short hair slipped sweetly and, as he soothed her, he found nothing but thin pyjamas between his hands and her collapsed body. The problem seemed to be her boyfriend – the revolting Bruce. Luke didn't feel up to solving boyfriend catastrophes, so he kept silent and opted for the simpler role of comforter. Anyway, his head was not in full working order. His body on the other hand...

'Luke? You haven't got a hanky, have you?'

She really was very wet. Luke reluctantly untangled himself, tried his coat pockets then heaved himself to his feet. 'Stay still.' He walked carefully down the corridor, into the bathroom, yanked the toilet roll and returned with a large handful of white paper.

She took it gratefully. Between comprehensive nose blowing, she asked, 'Are you drunk?'

'No. Yes.'

'Which?'

He took off his coat, but the answer remained unclear. 'I had four pints. I think. My head's not what it used to be.'

She glanced up at his forehead. 'You been in an accident?'

'Yup.' He didn't feel up to the full explanation. The important thing seemed to be to resume contact with her soft, damp body. He snuggled down beside her. Feeling a slight resistance as he pulled her close. He tried for a brotherly note, 'How long have you been with Bruce?'

She turned and clung to him, fresh tears spurting and wailed, 'Three years! Ever since finals. We were going to get engaged when we came back from Deepwater. And now there's this girl and I can't bear it.'

A door banged downstairs. Loud, slurred voices echoed in the corridor below.

'Oh God, I don't want to see anyone like this. Help me, Luke.'

Luke pulled out his own door key. His room lay at the end of the corridor nearest the stairs and the voices were already approaching. He looked at the key in his hand then at the distance to his own room and for no good reason turned back and fitted it into the lock of Melanie's door. He turned it; the door opened.

Falling into the room and shutting the door just in time, they clung together listening as the others shouted and giggled their way to their respective rooms. Knocking sounded down the corridor; someone called out 'Luke!'

Melanie pulled her face away from Luke's chest to say something. He dropped his head to kiss the open mouth before she could speak. After a moment she pulled away. Luke put a finger on her lips to stop her from speaking. He shook his head and whispered, 'Don't worry, that was just a friendly kiss to stop you giving me away.' He looked round the room; orderly – for a girl's room. He liked to create disorder himself but appreciated a certain sorted-out quality in other people. Her books on her bedside table, her suitcase clearly unpacked and stored, her undies on the chair but her jeans on a hanger. She was unlikely to let him stay; still you never knew ... He spotted the free bottle of local beer they'd all been given, still sitting on her windowsill. He'd drunk his on arrival last night.

'I think you need this.'

'I don't really like beer.'

'It's medicine.' Luke fished for his penknife and with a little difficulty opened the bottle. He pushed it into her hands as she slumped onto the bed. Then he settled down on the rug beside her, one arm flung comfortably across her hips.

Melanie sipped from the bottle, then sat up again suddenly. 'Luke, d'you think your key opens all the doors?'

'Well it didn't work in the corridor downstairs; perhaps there's just one key per floor. Very economical! Shall I go and give someone a fright?'

She gave a damp-sounding giggle. 'No, Luke.' She looked at his head as he leant against the bed. 'What happened to you – I mean the scars?'

Luke reached for the bottle and took a swig. This was a good cue, if he could tell her about his ordeal, he might get some sympathy and maybe something more into the bargain. He looked at the soft pyjama-ed limbs, then reached out and picked up her bare foot. Tiredness weighted his tongue. Better still would be to snuggle down with this girl and just forget all about the other stuff. He shook his head and brushed his mouth over the foot in his hand.

'Luke, don't do that. I keep forgetting that you're drunk. I can't ... I'm not ... Bruce ... ' Tears dripped down her face once more. He reached up and pulled her into his arms. She hung there limply, then after a while pushed him off.

'You've got to go, Luke. You've been so kind, but you've got to go. I'll see you tomorrow. Only ...' She took a deep breath and wailed, 'I can't face tomorrow.'

A few minutes later she finally stood up and pushed Luke gently, reluctantly out of the door.

18
Deepwater: A Walk in the Woods

Luke slipped out of the Birne Theatre at the end of his lunchtime session. He set off in the direction of the hostel, stopped, checked his mobile for messages, started a text, cancelled it and went back into the festival complex heading for the canteen. His head still ached. He had not seen Melanie all day. On the thought, her blonde mop walked past the windows. He abandoned his coffee and ran to catch up with her. She was dressed in her yellow mac.

'Where are you going?'

'For a walk. Coming?'

'A walk?' Luke surveyed the uninviting landscape. The sun was so thin as to be almost absent. The fields were brown/grey and the trees grey/brown. His urban soul revolted at the notion of deliberately setting off into this. Besides, his chances of a snuggling up to her would be improved in a cosier setting. 'It's freezing. Why don't you come back to my room? I've got the new Handel set, Theodora, with Dawn Upshaw, You'd like that.'

Her face scrunched up and she turned from him. 'Bruce was going to sing an aria from that in the gala at the end.'

'Oh! Well I've got a few other CD's with me. Come on, I need company.'

'No, I can't sit any longer, I need air. You come with me, Luke, the woods'll be full of leaves; we can crunch them. I promise I won't mention Bruce. I've just got to get some air.'

'Well, if I freeze, you'll have to keep me warm.'

In the half-light of the woods, they rustled though piles of leaves, stopping occasionally to jump on them for a sharper crackling sound. At first they moved quickly and erratically, but after a while their steps slowed and they returned to the faint path walking on side by side, implicitly accepting that the attempt to stretch back and recover the spirit of childhood had failed. Inevitably Melanie talked about Bruce again and then, as they emerged from the woods into farmland, stopped herself and turned to look at the hunched figure beside her.

'Luke, tell me about your accident. I mean properly. Ange was saying you were in that post office explosion, but you won't talk about it. I don't want to be a pain, but I've told you all my stuff, why don't you tell me yours? I'm not going to go around blabbing and … well I like you, Luke, if I can help … '

Luke looked down at the pale face beside him. Her pink-rimmed eyes looked so earnestly and kindly into his. This kindness and the strange open landscape made him feel undone, as though some covering had been stripped off him. He tried to assemble his story and for the first time thought about it as though it had happened to someone else.

He rejected his own starting point of the evening before the explosion, because recently the day of the explosion, though not the explosion itself, had slowly crept back into his memory. In the last few weeks, small moments had switched on, then receded, then switched on again, like a tooth waking up after an injection. He could remember working at the gym that morning; talking to Helga and, rather less vividly, talking to Sylvie on the way to the record store, he couldn't really remember going in to the post office yet, but maybe that would return too. He stopped walking, still undecided about whether he had the energy to tell the story again. In the end Melanie pushed him into the middle of it.

'Luke, on the boat the other day you said that Gulli was a sadist; was that because he gave you the Radames aria and it reminded you … '

She hesitated, but Luke shrugged. 'Yup. There's plenty of alternative tenor action in Aida, but he gives me the bit where the guy is walled up alive in a tomb. He is a sadist. He always said I should do Radames for this masterclass, but the fucking death chamber?'

'What really happened to you?'

Luke gave a bitter snort. 'I wish I knew. I can remember some stuff but, because of this bang on my head, I kept falling unconscious and nobody will believe the bits I do remember. I was there for a lot of hours. It was dark. I was stuck and hurting like a nightmare so … ' he sighed, 'I suppose I could have been hallucinating half the time. But the robot was real and I *know*, I know as well as I know my own name, that this girl was there with me some of the time.'

'What girl?'

'Heloise. She said that her name was Heloise. Dave thinks she may have given me a false name. Why on earth would she do that, for chrissake?' He shook his head and went on more quietly, 'Tell me why?' Then he stopped, brought his hands up to make a funnel for his mouth and hallooed into the woods, '*Tell me why.*'

They walked on in silence for a bit. Melanie spoke carefully, 'I know it's a silly question, but why does it matter so much?'

Luke leant one hand on the trunk of a beech, took off his shoe, shook it and put it back on again. Then he turned and leant back against the tree. Looking up at the open sky, he finally spoke, 'You know when you are singing opposite someone in a production?'

'Uh-huh.'

'Well, it's never perfect, is it? Either it's someone with a lulu of a voice, but she's got BO or she's over forty or she can only sing staring down the conductor's throat or it's a peach of a girl with a voice like a mouthful of lemon juice. Heloise wasn't a singer but – I can't explain – although I couldn't see or touch her, everything felt spot on.'

Melanie waited to see if there would be more, then said help-lessly, 'I don't know what to suggest, Luke. You *think* you would get on with her but if you did meet her, you might not even like her.'

'Or she might not have liked me?'

Melanie gave this the sniff it deserved and set off walking again. 'Some chance! Did you talk about afterwards?'

Luke followed, heading back into the woods. 'Well I'm not sure we expected to get out . . . you know, you can think two con-tradictory things at once. I never doubted that I had more life ahead of me and yet I couldn't see anyone finding us after all that time. But yes she . . . I . . . we made plans. We talked about what we would eat when we were rescued. She wanted a Knickerbocker Glory – you know an ice-cream pudding thing. She had one when she was little, while staying with an Aunt, but her parents would never let her have another. I wanted Mum's mushroom risotto, though mostly I wanted water, just water. I still drink water now, I never bothered or thought about it much before. Now, every time I drink, I remember how much I needed it. I must have been conscious for it to affect me so much, mustn't I?'

He stopped and stood staring at the distant building complex.

After a moment Melanie spoke. 'I had one of those ice-cream things once. Mine had tinned peaches in it and an umbrella on top.' She waited, then touched his arm. 'What else were you going to do?'

He moved off again, still staring ahead. 'We were going to ... she said she would come to the opera with me; she'd never been to an opera in her life. I promised to take her to Covent Garden.' Luke laughed suddenly. 'She said she would be frightened of getting lost, so I promised to hold her hand.' Luke slowed to a halt, frowning now. 'I wanted to touch her. My hands were stuck so that I couldn't touch her. I can't believe ... I just won't believe it will never happen. He turned his hands palm up, as if they might tell the story better than he. 'You want to laugh? I'm sure she said to me that she'd never made love and I said ... Oh God, Dave thinks I'm imagining that bit. He's probably right. There have to be answers out there. People don't just vanish.'

Melanie stroked his sleeve. 'Luke, I desperately hope you get some answers, but you have to find a way of accepting that there might not be one, or at least not the one you want. It's like me accepting that Bruce doesn't want to do all the things we planned together.' She paused as the tears started again. Then continued, sniffling, 'I can't make myself believe it, however hard I try, but I know I'm going to have to.'

Luke stuck his jaw forward. 'Well, I'm not going to believe it. I know Heloise existed ... exists. I'm not mad. Come here.'

He turned abruptly to pull Melanie into a tight hug. They stood for almost a minute, clinging to each other, then walked on hand-in-hand in silence. Rain started falling as they returned from the trees to the open ground. They stood at the edge of the wood, looking at the bleakness around them and then turned to each other and started tentatively kissing.

Half an hour later, in Luke's room, they achieved a form of oblivion by making love. Afterwards, Melanie lay laughing uncertainly. 'I feel so wicked, Luke. I'm angry and sad about Bruce, but I don't love him any less, so I shouldn't be here.' She sat up, pulling up the covers and hugging her knees. 'In fact, I suppose I am doing just what I've been blaming him for doing. I don't feel evil-wicked though, more sort of naughty, like kissing my cousin in the hayloft when I was fifteen. You're demoralising for a girl, you make it all seem so ... I don't know ... normal, inevitable.'

Luke leant over to kiss her lazily and finger the silk of her hair. 'I feel fine. No, I feel better than that. I feel good. We're not hurting anyone. Bruce can go ... whatever himself. It's his fault you're here, you owe him nothing.' Melanie reached out for her discarded clothes, a crease between her eyebrows. He caught her wrist and brought it up to his mouth. Speaking carefully as he kissed the inside of her arm, he said, 'It's the first time for me since the explosion. I planned to be with Heloise, but she isn't here either. Think of it as a rescue mission. "Girl saves (nearly) famous opera singer from going round the bend."' He pushed the arm gently back onto the pillow and laughed down into her face. 'It's going to take an awful lot of therapy to keep me sane.'

Melanie and Luke, arriving together ten minutes late for the evening gala, caused a roar of good-natured laughter. Melanie, still feeling like a traitor, found it difficult to relax and sing her best. Luke, on the other hand, sang like a young Caruso. His embarrassment came in the final speeches, when the impresario who had been the guest of honour closed the proceedings.

'So!' He started, his eyes sweeping round the assembled singers. 'I have had an entertaining three days. You have made me sometimes laugh.' He did so. 'Occasionally frown.' His brow duly clouded. 'And in one case,' his eyes stopped at Luke's tall, relaxed figure, and creased, 'you have made me envious.' A rustle and a small sigh of assent rose from the group. He continued. 'Yes, I envy Luca. Not, as you probably imagine, because he seems to have naturally what all of us strive for, but because he has learnt what we could all learn but wilfully refuse to. He is in love with his own voice. He listens to his instrument and plays it with tenderness and joy. If I say "more volume", does he inflate his lungs until the air spills from them, tighten his muscles and close his throat? No!' Everyone jumped. 'He *relaxes, drops* his shoulders, whispers exciting words to that engine within and *opens* his throat. Because of this love affair with his voice he will never mistreat it, always he will find quality before quantity. Go home now and remember to *seduce* your voices, then you will makes sounds like Luca rather than,' his eyes wandered across the company, each one of whom flinched in anticipation, 'a cat on the roofs.'

Luke curled a lip at Kes standing next to him. 'I'll do the cat aria next time.'

Kes drawled under his breath: 'Reelaax, Lucaa, sedoooce yourself.'

19

Wales & Scotland: Travelling in December

'Ruth, I need to go home.'

Puzzled, Ruth reached out to touch the worktop in the kitchen. 'This *is* home, Nina.'

'No, I mean my home in Scotland.'

'Oh, Scotland.' Ruth started to unpack the shopping, then stopped abruptly. 'Do you mean just to visit or ... ?'

'Well, I need to air everything in my little house and then close it against the weather, but I can't stay here forever. I only came to help you get better. I can't live in London, not all the year. I need the hills, I need my fat old kettle.' Nina put her arm round Ruth, 'I really don't want to leave you, Ruth, but I don't belong here any more. I did wonder if you might be happy in Scotland, but I don't know.'

Ruth stood quite still, then turned and reached towards Nina, clutching her sleeve. 'Could I come to Scotland too?'

'Is that what you want?'

'Yes, yes. I want to go away from here. I want to start again. You started again, didn't you? It worked for you.'

Nina stood silently, remembering the grim boarding house, in which she had lived for nine months, the sale of her parent's furniture and jewellery to cover the cost of a roof and windows for her cottage. That first winter, when her only heating had been the open fire and a paraffin stove, had been unspeakably grim. And the loneliness. The unspeakable dragging need to hold her little girl in her arms again, the fear of what Martha might be doing to her. Had Ruth suffered too? Could a child feel as she had? Had Ruth wept all those years ago over her loss as she did now over Martha and Dan's death? Perhaps then as now, she had sat in endless solitude on the bench in the garden.

She stroked Ruth's head, but her tone was dry. 'Yes, it did work – in the end.'

'Please say yes, Nina, please say yes.'

'Yes, of course ... though there are lots of things to think about. The cottage isn't big enough for two of us, we'd have to build or ...'

She busied herself among the shopping bags. 'Here, this is veg. and the rack is on your left.'

'Nina, I can sell this house. It's mine now. I could buy us a big enough house – I expect I could buy a castle in Scotland with the money from a London house.'

'But I love my cottage.'

'Well, I could build another one next door.'

'Yes, or we could build some extra rooms onto mine.' Nina stared at the bottles she had placed on the table. 'You would need somewhere to work, wouldn't you?' She turned and heaved washing powder and bleach onto a high shelf, then dropped onto a chair. 'Ruth, I think it might work, but you should come and stay to see if you like it first. We shouldn't rush.'

For the next couple of hours, they reverted to their old relationship, weaving happy plans for an expanded cottage with a workshop next door, or possibly buying the empty post office building, vacant since the Village Stores and the post office had joined forces, as a studio. Ruth had the inspirations and Nina tempered them with practical ideas. By the time Morris called to pick up Ruth to take her to the studio, both seemed to have shed ten years. They bubbled over with enthusiasm.

The shock on his face first alerted Nina to the enormity of their proposed plan. He took both of Ruth's hands, words pouring out: 'Ruth, you can't just go. Don't you remember? We've got exhibitions: next June in Rome and then in September in New York. We need to work together; we need to build another portfolio. We share our equipment. There are things I have to do for you. Who will check and sort out your threading? Who will tell you the colours you can remember.' He lifted her unresisting hands to his face. 'Who will listen to me talk through my designs? When I describe them to you, I have to visualize them fully and that's when they gel. Ruth, Sweetie, pleased don't go, I don't think I can work without you.'

Ruth stood quite still, her face draining of all the excitement and colour that had filled it while she and Nina had planned their escape and their new life. 'Morris, I'm sorry, I didn't think. I just wanted to get away and start again. She dropped her head miserably. 'I've made such a mess.'

'What is it, Ruth? Why do you want to start again? What

have you made a mess of? You're a brilliant weaver, breaking new ground. You have a future and a career. You do all this, even with the mountainous difficulty of being blind. Is it Dan? Or Martha? Is there something else? What makes you so unhappy?'

'No, no, I don't know. Mama was right, I'm being selfish and dissatisfied, I'm so sorry.'

'You're *not* selfish and,' he took a calming breath 'your mother was very rarely right. What is it you hoped to find in Scotland?'

Ruth got up and felt her way to the doors into the garden. She put both hands on the cool glass then pressed her forehead onto it too. She murmured, 'Peace of mind.'

'What's that?'

'Nothing. I can't change what's inside me by going somewhere else, can I?'

Nina who had remained silent so far, got up and faced Morris. 'Perhaps what you both need is a holiday. I must go and sort out my house before the winter sets in. Why don't you two come and stay nearby? Perhaps have Christmas there, or better still, New Year?'

Morris, seeing a little of the light come back into Ruth's face, agreed, though he had had a different kind of Christmas in mind. His personal life would have to go on hold for the time being; he couldn't afford to lose Ruth.

Nina went on more cheerfully, 'Morris, have you ever thought about moving yourself. I mean if Ruth can afford a house in Scotland, she could get somewhere big enough for you both to work. Come for a bit anyway. Just look around, see what the place feels like.'

Luke walked slowly through the carriage. He had taken to getting on at one end of a train at the start of a journey and walking to the other before finding a seat; testing, as always, the hope that Heloise might just possibly appear before him and by some miracle they would recognise each other. Perhaps she had only been visiting London for the day. Perhaps her strange parents had survived and taken her back to ... Cumbria or Cornwall or wherever – somewhere remote, with no opera houses.

He chose a seat with its mottled velvet cover relatively intact and pulled out his mobile before sinking down. Train travel had become a way of life for him since the end of October. The Verdi Requiem had spawned an immediate request for a last minute substitution in Leeds, then two requests for the Matthew Passion, one in Taunton the other in a Country House near Chester in November. A further Verdi Requiem had followed last week in Colchester and this one tomorrow in Swansea, where, happily, Melanie's parents lived in an old farmhouse. Best of all, he had been invited to sing the delightful Rossini, Petite Messe Solennelle, in Aberdeen on the 22nd December. He had lied when they rang him and said it was in his repertoire and that he had studied and sung it as an undergraduate. Luckily Gulli really did know it. Most of the fee would go to paying off Gulli for extra lessons, but it would definitely be worth it.

Tonight he would be staying with Melanie at her parent's house. Bring warm clothes, she had warned. Perhaps they didn't believe in central heating in Wales?

He hoped there might at least be warm duvets. What would his chances be of getting into bed with Melanie, he wondered? Deepwater seemed a long way off. They had been in touch most days since then, but the poor girl seemed unable to let go of the Bruce relationship. He sighed. He could hardly complain. Having seen off innumerable girlfriends with few pangs, the one girl that his hands at least had never touched remained constantly in his thoughts. In time he and Melanie might both get used to not having what they wanted. God, what a middle-aged way of thinking! Either I really fancy her, I get Bruce out of her hair and we make a go of it; or I call it quits.

With this laudable thought fresh in his mind, Luke paused at a booth on Swansea station and bought a bunch of roses. Melanie looked prettier than he remembered and her glowing face as she took the flowers, gave his heart a little kick.

'Oh Luke, nobody has ever brought me roses before.'

Melanie's parents were matter-of-fact friendly. Having three sons (Gerald, Donald and Jack) in various stages of not quite having left home, they treated Luke as just another large visiting male. The casual – show Luke the way, Melanie, love. I've put him next to you in Donald's room – boded well. Not so good were the uncarpeted, unheated corridors on the way.

'I hope you've got warm things, Luke. This house was built

before The Flood and last modernised in the middle ages. There's a fire in the sitting room and an Aga in the kitchen and that's it. Though you get a basin in your room and – surprise, surprise...' she turned on the tap with a flourish, '*hot* water comes out of the taps.' Luke, looked round at the expanse of what appeared to be uneven mud walls and suppressed a shiver. He'd been in station waiting rooms considerably warmer than this. Donald clearly came from the same Spartan mould as his parents: no rugs, no posters and worst of all – no duvet. Melanie, seeing his glance, pulled back the bedcover and shouted down the stairs, 'Mum, you can't give Luke Donald's hairshirt blankets, I thought we had a guest duvet now.'

A voice answered, 'That duvet's in Jack's room. Auntie Sue was under it for one night. Luke can have it if he isn't too fussy.'

Luke nodded forcefully. 'I'm definitely not fussy.' He scooped Melanie into his arms. 'We could always economise on bedding. I would be perfectly happy sharing with you – if it's allowed.'

She wrinkled her nose. 'Sort of. We all pretend it's not happening though.'

'In that case,' said Luke, reaching for the door with one hand and closing it carefully, 'how about a promissory kiss.'

Melanie went with him to Brangwyn Hall for the rehearsal. Glorious warmth enclosed him as he went in. An atmosphere of incurious friendliness seemed to be the norm. Luke, bracing himself for the usual overt or surreptitious attention to his scars, relaxed. The standard of singing also turned out to be a notch above his expectations. He stretched his performance that bit further and saw the conductor's eyes lift with pleasure. The next evening, after a night of little sleep but much comfort and a long lie-in the following morning, Luke sang (according to the local paper) like the Angel Gabriel.

He clambered onto the train the following morning after another satisfying but strenuous night, dropped into a seat without his usual restless prowling up and down the train, and fell asleep. The Petite Messe next, then Christmas. Melanie would almost certainly be able to join him briefly for New Year and then she planned to come and stay properly in London in February.

While Luke had been singing the Requiem at Swansea the night before, Morris had taken Ruth to King's Cross and put her on an overnight coach to Aviemore in Scotland. And as Luke, shivering, made hasty use of the bathroom and crept along the arctic corridor to Melanie's room to be tenderly warmed up again, Ruth, in the warmth of the coach, struggled with the complexity of the onboard facilities.

Ruth arrived to a sparkling morning in the Cairngorms. She turned her face towards the thin heat of the sun and sniffed the sharp air. Nina, with enormous pleasure, watched her greet the Scottish dawn, before stepping forward to hug her. This dream had finally come true. Half an hour later, when Ruth walked into her cottage and sat in her kitchen drinking tea, Nina found herself praying that the world would stop now. She watched Ruth as she sat at the table, her hands curved around a mug, the low winter light falling across the table, lighting her hands, but leaving the face in shadow. The same sense of being a moment in history, a painting perhaps, that she had experienced reading Morris's letters all those months ago, invaded her again. Ruth, who usually liked to investigate new surroundings, remained still and quiet, it seemed that the newness of the air was enough to occupy her senses at this moment.

As Nina did not have even enough room for a second bed in her house, she had arranged for Ruth to stay ten minutes walk away in Hugo's sister's Bed and Breakfast in the village. Morris would be able to stay there too when he arrived next week. Nina knew a moment's qualm about Morris's arrival in the village. Hugo and Geoff had been together for many years, but she could not help being aware that Morris, with his strange eyes, sometimes had an unsettling effect on susceptible people.

When Morris came, she realised that she need not have worried; the two older men treated Morris as others might treat an endearing puppy or infant. They gazed and took it in turns to get close, but in the spirit of mutual admiration not invasion and Nina relaxed. Morris played the role of privileged child to them and jealous guardian to Ruth.

'Nina, I'm not just being selfish, Ruth could not be happy in the long-term here. It would be months before she could set up her workshop. In the last ten years, apart from the spell in hospital, she has never been away from the studio for more than a day or two.'

'Relax, Morris, I'm not going to make decisions for Ruth. Let her have a holiday. She hasn't mentioned the studio once to me.'

'She has to me. She doesn't understand the scale of what would need doing to recreate it here. She can't imagine how small your cottage is.'

Nina laughed. The day before Morris had arrived, Ruth had walked round the outside of her cottage about ten times, running her gloved hands along the stony walls. Nina, with the kitchen door open, had listened, enchanted, to her childish commentary as it faded and grew louder with each tour. 'This is the bedroom, this is the bathroom, this is the sitting room and here is the kitchen again, and the bedroom, the window, the bathroom, the front door – where is the letter box?, the living room – what a funny small window – and *here* is the kitchen again!'

'Morris, only Ruth can decide. We mustn't ... we really *must* not fight over her. It's not fair.'

'Of course not.' Morris lied. He knew he would fight. His whole career depended on it, he decided, forgetting that he had managed to start and set up his career alone, before Ruth came to help him.

When Morris got back to their temporary home, Hugo's sister Clare sat reading the local paper out loud to Ruth. She had, at Ruth's request, looked up concerts and found an advertisement for the performance of the Petite Messe Solennelle in Aberdeen on the 22nd December.

'Please, Morris, *please* can we go?'

'Ruth you're insatiable. If you want to go to as much live music as this you will have to come back to London. I can't travel eighty miles to a concert more than once in a blue moon.'

'Please?'

He shrugged. 'Hey, why not, we're on holiday. Anyway, it's my fault for getting you to listen to so much music at home. I must admit, I wouldn't miss this for the world. Performances of the Petite Messe are all too rare,' he looked over Clare's shoulder, 'and – good heavens that's astonishing – it's being done properly with two pianos and a harmonium.'

'Who's singing? Anyone we know?'

'No, I don't recognise the names; they'll be locals. Oh, that's funny; one of them is called Luca Danford. Surely that's the same name as the guy who was in the explosion, do you remember, he wanted to talk to you, but you wouldn't let him? I wonder if ...' Morris looked up from the flyer he was reading. 'Oh, Sweetie, I'm sorry, I didn't mean to remind you. Don't look so sad.'

'No, not sad. It's just odd to hear ... to think about it all again. I really want to go to this. Please can we get there somehow, Morris?'

They had difficulty getting tickets and were only able to get two single ones at the back. Morris nearly turned them down, but decided that it wouldn't hurt Ruth to have a less than comfortable experience attending her cherished music in Scotland. When they arrived, the management, seeing their difficulty, put an extra seat into the space beside one of their tickets and they were able to sit together after all. When the soloists filed in, Morris was amazed to see that the tenor – stunning, scarred and with a slight limp – really was the Luke he knew. He almost clutched Ruth's hand to tell her and then thought better of it. No need to recall that time to her mind just at this moment. What a combination, though, looks and a voice.

As the music ended, the two cousins sat in a trance. 'Are you glad we came now, Morris?' Ruth whispered.

'Remind me about this if I ever object to a distant concert again?'

'I will. Was the ... did you know the tenor?'

Morris took Ruth's hand. 'Yes, it was Luke. I can't believe it; I met that boy. Wouldn't you like to meet a real opera singer, Sweetie? We could go backstage, I bet he ...'

'No! Never! Please don't make me. I won't ever go to a concert again, if you make me. I don't want to see anyone from that time.'

Morris, his hands gripped painfully in Ruth's, backtracked. 'Ruth, Ruth, calm down, it was only a suggestion. I won't make you do anything. We'll just worship from afar, shall we? All right?'

Ruth, still trembling, nodded. 'All right.'

'Come on, I've got a lot of driving to do.' He added with wicked intent, 'It's a pity Nina doesn't drive.'

20
Catford: Luke Crisis

'Luca, post for you. You'd better get moving, the bus goes in five minutes.'

Maria left the envelope on the shelf in the narrow hall and returned to her sewing.

Luke, thundered down the stairs, grabbed the envelope and stumbled out of the house into a murky January day. Standing at the bus stop, he stared at the unfamiliar writing on the envelope. Green ink? He opened it.

Dear, dear Luke, you've been so kind and lovely to me that I feel rotten, but I have to come clean now. You know I said Bruce rang on Christmas Day, well I didn't tell you but he drove to Swansea and stayed in a hotel over New Year. That's why I couldn't come to London. I wouldn't speak to him for two whole days, but in the end I gave in and we talked. We do still love each other and we are going to get married after all.

I don't know how I would have survived the last two months without you. If you were really free and loved me, it might have been different. But you aren't free – at least not free to love anyone for a bit. I think you are still searching for this Heloise girl. Until you've found her or accepted that you never will, I think no one else will really get close to you. Don't search for too long Luke, you could have any girl you fancied and it would be sad if you spoiled your whole life for something you can't have.

I know you don't really like Bruce, so you will probably not understand or even feel insulted that I'm going back to him. I don't really understand myself, but I sort of know where I am with Bruce. I think part of it is I'm not really in your league as a singer. You're going to have a brilliant career, travelling all over the world, living in Hotels in big cities, talking half a dozen languages, meeting new people every night. I couldn't keep that up. I'm a country girl. I want to succeed, but I shall stick to English venues so that I can get out and walk when I need to. I don't suppose this makes much sense to you, I just want you to understand that I'm being practical about who I am and what I want out of life. If I could truly have you instead of all that, I might not have gone back to Bruce, but I can't. You don't truly need me and Bruce does, but I think you are the most wonderful, talented person I have ever known. I am crying as I write this, and I can't believe what I am doing, but I know I'm right. I know it sounds naff, but a bit of me will always love you. Please keep in touch and I am sure your Heloise will turn up, or someone just as wonderful. Love you – and I'm so sorry – Melanie.

P S Because of this, I won't be coming to London next week, perhaps I'll see you at the Wexford auditions in March. Please don't be angry.

He put the sheets back into the envelope. He was on the bus. Somehow he had flagged it down and climbed on without being aware of it. Rejection? He couldn't remember ever being rejected before. It didn't feel like anything really. He sat looking at the green writing and thinking nothing. That was the worst thing. The nothing. What next? Where next? Who next?

He got out his mobile and after a few moments, put it away again. Dave had gone on his first ever visit to Antigua. The fact that he had gone so reluctantly did not diminish the sin as far as Luke was concerned.

That night, on his way to bed, Luke pulled the letter out of its envelope again and stared at the green ink without reading the words. The page slipped through his fingers and drifted to the floor. He left it there.

The following morning, another sunless January day, he got up early to catch a bus to Knightsbridge. This would be his fourth visit to give singing coaching. His pupil, William, aged eight, hoped to gain entry to Westminster choir school – or rather his parents hoped he would; William himself simply regarded singing as a better option than cricket or maths (for both of which he received extra coaching). Luke enjoyed these sessions. In particular he delighted in the coffee and homemade biscuits supplied by William's mum, not to mention the vast sum she was prepared to expend on achieving her ambitions.

Luke sat in the misted-up bus, so nearly asleep that he remained unaware of his ringing mobile until nudged by an irritated neighbour. The call was from William's mum to say that William had tonsillitis. Luke stayed on the bus for another two stops, unable to formulate a plan to deal with the rest of his day. Dave was still in Antigua. Ange had daytime work. He dialled Kes then cancelled the number. He could go to the gym, of course. They were always short-staffed and would be happy to give him an extra shift. He got off the bus and crossed the road. As he stood uncertainly on the pavement the return bus appeared. Having no better plan to hand, he climbed on to it.

Once home, he found his mother had gone out. He resolved to fill the time with a little work on his audition pieces and went up to his room to fetch some music. In the doorway of his room he paused, distracted by the sight of Melanie's letter on the floor beside his bed where he had dropped it last night. He sat on his bed and read it again, then went downstairs without the music. He switched on the television and flicked through the channels. A programme showing an MG in pieces in a garage caught his eye, but the story seemed to concentrate on the search for elusive spare parts and there was little about the quality of the car or its paces. Luke dozed off.

When he woke again the television screen showed a child carefully building a tower of bricks. Luke watched with minimal interest as the tower, reaching the limits of the child's skill, tee-tered and tumbled over. The fall was so slow and inevitable that Luke was unprepared for the jolt that swiped away his insides. The small screen showed red and yellow bricks scattering over a white floor. The child, equally unprepared for disaster, stiffened and took an endless breath. Luke and the child sat mirrored; their mouths open staring at the devastation before them.

Eventually the child found her voice and howled out her dismay. Luke shut his mouth as if swallowing solid air. Frothing around in his mind was an elusive sensation, too misty to be called a memory. The tumbling bricks had been unreasonably familiar and even more unreasonably frightening. He tried to hold on to the end of the thread that dangled in his mind's eye, and thus climb back to the truth, the real truth of what had happened on June the ninth. He held his head tightly as if the memory might be caught between his two hands, but already it was too late. The sensation that might have been memory had imploded into the hidden centres of his brain. He dropped his hands slowly, and as his fingers brushed over his mouth he felt, yet again, the impression of Heloise's touch.

This memory of her touch had so far been a potent consolation to him, because it reinforced his belief in her existence, but now, for the first time, the endlessly reformed equation in his head included the possibility of defeat. He sat very still, looking down at his own hands in his lap, waiting for this moment to pass.

'Luke?'

He flicked the remote control and the child disappeared in a pinprick of light, but he did not answer. Claudia's shout had had no gentleness in it.

'Luke, where are you? Ah, here you are.' Her small figure stood ominously compact in the doorway. 'Is it right you shouted at Mum this morning? For heaven's sake, it's bad enough having you drooping around the house at your age without...Hey, what's up, now?'

'Nothing.'

'Oh come on, don't be like that.' She moved into the room, becoming less solid, more accessible. 'What is it? You used to be so like a tanker, Luke, so undentable. I could shout at you, I could even slag off your voice, and you wouldn't turn a hair. Now, I suggest you could have been nicer to Mum and you...you look like I drowned your pet kitten.'

Luke laughed briefly, and moved over to pick up his mobile. 'You used to slag me off all the time, and now you don't. Perhaps I just got out of practice.' He sounded both casual and brittle. Claudia stood still, hands on hips, waiting for him to sit down. Trying to find a way in, trying, she suddenly realized, to 'diagnose' his problem. As had happened several times in the past months, her stomach rose and shivered. This man, her brother, was sick. Not sick in the usual medical sense with wounds that could be stitched, fevers that could be medicated, but with an insidious worm in the bud, a worm that could not be located or excised because it was a phantom, the creation of a sick brain. It was also out of bounds, like a ghost that could never be laid to rest because no one except Luke could see or hear it. She was very nearly sure that he thought about this phantom every day, though he gave no sign any more. He, who could walk unashamed into a room as a child saying, I've eaten that peach you had on the windowsill – you don't mind, do you? Now he would say he felt happy and look away as his eyes filled.

'Luke are you thinking about her, now?'

'Yes.'

He did not look up, just went on tapping his mobile. She sat down next to him. 'Why are you more unhappy now than before.' He was silent, still scrolling through the phone's menu. 'Stop it Luke! Talk to me. I can't help you if I don't know what's wrong.'

'You know what's wrong.'

She started to speak, but he lifted a hand to stop her. 'You know what's wrong and this time you can't do anything about it. If Heloise is dead ...' She shifted in exasperation, 'you can't bring her back to life; if she is a figment of my imagination, you can't make her appear, and you can't cure me of this figment – this sickness – because she's there – alive – in my head, in my ... everywhere. I can feel her hands on my sleeve, on my cheek, now, this moment.' He looked at his sister, but she hadn't an answer ready. 'That makes me pretty sick, huh?'

'Luke, please let me try just once more to explain about the brain?'

He flung himself away from her into the sofa, with his hands over his face, but said, 'OK, go ahead, I don't think anything will work, but I'll listen. I will listen.'

Claudia, twitched down her skirt, and sat on the edge of the sofa, she turned to face him, her small head thrust forward, thoughts running fast and almost visible behind her eyes as she sorted them into a language he could comprehend.

'Luke, you remember that book I gave you about the brain?' He looked up, alarmed at her earnestness. This was quite different from the fierce but indulgent tickings-off that she periodically gave him.

He sighed. 'Yes. And no, I haven't read it. Did you seriously think I would?'

Claudia shrugged. 'Well, I gave it to you because it tells you about real cases; people who have had injuries or diseases of the brain, and the particular things that changed for those people. You know how some people, when they've had an arm amputated, think it's still there because they can feel it. The brain tells them it is still there even when their eyes tell them it's gone.' She waited for him to nod; even this gesture told her that he felt that what

171

she was describing was irrelevant. She went on, 'There are people who are also convinced that they have an *extra* arm, because their brain tells them so. They can see two arms, but they can feel three, because the brain is making an error. *Listen* Luke, this is the important bit. The inside evidence – that is what their brain tells them – is the one they believe. Not the outside evidence, even of their own eyes, not what everyone else in the world can tell them, not any arguments they make with themselves that people only have two arms. Nothing, *but nothing* is more convincing than the messages from inside your own brain.' She gazed at him as he lay back staring up at her. He was paler than usual, or maybe he always was pale nowadays, his eyes wide and sombre. In the old days he would have laughed at her zeal. As she realised that the old invulnerable confidence had gone forever, rare tears pushed under her lids. She stood up, opened her mouth, shut it again and brushed past Luke, giving him a quick smile as she left the room.

Two days later, as she pulled her clothes out of her hospital locker at the end of a heavy shift, a colleague called out: 'Claudia, phone, it's the police.'

'Dr Danford? Hello this is Police Constable Graham Leigh here. I'm speaking from Tottenham Court Road Police Station. We have your brother, Luca, with us in a somewhat distressed state. We would have called an ambulance, but he assures us that you're a doctor and that you will understand his problem and will know what to do ... Yes, he's right here. I'll pass you over.'

'Claudia? I'm all right. No ... I ... there was a car. It backfired right beside me. I couldn't ... Of *course* I freaked. The stupid thing is, I can't seem to stop crying ...'

'Wait there, Luke, just wait for me. I'm coming, in the car.' Claudia scrambled into day clothes and hurried to the car park, hoping to catch Luke in a sufficiently malleable state to agree to some help. It all took too long. By the time she had negotiated the London traffic, Luke had replaced his armour and looked cool and distant again.

'Luke, you've got to see someone, I mean a specialist. If I hadn't been coming off duty, they'd have had to call an ambulance; it might have been better in the long run. It's getting worse, not better, isn't it?'

'I'm fine. It's nothing. Don't make a fuss. It's just sudden noises.'

'And what about the Underground?'

'There's nothing wrong with buses.'

'Mum says you get up in the night – most nights.'

'Well, you would if you had things on your mind.'

'That's the point, you need someone to help you deal with those things.'

'I don't need a shrink. I need a decent fucking detective!'

'*Luke*! I give up.'

Claudia drove through the London streets in unusual silence. Problems existed to be solved, though not everyone, she had come to realise, actively sought solutions. She attempted to process the environment as she imagined Luke might: aware of car horns, music spilling from burger bars, a busker with bagpipes, the shouts of a fanatic of unknown persuasion. The January night was unnervingly warm. Eight months since Luke's brain op. Most brain repair occurs in the first six months, though there was a certain amount of dispute over this and it was true that some stroke patients made further amazing strides years after a stroke. At the next traffic lights she looked at Luke's now serene profile. He turned and grinned at her in a way that over the years had successfully disarmed her. She shook her head and turned again to the outside world. A leering motorcyclist made her hastily turn back again.

Luke, to please Claudia, went back to a couple of the survivors' meetings and phoned one of the counsellors listed on the leaflets there. The counsellor turned out to be very pretty, very warm and extraordinarily sympathetic. To his own surprise, Luke enjoyed his sessions. She made no attempt to convince him that Heloise did not exist. She did, however, persuade him to get to grips with his dislike of the Underground and lifts and sudden noises. Using desensitisation methods, she took him to underground stations and waited patiently with him; later she travelled with him until, one day, he found himself alone and unafraid on the Underground. She encouraged him to talk about Heloise, neither believing nor disbelieving his story, simply trying to persuade him to accept the current situation – that is to live with her absence. She encouraged

173

Luke to talk about his other girlfriends and to realise that each of them had seemed ideal at first and then, further down the line, just ordinary. Luke began to sleep better.

Claudia also began to relax. Luke would soon set off to Rome for three months on a visiting Scholarship, finishing up with the three performances of Rigoletto at the Baths of Caracalla. He would be thoroughly busy, distracted and away from all reminders of the wretched explosion. The press, like a dripping tap, still ran articles intermittently on the subject. They hurtled from the quality of Intelligence sources via endless re-runs of the Nairobi explosion last year to the lawsuits rumbling around among the Water Board, the post office and the National Car Parks Association or anyone else who had an interest in the properties affected by the explosion. Each article carried pictures of the devastation or the dead or the injured.

Luke would, of course, be back for Barbara's wedding in May, but in Italy again by the time of the anniversary of the explosion. Perhaps Mum could take a holiday after the wedding.

21
Heathrow: Relatives

Dave's face, distant and preoccupied, finally appeared through the arrivals gate at Heathrow. He was only a couple of metres from Luke when he registered who had come to meet him. He stopped dead and a slow smile took over his face. 'This is very touching, Luke. What's with the spare clothes?' he asked, indicating the heavy coat and scarf over Luke's shoulder.

'Don't be an idiot, Dave. It's minus four outside, you'll be frozen even with these.' Luke handed them over. 'It was Mum's idea anyway.'

Dave's face broke out in an understanding and affectionate grin. Maria, with Luke's welfare ever a primary aim, had provided Luke with an excuse to make the trip to Heathrow. No doubt she thought it would do him good in some way? Dave shrugged himself into the coat, wound the scarf round his neck and heaved his rucksack into place.

'Thanks. Anyway, Happy New Year – a month late. I'm sorry I missed the Millennium Celebrations. I gather you had the most almighty firework fest.'

'God yes, that seems ages ago now, London blazed; it was thoroughly Wagnerian. That's the first New Year I've spent at home since I was a kid. At least the hangover was manageable. Did you celebrate big time in Antigua too?'

'And how; a street party to make Notting Hill weep with envy.' Dave paused. 'Coffee here or back at my place?'

Luke jerked his head towards the exit. 'We'd better get the car out of dock. It's a fiver a minute in the short-term car park.'

Dave, pushing his own memories and experiences into the background as he watched Luke negotiating his way out of Heathrow, tried to re-orientate himself in time and space after a ten-hour flight and an absence of eight weeks. This is how life would be for the two of them from now on; an odd hour's conversation here or there, brief meetings at airports between engagements. He would be in England until October, but Luke would be in Italy for a large slice of the year.

'When are you off? To Italy, I mean.'

'Oh about three weeks, March 14, but I'll be back in April for the Wexford second call auditions, and of course in May for Barbara's wedding.' A swagger entered Luke's voice. 'I've definitely got Macduff at Glyndebourne and a probable Bohème for 2003.'

'Hey, man, going places now!'

'Mmm.'

Dave glanced across at his friend. The swagger had not been as pronounced as it should have been for the news. Under the natural all-year-round tan, Luke's skin showed an unusual pallor, with shadows under the cheekbones. He had never fully regained weight after the explosion, or maybe it was simply normal aging that had hardened the edges of his face. Around the eyes tiny lines had appeared and somehow – perhaps it was all those stitches on his forehead – a faint suggestion of despair seemed to lie in the set of his eyes. Dave sighed, this time last year Luke had shed stardust wherever he went, now the sparkle seemed to have been extinguished. Maybe the Melanie girl leaving him had knocked him back again, but Luke had always been easy-come easy-go. Surely this girl had been no more than a filler? And then there was the therapy business. In his last phone call, Luke had joked about his dishy therapist; the trips on the underground and her resistance to seduction (for ethical reasons). He had sounded positively chirpy. But therapy? Did Luke really need therapy? Heloise seemed to have disappeared from the conversation. Did that mean she really had been a figment of Luke's imagination? If so, then he too had been deceived, he could have sworn that Heloise lived, breathed and had been beside Luke in that smashed up building. Whether she'd have been the answer to his prayers and whether she had told the whole truth there, seemed more questionable.

Dave, mid-reverie, watched Luke settle onto the motorway. With his thoughts acting like confetti, he missed the question.

'What was it like?'

'What?'

'Meeting your folks, I mean? You know, seeing relatives you didn't know existed? Did you find a gene-mate, you know, someone you felt close to, without ever having met them before?'

Dave flipped his mind back to the hot island he had left late the previous evening. In the years since his mother had died, he had resisted all invitations to meet his remaining West Indian relatives – his mother's mother's family – a quarter of his genetic inheritance. This year he had run out of excuses and perhaps also, with Luke's near death he had come to realise that maybe blood ties mattered. His father, a Scots music student in 1960s London had (according to his mother), never known of his existence. His grandfather, a white petty criminal (according to his mother) who had married his grandmother just for the bed and board, then drifted off when it suited him, had died after being hit over the head in a brawl when Dave was three. The idea of meeting the remaining relatives had never greatly attracted him. How unlike his forebodings they had all been. How easily he had slipped into their comfortable, respectable lives. How closely they had drawn him in, in those few weeks. His Aunt Jasmine (his mother's half sister) sitting across the kitchen table, holding a blue checked mug might have been his mother. Duncan and Rom, the neighbours and, they insisted, some kind of distant cousins, had taken him nightly to the Sousmarie bar. He had found himself singing madrigals at two am with these neighbours and Jasmine's daughter, Althea, and a number of other people, who all seemed happy to call him friend or cousin, and he had felt part of a community. Madrigals? Surely he must have dreamt that.

Luke snapped his fingers. 'Dave, you asleep? Did you meet anyone?'

'Yes, sort of.'

'Well? Sort of how?'

'There was a cousin – Althea. We had actually met before. Her mum says she bathed us together when we were three when she came to London to stay with Mum, but it doesn't figure in my memory. Anyway Althea's only been to England a couple of times when she was little, she did feel familiar; like someone who has lived through the same stuff as I have. Well I suppose our mothers being sisters would explain it. Still it seemed wild to me, like talking to Claudia or Barbara or someone I've known since I was little. Odd to think I could have walked past her in the street without knowing.'

'Will she be coming to England at all?'

'Yup. And no, she's not your type.'

'I wasn't going to … Anyway, how can you be sure.'

'Trust me. Anyway, you'll be living it up with some Italian bimbo by the time she arrives.'

'Sure.' Neither Luke's grin, nor his voice seemed wholehearted. 'My cousin Carlo's on the case. This cousin of yours, does she look like you, too?'

'Althea? No, thank God. She's neat; she's got style. What about that therapist you were so keen on?'

'Well, she says I am doing fine and of course she won't be able to do any more after I've gone to Italy. Anyway it's one of the big no-nos for therapists and their 'clients' to get together, apparently.'

When they got to Hackney, Luke came in for a coffee, but continued to be uncharacteristically reticent about himself and surprisingly interested in Dave's experiences in Antigua. After he had waved Luke goodbye, Dave stood for several minutes puzzling over the last hour. Never, in all their years together, had Luke deflected personal questions or shown persistent interest in people with whom he had no direct connection. Is this what therapy did for you? Had Luke suddenly laid his ego to one side and become thoughtful and empathetic. If so, it didn't seem to have made him happier. Dave mourned for the lost self-centred, sunny Luke. Then he laughed at himself. Why this reluctance to accept a grown-up friend?

Shaking off his melancholy, he set about reacquainting himself with his tiny flat, trying to get back into his old routines. He disembowelled his rucksack, but there was nothing to wash. Loving, if distant, relatives had sent him off with clean underwear and all his buttons replaced. He had shopped for milk and cheese on the way back with Luke, but somehow his stomach still felt weighed down by the stream of time-detached in-flight meals he had consumed. He picked up the scores for his next performance. He had not practised for more than the odd hour in the last three weeks. He leafed through the pages and put them down again. Jet lag – that must be the problem. He flung himself down on the bed and stared up at the photo pasted to the low ceiling above his head. It was a still from the cabaret act they had done at the final Gala at college: Luke, Kes, Angela, Mike, Judy, himself and another couple of friends. Angela had been drunk and relaxed and to everyone's surprise had had the audience laughing at every move; a pity she was so uptight the rest of the time. She took herself so seriously and yet seemed to have a natural turn for comedy, whereas Luke, who seemed to touch life so lightly, could draw tears out of a Scrooge.

Dave corrected himself, Luke who *used* to touch life so lightly. Jetlagged, troubled by the changes in his friend and with his only living relatives now almost four thousand miles across the water, Dave found tears swarming in his eyes and closed them.

A month later, across the Thames in Greenwich, Morris, standing in the damp March bleakness of his London garden, found himself also threatened by tears. He refolded the letter from his parents. They wanted to sell their London house – his home, his studio-workshop – to raise extra money for their planned retirement home in the Seychelles. Now that they had finally decided not to return to England, this house would clearly be their best source of cash. Morris had had the benefit of paying them a nominal rent all these years, and now they both felt that since his strange career seemed to be paying dividends, he could surely afford to rent his own apartment or, if not, perhaps he could share with Ruth now that she was the only inhabitant of that vast house in Blackheath, bought by Martha's grandfather in the days of servants and large families. There didn't seem to be any point in them coming back to England at this time of year, so they had put the sale in the hands of competent agents (Bosun & Cairns). The tenants on the two upper floors were on short-term leases falling due in April and June respectively, so, after a little refurbishment, Bosun & Cairns should be able to have it on the market by July or August at the latest. What did Morris think?

Morris found himself unable to think. Every time he tried, the sense of being on the brink of a crevasse overwhelmed him. He walked from his studio to Ruth's then back and out into the garden again. He reached out a thin hand to touch the damp leaves. Did he really love ivy? The idea of parting from this gold splashed nest with the sky above it seemed to cause an even fiercer contraction of the heart than the notion of Ruth leaving him for Scotland. Of course, he didn't think that Ruth really would go and anyway it was in his power to alter that decision. Against his parents' decision he had no defences.

He walked upstairs to his own tidy rooms on the floor above. For ten years he had lovingly painted a wall here, screwed up a shelf there, nothing spectacular in the design line, but all neat and to his personal taste. He had slowly replaced all the dark floral scraps of carpet with polished or painted floorboards and plain carpets. The walls acted as a gallery to his and Ruth's weavings. Where would he ever find another place like this? His income would not run to more than minimal living space and Ruth's work needed a whole room. Of course Ruth could contribute to the studio costs now – if she didn't move to Scotland, that is.

On the other hand she might want to take the big loom to Scotland. What would it be like working alone again? Her busyness so close to his space kept him working. She needed him for all the little things: difficult threading tasks, colours decisions, detecting snags. Her needing him made living necessary and worthwhile. No one else minded if he existed or not. Douglas, Joe, Kish ...and nameless other men in his life tended to be transient; Ruth and the weaving were the only things that really mattered – *and, of course*, the house. He walked back down to Ruth's studio and spent half an hour fingering the miniature bumpy labels on all her wool pigeonholes. He oiled the small sewing machine they used in some collage works. He wound several bobbins and tidied a drawer of tangled cotton reels. Then he wandered into the garden again.

For the rest of the morning Morris worked on his loom, still unable to face his situation to the point of taking action. He did think of phoning his parents, but they would not understand his attachment to bricks and mortar. They had moved cheerfully and willingly with each change in their diplomatic fortunes and now, quite reasonably, looked forward to cashing their investments and enjoying a more leisured existence in the place of their choice. They had never asked for a realistic rent, they had disapproved of but not attempted to dissuade him from his chosen work. What aspect of their decision could he possibly argue over?

He went up to his kitchen to prepare lunch, but found himself sitting on a stool in front of the phone. Eventually he grabbed his jacket and tramped though the icy rain to Ruth's house in Blackheath. Ruth and Nina had come back from Scotland the week before, but he had had no chance yet to talk to Ruth privately about her plans.

Nina was out and Morris, unable to contain himself, hurried Ruth into the kitchen and stood shivering. 'Ruth? Something important has come up. It's my parents; they want to sell the house – our studio. They need the money. We'll ... I'll have to move and find somewhere else to work.'

'Sell the studio? Oh no! Your flat as well? Is there nothing we can do? My room! I don't want to leave my room.' Ruth reached out to put both hands against his chest in protest.

Morris immediately felt better; his feet touching solid ground for the first time since he had received the letter. He was not entirely alone. 'I don't want to leave either, Sweetie, but I don't have the money for a deposit on a house, never mind a steady income to pay a mortgage. You know the house next door to me is up for sale? Well it's in a terrible state and they are asking £320,000. They'll probably ask double for mine. I suppose we could both work somewhere here.' He stopped and looked around uncertainly. 'I'm not sure I could live here though. Well, of course I could if I had to, but it depends on what you want to do. I mean this idea of working in Scotland. There's the exhibition in Rome coming up. There's a lot of work to be done before we're ready for that and Mum and Dad want the house on the market by July.'

'Morris, you're shaking. You must be so cold. Let's go and put the heater on in the drawing room.'

'Why aren't all the heaters on in this weather? No, don't tell me – Martha. I couldn't live in this place again.'

'I'm sure we can do something. Can't we swap this house for you studio?'

Morris marching through the hall, spoke impatiently. 'Ruth, it doesn't quite work like that. Anyway you still don't have probate, so we can't do anything.' He stooped over a fan heater, then paused and lifted his head. 'Still, it's a thought. We're seeing the solicitor a week this Friday on April 6th. We could mention it.'

'Good. How long have we got before something happens?'

Morris shuddered. 'In house selling terms, no time at all.'

Eight days later, after several unfinished conversations about looms, house prices, live-in carers and Scotland, they found themselves in Lewisham climbing the stairs to the dim solicitor's office, above J.S. Macrae – Funeral Directors. They had met Mr Clarke and his partner Miss Dalton of Bright & Goldman several times in the immediate aftermath of Dan's death and had become used to his musty office and to being told to be patient. They didn't expect too much from this meeting.

'Please take a seat Miss Gardiner, Mr Gardiner.' Addressing himself solely to Ruth, the solicitor continued, 'I'm sorry we've been taking so long to prove your parent's will, Miss Gardiner, but there have been several complicating factors. I hope you have managed on the interim allowance.'

'Yes. Yes, thank you. Well, Morris has done it all, with that power of Attorney thing we all signed. I've never learnt about bank accounts.'

'Hmm, well I think it would be as well if you started to involve yourself in that side of your affairs.'

'Morris thinks I should get a Braille computer and then I'll be able to do things on this Internet system.'

'Hmm, well I don't know about the Internet, but certainly being able to use a computer would be a skill for you in the future.' He caught Morris's puzzled glance and hurried on, 'Anyway, let's come back to your parent's wills.'

Morris frowned. 'Is there more than one will?'

'Yes, well, this has been one of the complications. Your mother and father made other very different wills from the ones that we hold. They placed them with Drewitts in Guildford. Do you have relatives in Guildford, Miss Gardiner?'

'I don't think so. I don't think we have any proper relatives apart from your family, Morris.'

'Nina was related to your mother, but only by marriage. Anyway go on Mr Clarke, what did these wills say?' Morris began popping and unpopping the tie on his umbrella.

'Well, as I say we only discovered them recently and it set us back for a bit. You see these wills, signed by both your parents, left the entire estate to the Sure Sign Temple Foundation...'

Morris jerked upright. 'The witch! Did she leave nothing to her daughter?'

'...or to whichever of them survived the other. Relax Mr Gardiner, Miss Gardiner's father seems to have taken his own steps to deal with this. Less than a week after signing that will, your father placed a new will, the one you have already seen, with us. It most clearly states that he revokes all previous wills. He leaves his entire estate to Miss Gardiner and it names you – Mr Morris Gardiner – as trustee, and us as executors. There is still a problem, as the accident in which your mother was killed is the same as the one resulting in your father's death. Luckily,' Mr Brown flushed and corrected himself, 'I'm sorry, I mean unfortunately for her, but of material advantage to you, Miss Gardiner, is the fact that Mrs Martha Gardiner predeceased Mr Dan Gardiner by thirty days.' Morris relaxed back into his seat. 'Well, to cut a long story short, Miss Gardiner, you will be, once probate has been granted, the owner of a property worth something in the region of a million plus...'

Morris dropped the umbrella. 'Mama Mia! Is that monstrosity worth that much? It hasn't been renovated in forty years.'

'Well, it has eight bedrooms, the location is extremely desirable and then there's the land – something over an acre. To continue, there are also bonds worth in the region of £10,000 in your mother's name and a mixture of stocks and shares amounting to approximately £25,000 in your father's. We have applied for probate and, presuming that the Sure Sign Temple Foundation does not contest the will, you should be able, even after death duties, Miss Gardiner, to live very comfortably.'

Morris, uneasy still, asked, 'Could they do that? Would they be able to overturn a later will?'

'They could try. I don't think there's any legal likelihood of them succeeding, but it's a large sum and they can afford the legal fees, so they might try. Ideally there should have been a longer period between the death of Mrs Gardiner and Mr Gardiner, but I can't see any court in the land finding in their favour under the circumstances, so I wouldn't start worrying about it.' Mr Clarke turned once again to Ruth. 'There will in all likelihood be some compensation due to you from the explosion disaster fund – and this should be substantial in your case as you were dependent on your parents. Then there is a possibility of further compensation from the liable parties if they ever come to an agreement, though I wouldn't hold your breath on that one. Have you any thoughts about what you would like to do with your assets and would you wish us to continue to manage them for you?'

Morris, still stunned by the sums involved, lifted his palm defensively. 'I think we'd better go away and think about all this.'

Ruth, who had sat quite still during Mr Clarke's revelations, smiled confidently. 'I know exactly what I want to do. I want to sell Temple Lawns – the house, as soon as I'm allowed to, though I shall be very sad about the garden, and I want to buy our Greenwich studio from your parents, Morris. I'll be able to do that, won't I?'

'You'll be able to do anything you like, Sweetie. You'll be able to buy the whole house – and the house next door as well, I shouldn't wonder.'

'All right, Morris, I think that's a good idea, then I can live next door and still get to work.'

'Ruth, I was only joking. What about Scotland?'

'The trouble with Scotland is that it's too open. I can't feel my way around like I can in London. And the sounds aren't the same; I can't hear what's happening around me. I'd have to learn them all over again. It's like another language, I speak London not Tomintoul.'

Under Mr Clarke's blushing gaze Morris, his mouth wobbling like a frightened child's, stood up and pulled Ruth up and into his arms.

22

St Mark's, Catford: Barbara

Barbara knocked and listened for a moment before opening Luke's bedroom door. He lay curled away from her, still apparently asleep, although sunshine streamed through the curtains. She put the coffee mug down on his bedside table, sat on the side of the bed, and stroked his shoulder.

'Luke ... Topo, Mum said to wake you. She said to remind you that Grandpa-Carlo, Clara, Paolo, Caterina, Pepi, Teddy and Carlo-baby will be here in less than an hour.'

'Oh God!' He groaned and rolled over, reaching out for the coffee. Barbara put it into his hand. 'You'd better remember that Carlo-*baby* is twenty-six now. He nearly hit me last time I called him that.'

'OK, I'll remember.'

Luke sank back under his duvet. 'Can't I be excused lunch?'

'Nope. Luke ... ?' Barbara, looking at the hunched shoulder, made a decision. 'Shall I tell you a secret?'

'Uhhuh.'

'You're going to be an Uncle in January.'

Luke, eyes wide, emerged from the bedclothes again. 'Ba!'

'Sssh.'

'Why the secrecy? Mum'll go wild.'

'Precisely. I don't want anyone to know till after the wedding. It's very early days yet and Mum ... Oh God, I've just thought ... Dad'll be even worse.'

Luke grinned, reaching out to stroke her flat tummy. 'Glad you're the first, by the time I get there you and Claudia will have worn off the edges of their excitement.'

'D'you think Claudia will? – have babies, I mean. I sometimes wonder.'

'What did she say? ...' He stopped, his brow wrinkling. 'You haven't told Claudia, have you?'

'Not yet.'

Luke took a sip of coffee and lay back again. Having flown in late the previous evening, he began to think that his brain might still be somewhere over the Alps. He stared up at his sister. She looked her usual mischievous, alluring self, but with something extra overlaid: self-consciousness, guilt? Wedding nerves perhaps? This baby thing...why tell him first? Sure, he was excited to hear it, but as news it would make a bigger impact on pretty much every other member of the family. Barbara, the maestro of impact, must have had a reason. Weird the way he had started to question everyone's motives; a year ago he would not have bothered with any of these concerns.

'What's up, Baba? Why are you telling me first?'

Barbara burst into tears. 'I just want to make you happy again and I can't think of anything else.'

Luke, astonished, pulled her into a tight hug. 'Oh Ba, you fool. I'm all right. I'm perfectly happy. I'm fine. What's all this about?'

'Unless Dave is with you, you don't go out at all. You don't even go to the gym.'

'Listen you nutcase! Perhaps you haven't noticed; I've been in Rome for the last two months, working too hard to go to gyms and suchlike. Seems to me you've been so occupied swanning around and getting your frills together you never even noticed I was gone.'

'No Luke, I know. Carlo-baby – sorry Carlo – came round last night. He says you don't go out at all. You don't talk about Melanie or ...'

'Melanie ditched me months ago. She's going to marry Bruce – who's a dork – after all.'

'No! Why didn't you say?' Barbara's horrified face comfortably reflected Luke's humiliation. To be rejected was one thing, but to be turned down in favour of someone you despised, left you crawling among the slugs and snails. After staring at her brother for a moment, Barbara looked a bit more cheerful. 'Well, at least that makes sense. When did this happen? Was she a dork too, really?'

'Way back – January. No, she wasn't a dork. I really fancied her. Though she was a bit ...well mother-earthish. You know, inclined to the outdoors.'

'D'you miss her?'

'I miss that she was there, if you see what I mean. I don't know what – who to think about now. I quite fancied that counsellor,

186

but she is off limits. So that leaves ...'

'Think about my baby; don't start on ...Don't think about ...'

'...Heloise?'

'I think I'll hate that woman, if you ever find her.'

'I don't suppose I ever will now. But don't worry, Ba, I am *not* round the bend and I *will* think about your baby. Hey, smile now. You're getting married tomorrow. Now move yourself, I've got to get up if the entire mafia are on their way here for lunch and I must rehearse my song for you. I'm sorry I missed Lewis's stag night.'

'What stag night?'

'Oh ah! Perhaps he didn't have one. I just assumed ...'

Maria walked into the fast filling church, smiling and waving her way down to the front pew. Lewis and his best mate, Steve, were already hovering there. Lewis looked down with the calm certainty that his six foot five seemed to have conferred on him. He smiled at Maria, then looked beyond her and moved swiftly up the church aisle to gather up his less than confident parents and his one uncle, these three constituted his entire family. He parked them, beaming, in the right front pew. Maria smiled across, wondering yet again how such sparrow-like people had produced and nurtured a cuckoo the size of Lewis. The rest of the groom's side were filled with Lewis's other family – firemen and (one) firewoman.

Bubbling with anticipation, Maria gazed at the magnificence of Luke and Dave in the choir stalls, as she waited for her daughters and husband to appear. She did not for an instant doubt that they would look anything less than beautiful. She had made Barbara's wedding dress and Claudia's bridesmaid dress. She had taken Gordon to buy a suit and taken Luke's suit to the cleaners. If Gordon's jacket stretched a trifle across the midriff and Luke's hung a little loosely, these were minor matters. For Claudia she had chosen a deep and flattering rose colour and Claudia (to her surprise) had submitted like a lamb. Barbara had been a joy to dress, from the choosing of patterns, through three delightful expeditions to fabric warehouses where she had been able to feel every cloth from weighty damasks to gossamer silks, to the careful construction of the dress itself. Many fittings had given her happy hours with her daughter. Barbara's work friends had filled the church and reception hall with flowers; her own friends and two of the choirboys' parents had prepared plates of mouth-watering food; the smoked hams, fresh olives and cheeses brought over by Clara from Italy making all the difference.

There was nothing more to do except watch her beautiful daughter marry a man she felt very comfortable around and who lived and worked a ten minute bus ride away from her home. What more could a mother ask? A husband for Claudia, perhaps? A return of the old Luke? Maria crossed herself surreptitiously; it did not do to be greedy with wishes. It was surely enough that Luke stood there now amongst the choir in his old surplice, nearly a year after he had lain under that mashed up building. She thanked God.

The organ paused and started up again, everyone turned and a collective catching of breath greeted Barbara as she drifted in; a snowflake against the darkness of Gordon's suit. Through the light veil, her smile reached first for her brother, then her mother and finally her bridegroom.

Dave, who like Luke had rejoined the choir for today, also received a glancing beam and marvelled. What tiny action of fate had made him part of the Danford family? He was unrelated to any of them, merely Luke's friend at primary school and in the church choir. Was it just that as the family spun around Luke they had simply absorbed him – a minor planet – into their solar system? They had been kind to his mother too, and then when he was fifteen and she had died, they had casually, but firmly taken him in until he was eighteen, rather than allow him to be taken into care or sent to his grandmother in Antigua. He shook his head in wonder. His guess was that Maria, being practical, had simply decided that someone should keep an eye on Luke all those times of the day when she or his sisters were not at his side, so she had co-opted him as a brother for her darling. No other family, thought Dave, had such simple and selfish priorities: each other, food and clothes, in that order. He looked down at his new shoes and grinned. When Maria had firmly checked his intended clothing for the day, he realised that, as far as she was concerned, he counted as one of the family.

Dave looked up again to see Luke gazing at his sister in transparent delight. He watched Barbara turn once more to smile at her mother. Maria looked serene and rested, as though she had scarcely lifted a finger in the last few weeks. Most other families would have worn themselves out with the preparations. Noise had certainly featured in the Danford household recently, but it was the noise of information being exchanged. Yes, Louise and Katherine do know that Barbara loves anemones. No, Claudia had not found any pink shoes, would Mum come with her on Friday morning when she was off duty. Yes, Luke could still get into his choirboy surplice but it needed washing. Yes, definitely some coffee now. Each picked a task they could accomplish; each lived for the moment in the moment. Dave, catching sight of Claudia, behind her sister, corrected himself. Claudia, like ordinary mortals, carried the past with her and also peered with concern into the future. She was the less sunny for it, yet he loved her as much as the others. He loved them all. He loved them for loving him. He would sing out his love in a moment.

In growing but well-hidden excitement, Dave waited for his part in this wedding. He watched Luke, who stood relaxed and with a smile curving his lips that almost reminded him of the old Luke. The priest moved gently but inexorably through the phases of the Sacrament of Matrimony. It was a full mass, but it seemed to Dave that it was over in the space of a few heartbeats. The organ changed gear. He flicked Luke a glance and moved to the centre of the church facing down the aisle. His deep rumble joined the incense-filled atmosphere in a soothing bass rendition of Schubert's *Ave Maria*. Barbara, whose favourite song this was, started crying.

As the last notes of Dave's solo faded into space, Luke beamed at him, then stepped forward and exchanged places. The chords from Puccini's *Messa di Gloria* rang out. Luke's first notes sounded as if they had detached themselves from the vaults of the chapel and chosen to float, just at that moment, into the air around his lifted head. *Gratias agimus tibi propter magnum gloriam tuam (we give thanks to you ...)*. How does he do that, thought Dave? So high, so exposed, the notes needing to be placed so perfectly in the uncharted spaces of the air. For himself, as a bass, Dave had the sensation whenever he sang of pushing the air gently to one side allowing his notes to take up their natural resonance in the atmosphere. He felt that he could have a discussion with the air about the correct placement of the notes before committing himself, whereas a tenor had to have each note in a state of perfection from the moment of release.

Dave breathed in deeply; around him the faces in varying states of bliss of the people he most cared for. This would be a good moment to stop the world.

Ruth lifted the scissors, took the first two warp threads between the fingers of her left hand, snipped, knotted and smiled to herself. Knotting off constituted the finishing act for one piece and the start of the delicious interval between weavings. Delicious, not because she could stop weaving, but because she could consolidate the dream of her next weaving, in this buffer state she need not worry about how to set it up or where to get the materials. Dreaming without restrictions. She picked up the next two threads, snipped and knotted.

The door clicked. Before Morris came through Ruth knew that he would be pressing her yet once more to come to Rome in June. Just now, she didn't ever want to leave the studio again. She felt centred here, this was her box and she fitted it precisely. Scotland had been exciting, but so...so hard and full of edges: everything waiting to be bumped into, every sound needing to be translated. Living becomes tiring if you need to be aware from moment to moment about whether you can raise your arm safely. She must remain firm.

'Ruth, you *do* have a passport. You remember, we were so surprised when it came through the post six weeks after the explosion.'

'I don't need it now.'

'You were supposed to go on holiday'

'I had a holiday in Scotland. I couldn't find my way about there, I had to have someone with me all the time.'

'Rome is a city; much more like London than a Scottish village.' Morris tried another tack. 'Nina once said that she longed to travel. She has never been abroad, you know. It would be a way of thanking her, now you have the money.'

'Well you could take her, Morris, though she doesn't like cities much. Anyway, what use would I be in Rome.'

'You can promote your work.'

'I will just be a problem for you, Morris.'

'I'll get lonely promoting it on my own.' Seeing her resisting still, Morris decided to play his trump. 'You know that boy you heard singing in Aberdeen, Luke Danford? Well he's singing in Rome when our exhibition is on. If I get tickets for that, will you come to Rome?'

In Rome? Luke? Ruth, bent down to concentrate on tying off the next knot. If she sat in an audience, she could listen in safety, be near him. What if Morris should try and make her meet him again? She tried to still the thud in her chest and sound casual.

'I still don't want to meet him.'

'I'm sure we couldn't get near him, even if we wanted.'

'Oh! What's he singing?'

Morris hearing the tremor in her voice, knew that he'd won. 'Nothing you'd be interested in really, shall we not bother?'

She lifted her head, eyes big. 'Morris! Tell me!'

'Rigoletto. He's singing the Duke of Mantua for three out of the ten performances of the production in the Baths of Caracalla.'

'Oh!' she sighed. 'Can we get tickets, Morris, please?'

'I knew it! You really are hooked on that guy. I've never seen you like this before.'

'Don't laugh at me, Morris, you're keen about him too, aren't you.'

'And how! But that's different.'

'I know. You prefer men to women.'

Morris stayed silent. With Ruth, you never knew if childlike curiosity or Martha's bigoted opinions would emerge on life issues.

Ruth reached out to touch him and he let her take his hand, she spoke cheerfully. 'I don't mind, Morris, Nina says her best friends in Scotland are like that too. In Aberdeen, when we heard him -- Luke – sing, I began to understand about fans and why people go crazy about pop-stars. I just wanted to make him go on singing all the rest of my life.' She turned over Morris's hand. 'I even wanted to touch him. You met him, didn't you?' She took an audible breath. 'Tell me what he's really like.'

Morris held her hand loosely in both of his, as he tried to summon the image of Luke on the two occasions when they'd met. 'Well he's almost edibly good-looking. Even when I saw him in the hospital and he could hardly walk and his face had great red marks all over from the stitches, he looked ... ' Morris let go of her hand and went over to the tool rack above Ruth's work bench. 'I don't know what it is, he seems to move inside his skin in a way that just makes you want to stare and stare. I was hooked and I didn't even know he could sing then. I don't think he smiled at all that first time, but when he came to our exhibition ... ' A pair of scissors fell clatteringly off the hook under his restless fingers and Ruth jumped. 'Sorry. He looked so much better and he smiled straight at me – I suppose I was the only person there he recognised – it's really corny, but I felt like I was the only person in the room. I nearly melted on the spot.'

Ruth laughed, clearly not believing him. 'Don't be silly. Anyway, can we get tickets?'

'We can try, but we may have to get them out there.'

'I'll come.'

23
Rome: Luke

Sunlight in June in Rome, Luke opened his face to this blessing, glad not to be in England. The morning rehearsal had gone better than expected; Amira was fine – no, better than fine, a sweet-voiced singer. A little old perhaps, but that didn't seem to stop her switching up the heat between them. He didn't mind any more, it was just good to be wanted; he would go with the flow now. He would do what people wanted, sing what they wanted. He was lucky to be in such demand. The anniversary of the explosion had passed. Mum and Claudia had come over for a few days, but he had not felt any renewal of his fears. In a way he had felt some of the chains of the last year slipping away. Bathed in general approbation, with time doing its healing stuff, the Heloise pain, once a whole-body sickness, had condensed into a small nut – a piece of grit lodged somewhere central, but undefined, within him. It was no longer in every pathway of every nerve. When occasionally it gripped him, there was a comforting familiarity about the small ache.

He was in Trastevere now, the hotel only five minutes away. Strange to be in a hotel, his uncle and aunt had let their house for the summer and gone to their chalet above Locarno and his cousin Carlo only had a miniature flat. Anyway, the role came with accommodation so why not? Luke lingered in the sunlight, looking into shop windows. Windows filled with cheeses beyond the imagination of an English shopkeeper; shops full of packages glinting with cellophane and ribbon next to mundane ironmongers' and stationers' shops. There was even a small art gallery. Luke glanced in as he passed to see what paintings were on offer, but there were no paintings today. He walked on towards his hotel then stopped as the little piece of grit near his heart caught him unawares. The exhibition was of weaving. Weaving; the Exhibition in London with torrents of colour on the walls, all made by Morris Gardiner and the blind woman; the same woman, sick in Lewisham Hospital; the lifts; St Thomas' Hospital; the explosion and, like an arrow to the gold, the thought of Heloise. He had still not spoken to Ruth Gardiner, the woman found in the hours before they rescued him. He stopped on the pavement, in the perfect state of two minds; to go on to his Hotel and lunch and not allow the piece of grit to irritate unnecessarily, or to go back just to pick up that one loose thread. He stood staring up at the sky, unable to move his feet, but swaying his head from side to side, the victim of an invisible tug-of-war game. He leant against the lamp-post and let them fight it out.

Retracing his steps, he gave a quick glance at the posters. They told him that Ruth and Morris were indeed the artists. Not a waste of time then. He paused and peered through the glass. There behind the desk at the end sat the woman depicted in the posters. Luke paused to assess her. Late twenties, perhaps? Not much to look at: shapeless, dark hair, enveloping clothes, unfocused eyes – of course, the blindness. Did he really want to meet her? He tried to look at the weavings, but sunlight on the glass obscured all but one. This one with dark smoky rectangles covered in drifts of bright specs reminded him of something. He moved into the doorway. New York at night; that was it.

Morris, his back to the door as he fiddled with a stand of posters, was speaking, 'I'll go and get us a couple of panini, shall I?'

Luke, who had taken half a step to leave the gallery again, warmed to the thought of Morris's welcome. He stepped through the doorway.

Ruth spoke: 'Morris, let me do that. I want to feel the sunshine. I'll be fine.'

Luke leant against the doorframe, his heart slamming against the wall of his chest, a tidal wave in his ears, so that a blackness seemed to be about to engulf him. The pain struck again. In an unstoppable cascade, memory ripped open spilling images, sensations, words and sounds. Ruth Gardiner sat there: unattractive, no longer young, sightless and speaking with Heloise's voice.

Ruth spoke again. 'I've got enough money. I won't be long.'

Certainty gripped him. Voices were his trade; he couldn't be mistaken. She had such a strong small voice, slightly husky and sort of young/old. She stood up, a lumpy cardigan reaching to her knees, her badly cut hair obscuring her face. Everything about her alien to his dreams – except the voice. *Except the voice.* As she walked confidently towards the doorway, unfolding her white stick, he put a convulsive hand on her sleeve. She stopped dead; instinctively assuming someone was trying to protect her from an obstacle.

'Hel ... ' he cleared his throat and tried again. 'Heloise?' She put her head on one side, puzzled and showing no understanding. 'Heloise ... it's Luke. Please remember,' he begged, a fresh horror rising in his mind. Maybe she had had a memory loss of the whole traumatic event. People did. 'Heloise, please don't deny me.' Morris reached her and took her elbow, his face alight with pleasure.

'It's Luke, isn't it? How wonderful to see you. This is Ruth.'

'Luke? No!' she whispered, and nearly fainting with relief, Luke saw that she knew, she had remembered.

'What ... ?' Morris began, but her hand moved swiftly to silence him.

'Shhh.'

She stood quite still, her head tilted, listening. Luke, a victim of total white noise both in and outside his head, simply stood. The fates had snatched his script, given him this lanky woman and filled his mind with cotton wool. The fates had also walked off with his dreams and the resultant empty pit was too frightening to look into.

She spoke with barely a tremor. 'It's all right Morris, I've already met Luke. Could you mind the shop while I ... while I catch up with him.'

Morris looked from Luke's pearly sweating face to Ruth's frozen one. 'I don't understand. When did you meet?'

'I'll explain later. I just need to talk to Luke for a moment.'

Morris walked reluctantly back to the desk at the rear, and Luke, picking up this new script, said politely, 'I'll walk with you to the *panetteria*.'

Ruth, tapping her stick efficiently against the wall, left the gallery, she skirted obstacles smoothly, while Luke, the master of natural movement on stage, stumbled behind her. They walked in silence to the queue outside the little sandwich shop.

'Luke?'

'Yes?'

'We're coming to your first night at Caracalla.'

So she had known he was here. Her silence, her vanishing, her lies beneath the rubble were deliberate? Like the feeling of blood flowing through a new wound, sensation began to return and with it a dragging ache. An ache with both physical and mental properties, an ache on its way to somewhere else, somewhere much bigger and nastier. An ache it would be exceedingly dangerous to investigate. He had so often planned her first visit to the opera. He tried smiling politely, forgetting that she could not see. 'So you will actually go to an opera at last.'

'Oh, I've been lots of times.'

'I thought you said ...' another lie perhaps?

'I did, I never went to an opera until last summer. Mama wouldn't let me. Morris takes me now.'

Luke took a quick glance into the empty pit of his dreams. It was filling up fast. It was filling with an anger of such vast and brutal dimensions that he would not, he knew, contain it long. His mobile rang.

His cousin Carlo, sounding urgent; where was he? 'I'm in the Via San Martino but ... sure I am only five minutes from the Hotel but ... yes but ... Bloody hell, *tonight*? Jesus, that's hundreds of miles away. You're crazy! I've never been in a helicopter ... and they want me to sing at the other end? But Carlo I've just found ... Oh God! Yes, yes I'm coming. I hope the fee is astronomical . .. Sure, I might have guessed. OK, OK, I'm coming!' He shouted the last words then turned to the silent woman beside him. 'I have to go Hel ... Ruth. I have to fly to Piacenza and sing the Duke in Rigoletto tonight in some godforsaken castle on a crazy mountainside.'

'You should not swear so, Luke,' she said gently.

Tears instantly swelled his eyes. There was no way out of this and back to his dreams. Heloise, strange, dark and blind stood in front of him and said the same things in the same voice that his beautiful fair companion had said in the darkness a year ago. A car drew up and Carlo leaned across and opened the passenger door.

With his usual carelessness, but luckily in colloquial Italian, he called to Luke, 'Oi Luca, hop in, I'll drop you at the hotel. Come on, leave the girls alone. She's not your type anyway.'

Panic stricken, Luke finally touched Ruth. He took her by the shoulder, looking for the first time into her dark, wandering eyes.

'You won't disappear? Where can I find you? Tell me . . . truthfully.' She opened her mouth on a small gasp as his hand bit into her arm. Then she fumbled in her bag.

'My card – we have a card now. I . . . I live in London. I'm returning after your first night, on the Saturday.'

'Luca, for Chrissake get in! I've got you to Roca's hotel in forty-five minutes. Plenty more fish in the sea! What was all that about?' He added as Luke slid into the passenger seat. 'She didn't look like your kind of bimbo. Didn't she have one of them white sticks?'

'Yes, she's blind. She . . .' Luke made an instant decision. 'She's a weaver. I just like her work. I saw it in London last year.'

Carlo was silent a moment, struggling with a complex thought. 'That can't be right. You can't do those weaving things if you can't see. I mean how would you know which colour to use?'

Luke said automatically, 'Some of the colours have different textures; it's the dyes. You can feel them with your eyes closed.'

'That so? How d'you know a thing like that?'

'She told me.' In that instant another slice of memory from their lost hours underground flooded into his conscious mind.

She told me and I didn't listen, he thought. She had a watch that *spoke* the time. She asked *me* if it was dark and she laughed when she said she couldn't see anything either. She knew opera, but had never *seen* one. He had missed all the signals. His legacy? Rage. Where his dream had cracked apart, nuclear fission had taken place; explosion after explosion lighting up nerves and contracting muscles. People talk about blood boiling, thought Luke in amazement, and this is how it feels.

He had thirty minutes in the hotel to get his things together. Seeing Carlo about to come and help, he pushed him towards the bar. 'Wait for me here. I'll be quicker alone.' In desperate need of action, he ignored the lift and ran upstairs. Anger propelled him into his room and he heard, with satisfaction, the crack of the door slamming behind him. His jaw ached with aggression and he found himself, as he dashed his arm across his face, gripping his sleeve and almost tearing it with his teeth.

Fearing that he might wreck the room in spite of the time restriction he stripped, jerking his clothes off haphazardly, and switched on the shower. In the shower he lifted his face to the stream making strange wolf-like noises. Whatever he had hoped to wash off remained stuck to him. He had five minutes to dry, dress and pack for this crazy one-night substitution. His throat felt like the skin of an elephant.

He entered the lift, ignoring the friendly attendant, his brow still dark, then climbed into his cousin's waiting car. Carlo, after a couple of light questions, shut up. Luke scowled unseeing at the passing panorama of Rome. How could he have been so obtuse? How could he have let so much pain build up around a person who never really existed? He had lived a year of agony – for nothing. Ruth's insignificant statement that she had already been to an opera provided the catalyst to some annihilating chemical change in the fibres of his being. He might as well have swallowed a lethal cocktail and his insides began to rebel. He forced Carlo to stop while he dived into a bar to use the toilet. His thoughts, equally out of control, slopped around his mind, returning again and again like poisoned bile.

Who could he tell that he had found his dream and didn't want her? Dave? Mum? Claudia? They needed to know that he wasn't mad, that someone else was the liar in this farce. Yet he felt more of a fool – more of a sick man – now, than in the whole of the past year. And to top it all, Heloise's voice came from this lying, un-appealing woman; a voice woven inoperably into his nerves and muscles. He groaned aloud.

'Jesu, Luca, what's the matter? Don't you *want* this Rigoletto? I thought you would be in heaven at the call. I've never seen you like this.'

'Rigoletto? No, it's not that. Dear God, I'm performing a major role tonight I keep forgetting.'

'Forgetting? Has someone died?' The laughing groan that issued from Luke alarmed Carlo further. 'Who is it? Tell me instantly.'

'Nobody important, just a dream – God help me! – just a dream.'

24

Montevitano: Rigoletto

Three-quarters of an hour later Luke sat in a noisy tin box, ten thousand feet above Bologna, a vocal score of Rigoletto in his lap. A woman, whose name he had failed to catch, talked at him non-stop from one side and across the tiny aisle a morose man stared either at him or out of the window. In spite of the blasts of information from the woman, her role in tonight's performance, or indeed in Luke's life, remained mysterious to him. The only enlightenment he gained was that the tenor he would be replacing had suspected appendicitis, his cover was attending his mother's funeral and that the impresario Dmitri Dvoran and some political VIP would be in the audience. Half an hour into the flight, the woman dived into a briefcase and produced some photos; these appeared to be of a cast of South Pacific or some beach party and not the production he was about to take part in. He glanced through them. Then hoping to silence her, he handed them back and started to leaf through the score. Speech continued to pour from her, so he leant back and shut his eyes.

Luke stood in the wings. Wings really meant that here. He had seen open-air stages like these before, with the auditorium erected on a complex weaving of scaffolding; they appeared all over Italy in summer season. This was in a dramatic league of its own, though. The castle occupied the narrow summit of a mountain, so that the stage had to be hung from the battlements of a castle, with the auditorium floating on its steel structure over the courtyard below.

He had survived the first act. His antennae told him that the audience, although not yet thrilled, wished him well. Now for the big act with Rigoletto's daughter, Gilda. In his part as the Duke of Mantua, Luke would be trying to seduce Rigoletto's innocent and secluded child, Rigoletto being his court jester. He ought not to have been surprised to find Angela playing Gilda. She had rung him from Piacenza only a couple of days before to complain about the costumes in her touring production. When her opposite number took ill, she put Luke's name forward. Luke being young, mobile, in Italy, in rehearsal for the very part they needed and only a few hours away, was clearly the answer to their prayers. Once again he would be grasping Angela's skinny body, and listening to her tightly controlled *bel canto*. Her complaint about the costumes turned out to be justified; they provided the last straw to this nightmare that ought to be a triumph. The designer belonged to the wisps-of-gauze school – the poorer the character, the fewer and less colourful the wisps. All very symbolic no doubt, but unlucky individuals became fiendishly exposed. Angela did not respond well to this baring of flesh, waves of discomfort poured off her even in their hurried rehearsal.

She started her big aria. He waited, hoping, as he did each time he heard her sing, that she might for once let go; let her voice fill the sail. She still treated every aria as a recitative, a preparation for the real thing. Why hold back at the moment you had the audience in your power? They would be somewhere else tomorrow. He must not allow irritation to spoil his performance. Still, better to be bothered about Angela than furious about Heloise. He stepped on stage again, a Duke disguised as a poor student (qualifying for a costume of three wisps of gauze); perhaps it was a good thing that Angela did not turn him on.

Luke set about seducing the audience instead. For fifteen halcyon minutes he forgot Heloise and his broken dreams. He wickedly infringed Angela's modesty, forcing her into better acting of shocked innocence, he wooed her and the audience with brazen confidence masked as modesty. With all the notes falling comfortably into his middle and upper register, he could hardly fail.

The interval was spent pacing the moves of the next scene backstage – a big scene this one, with an exposed solo at the beginning. His part could be interpreted in a variety of ways. This director wanted a sad, misunderstood Duke; a man in a desperate state of beautiful melancholy because the first woman he had truly loved had been stolen from him. Well he could do that all right. The only trouble was that his thief was the woman herself. Once Heloise had crept into his thoughts she lodged there like a lethal tumour reaching towards every corner. On stage again, his voice ripped into *Ella mi fu rapita ... (they stole her from me ...)* and turned over with the agony of his loss, *parmi veder le lagrime*

... (*I can just see the tears ...*), with all the outraged innocence the director could have imagined. Underneath this full sound, however, the anger washed dangerously, hardening notes, edging consonants. He fought to control it, aware at the same time that the audience appreciated the robustness after Angela's slightly saccharine Gilda.

Luke, released from the remainder of the scene, did not return to his dressing room. He prowled restlessly backstage. Between acts he found and sat on a tall stool (a prop for the next scene in the bar) in an unlit corner. In some curiosity about his body's wild fluctuations, he waited, listening to the blood moving fiercely around his chest. The anger refused to recede. He would be on again in a moment. Fine, he couldn't wait. *La donna e mobile ... (women are fickle ...)*. An aria which had, until this very minute, seemed the ultimately stupid male statement, the exposure of the most fickle character in opera. Tonight it was different. Tonight ... he clenched his teeth, then jumped as a hand touched his shoulder.

Maddalena (he did not know her real name), the innkeeper's sister in the next scene, held a finger to her lips. She moved in close behind him, her fingers skilfully kneading the hard muscles at his neck's edge. He sighed gratefully. Not all women ... Her thumbs rose through the hair on his nape releasing the blood pounding around his ears. If the blood started to pound elsewhere that would be fine in the coming scene. Like Gilda, she was wearing a costume in which bits of gauze studiously failed to cover any part of her anatomy fully. Unlike Gilda, she had a smell, a roundness that invited handling. She also had that quality of depth in her voice that worked magic in his brain.

They were called; he leant back, and mouthed the word 'grazie'. She blew him a kiss. One more river ... the most worn aria in operatic history, then a leisurely interrupted seduction and he could go home. Home? Some hope! As it was the first night, with the audience full of local bigwigs and, apparently, an important politician, there would inevitably be a party. He could anticipate it all, Angela drunk, weeping all over him, no bed until 4 am. He moved towards the stage, anger rising once more, belly to chest, and caught the tail end of Maddalena shaking her head at him.

The first bars of *La donna* ... came out like the baffled cry of a hurt child. Appalled that he might wreck such an exposed piece of singing (every note of which this audience would have known from infancy), he opened his chest and thrust in every ounce of steel he had. At the end of the first verse Maddalena, in the wings, mimed self-strangulation, and flapped her hands gently up and down. Grasping the message, he made a stupendous effort to lighten and soften the next verse. Falling a long way short of the cheery Casanova he was aiming for, he produced a sinister jollity and was consequently shaken by the tumultuous applause that followed. He had expected a silent pillory for his burning and sacking of their pet aria.

He stood, aghast, for several moments, missing his cue to reach out for Maddalena as she came on stage. She, bless her professionalism, swerved as if he had, and he made a late laughing lunge.

Already unnerved, there followed for him the most bizarre experience of his (or surely anyone's) stage career. Maddalena pretending to seduce him while apparently resisting his advances did precisely that. Acting didn't enter into it. She moved her barely clad hips against him until he was thoroughly aroused. Let his wandering hands through the gauze and around her breasts. Let her own hands drift suggestively over his bare chest and barely covered groin. His breathing started to clot and he held on to her unable to let her go for fear of what might be visible through the gauze. Her eyes, provocative and merry, laughed at his difficulties. Luckily, the singing in this scene comes in breathless snatches, interrupted by the despairing Gilda and the triumphant Rigoletto outside the bar.

By the time he had thrown himself on the attic bed to feign sleep, his anger and desire had mixed a volatile cocktail and had Maddalena appeared he might have handled her violently. There was no need. After the stabbing of Gilda, while Rigoletto is crowing triumphantly over the supposed body of his enemy, Maddalena appeared with a torch to lead him up to the castle parapet in order to sing his last reprise of *La donna* high above the stage. He had never actually rehearsed this bit. She grabbed his hand and ran with him up a cold stone staircase until they suddenly hit the night sky. Light shot between the crennellations, but dark shadows filled the spaces between.

He pulled her into the shadow intending at the very least

to kiss her savagely, but she whispered, *'Si, si, giovane,'* as she slipped off her pants. His instinctive professionalism made him resist momentarily. She misunderstood, mumbled about the pill into his ear, and in seconds he found himself inside her. His alter ego danced round the edges of his consciousness shrieking: 'You fucking idiot, you're in the middle of a performance, you've got to sing, now. Stop! For Christ's sake stop!', while his body thrust relentlessly into the accommodating flesh. As Rigoletto hit the climax of his revenge *'O gioia!'* Luke groaned his own revenge. His knees sagged and he let go of the pressure inside him. Staggering free of Maddalena, hidden from the waist down, he faced the blinding spotlight as it picked him out between the battlements.

His voice, softened and relaxed at last, finally obeyed his commands. He sang the reprise of *La Donna* ... as if mermaids danced before his eyes. When the spotlight released him, he found Maddalena still in the shadows. She took his face between her hands.

'Sta meglio, giovane? Better now?'

'Yes, oh yes.'

A slurred English voice exclaimed, 'Shit, it's raining!'

Luke, left for a few seconds to himself, escaped from the party into the street. Rain was indeed falling. He lifted his face to it in a vain attempt to change his mood. He should be enjoying bliss; everyone in the cast and, as far as he could tell, most of the audience, had hugged and congratulated him on his performance, thanked him for saving the day and told him what a beautiful young man he was. Sadly, the only woman who seemed not to be available was the understanding Maddalena. She appeared to be locked to the side of a forbidding middle-aged man. She had given him a wink, but that seemed to be that.

The wet street gleamed under thinly spaced street lamps. Luke, gulping the air, walked down the steep slope away from the Castle entrance. Beside him the scaffolding supporting the seating rose like steel knitting. The rain, already dripping through the wooden boards above, pinged on the metal and shone on the great yellow plastic knuckles that housed all the joints of the structure. As the rain grew heavier, Luke ducked under this scaffolding. He laid his head against the cool wet metal bars and found himself sobbing without tears. For the first time in his life, Luke felt sorry for himself. As far as he could see, tonight he had been given every-thing he had ever asked for and it tasted like darkness or the space that lay between stars – everlasting emptiness. Even the anger had slipped away leaving nothing in its wake. He had once, aged about seven, spent nearly an hour watching two parallel lines, waiting for infinity so that he could catch them meeting. As hope of witnessing this miracle slowly drained out of him, and he knew he had been duped in some way, he had felt this lack of desire to go on, to bother with tomorrow. He pressed his mouth against the cold metal wanting to feel *something*.

'Luke, here you are! I've got a bottle of Champagne here.' Her eyes shining, Angela moved hazily towards him. 'You look funny, Luke, are you drunk?'

'Probably.'

'Isn't this the best night of your life?' The satisfaction in her voice invited only a positive answer. Luke, who never disguised his feelings except on stage, faked a smile, took the bottle out of her hands and took a swig from it. She burbled on, 'I knew you would stun them. You know that was Dmitri himself, talking to you back inside, the man beside Careno, the producer. You'll never be out of work again in your life. They're looking for you in there; I crept out. Aren't you pleased with me for making them call you up?'

Luke, playing the part of Luke, reached a lazy arm out and hugged Angela. 'Brilliant!' He took another swig. 'Fucking brilliant!'

Angela laughed. 'You really are drunk, Luke. Well you deserve it. Hey, you're not singing tomorrow are you?'

'Technical.'

'Dear god, you ought to get some sleep. Let's go find Rosina. I think you're staying with her. I'll look after you, Luke. I've got some aspirin in my bag.'

Luke, playing on in the role she had given him, allowed her to take him back to the party, find his hostess and take him to his room. She even started to help him undress too, but Luke, seeing further comforts in her eye, suddenly became competent again, kissed her goodnight and shut the door. He drank the water she had left him, ignored the aspirin, lay down and turned his face to the wall.

25

Caracalla: Heloise

With his hands on Ruth's shoulders to stop her slipping away, Morris spoke firmly. 'You have to tell me what happened. I can't help if I don't understand.'

'No, no, no, no Morris, I can't. I want to go home.'

'You don't want to go home before Luke's first night, do you? Don't cry, Sweetie, someone might come in to the gallery.' He pulled her into his arms. 'Come here.'

As Morris stood there hugging and petting Ruth, he looked over her shoulder at the doorway through which Luke had appeared only yesterday. Luke had paled so sharply during his brief moment in the gallery that Morris had thought he might faint. Then the two had set off together. Minutes later Ruth had returned, almost equally pale, and without the panini, but he had been unable to get her to talk. As he tried to coax an explanation out of her, clients appeared and the whole bustle of selling two big weavings took him up completely. Since then, what with Nina arriving that evening, and Ruth's determined silence, all he had gathered was that Luke had had to leave in a hurry to go in a helicopter. Sometimes Ruth baffled him completely, he almost felt like shaking her. If she met Luke in the explosion, why on earth would she have denied it, yet when else could she possibly have met him and why were they both so devastated to meet again?

He sat Ruth down at the desk at the back of the gallery and tried another tack. 'Have you talked to Nina about it?'

'No.'

Morris looked down at the bent head. What if Luke should appear and demand an explanation from him? He needed to have some clue about what was happening. He spoke more gently. 'Just tell me when you met Luke before? Is this something to do with Martha? I mean, why did he recognise you? ...Did you know him before...'

'No.'

'He called you Heloise ... Jesus, you *did* meet him in that explosion!'

'Yes.'

'Ruth! Why couldn't you say so? Quick, blow your nose, someone's coming in.'

Luke, back in his hotel room in Rome and with only two hours to spare before the technical rehearsal, flung himself on his hotel bed and fell asleep, his mobile phone in his hand. Waking, an hour or so later, he stared at it. Who should he ring? Dave or Claudia, or perhaps Barbara? Maybe Mum? In the twenty-four hours since he had found Heloise, he had not yet phoned any of them. He had been waiting for over a year to make this phone call. What could he say? I'm not mad, Heloise is real and not a dream, I was right all the time – when he had clearly been so wrong. What price his mental state now? Who would cure, or even limit, this anger? Where in the whole wide world would he find an antidote for this poison now coursing through his veins?

He needed a shower. He went into his bathroom, half-undressed then returned and flung himself back on the bed, grabbed his mobile and dialled Dave. No answer. Barbara would be at work and wouldn't be able to talk. With Claudia work and sleep followed no visible pattern; he tried all the same. The answerphone. The screen clock read 13.30. In half an hour Carlo would pick him up for the next rehearsal. He showered very briefly then, still wet, tried Claudia again. No luck. He tried home. No answer. Mobile in hand he moved to the wardrobe and pulled out a shirt then, on an impulse, he rang Melanie.

He could hear a hubbub of voices in the background before she spoke: 'Hi, I thought you were in Italy.'

'I am. Something's come up … where are you? Can you talk.'

'Not really. I'm in John Lewis. Bruce is helping me choose a silver wedding present for Mum and Dad.'

'Oh! OK I'll leave it then. Sorry.'

'What is it …? You're not ill, are you?'

'No, I'm fine.' Why had he phoned? What could he possibly ask of Melanie now? I've found Heloise and I don't want her after all? Please leave Bruce and come and console me? 'Just thought I'd tell you about my helicopter ride to do a last minute substitution yesterday. I'll tell you another time. Get back to your shopping. Give Brucie my love.'

'Better not. Sounds exciting. Speak to you later. Bye!'

Luke flung the phone on the bed, pulled on a clean shirt, opened the minibar and grabbed a can of cola. He took his shirt off again and put on a less formal one. Carlo would be here in ten minutes. After a frantic search through the pockets of his leather coat he found Morris and Ruth's card. He dialled.

'Morris, it's Luke. I need to see ... Ruth,' (Ruth, for heaven's sake, not Heloise), 'I need to talk to her. I'll come late morning tomorrow. I can't talk now; I've got to go. I'll see you.'

He had hardly put the phone down, when it rang. Carlo, parked dangerously outside the hotel, called to him from reception to come immediately. They set off across the city to the temporary opera stage set up in the Baths of Caracalla; Carlo, slicing through the traffic in true Roman fashion, whilst arranging his prospective conquests on the phone. Eventually he switched off his mobile and demanded a full account of Luke's adventures. Luke, looking across at his so competent cousin as he slipped his small Renault in and out of impossible gaps, gave him, perhaps unnecessarily, the cleaned up version of his triumphs. Carlo would probably have been the only one of his relatives who would both believe and not be shocked by the Maddalena episode, yet he felt reluctant to tell him. Discretion formed no part of Carlo's expansive and cheery character. He was an organiser, a networker, the nearest thing to an agent Luke possessed in Italy, an uncritical and reliable supporter, but he would be unable to resist telling his crowd about such a juicy event. Luke wanted to be known as a singer not a womaniser.

The technical rehearsal ran over; they always do. The noise of hammering and shouting interrupted every aria. The bells of Rome announced midnight and the crew were still messing with the lighting of the last act. By the time he reached the privacy of his hotel room again it was too late to ring Claudia or Barbara. He did try Dave again but got nothing. Fearing he would implode if he could not talk to someone who might understand him, he set the alarm for eight am the next morning.

He regretted this decision when it dragged him out of sleep at what felt like dawn. He groaned, picked up his mobile and dialled his sister.

'Claudia? Thank God!'

'Why are you ringing at this hour?'

'I have to talk to someone.'

'What's happened? Are you in trouble.'

'No, no. Nothing bad, just...' Luke rolled out of bed and went to peer through the shutters. 'You remember that weaving show I took Mum to not long after I came out of hospital...?'

'No, should I?

'Never mind. I did take her and one of the weavers was the blind girl who had been rescued from Cardon Street before me.' With the phone clamped to his ear, Luke walked in to the bathroom, peered at himself in the mirror and returned to the bedroom. 'Only she wasn't at the exhibition because she had pneumonia. They wouldn't let me talk to her because she was too ill and later because she refused to talk to anyone about it. At least that's what they said.'

'What's this all about, Luke? You sound funny, you all right?'

'She's Heloise ... Claudia, you there? I'm not making this up. I've met her here, in Rome.'

'What d'you mean? You mean you've found Heloise.'

'Yes, but...'

'Oh Luke, that's fantastic. Are you quite, quite sure? Have you talked to her? What does she say?...What's the matter?'

'I talked to her, but I had to rush off. I sang in Rigoletto on some crazy mountain top the night before last. Never mind that...' Luke had been walking in ever decreasing circles round the hotel bedroom while he talked to Claudia in the wild hope of keeping a lid on the seething tears that threatened to overflow. He gave up, stopped by the window and clung to the curtain to keep himself upright. 'She's all wrong, Claudia.'

'Luke? You're crying, aren't you? What's wrong with her?'

'She's blind. She looks like ... well she looks odd and ... she's called Ruth for chrissake'

'Oh Luca! Are you quite sure it's Heloise?'

'Yes, she admits it. She lied to me.'

'Poor Topo. Listen, the important thing is that she's real. This means you're not sick, Luke. There's nothing wrong with your mind. Your brain is not injured.'

'But don't you see, Claudia, my brain was never sick before. I was fine. It was you who'd got it all wrong. The trouble is, *now* I feel sick. I feel sicker than I have ever felt in my life.'

'Luke, Luca, it's all right. Mum will come. I can't, nor can Barbara and Dad's in Portugal – I think. But Mum could come. Don't do anything crazy. Is Carlo there? What about the performance? Are you on tonight?'

'Yes. I performed totally unrehearsed the other night. Don't hassle me, I'll sing – whatever. It's the dress today. It's not the singing that's the problem. It's inside me, I feel as though there is an explosion about to take place in my chest.'

'Luke, you're to ring Aunt Clara's cousin, Doctor Vitorelli *now*. You must have a check up. It may just be psycho ... it may just be shock, but you should have a check-up. *Please* Topo.'

Luke sighed. 'All right, Claudia, but this time I think it is a shrink I need. My mind feels like someone drove a motor through my brain. My body's working fine really: in the last forty-eight hours I've been to Piacenza and back, I've been in a helicopter, I've sung a major role in a public opera venue for the first time, I've even made ... I'm talking crap. I know; you've got to go to work. I'm going to see Heloise or Ruth or whatever she calls herself later ... Yes, yes, don't worry, I'll see Vitorelli. I'll be all right. Anyway, at least the performance on the mountain seems to have been a blinding success. I was 'bravoed' to the stars.'

Luke, hiding behind dark glasses, walked up the Via San Martino again. He peered into the Galleria Botticelli, hoping to surprise Ruth, but only Morris and a middle-aged couple stood there.

'*Si, vende*, yes, for sale.' Morris pointed to the ticket. The couple talked to each other in a strange language. Morris flicked Luke a glance to say I'll be with you presently, then stood with his head inclined towards the couple and his eyes on Luke, his feet and fingers twitching at intervals.

Luke looked at his watch. He had an hour, yet this infinitesimal delay felt like a personal insult. He reached out and let his fingers wander up the rough surface of the great weaving beside him. Morris flinched, though he could barely have seen the movement. Satisfied to have gained a reaction, Luke moved until he could not be ignored and put his whole hand on a silk weaving in pale greens and blues. Morris's sharp intake of breath, gave Luke acute satisfaction.

'Scusi!' Morris turned from the couple. 'Please *non toccare*. Luke, please ...Don't handle them.'

Luke kept his hand on the delicate cloth. Morris, his eyes flicking from the trespassing hand to Luke's face, hurried over. 'You want to talk?'

'Sure I want to talk ...to Ruth.'

'She's not here until later, can I help? Please, the silk can absorb moisture very quickly.'

Luke lifted his hand. 'Did you *know*? Did *you* know?' Morris opened his mouth. 'Did you know Ruth was Heloise?'

'No, I swear it! You're mad with us aren't you? Please don't be mad with me. I don't know what's going on with Ruth. She's been different ever since the explosion. I knew something was wrong, but her parents had died, she'd lived through that nightmare – I thought that was it. I never knew she'd met you, I swear it. I tried to persuade her to see you, honestly, and Nina's been on at her ever since you talked to her. Ruth just clammed up. She ...we ...'

The couple who had been looking at the weaving left the shop in a huff. Luke watched them with a sense of detached satisfaction. The only thing that mattered was getting his hands on Ruth; their exit represented one obstacle less. He just had to deal with Morris now.

'Where is Ruth?'

'At the Pensione.' Morris, his hands perpetually smoothing the leather strap of the bag on his shoulder, kept his distance. With one foot he began tracing a pattern on the floor like a child. He looked up at Luke in snatches. 'She won't come in. I don't know what to do.'

'Give me the address.'

'I can't do that, Luke. She's frightened.'

'Christ! What's she frightened of?'

'I don't know. You, I suppose.'

'She didn't seem frightened yesterday; she seemed pretty cool to me.'

'She was all shaky when she came back. Anyway, she's frightened about something now.' Morris suddenly planted his feet and looked directly up at Luke's menacing figure. 'Luke, I haven't the foggiest notion what all this is about. Could you just fill me in?' he pleaded. 'Ruth just cries and says she wishes she'd died in the explosion. How can I help if I don't know what the hell is going on.'

Luke flung himself in the chair behind the desk and muttered, 'If she dies before she's explained what she was up to, I'll kill her.' He looked up at Morris, challenging him to laugh, then leant on the desk, his head in his hands and continued indistinctly, 'Sorry, Morris, I guess this is nothing to do with you. If she lied to you too, you wouldn't know. She saved my life, you know. I should be all over her with gratitude. I've spent a year searching for her to say ... to thank ... to go on with conversations we started, plans we made. She was with me the whole fucking time in that building – the post office.' Luke took off his dark glasses, pushed back his hair and looked up frowning. 'No, that's not right. She found me soon after I woke up, but she said that I'd been unconscious for hours. I've got to talk to her, Morris. I ... they ... the doctors, my family, they think ... thought I was mad, that my brain was damaged. They thought I had made it all up because no such person as Heloise existed.'

Morris, seeing Luke limp and submissive, ventured to approach. 'I didn't know any of this, truly. I can tell you that Ruth's been unhappy, that she's had something on her mind. I just thought it was her parents dying, especially Dan. I mean, Christ that's enough to throw anyone, it was appalling to see him in such pain. I didn't have any idea about her being with you. I mean, why wouldn't she tell me about that?' Morris put a hand on the desk and leant over Luke. 'How about you telling me the whole story and maybe I'll be able to understand what's got into her? Maybe I'll be able to persuade her to meet you.'

'Only Ruth knows the whole story; that's the trouble. I wasn't always with it – because of the bang on my head ... and my hands were trapped. She stayed with me, she ... she looked after me. When everything seemed unbearable she distracted me. But she said her name was Heloise, she said she was twenty-five and that she had fair hair. At least that's what I remember, but I fell asleep sometimes. Then she heard noises, she left ... she had to leave me.'

Luke hastily replaced his glasses just as a customer walked in. He looked at his watch. 'I have to go now. For God's sake get her to talk to me.'

Luke dragged himself through the dress rehearsal, distracted by the need to see Ruth and the fear that she would slip out of his grasp again. While he was off stage during a break he tried Morris's number again.

'Well?'

'Luke, I'm sorry, I'm not doing very well here. There isn't a good time between now and when Ruth and Nina fly back on Saturday. Besides, Ruth is still resisting. All she will say is that it's too late and she can't change anything now. She knows you will hate her and there is no point in meeting.'

'Jesus! Tell her . . . tell her I don't hate her; she saved my life for chrissake. I just want to understand. I need to know. Please Morris, she's got to talk to me.'

'Look Luke, when are you back in England again? Come to my place when she's working, or come and eat with us. I'll make sure you get some time with Ruth and I'll tell her she owes you an explanation.'

Dancing with frustration Luke said, 'I'm not back for three weeks; I can't wait that long. What about tomorrow at ten.'

'I'll try again, but I don't think . . . and there's Nina. You can come and harangue me if you like. I shall be in the gallery again tomorrow.'

'OK, I'll come. I've got to go now, I'm on again.'

The next morning Luke had a costume refit. He was occupied all day and found himself, still in a state of turmoil, about to go on stage for the first performance of the Roman Rigoletto. How would he obliterate the knowledge that Heloise/Ruth would be there in front of him listening and yet refusing to speak to him? His mobile pinged to alert him to a text message. With slippery hands he pressed the buttons and read, "Gordon says you found Heloise. Great news! He and Maria send love. Show the Romans how it's done. Dave".

Ruth sat between Morris and a perspiring Nina dreaming of a miracle. The scales would fall from her eyes and Luke would be there in front of her. Whatever else happened she would have this evening. Luke would sing. She could re-live moments in that echoing, clammy nest a year ago, when Luke's voice did not just go into her ears, but surrounded her head; she could even breath it in. In spite of the mess she had made of everything, she could hang on to the one precious residue from those hours under the rubble: for that short period, for the only time in her life, she had been the most necessary thing in the world to another human being. Hours when she became familiar with Luke's soft skin. Strange that a man's skin should be made of the same stuff as her own, yet feel so deliciously alien.

A brief overture – then Luke's voice. Bright, casual and care-free, it sounded unlike the voice she clung to in memory. She had to wait until the second scene where he woos Rigoletto's daughter to hear again the tones that returned her to the past. With this voice her body remembered the soft sculpture of Luke's body. Her mind remembered the discovery of his fragile humanity, which like footprints in virgin snow had immediacy and wonder beyond her experience. Minutes later, as Gilda sang her besotted hymn *(Caro nome...beloved name...)* to the false name of the man she has fallen in love with, Ruth sat overwhelmed by layers of revela-tion. Like Gilda she was in thrall to someone who could never be hers, who belonged to a different world. Just as Gilda had lied to her father and would end up paying with her life, Ruth knew she could not escape from the position she had placed herself in; she would be always longing for something out of reach. She would not meet with Luke again. There was no point.

By the time Luke was next able to visit the gallery neither Ruth nor Morris were there. By this time, too, the media had caught up with him. His youth, his looks, his glorious last minute sub-stitution in the mountains, his recent debut in Rome, the older story of the rescue in the London explosion all combined with his golden voice to bring the hungry press to his doorstep. Carlo did his inexperienced best to manage the flood of interest and Luke flourished in the warmth of attention. He even found the endless interviews a distraction from his trouble over Ruth. The only dif-ficulty came when an English interviewer asked, 'Did they ever solve the mystery of the girl in the post office with you – the one who went missing?'

Luke's easy flow came to a halt. He stared at the avid woman in front of him, thinking fast. Eventually he said flatly, 'She died.' Seeing further questions in the reporter's eye he added, 'I've been to see her parents.' As soon as he could, he signalled to Carlo to finish the session. After this he gave Carlo an ultra-simplified version of his encounter with Sylvie before the explosion and his visit to her parents afterwards. Then he mentioned, as casually as he could, that the blind weaver had been rescued from the building too. Carlo had little interest in Ruth, who he had seen and discounted on looks alone. He decided that the press should be allowed the Sylvie story though not, he promised Luke, her name.

From then on, in an attempt to make the loss of the image he had built around Heloise more bearable, Luke began setting about a mental substitution of Sylvie for this mythical being. He could accept and mourn for the dead Sylvie; he could not cope with the living Ruth.

A week later Luke managed to get to the little gallery again. This turned out to be the last day of the weaving exhibition. He found Morris alone and beginning to pack up. Nina and Ruth had already been gone for a week.

Morris, after a cautious glance, seemed pleased to see him. 'Luke, I'm so glad you came before I left. You're a busy man these days. I wanted to tell you how brilliantly we all thought you sang in Rigoletto. I think you were the only thing Nina liked about Rome and as for Ruth, well ... Anyway we could have listened all night, you sang beautifully.'

'Thanks Morris, better, I think, than I sang the role up on that mountain, though the press are hooked on the drama of that one. This is a better production to start with. Anyway, I came hoping to sort something out about meeting Ruth. It's crazy that she'll come and hear me sing, yet she refuses to see me face to face. I must talk to her.'

'Look, I've been thinking about this, like I suggested, your best bet is to come to lunch at my place as soon as you're back in England. Ruth works there most days. We'll be flat out because the Grosjean are showing us in New York in three month's time.'

'I'll be in New York mid September too, I've got a couple of days on my way back from Chicago.'

Morris grinned. 'Our paths seem bound to cross, don't they? I won't tell her you're coming. I don't like to deceive her, but I can't think how else to do it. If she's scared I'll stay with her. Do you know, I think she's more embarrassed than anything else.'

Luke laughed dryly, 'That figures. I mean if you'd told a stranger several almighty lies and then been found out ... But we were there for so long. We got to know each other, we ... ' Luke stopped.

'If you got to know Ruth you're doing well. She isn't like other people. She's half grown up, half a child still. Her visual world faded out between the ages of seven and nine. It doesn't help either that her mother was a maniac.'

Instantly suspicious, Luke snapped, 'She said her mother was religious.'

'Religious nothing, she was a witch. She just used religion like a power tool to demolish anything or anyone in her way.'

'Oh!' Luke paced over towards the desk and picked up a flyer with Ruth's photo on it. He stared at the uncommunicative face with its dark frame of hair. This person just would not join up with the Heloise he knew. 'It still doesn't make sense. Why did she lie to me in the first place?'

'Look, it's no good grilling *me*. When are you back in London? Friday week? OK come to my place in Greenwich – we have our workshop in the basement of my house – on the following Monday. I'll make sure she's there. And Luke, I'm sorry about all this. Please try not to blame Ruth too much, she's had a rotten deal, but she's all right – extraordinary really.

26
Greenwich & Richmond: Ruth & Sylvie

In the doorway of Luke's house in Catford, Dave paused. He looked back at the hunched figure sitting on the bottom of the stairs. 'Do you want me to come with you? I can spare an hour round lunchtime.'

'No Dave, thanks but I don't want to involve Ruth with my friends. I must try and lose her, you know, undo all the stuff that links us.'

'I suppose. Though frankly I'm curious to see this phantom of yours. There must have been something about her that made you so...obsessional.'

'Her voice. That's all, there's nothing else left. OK, so I'm crazy, it's just that the sounds coming out of her throat they ... they make me want to lie down and purr. Anyway, my plan is to see her; make her to explain what the hell she was playing at; look at her until I'm cured of this weird sickness. Then I'm going to start my life again.'

'Yea, well, tough guy, I hope it works out.'

'What d'you mean.'

'Well, she sounds like a siren to me. This enchantment of yours has lasted a fair while; I'm not sure you can expect an overnight cure. How much time have you spent with her so far?'

'I don't need time. One look was enough.'

'You've seen her just the once?'

'Yup, for about ten minutes. I was talking to her when I got called for the Rigoletto substitution.'

'Jesus, man, ten minutes? You can't undo a year in ten minutes!'

'How long does it take you to decide you fancy someone, then?'

'Luke, you're looking at this from the wrong end. This isn't some chick you've just met and you're wondering whether she's on or not, this is a long relationship – at least from your end – that you're trying to wrap up. Undoing is more difficult than starting.'

'Dave, I've thought this through. I am dead sure about it. This woman is in a different zone from me. We've got nothing together.' Dave opened his mouth, then after checking Luke's face, shut it again. There seemed little point in reminding him that for the last twelve months he had been repeating *ad nauseam* his belief that he had something special in common with this same woman.

'All right, play it your way. Give me a call if you change your mind about my coming. OK?'

Luke looked at his watch. He had a couple of hours before he needed to catch the bus. He decided, uncharacteristically, to walk from Catford to Greenwich, something he had done occasionally in his teens as a way of accruing cash, by saving his bus fare. It would also mop up the waiting time. The August air turned out to be damp and heavy in his lungs, quite unlike the dry Roman atmosphere and with the addition of traffic fumes he began to regret his decision. Still, Blackheath felt pleasantly open and by the time he found himself descending the hill into Greenwich the sun freed itself properly from the surrounding cloud and the day suddenly improved.

Luke arrived at the tall, dilapidated Georgian house in Borrow Crescent and met Morris on the doorstep. He was shown in and taken straight down narrow stairs to the basement.

'Ruth, I've brought Luke to see you. He needs to talk to you, he needs to understand why you told him the things you did after the explosion.'

Ruth froze, she had just pushed the bobbin back into the shuttle and she stood, with it still gripped in her hand. She whispered, 'Luke?'

Morris patted her shoulder. 'Yes. I'm going to leave you two to talk for a bit. I'll be in my workroom. You can call me if you need me. Luke won't eat you, just tell him the truth.'

Neither spoke as Morris left the room, but Ruth looked towards Luke as if she knew exactly where he stood. 'Ruth,' he said as calmly as possible, 'I just need to know why, when you knew I was searching for you, you refused to see me and let everyone think I was mad?' Ruth took a breath but seemed unable to speak. Luke pressed, 'Why?'

She bent her head. 'Because I am not the person you thought I was.'

Amazement held Luke speechless for a moment, amazement

not at what she said, but that this unprepossessing stranger should own the voice of the woman he had been so utterly convinced that he loved. Her voice still flowed instantly to the pleasure centres of his mind, while her unfamiliar form stalled in his vision. This aching reminder of the sensations from those hours underground perversely made the anger that he had so successfully repressed during the intervening weeks begin to bubble up again. He gripped an upright wooden beam and tried to keep his voice even. 'Why on earth did you act as someone else in the first place?'

Ruth muttered. 'I was just pretending.'

'Pretending?'

'Yes, I...'

'Jesus! You find this poor mug trapped in a trashed up building and you think it's a good time for playing games. You think I'm some kind of dupe? Christ!'

'Luke, no...'

'And don't you dare tick me off for swearing.'

'I wasn't going to. It wasn't like that, really. I didn't think of you as a . . . as a dupe. None of it seemed real. I thought . . . It seemed more like a story than real life; a story we would never get out of. So I thought we...I...could pretend a bit. I'm sorry. I'm so sorry. I would do anything to change it, but it's too late.'

'You've had a year to do something about it. You refused to see me.' Luke heard the sneer in his tone and couldn't stop it. 'They thought I was mad, you know? I had to see shrinks...God how humiliating.'

'Shrinks?' the wobble in her voice gave him satisfaction.

'You know, psychobabble artists, psychiatrists, counsellors, therapists, sick-mind doctors. Claudia – my sister – strewed them in my path at every turn. *You're* the one who should be seeing a shrink.'

'I didn't mean...never mind.' Ruth, silenced, sat with the shuttle in one hand the other spread flat, fingering the warp threads of her work. Luke looked down at the hand, at the newly filled and the still empty areas of weaving, at the complex arrangements of wools and bobbins, impressed in spite of himself.

Speaking more naturally, he tried to get back on track. 'Why did you tell me your name was Heloise?'

Her voice almost inaudible, Ruth went on. 'Well I had this doll...'

'This what?'

'A doll. I called her Heloise and ...'

'A doll? *A doll?*' He ran his fingers through his hair gripping it in exasperation. 'I don't believe this. You really are living in cloud-cuckoo land.' Ruth shrank as if expecting a blow. 'I'm sorry!' He turned his back on Ruth and walked over to the glass door between the studios. 'Go on.'

Through the partition came familiar sounds. Morris had put on the Verdi Requiem. Luke concentrated on the sound urging his mind to be diverted into guessing which recording Morris had chosen. Cupping his hands around his eyes as he tried to peer through. *Dies irae* ... Who was conducting? Giulini?

From behind him Ruth spoke. 'It's the Karajan recording with Carreras, Baltsa and Van Dam. I forget the soprano.'

Once again Heloise's voice, like a glass of brandy swallowed too fast, flooded his senses. He leant his head against the coolness of the door. 'How ...' bitter confusion edged his tone, 'how did you guess that's what I wanted to know?'

With an anxious laugh, she answered, 'I heard you listening. You went over to the door. We've got the other Karajan too, with Freni and Ghiaurov, but this is my favourite recording.'

Luke turned slowly, only to be rocked by the discrepancy between the voice that matched his inner image and the stranger's face. Unable to quell his anger or think how to get Ruth to give him answers he could bear to listen to, or to marry up her voice with her appearance, Luke simply opened the door to Morris's studio and walked through it. Morris, startled, got up from his seat at the loom and came over. 'Luke! That was quick! How's it going?'

Luke slapped his open palm to his forehead, 'She says she was pretending. *Pretending*, for Chrissake! And Heloise turns out to be a doll. Talking to her is like ...' Luke shook his head.

'Interviewing a kitten?' Morris suggested. As Luke snorted, Morris raised his eyebrows sympathetically. 'I do know what it's like. Most of the time I rather like not knowing what is going to come out of her mouth, but sometimes it can be exasperating as hell.' He hesitated, then making a decision, loosely knotted the threads he had been sorting and put his head through Ruth's door. 'All right, Ruth? I'm just going to take Luke up to the kitchen.

219

Lunch in a minute. I'll call you.' He closed the door and led the way into a passage with stairs up to the next floor. 'Come with me and, I'll try and explain some stuff you need to know if you're going to make sense of Ruth.'

He ascended the narrow staircase, talking as he went. 'It's one of the many conundrums in my life – Ruth's personality; I sometimes think she's an alien. You'd expect her to be like one of us, I mean Dan, Martha, me or even Nina, I mean we're pretty much all the people she's ever met, unless you count her one month in the blind school.' He started getting stuff out of the fridge and Luke dropped into a chair at the kitchen table. 'I don't know what happened to Dan and Martha's genes. Ruth seems to be completely independent in her mind and it's not as if anyone else has had much input. Martha was a raving lunatic – sort of self invented Christian fundamentalist. She re-interpreted the bible according to some mysterious agenda of her own,' Morris turned to Luke, 'that all sounds too warm, she was cold, callous and bigoted. She could out-argue a Machiavelli and she was about as motherly as a snake . . . never mind. Dan – he's my uncle – would have been normal except that Martha scared him rigid. Nina's OK, but not exactly mainstream late twentieth century, a bit Mrs Tiggiwinkle, and then there's me – I'm the nearest thing to normal that Ruth knows and, well, I'm a little off-centre too.'

'She never went to school. Martha fooled everyone, even the odd inspector. I mean the girl doesn't know an atom from an anteater. I told her stuff in the holidays, but she's not grounded in the same kind of reality as the rest of us. Add to that the fact that she hasn't *seen* the real world fully since she was six or seven. The blindness came on slowly, between seven and nine. Martha and Dan didn't understand at first why she crashed around hurting herself all the time, and grew so introverted. The more irritated they became, the more she closed in on herself. You begin to get the picture.'

Luke sighed. 'I suppose. But under that building we were both in the dark and we talked about everything. I mean we got close. Why hold me off for a year? If I hadn't walked into that gallery, I'd still be considered crazy.'

'There's no way back now, Luke. Just hang on for a bit, she may be more forthcoming when she has got used to you being here. I'm going to call her for lunch now.'

They sat, the three of them, in the cool light of the East facing kitchen, eating bread and soup. Morris talked to Ruth about her work and their timetable. They would overlap for one day with Luke in New York. Luke watched Ruth intently. She appeared, to his surprise, to be able to eat as if she could see. A part of him did not want to observe this competence; he needed negative input so that he could cut this incubus out of his being.

Morris leant across the table; 'Luke, you know Ruth made me drive over eighty miles to hear your Petite Messe in Aberdeen last December. That's when I realised you were *you*. I mean when I met you in the hospital looking for this girl and again at our exhibition I didn't know you were a singer.'

'You were there? In Aberdeen?'

Morris nodded. Luke worked out that if they had come up afterwards and spoken to him then, he would have known about Ruth by Christmas. Maybe he would have been able to convince Melanie that he was serious, he would have been able to show Claudia that his mind had not been affected. He would not have sung his first big role while battling with unappeasable anger.

Almost as if she wanted to provoke him, Ruth added, 'Morris wanted to come and see you after the performance, but I wouldn't let him.'

Exasperated, Luke flung back his fist and hit the wall sharply. It made a surprisingly loud noise.

Ruth jumped and drew a ragged, frightened breath. 'What was that?'

'It's all right, Ruth; Luke just thumped the wall and hit the spot over the old hatch.'

Ruth pressed her palms against her cheeks: 'You're still angry with me, Luke. But you see, when I found you, I *knew* you were going to die. You had blood all over your head; you'd been unconscious for hours. I didn't think it mattered what I told you. I just wanted to make you happy ...'

Still propelled by anger, Luke interrupted. 'So, it was all right to lie to me when you thought I was dying. Not so good when I'm walking around no longer at your mercy?'

Morris put an arm round Ruth. 'Steady on, Luke. She did what seemed best at the time. Don't make things worse now.'

Ruth reached out seeking to touch Luke, but he had pushed back his chair. She turned instead to Morris. 'No, no, it's not Luke's fault. I understand that he's angry. I just don't know what to do about it now.'

Appalled at himself, Luke spoke jerkily. 'I'm sorry. I didn't mean to alarm you. I leap like crazy at sudden noises these days. I just seem to be more jittery than I used to be.' He pulled himself up from the table. 'I didn't mean to be rude either. It's just that I've been waiting a year to make sense of all this and I still feel as though I'm in the dark ...' He stopped abruptly staring down at Ruth's unfocused eyes. 'O God, that was stupid. Sorry! I think I'd better go now. I'm supposed to be seeing ...I've got to go. I'll give you a ring.'

Feeling ruffled and guilty, Luke left the flat and strode down into Greenwich proper. He still had two hours before he was due at Sylvie's parent's house. He wondered how he could have agreed to see them both on the same day. He texted Barbara to say he had made a mess of things and been horrid to Ruth.

Leaning against the railings of the National Maritime Museum, he stared at the Queen's House, serenely occupying the centre of a giant lawn, and the classical buildings to either side. Everything spoke of symmetry, with the great colonnades flanking the Inigo Jones masterpiece, each pillar locked to its plinth and the plinth to the land beneath. The whole structure stood there, sure of itself and convinced of its central position in the scheme of things. Only a year ago his life had had this same grounded, balanced quality. Now, the very paving beneath his feet could barely be relied upon.

How could Ruth speak with Heloise's voice? How could Sylvie have looked as she did and be so very dead, so absent, so wiped out? What about Sylvie's parents, expecting him this afternoon? What if he messed up there too? Yet he had to see them, it must have been Sylvie he'd been thinking about all this time. Since meeting Ruth the possibility that he had confused the two women swept in and out of his mind. To admit this would mean that his brain had been affected by the injury, so that he had exchanged parts of his memory under the building. To deny this possibility would mean that Ruth was all he had of Heloise.

After dithering some time, and being reminded by his mother that he had promised to see them a year after his first visit, he had finally rung Sylvie's parents yesterday. He half hoped there would be no answer; that they might have moved. They had not. Gulda answered the phone on the first ring. Luke had the unnerving sensation that she had been waiting all year by the phone for him to call. Yes, she said calmly, they would be delighted to see him, what about tomorrow? Luke agreed, thinking he could get all the explosion stuff sorted out in one day and then start his life afresh when he got to Chicago the following week. He must have been crazy. Luke let go of the railing and stared at his hands imprinted with the iron bars he had been gripping.

His phone pinged with a text. send ruth flowers. Ba x. He walked back into Greenwich and stopped at a florist. He hovered over some crimson roses then imagined Ruth receiving them and sent freesias instead. Then he bought the roses as well for Sylvie's parents. Feeling marginally lighter, he walked on towards the bus stop.

In the same blinding sunlight on nearly the same day as the previous year, Luke walked down Rosemary Road again. His eyes swept up and down, looking for the anomaly in this pastel suburban street, the stark red, white and green of Sylvie's parent's house. Nothing had changed. The window boxes looked as if they had been planted freshly the day before. Luke let out his breath. He would not have been entirely surprised if Peter and Gulda had stopped bothering with the surface of things when their world cracked apart a year ago.

Luke knocked and stared down at his extremely clean and respectable shoes. His abiding image of his last visit had been the balding grey/brown of his trainers against the new-sheet whiteness of their sofas. He felt he had been discovered in bed with his shoes on. Luke lifted his hand to knock again, half-hoping that they had misunderstood his phone call and gone out.

He heard footsteps at last and the door opened. The man in the doorway had shrunk. Last year he had been thickset with rounded, high coloured cheeks. Now, still dressed in what were clearly his original clothes, he almost rattled inside the fabric. Luke looked at Peter and in a parody of their last meeting stumbled and nearly fell over the doorstep, so that Peter had once more to grasp his arm. He led the way into the sitting room, then turned and clasped Luke's hand in both of his. 'Luca, you look well, you look very different from the sick young man of a year since. I am very pleased.' He shouted, 'Gulda, he is come.'

Luke, unable to return the compliment, said, 'I've been in Italy for the last three months, so I've had a bit of sunshine.'

'Yes, it's good. It's very good. Ah Gulda, see how this young man has become so well again since last year.'

'I am happy,' she announced, also clasping his hand between her warm palms. 'Sit you down. I shall get some tea and cake, yes?'

Luke checked her with an outstretched hand. 'Do you mind if I have coffee instead? I'm not used to tea.'

She smiled. 'Yes, coffee we have. You shall have some.' She leant over suddenly and patted his cheek. '*So* handsome, Sylvie would have been very happy. Coffee? Yes.' She trotted out.

Luke and Peter sat in silence a heartbeat longer than was comfortable, then Peter spoke. 'Helga tells us that you came to see her.'

'Yes, we met up. She was very kind and showed me the sights of Copenhagen. She told me about that day in Cardon Street. Now that I've spoken to her I remember better. I *did* talk to your daughter – to Sylvie. I went into the post office, just to be with her.'

Peter nodded. 'Yes, we know.'

Gulda returned carrying a tray. Luke tried not to look startled. A strawberry-topped cake, large enough to feed the chorus of Nabucco, occupied the centre of the tray; four or five other rose-decorated plates held sugared biscuits, tiny buns with iced wings, chocolate slabs and smartie-covered sticky cakes. Had he strayed into a children's party? Had she made all this just because he was coming today? Who would eat it all? He had a fair appetite, but Peter clearly lived on air these days and Gulda's proportions indicated a perfectly normal desire for food.

Puffing slightly under the weight, she deposited the tray on a central table in front of Luke's popping eyes. She smiled confidently and his memory stirred. Last year, they had been trying to cope with Birthday Cards arriving for Sylvie from people who still did not know. They thought he had remembered.

'You would like some cake?' He nodded, trying not to look daunted. Gulda bustled about supplying each of them with a plate, a cup of tea or coffee, a little table to put these on, a napkin to cope with the sticky fingers and a fork for the cream-filled cake. Then she filled the plates and finally sank onto the sofa beside Peter, saying to Luke as he took a large bite of cake, 'Now, you tell us about your meeting with Helga.'

Luke settled back into the sofa and, while working his way with pleasure through a plateful of sublime home baking, talked about Helga. Then listened to them talking about Sylvie and finally he talked about his own work and his family. He spoke more freely than he had for months. Here were people who lived in the same shadow that he now lived in. A shadow that others could not comprehend or assumed had vanished with the shovelling up of the rubble. The bruising encounter with Ruth earlier today became overlaid with the enveloping tenderness of these two people and Luke, who a couple of hours ago had begun to seriously dislike himself, felt a fragment of self-respect seeping back in.

Laden with cake and soothed by their overwhelming warmth, Luke asked if he might see the photos again. He turned over page after page saying little. He had to stop himself whimpering out loud. The mismatch between the bright-eyed, glowing girl inhabiting the albums and the dark, lanky woman with hazy eyes who had enraged him this morning, made him shudder. That the first had died and the second lived, struck Luke as a piece of divine bad taste. Becoming aware of his thoughts, he looked up blushing. Sylvie's parents sat watching, heads tilted, eyes begging for something out of his power to supply. Luke dropped his eyes again.

'Luca, did you ever find the girl you first came to ask about? I forget the name.'

With an overwhelming sense of relief, Luke said, 'Yes, I found her in Rome. Only a few weeks ago, actually.' Dear God is it really only weeks? 'She's blind.'

'Blinded from the explosion? Poor girl!'

'No, no! No. It happened when she was a child, I think. She didn't tell me about the blindness when we were stuck under the building. She…well she told me stories. That's why I couldn't find her afterwards; she didn't want me to find out she hadn't been telling the truth. She's a weaver, she lives in London, but she had an exhibition in Rome – really fantastic work – and I went to see it. I recognised her voice. She knew I'd been searching for her. She let me go on thinking that she was ... she was just imaginary or something or that I was sick in the head.'

Gulda wrinkled her brow. 'She must be very clever but also a strange, unhappy girl.'

'Yes, she's a bit odd. She has a special voice and her work is astonishing.' What else could he say? Luke stared at the pale carpet. When he looked up again Peter nodded.

'Hmm, you are angry young man, yes?'

'I don't understand why she had to lie. She knew I was searching for her. We talked under that building, we made plans, we ...' Luke stopped. Perhaps they hadn't kissed; perhaps he had muddled Sylvie and Ruth. He looked down at the album in his hands; it must have been Sylvie's lovely mouth he could almost still feel. And yet, he could remember his conversation with Sylvie now; they had not had time to kiss, surely. He sighed. 'I'm sorry. I was foolish to make plans in the first place. This is not important to you.'

'It is important, Luca. We, too, are foolish. We too pretend. We say to ourselves, maybe Luke would have been together with Sylvie, maybe they would have married, maybe they would have had babies,' he stroked his wife's hand as two tears tracked through the powder on her cheeks, 'so we want you to come and see us, then we can go on with this foolish pretending. And you did come. You come to share Sylvie's birthday with us.' Peter beamed. 'Sometimes it is better to be foolish.'

27

New York: Luke & Ruth

Luke stopped the taxi. He walked the last two blocks along the edge of Central Park then turned towards the hotel where Ruth and Morris were staying. Whatever he had expected from this brief walk, it had failed to materialize. Neither the exercise nor the crowded pavements nor the vast buildings answered the overriding question in his mind; why had he committed himself to an evening with Ruth? Why, just when he was feeling good again, with the auditions in Chicago going like a dream and the two days of informal meetings in New York yielding engagements not only for three years hence, but a big role-share for next year, had he set himself up for another dusting? He had a miraculously clear evening because of a rescheduled flight. He needn't have done it. He had merely phoned Morris to find out where their exhibition was being held, then, when Morris had said he was occupied but Ruth was on her own that evening, he heard himself suggesting he take her out. He must have been mad. Morris would have found someone to look after her; the Gallery had permanent staff in New York, for heaven's sake. Although he had managed to make things better on the phone after their last disastrous meeting in London, it was unlikely to be a bundle of fun. Maybe it was that; maybe he had to exorcise that visit in case it had been his fault. Of course it had been his fault. So why was he out here looking for more trouble? Some confused idea that New York might be neutral territory, perhaps?

He walked past the hotel. For a moment he imagined ringing Ruth, saying sorry, but something important had come up. He stopped to consult his inner demons and found himself staring at his reflection in a shop window – a drugstore. His image veered to the left in the misshapen glass. As a small child he had once been taken to a room with distorting mirrors in some museum. The images wobbled and showed him first a Rubens then a Munch version of himself with several oddities in between. In dismay he had run out of the Hall of Mirrors and for months afterwards had checked out his six-year-old body in every possible reflective surface. Why should a few seconds of image disturbance need so much repair and reintegration? Now his mind, like those mirrors, offered three unsettled internal images of himself: carefree pre-explosion Luke, angry post-explosion Luke, and finally the heart-sick fool who lived in a ruined building, chained to a disembodied voice called Heloise. No amount of mental blinking seemed able to make the mercury coalesce and bring unity. He had told Dave that he would look at Ruth until he was cured of Heloise. Well, that day in London had not been enough; he just needed a little longer. So he *did* need to see her tonight. He frowned and felt, as he sometimes did, a tiny pull from his scars.

He went into the drugstore for five minutes of air condition-ing and on a whim bought a cooled half bottle of Champagne. That should make things feel better. He would take it up to her and they would drink it before going out. He left the shop feeling better pleased with himself.

Uncertainty overtook him again as he stood in the repressive entrance hall of the hotel. The receptionist phoned through to tell Ruth he was here, staring all the while at his carrier bag as if she suspected a sinister motive. 'You're to go up,' she said finally, 'forty-ninth floor, room 4927. You're to go straight in.'

When he entered the room. Ruth was sitting in a cream-up-holstered chair, which someone had placed to catch the last rays of the sun. She was still wearing the inevitable shapeless cardi-gan but her dark hair, recently cut, dropped silkily, almost pret-tily onto her shoulders. The rather bare decor had acquired a bit of a golden sheen too. Ruth turned towards him, hands white as they clutched the arms of the chair. He was glad, after all, of his purchase.

'Hello Ruth, I like your new hair cut. I've brought a little bottle of Champagne with me.' He saw her head tilt and her hand lift as he moved towards her, unwrapping the bottle. 'You know, the stuff with bubbles.'

'I do know, you told me.'

'What d'you mean? When ...' Luke, bottle in hand, stopped half way across the room to hold onto the bed end. 'Yes ... Yes, I remember. I tried to sing the Champagne song from Fledermaus. I'd forgotten.'

'I've never drunk Champagne. Morris wanted me to drink

Champagne at the London Crafts festival prizegiving. Then I remembered that you weren't pleased that I went to my first opera without you. So I waited to drink some with you.'

Luke, reaching her side, opened and shut his mouth. Then, taking her hands, placed the cool bottle in them. 'Hold that a moment, while I find some glasses. Can you feel the funny cork? Do they have Champagne on the opening nights of your shows?' He *would* get used to that voice, he just had to see it coming out of Ruth's mouth for a little longer then the heartsick fool would stop tugging at his innards. He looked around the darkening room. 'Where's the minibar? There should be some glasses somewhere near it.' He saw it on the far side of the bed and went to turn on the light, then stopped. Ruth didn't need lights at all and the minimal lighting gave a pleasant backstage feel to the room.

Ruth, behind him, spoke again in Heloise's voice. 'I went to the Private View of our exhibition in Rome, but I didn't enjoy it very much; too many different things happening at once.' Luke turned to join up Heloise's voice with Ruth. 'They gave us some wine. I tried one sip and then left it.'

The rounded pop of the Champagne cork sounded out suddenly. Ruth jumped, 'Oh! What was that?'

'Sorry, I should have warned you; it's just the cork popping. There try that.' He put a half full glass in her hand, then held it and clinked her glass on to his. 'To your success in New York! Your weaving will sell out again.'

Ruth chuckled. 'Not all, I hope, we are running out of stock and I've done so much less work over the last year.'

'Well I hope you have a critical success then. Cheers!' As Ruth lifted the glass to her mouth, she pulled her head back suddenly, and Luke laughed. 'It's just the bubbles Ruth. Fight your way in. Go on. They just cool your face for a moment before the Champagne starts to warm you up.' Luke dropped on the corner of the bed, laughing at Ruth's screwed up face.

Ruth, hearing him, joined in. 'But Luke, do people *want* to drink this? It's so ... wet!'

'Oh Ruth, you do look funny. Just take one sip. Go on, that's a good girl, let it lie in your mouth for a minute to taste. Can you feel the bubbles pinging on your tongue?' She nodded. 'That's right. Now swallow it. Come on, it's not that bad. I bought the best – well nearly. Now have another sip. That's better.'

Ruth, blinking hard, her face eloquent with distaste, took three or four sips. He watched her, grinning. Finally she lifted her head towards him in surprise. 'Oh! You *are* right Luke. Once you get used to the bubbles it's ... it tingles. I like that.'

'Great.' he said, relaxing back onto the end of the bed. 'Got your gallery set up all right then today?'

'Yes, Morris seems quite happy. The press are coming tomorrow evening. I'm supposed to have bought a dress today, but there wasn't anyone left to help me.' Luke shook his head; someone should have been with her and sorted that kind of thing out. Almost as if she had read his mind, she added, 'It's no one's fault, Nina was going to come with me and help me choose, only she suddenly got called for her knee operation last week and she's been waiting eighteen months so she wasn't going to turn it down. She'll be joining us tomorrow.' She added half-jokingly: 'My last night of freedom. Luke ... ?'

He interrupted. 'Does Nina choose all your clothes?'

'Yes, she does now, Mama did it before.'

'I'm not sure she ... has kept up with the fashions, you know. Why don't you ask one of the others, one of the Grosjean Gallery people, surely Morris ...'

Ruth chuckled again. 'Morris is always wanting to get such funny clothes.' She took a breath. 'Luke?'

'Yes.'

'Luke, I want to ask you something.' She took another sip of Champagne then sat for a moment running her finger round the rim of her glass.

'Go ahead.'

'I know you said we could go out to supper, but we could have it brought up to the room.'

Post-explosion-Luke relaxed, he wouldn't have the complication of going out with her. He protested lightly. 'If you'd rather, but it's OK to go out, we can go by taxi. I've got a nice place in mind.'

'It's not that I mind going out.' She took another sip. 'I want to do something and you're the only person I can ask really. You remember, when we were stuck together after the explosion, when we ... when we talked about afterwards and you said that one day we would make love.' Luke's mouth opened, but nothing came out. 'I know everything is different now; but I'm nearly thirty, Luke. I've read about making love and it sounds...but it is never going to happen to me is it? Nobody else will ever ask me now. You remember, you told me you would show me?' Luke goggled at her, but of course she went serenely on. 'It's bad enough that I can't do things because I can't see. I want to make love just once. Not being able to see won't matter, will it?' Luke cleared his throat. After a moment Ruth continued a little less certainly, 'I thought men were always wanting...I thought you'd be pleased if...'

Luke cast a horrified glance at her glass of Champagne, but there was nothing spur-of-the-moment about her request. A deep and quite genuine shock turned his knees to sand. He wasn't sure where to start. Every possible opening that came to mind seemed to suggest an insult to Ruth. He cleared his throat again. 'Ruth, it's not as simple as that. You can't...you don't just ask any guy to...to sleep with you. I mean, you need a relationship of some sort first.'

'Don't we have a relationship?'

'No! I mean not that kind of relationship. I mean, you don't start sex with...sex,' he said in desperation. 'You have to do other things first, you know...I suppose you don't know.'

'We kissed, Luke. Don't you remember? I thought you liked it.'

Luke clutched the end of the bed, whispering, 'I thought that was just part of my dream.' He shook his head as if to resettle his memories. 'Heloise...I mean Ruth you still can't just...*do* sex all of a sudden like this.' He stared at the pale woman in the lumpy cardigan seated in front of him. 'Are you sure about the kissing?'

'Yes.'

He wondered if he was being punished. 'Are you teasing me? You can't be this naive, Ruth, is this your idea of a joke?' She shook her head, dumbly. He floundered. 'Anyway I...I don't even have any protection on me.'

'Protection?'

'Contraception ... ' seeing Ruth's face still unresponsive, he went on, 'er...baby stoppers?'

'Oh that won't matter. I had an operation when I was a

child. Mama explained, when I was much older of course, that I wouldn't ever have babies. She said it would be better. The blindness is genetic, you see. So it makes sense.'

Was there a bitter note under the appalling matter-of-factness? His thoughts, wandering hopelessly, met visions of Barbara's swelling tummy. Even Claudia planned to have several children and, without precisely dreaming of such a thing, he fully intended to have a family. So, instead of reassuring him that he could have safe sex with her, Ruth's admission made her even less a whole woman to him. She might as well have turned on a cold shower.

In the ensuing silence he watched her helplessly. Her sightless eyes pinned so convincingly to his face, took on doubt. 'Come near me, Luke. I can't feel what you're thinking.' Luke let go of the bed end, pulled the dressing table stool nearer to her chair and sat down beside her. He stared at the great white-covered bed. He was perplexed in an area that had always seemed straightforward to him.

Ruth put her hand out; it brushed his neck and settled on his shoulder. Sweat rose on his forehead. His body was in the process of being aroused and repelled in measures so finely balanced as to deprive him of further speech or movement. Her voice, and now her hand, as its warmth reached through his shirt, stirred all his fantasies; of course they might not be fantasies or even dreams, they might be real memories. Memories? Had this unfamiliar, gauche woman on the chair beside him, once kissed him into a state of acute excitement?

He had to know; he had to ask her exactly what she remembered; yet to do so would make this crazy proposition of hers inevitable. His mind screamed out warnings to him. You want another dream crushed? Go ahead then, Luke. Go for broke. You're fucked up enough already, what does one more wrong move matter?

A slight pressure from her fingers interrupted his tumbling thoughts. 'Luke, when you taught me how to kiss, you talked about other things, things we would do one day. You said it would be fine, and you would teach to me to enjoy that, too.' Luke sat on, incapable of speech. In a whisper, with tears behind it, she went on, 'I thought you would be pleased, because I've not been with anyone else.'

He leapt up suddenly, wailing, 'But I thought you were Heloise.'

She paused for a moment head to one side as if she were re-running his words and then said flatly, 'Heloise was beautiful and Ruth is not.' It was not a question.

He waved his hands about helplessly. 'No, no it's not that. It is just that Ruth is someone else. I don't *know* Ruth.' He stopped suddenly as a truth walked in through the door he had just opened in his mind. He went on speaking more slowly, as he sat down next to her again. 'I didn't know Heloise either, of course. Heloise is made up of *your* voice, *your* hands, *your* words and *your* stories. The rest – all the rest – it's just from my head.' He pushed his hair away from his face, feeling the scars under his fingers.

Her hand settled on his shoulder again. 'Luke, all those first things you said, they're true still, they are Ruth. Was the stuff from your head so different from how I am? And is it so much more important?'

He dropped his head into his hands. 'Yes.'

She lifted her fingers and softly stroked his cheek with the back of her hand. 'I'm sorry.' Her hand encountered dampness. She pulled it away and turned from him, both hands covering her own face. They sat side by side in the shadowy room, closing in on their own pain, each trying, too late, to snatch back some part of their dreams.

Luke moved first. He heard her whimper and realized when he turned that her shoulders were shaking with barely controlled sobs. He reached his arms around her and held her. They sat huddled in the dark.

28

New York: Night

Minutes later Luke fished around in his pocket; found a napkin from lunch and gave it to Ruth.

She took it, still gulping. 'I'm sorry. Thanks. There are tissues somewhere. Oh I know.' She stood up and felt her way over to the bed, found the tissues and blew her nose. Then, sniffing gently, she pulled off her shoes and curled up on the bed like a wounded animal.

Luke, feeling a year older than when he had entered the room, reached for the bottle and topped up her glass. 'Here, drink some more Champagne. It'll make you feel better, honestly.' Like an obedient child she sat up, still catching her breath, and accepted the refilled glass.

Luke put out a hand to switch on the light, then once more changed his mind and went over to the window. New York lay sprinkled like a heap of jewels all around him. He stood, hand on the blind cord, unable to move. There was a sigh from behind. Luke continued to stand, shaken by one of those moments when the essential non-fairness of life forced its way in to his consciousness.

'Ruth, I wish you could see. I'm looking out of the window. It's dark now and all the million lights in New York have been switched on. It is like floating in stars. You can see the buildings too, but they seem to be just a backcloth, quite light and airy. It's the lights that are the solid things.'

'Tell me more, Luke, I want to *see* it.'

Luke swallowed. Heloise – or rather Ruth's – voice and the sight outside moved some part of him that belonged on stage: the visionary, the child who knew he had the power of gods to shift and sway the world by his own actions. I am the person who can interpret *this* world for *this* audience, he thought. Speaking slowly as he thought on-line, he said, 'When you were little, you must have had bricks.'

'Yes, of course.'

'Be little again and take those bricks and build a tower as high as it will go, and then another one and a third one and put them in the middle of an empty room, then with hundreds of boxes of bricks go on and on building all across the carpet until the whole room is full of towers as tall as they can go.' Luke paused to adjust his mind to the world of vision that Ruth had last seen, aged six or so. 'Did you ever have those little stick-on gold stars?'

'Yes?'

'Well, these towers of bricks are covered in hundreds and thousands of tiny stick-on gold stars. Do you remember Christmas tree lights, all different colours?'

'We had white lights, but Morris's parents had coloured lights with petal frills. They were so pretty in the dark.'

'There are hundreds of lights like yours and Morris's thrown all over your brick towers, some of them on a timer, blinking on and off. Now, here's the difficult bit. Think about the ceiling of this imaginary room flying away into the sky and the walls falling away backwards, so that there is nothing but black sky above. It's black in the distance but sort of milky and steamy nearby. There are no stars, because the shining from all your million little lights is too bright. Now imagine you could shrink to the size of a ... a grain of sugar and walk around like an ant between your towers of blocks.

'Hundreds of Christmas tree towers?'

'Ye-es. On the ground there are cars and noise and smells; up here, with the window shut, it's all just picture. A light show. We're just suspended somewhere inside it like ...' Luke paused in astonishment as an image rose before him of the piece of weaving that had caught his eye in the window in Rome. He had noticed it because it reminded him of New York at night. 'There's a piece of your work that feels a bit the way this looks. Lights in a three dimensional space.'

'Oh, Luke! Which one?'

Luke abandoned the window, picked up the remains of the bottle of Champagne, came over to the bed and emptied it into the two glasses. There was just enough light from the window to see Ruth lying back now against the white cover. He lifted her hand to put the refilled glass into it. 'You had it in Rome.'

She pulled herself into a sitting position, her knees tucked up, without spilling the drink and Luke sat down on the bed near her feet.

'Whereabouts was it in the gallery?'

'Well,' he took his mind back to the moment, 'I walked past the front window, and suddenly realised that the poster in the corner was for a weaving exhibition.' Dryness crept into his tone as he remembered the months of his search. 'So I stopped. It looked vaguely familiar and I very nearly didn't bother to turn back.' His voice changed again as he realised how great had been the role of chance in his rediscovery of Heloise. 'As I stood, trying to make up my mind, all I could see, because of the sunlight on the window, was the piece hanging on the left wall and I thought, "that reminds me of New York at night and anyway I *like* weaving, I might as well go in".'

Ruth, her head tilted to one side as she listened to the fluctuations in Luke voice, put her glass down and reached out to touch his shoulder. 'Now you wish you hadn't. I'm sorry, Luke, I didn't understand. I'm glad, so glad you did come in. Are you still angry, Luke?'

'Sometimes.' He answered truthfully. Then consulting post-explosion-Luke he went on slowly: 'If I hadn't found you in Rome, Claudia would still think I was crazy. I might think I was crazy, but … I would still have the image of Heloise I so stupidly created for myself. No, don't cry, Ruth, I am trying to sort this out in my own mind. It's not you; it's me. There's Ruth and Luke and then there's Heloise and another Luke and both those last two are not real and I don't know what to do about them.'

'Is that why …? Luke, please sing … sing to me again?'

Luke finished his Champagne and turned to sit more comfortably. His hand brushed her stockinged foot, and he picked it up. Then he hitched himself further onto the bed and pulled both her feet in his lap. 'If you like. Drink up, Ruth, before all the bubbles disappear.' As she drank, he ran his hands over her feet. Ruth's feet, smooth in the stockings and no longer bearing her weight, were suddenly the most intricate and fine structures he had ever held; like complex sculptures with the working parts so barely, yet precisely, covered in soft, elastic skin.

Her rich chuckle sounded. 'You're tickling!'

His hands stilled and he clasped the feet loosely. 'Sorry! Feet are amazing things. What would you like me to sing?'

'Something old, and not too heavy.' After a moment he started singing; his tone light, relaxed, *'Did you not hear my lady go down the garden singing, blackbird and thrush were silent to hear the alleys ringing. But saw you not my lady out in the garden there, shading the rose and lily for she is twice as fair. Though I am nothing to her, though she must rarely look me and though I could never woo her, I love her till I die.'*

Out of the near darkness her voice, sounding detached and separate from the body lying against the distant pillow, floated back to him. 'When you sing softly like that I can hear the sound like a wind in your chest. I can feel the air vibrating. It makes my breathing-in feel different, as though the fragments of your voice were still inside the air as it goes into my lungs. Another?'

Luke, let go of her feet, kicked off his own shoes and lay down beside her. Songs that he pretended to despise rose and he let them free for this supremely uncritical audience; *'O Danny Boy, the hills are ever calling . . .'*

Like a child, she curled towards him tucking her feet under his thigh and resting her face lightly against his arm. *'There's a place for us, somewhere a place for us . . .'*

Ruth closed her eyes.

'The water is wide, I can not get o'er, and neither have I wings to fly . . .'

Luke began to feel as though he had been lying on the bed for hours and at the same time as though he had just arrived at an oasis after a journey of years. The slight roughness of the cloth under his bare arm, the small anomaly of Ruth's feet under his thigh, the faint pleasing smell of whatever soap she used, felt like sensations that he had lived with all his life. For the first time in years he had nowhere to get to, nothing hanging in the in-tray of his mind, no other agenda. He listened to the sounds of his own voice, correcting the tone, raising the volume, smoothing the line and let go of every other consideration. Turning his face into the slippery warmth of hair beside him, he listened to the muffling of the sound. An oceanic space spread out around him as if they were both lying on some benign wave.

He could only just see her face in the near dark. Such a pale face under that dark hair, with her eyes closed, she looked like any other woman – a soft blur of pale flesh. No lipstick even. Her mouth? Half hidden by a strand of hair, as her face lay tilted towards him.

She spoke sleepily. 'No more?'

Lifting aside her hair he leaned over to look and when her lips parted in surprise, he dropped his own mouth to meet hers. The first few seconds, as her hands reached for his head and her mouth responded, seemed infinitely familiar. Then she gasped, pushing him away. 'Luke? I don't understand, you said…'

He picked up her hand, pushing his fingers between hers. 'Ruth …Heloise?'

'Luke?'

'It's all right,' he smiled at the tremor in her voice, 'I know. But you're both to me.' He placed his mouth softly over hers again, feeling her uncertainty. Did she, like all his loving relations over the last year, think his mind was affected? He would prove them all wrong and his own instincts right. Slowly pushing her hand back until it rested on the pillow, he leant over and tried to melt the resistance he could feel. She caught her breath, still tense, still thinking. He stilled himself, turning his mouth from hers and into her hair. They lay full length together, their bodies speaking one language, their minds with the weight of the intervening year confusing the issue.

Speaking urgently he said, 'Just remember being Heloise, *remember.*'

The structure across his chest seemed to tighten against him every time he breathed in. Possibly, as it settled it would squeeze him to death millimetre by millimetre. In his nose the thickened air, like sandpaper, rasped at the soft tissue. His ankle, so far away and out of reach, kept sending grinding messages jolting up his leg to remind him of its needs. None of these discomforts reached anywhere near the terror in his throat, the craving for wetness; the dream images of water drops landing on him. He and Heloise had tried not talking about water and then talking about it. He had toured round the fountains and waterspouts of Rome with her. The silences grew longer. Then Luke whimpered, 'I can't think of anything except water. Every second I imagine it trickling, somewhere near, I imagine you gathering it in your hands and opening them above my mouth. I just dream of being wet again.'

'Luke, Luke, shush! I would do it if I could, I would empty the water out of me and into you, if I knew how.'

'Lick me...please.'

First a little cool puff of breath above his face, then a tentative dab of wetness, so light he could only feel it as it withdrew, on his cheek.'

He moved instinctively towards it, like a baby to the breast. 'Please – on my lips, please.'

Her tongue, sticky with it's own deprivation, yet still blessedly damp, moved delicately across his mouth. 'Like that?' She half laughed. 'The trouble is, that my mouth is so dry too.'

Luke whispered. 'Kiss me, we'll give each other water.'

As her lips bumped softly against his waiting mouth, Luke knew instantly. 'You've never done this before have you?'

'No.'

'How old are you really, Heloise?'

'It's not that. I...my parents...I don't really go out much.'

'Never mind. Come on, I'll show you. Kiss me again and open your mouth a little...that's it...see? I give you a little water and you give me some...It's good isn't it?'

The distraction, the excitement, the miraculous wetness and the frustration of not being able to touch her or to move things on as his body demanded, swept in succeeding waves over him as he lay under the sweetest assault of his life. He begged, cajoled, instructed her innocence and promised such things on their release as his body demanded now. Eventually Luke slid into blessed oblivion.

Luke stared down at the blur of her head against the white pillow. 'Remember now, Ruth?'

'I never forgot, Luke.'

'I did. At least I thought I'd dreamt it. If this is really what you want, we'll make that promise come true. Just this once. Are you sure you want this?'

Her fingers brushed his cheek then traced his forehead, his nose and his lips. Satisfied, she answered, 'I'm sure.'

Afterwards, she lay thoughtful beside him, more surprised and relieved than enthralled.

'It only hurt a little Luke. I think I like it, but it's a very funny thing to do. I didn't realise it would be so ... so wet.'

Luke smiled. 'Well you wanted to know and now you do. We'll have a shower in a minute and you'll get even wetter. I love water now, don't you?'

'Mmm. Kissing is the bit I like most.'

'Kissing is good. You're good. Hey, what are you doing?'

'I just want to feel you. I have never felt a man before.'

'I should hope not, at least not like this.' He drew in a sharp breath, as her hands pursued their delicate investigation. 'If you do too much of that I shall have to ... ' He captured her hand, torn between a lazy spreading return of his earlier ache and an increasingly empty feeling inside. He sat up. 'Come on. Let's have a shower and get something to eat.'

He switched on the reading light and lay watching the unself-conscious way Ruth disentangled her body from the sheets. She started feeling around, laughing. 'My clothes, I don't know where they are, Luke. We didn't put them beside me.'

He slipped out of bed behind her. 'We don't need clothes for a shower.' He enclosed her body feeling her heavy breasts sag against his arms and her bottom touch softly against his thigh. With another effort he let go and led her to the bathroom. The shower was big and it seemed simpler to get in together. In the bright lights of the bathroom another revelation awaited Luke. There was nothing unattractive about Ruth's body: tall and evenly pale, all the lines running in smooth curves, and the kind of breasts he fancied. It made no sense that she managed to look so unappealing when dressed. He put this problem aside for solution at a later date. Tearing open a sachet of shower gel with his teeth he poured it over Ruth, then he let her soap him. The calls of hunger grew fainter as they stood skin to skin enclosed by water. He quelled her protests at getting her hair wet and they stood directly under the showerhead, fulfilling that most desperate of all their needs under the building.

Just as in that earlier time, they talked as their mouths grew more and more involved with each other. 'Remember dreaming of this, Ruth, drinking and kissing together? Do you drink more now than you used to?'

'Mmm.'

'I drink all the time. I can't get enough. I fell in love with your tongue ... What are you laughing about?'

'Well, I can feel you changing shape, Luke.'

'Yes. Come here.' Luke, switched off the shower, reached out and wrapped a towel loosely round Ruth, then lifted her in his arms.'

'What are you doing? I'm still all wet.'

'We need a little more practice.'

'Luke! We'll make the bed all wet.'

It was Ruth who pulled the sheet over their cooling bodies. Luke lay half asleep, slowly re-engaging with the here and now, following that brief moment when both mind and body are wiped of all concerns. Some of his famished dreams over the last months had after all come true, the last icicles surrounding his memory of the explosion melting away. There was something so unexpected about sex with Ruth – in contrast to his overworked images of union with Heloise. Perhaps, simply that he hadn't expected it, so it was in a sense a bonus, and he hadn't had to strive and plan and work for it. He remembered Maddalena, he hadn't had to work for that either, but that had been terrifying and only very momentarily satisfying, followed by more terror. No, this was different. It occurred to him that he had never before made love to a girl who was without prior expectation. Ruth, accustomed to being led, simply went with the flow like a trusting child. Usually sex with a new lover involved some necessary adjustment, some discomfort and rearrangement – there had been little of that. Of course, with other lovers he could never have issued the stream of quiet information along the way that he had given Ruth – as he had once with Heloise. Tomorrow? Well tomorrow he would be flying home of course and Ruth would be staying in New York. And after that? There would be time to think about that tomorrow ... or the next day.

29

Pimlico: Dave's Flat

Morris didn't get back to the hotel until late that night. He knocked on Ruth's door to check that she was all right but didn't come in. At breakfast next morning, still fizzing with excitement over an artist called Jay Carlyle, whose Private View he had attended the evening before, he talked non-stop.

Ruth, waiting for the right moment to tell him that she and Luke had been in bed together, had difficulty finding spaces in his rapid flow, never mind spaces big enough for her to convey such momentous events. Anyway, what language should she use? She had talked to no one (except Luke) about sex – if that is what it was. Sex, making love, sleeping together, mating? None of the words she had come across in her restricted reading quite applied to those hours in the hotel room. And where exactly would this lovemaking fit into the pattern of her life after this? Would it happen again? Had Luke just done it because she asked? What did it matter so long as Luke's anger had been appeased? The man she remembered had come back to her. Underneath this rationalisation her starved senses swam with reminiscent delight. The bigger sensations had come and gone swiftly, defying remembrance. Other moments had been suspended in time: the weight of his arm, relaxed across her stomach, the feel of shoulder blades moving under skin, Luke's breath in sleep arriving in warm pulses on her neck. These joys she could hug to herself, stowing them safely in her memory; they would last forever if necessary.

'What are you laughing at?'

'Sorry, Morris, I was remembering Luke banging on the wall that day in London.'

'I thought you said he was fine last night.'

'He was ... lovely, like I remembered him when we were stuck in the post office. I laughed just now because I realized why his thumping on the wall frightened me so. When I was little ...'

'Ruth, sorry, tell me later Sweetie, we must order a cab and get to the gallery, we're due in forty minutes.' Morris took her arm and guided her to a seat in the main entrance. 'Wait here a sec. I'm just going to leave instructions with reception for Nina.'

Ruth fingered the leather of the bench and remembered the hard wooden seats of the church hall. She had been about eleven, attending a lecture with Nina. Nina had been allowed to take her on educational outings, classical music concerts and, of course, religious events. Funny disjointed scraps of information from these outings had stayed with her. Nina chose this lecture because the subject – milk yields – would be useful for the smallholding she hoped to own one day.

Ruth, finding the speaker's voice scratchy and the room smelling sharply of polish, had lapsed into a daydream. Then had come a hiatus with funny noises. Nina said reels of film were being loaded onto a projector. As the film started Ruth settled back into her dream, but a dry, thudding, banging jerked her back. She clung to Nina's hand convinced that a monster had entered the room. The thudding continued along with strange hooting, groaning sounds right there in the room.

Later Nina explained it all carefully. The noise had been an angry bull shut in a stall. If a bull is kept shut away from cows, he becomes angry and frustrated. However, if he can fulfil his natural urges he becomes calm and noble. At this point a much younger Nina had giggled and said, "just like men, really, but for the Lord's sake don't tell Martha I said that, in fact you'd better not tell her anything about the bull, just about milk yields." When Luke had banged the wall in Morris's room that day, the hollow thud echoed just like the bull in the stall. Of course men and bulls are different.

Morris reappeared, took her elbow and led her out onto the hot sidewalk and into a taxi. She listened to him giving the driver directions, and the driver failing to understand them. When he finished she would tell him about Luke. Meanwhile her mind still tugged at the scraps of information that were all she had to go on when it came to understanding men and sex. Luke's actions last night did not fit with Mama's only lecture on the subject. In this the evils of the body or men or possibly both had jostled together and contrasted with the preciousness of virginity. This last was to be saved for God, but God would clearly have no use for it and, as Morris pointed out, if everyone did that no children would be born. In his view God either didn't exist at all or was the product of a vague collective human instinct, utterly uninterested in her or anyone else's well being. Luke, on the other hand, angry and damaged, belonged to the here and now and she felt she owed him something precious.

Maybe what she and Luke had done together in that hotel room was wrong. Yet those hours meant she could join up all the different people that seemed to be Luke. She had met him in such contradictory states: confused in Rome, angry in London, shocked last night, then later on, when he sang, the Luke she remembered from under the building. This last persona, the glowing physical one, whose singing let her float free of her darkness, this Luke she must find again – if he ever gave her the chance. Perhaps now at least they could be friends. The kissing felt special, the rest – well it was good to have experienced it, but the whole evening had been full of extreme sensations, and perhaps she wouldn't be sad if some of them never happened again. Funny how things had just slipped from one moment into the next last night and yet refused to be bundled together this morning, leaving her with all these thoughts and the most enormous unanswered question; what had Luke made of it? Was he thinking about her now?

Luke, had she but known it, was equally unsettled about what had happened and what lay ahead. He had not meant to make love to Ruth and most emphatically did not want a long-term relationship with someone who could never have children. He did not even want a short-term relationship with someone as vulnerable as Ruth. No matter how novel sleeping with such a frank and innocent person turned out to be, he could hardly have fun for a few months with Ruth and then move on.

Had he made things worse? His body told him otherwise. As if on an agenda separate from his conscious thoughts his body, temporarily satisfied, seemed also to be warning him that, like an addict, it might want more of the same. None of the trappings of his standard relationships were available. He could not send cheerful or impudent text messages to keep her interested and anything he wrote in the way of a letter would be read by Morris. He blushed, thinking of the complications of communicating intimate thoughts through someone who, even he had realised by now, was gay.

Luke, without bothering to find reasons, also failed to mention his fling with Ruth to Dave – or indeed to anyone else. Fling? No. Clever solution to an odd situation? Therapeutic arrangement? He put the exact description aside. He had plenty to tell his family. Next year, 2001, was already full of engagements; Bohème in Chicago next July and a cover, with two definite performances at the New York Opera House in September then several bookings into 2004. A local patron had sponsored the Chicago appointment, so he would get funds for a whole month not just performance fees. Luke had never doubted that he could earn a living as a singer, but he had expected to be working at the gym and stacking boxes in the market a whole lot longer as well. It looked as though those days might already be over.

No, he rationalised, he had fulfilled Ruth's very strange request and that would probably be the end of it. Occasional visits, when he came home would be in order. He could drop in from time to time, admire the weavings, persuade her to give her opinions about a concert or opera, then, when he had listened to her voice and perhaps sung a little in return, nothing further should be necessary. Almost as if he heard his body laughing at him, he continued to argue with himself; sex is easy to come by, there's no need to seek it out with difficulties attached.

Luke landed back at Heathrow late the following day and returned home with enough of his old *joie de vivre* to make Claudia ask, when she saw him that evening, what had happened. He satisfied her with the story of his singing successes and mentioned in passing that he had seen Ruth. His family, ever loyal, had more than happily consigned Ruth to oblivion at his request, so she was more interested in his talk of finding a flat on his own. Dave, his previous lease up, had moved to a rather large and too expensive first-floor flat in Pimlico, but was looking for another more reasonable place. Perhaps he could share with Dave, that way Dave could afford to stay on.

Dave, in response to this proposition looked at him, amusement in his eye, 'Why the breakout, Luke? You live the cushiest possible life at home. You planning to cut loose and go on the razzle? What's happened?

'Well, I can't live at home forever. Anyway, I saved up some of my Roman scholarship, my agent has a string of concert performances and teaching lined up between now and February; then in

2001 there's Glyndebourne in May, a summer travelling season with Opera North, Chicago again and New York in September.' Looking at Dave's face, on which the question still lingered, he protested, 'Dave, I can't live at home forever, I don't want to be there when I turn thirty.'

'I'd stay until they kicked me out if I had the chance.'

'Well you did – have the chance, I mean.'

'Yes, well, there were good reasons for me to move out. You haven't really given me one, though. What's happened? You never mentioned moving when I last saw you.'

'Why the third degree? I don't know why. It's just time to go. I can't play the piano all night, never mind singing. Then Mum looks at me these days when I sleep late ... '

'And?'

'Well I saw Ruth again in New York,' Luke saw the look of satisfaction on Dave's face, and thought, bullseye, this will satisfy him, 'and we sort of came to an understanding. I think I can go on from there now. We can be friendly without too much else. I want a new start now.' To prevent further questions, he went on, 'You've never seen her work or Morris's, have you? Ba reckons Morris is gay; she's probably right. Anyway, I'll take you to the studio, when they get back.' Thus, he thought, making it clear to Ruth that he wanted to be friends and yet preventing intimacy.

'You look exceptionally pleased with yourself, this meeting of yours must have gone well.'

'Yes. Yes, it did. I now know which of my memories from those hours under the building are real. So, apart from when I was actually unconscious, I know what happened that day.'

Dave grasped his shoulder and shook Luke slightly, he spoke with satisfaction, 'Finally. I couldn't be more pleased.' He walked across the living room and opened a door on the far side. 'Well, you can move in here for a bit and see what real life feels like. This second bedroom isn't as big as mine, and you'd have to come through here to get to the bathroom. You can play my new Yamaha keyboard – silently if you want – but no sound you make will ever trouble me.' He gave Luke a considering look. 'Only thing is ... I'm not entirely sure my lifestyle will be any more compatible with yours than your parents. Of course, I've only taken the lease for three months because I can't afford to keep it and I guess you should know before then if you can hack life with me ... or without Maria and home.'

Luke waved aside any doubts and a couple of weeks later, after innumerable to-ings and fro-ings across south London in Dave's Fiesta, even Luke's collection of old LPs had been safely installed. Luke planned to finally move in the following week on his return from a two-day music workshop in Birmingham.

Fulfilling his earlier promise, he rang Morris and suggested bringing Dave over to see the Greenwich studio. 'Luke, that's splendid, we'd love to show your friend round. Though I'm afraid we don't have many hangings to show after New York. Ruth will be so pleased, she really enjoyed her evening with you.'

So Ruth had not confessed all to Morris, then. Well that would make life even easier. 'You do still have that sunrise coloured weaving inside the front door, don't you?'

'Of course, that's mine. I mean Ruth made it, but she gave it to me. I wouldn't sell anything like that. In fact, Ruth has a hanging she refused to sell because she wanted to give it to you, Luke, but she isn't sure if you will want it.'

Luke tensed with pleasure. 'If I will want it? I think they're stunning. I'm just about to move into a flat so I've even got a wall. Mind you, the wall's not quite up to the scale of most of Ruth's work. When can I come?'

Mid-morning two days later, Luke and Dave walked into the quiet crescent where Morris lived. As they arrived they found Morris saying a lingering goodbye to the owner of a gaudy Alfa parked outside the house. Luke whispered, 'Clock the Alfa!' Dave opened his mouth, but they were now within earshot and he shut it again.

Morris turned, his gaze moved from Luke to Dave and back again as he lit up with pleasure. Dave, to Luke's surprise, went into his silent mode. He was not rude or even unresponsive, merely withdrawn. Morris led them down to the basement where Ruth stood working at an almost finished piece stretched on an upright frame. She had a giant needle threaded with some silvery ribbon-like material, which she was stitching in to the surface of the hanging. The low south-eastern sunlight threw a pattern from the bars on the basement window across the work. Almost as if she could see, Ruth wove her glittering ribbon in mimicry of this pattern.

Luke kissed her and introduced her to Dave. She smiled and leant her cheek towards him for the kiss, but did not put down her work.

'Do you know that your needle is following the sun?'

'Of course, Luke,' she answered without pausing, 'I can feel the heat on my hand, but I have to work quickly. The sun only comes in like this occasionally. In fact,' she chuckled, 'I think maybe you're standing in it now.'

Dave and Luke moved quickly aside, Luke saying, 'Go on, don't mind us, I'd like to watch for a bit.'

With a total lack of self-consciousness, Ruth continued to work, catching the sunlight on her weaving canvas with what seemed to Luke astonishing expertise. With her shorter hair, now tucked behind her ears as she worked, her cheeks showed smooth and pale as she leant into each stitch. Morris joined them with four cups of coffee. He seemed restless, inviting them into his studio, then taking them out again and into the garden before they had time to look at anything. They stood around in the Oc-tober sunlight. Or rather Luke stood, Dave walked slowly up and down gazing at ivy and rosemary like a botanical expert, while Morris pointed out features, or nipped in to see how Ruth was getting on. He looked pale and tired after the trip to New York, and complained of jet lag, although the exhibition had been a suc-cess. Ruth, on the other hand, looked better than Luke had ever seen her before.

When eventually Ruth came out, they decided that it wasn't warm enough and returned to the kitchen, deposited their cups and followed Morris to his spare bedroom. There on the wall of the high-ceilinged room hung the weaving Luke had noticed in Rome. The one with a myriad of tiny lights clustered onto dark columns that reminded him of New York at night. This turned out to be the hanging Ruth wanted to give Luke. It was more than five feet tall and he had no wall he could sensibly hang it on. He also felt guilty about accepting it, having seen the price stickers on the exhibits in the show in Rome. On the other hand he could not disguise his delight. It was agreed that it would continue to live with Ruth, but be nominally his.

Ruth's mouth curled mischievously. 'You will have to come

and visit it, Luke, whenever you are in London, or it will become lonely.'

He smiled and touched her arm. 'OK, it's a deal.'

Returning to South Road, Pimlico in buoyant mood, Luke became aware that Dave was unusually silent. 'What's up? You've gone into deep, dark Dave mode. Didn't you like them? Don't the weaving things do it for you? I know Ruth is not much of a looker, but she's not such a turn-off as I first thought. What do you think?'

Dave flung himself into a chair and sighed. 'What do I think? Mmm. Well, you're right the weaving is something else, though personally I prefer his to hers.'

Luke smiled in triumph. 'I knew you would. The softer palette has always been more your thing. What d'you think of Ruth?'

'I think you did her an injustice. She's sweet looking, once you get used to the eyes.'

'Yup, I know, but she looked so . . . she was such a stranger that first time. I can't explain, but when I saw her in Rome it was like I'd walked on stage to sing the Duke only to hear the opening bars of Carmen. I knew there had been the most terrible blunder. And . . . she's cut her hair and looks a bit different now – better. Anyway, why the heavy silence? What didn't you like? Morris?'

Dave stood up again, closed his eyes for a moment then spoke with deliberation, 'Oh no, I liked Morris all right. In fact I liked him a whole lot more than that.'

Mystified, Luke said, 'Dave, have you lost your marbles? What do you mean?' Then when Dave didn't answer, but just looked stolidly back at him, he asked on a rising note, 'What could you possibly mean?'

'Luke, you half-wit, I'm gay.'

'Gay?'

'Christ, man, where've you been living?'

'You're telling me you're . . . *you're gay? You fancy Morris?*'

'Yes.

30
South Road: Dave & Morris

Half an hour later Luke, wandering restlessly round Dave's sitting room, continued to grapple with this revelation. 'But Dave, I don't understand. Why didn't I know? Does anyone else know?'

'Yes, of course.'

'What about that time ... I mean when I split with Bridget, you and she ... ?'

'Yes we did. She was sweet. I thought for a bit I might be bi, but I couldn't hack it, and I knew really.'

'You could've told me.'

'Well, I could, but you're such an idiot and I love you so.' Luke's mouth hung open and Dave cracked up. 'Luke, I've known you since we were four years old. I don't go in for incest. I meant what I said. I love you. You're my brother, my friend. If you looked like a rat, I'd still love you. But I don't mind that you're drop dead stunning as well. Relax, don't go coy on me. Nothing has changed. You know something you didn't know yesterday, but I've known for sixteen years and I'm not planning to change.' He looked at Luke's flushed face and said mockingly, 'Love and sex are not the same thing. You should know that.'

Luke looked up at the familiar row of prints on the wall. All the solid things in his life seemed to be melting away leaving only small islands of known territory. You couldn't rely on some overblown peonies to get you through the day.

'Well, but ... sometimes ... I mean your reaction to Morris ... that's not just ...'

A dull flush rose on Dave's skin. Luke saw with surprise that even his hands showed red. Silence stretched between the two men until Dave, a thin sheen of sweat on his upper lip, looked at Luke straightly. 'No, you're right. This feels different. Don't laugh, Luke.'

'I'm not laughing, I'm feeling hysterical. You know a guy for twenty-five years, then find you didn't know him at all.'

'I am exactly the same person as I was thirty minutes ago or come to that twenty years ago.' Dave turned and dropped into a chair. 'Actually, I do feel odd just now. I feel like I'm fifteen years old again and it's the first time. You couldn't see your way to asking him here sometime soon, could you?'

'Dave, why the mad rush? I've never known you like this. You said you hadn't changed, but you've gone outright bananas.'

'I'm sorry. I just know I must act fast. Some chances only brush you on the shoulder, the old butterfly an' all that. He could be about to ring that sod with the Alfa, for all I know.'

'I can't just ask him here. Anyway, I'd have to ask Ruth, too.'

'Can't we all meet up for something? A meal, a concert?' Luke, reaching wildly into this uncharted territory, suggested. 'Well you can send them some of those comps they gave you for your Hackney gig on Friday. You can make nice to them afterwards.'

Dave grimaced, then frowned, head on one side as he reviewed the programme – excerpts from Carmina Burana, the Hallelujah Chorus, two choruses from the Creation and a couple of spirituals. He would be singing solo bass for the local combined church choirs. Suddenly he grinned. 'That's not such a bad idea, Luke. Ring them and ask if they'd like a couple of free tickets.' Looking at Luke's astonished face he added, 'Please.'

Luke shrugged and picked up the phone. 'Morris? Do you fancy a couple of free tickets to a concert this Friday? It's four soloists including Dave – the Dave you met today – and the choirs of Hackney Wick? ...No, I can't go; I'll be in Birmingham, but Dave would love to see you afterwards. OK, he'll drop them round sometime,' He looked at Dave, who mouthed "now", 'probably today.'

He put the phone down and turned to see Dave, now sunk on the uncomfy sofa, looking anything but grateful. Luke, still navigating without a compass, stared down at his friend. He had leant against Dave's supporting bulk, both physically and metaphorically, for more than twenty-five years, finding him always there, like the walls of his home, his history; to be preserved, naturally, but existing mainly for his benefit. In a few hours this bulwark had become vulnerable, strange and, Luke noted with an amazed detachment, not bad to look at. All Luke's girlfriends had seemed to think so. That didn't make sense. What was it Barbara had said? When men were too good to be true they were always gay.

Did women like gay men? Was Dave really gay – all these years? Women seemed to like that he was big; Sophy, his last girlfriend before the explosion, had always claimed he was the gentlest most dependable man she'd ever met. Did Mum know he was gay?'

'Does Mum know?'

'Sure.'

Luke shook his head. What would a man see in Dave? He struggled to reverse his male orientation: the corded brown arms, the frank, slightly mocking gaze? If Dave were a woman, thought Luke, I could make a list of things that were attractive and things that turned me off, but he's Dave, whole and indivisible. I give up. Dave hadn't moved during this scrutiny. An unattractive pallor lay on his skin.

Luke shrugged and flung himself down in front of Dave's new piano keyboard. 'You'd better have a drink, man. You look like you're wishing I hadn't rung now? What's happened to all that get up and go? OK, we're going to get this instrument working. I'm Gulli and I want to hear you ease into that lower register.' He marked the beat for the exercise with his head, as his hands began to play a scale. To his momentary astonishment trumpets sound-ed. He hit a few random buttons, and eventually found something that sounded more or less like a piano. Dave, feeble at first, ran over some scales. After a while the familiar exercises took over and they both began to get a rhythm and Luke to get the hang of the piano.

Twenty minutes later Luke broke off, 'I suppose I'd better get my stuff together for Birmingham, my train leaves in a couple of hours. You've got tickets to deliver.'

'Sure.' Dave shuffled through the pile of papers on the tiny table that did duty for a desk, then pulled his coat off the hook.

Luke, puzzled, asked, 'Don't you want to do anything?'

'Like what?'

'I dunno. If I were planning to … if I wanted to impress a babe or something, I'd be showering and changing – at least shaving? Don't laugh. How am I to know how you go about these things, you secretive git?'

'You are unbelievably innocent, Luke. I'll be half an hour.'

Dave had his hand on the doorknob when the phone rang. He paused, shrugged, and picked it up. 'Morris? Sure, we'll be here for the next hour.' He replaced the receiver carefully and turned to Luke. 'Morris, is on his way to the West End with a car full of weaving, so he'll drop by for the tickets.'

'Wow! That was powerful bait.'

'Mmm, possibly.'

The two men returned without further comment to the voice training exercises.

Half an hour later, hearing a car, Luke got up and went towards the door. Dave grabbed the tickets and pushed past, shutting the door smartly behind him. Luke returned to the sitting room and without hesitation watched from the window. Morris was parking on the pavement on the far side of the road. He came round the side of his car, scanning the houses for the right number. He stopped, his gaze halting and widening, presumably at the sight of Dave's solid form at the top of the steps blocking the way to the front door. He looked momentarily alarmed, then puzzled and watchful. He approached slowly and Dave went down the steps to meet him.

Luke, half fascinated, half appalled, stared motionless. The two men stood close, but not touching. They did not shake hands. Dave seemed to tower over the smaller man. He stood quite still, apparently relaxed, hands in pockets, eyes fixed on Morris's face. Stage technique, thought Luke, that's not really fair. Morris, meeting the unexpected, spread his movements over quite an area of pavement. He held the lamppost with one hand, studied the ground then looked sharply up at Dave, as if perhaps to catch him looking elsewhere. Then he spent a few minutes apparently pointing out the virtues of Dave's battered Fiesta, his hands touching the roof, the windscreen wipers, he even leant down to look at the hubcaps. Dave remained rocklike during the whole performance. Finally Morris leant against the wall that bounded the steps up to the front door. His fingers lightly tracing the brickwork; his gaze absorbed by the basement area. What on earth could they be talking about all that time? How did a bloke chat up a bloke? Suddenly Morris levered himself off his prop, held out his hand and took the tickets, gave Dave a blinding smile and set off across the road. Dave returned to the flat, grabbed his coat and before Luke could demand to know what on earth they had been talking about, said abruptly, 'Going for a walk,' and vanished.

Dave did not return to his flat that day. He also switched off his mobile. Luke had to set off for his workshop in Birmingham, his world still unsteady on its axis and his curiosity unsatisfied. When he got back to the flat a couple of days later, he asked impatiently, 'Dave, how did things go?'

'What things?'

'Don't play dumb; you and Morris. Did he come to the concert?'

'Of course.'

'Well?'

'Well what?'

'Jesus, you're uncommunicative. OK, just tell me, for instance, before I go wild with curiosity, what did you talk about the other day all that time outside the flat?'

As if he were scanning a shopping list, Dave ticked off on his fingers and recited, 'Squirrels, baseball, cars, omelettes, the colour green and ... you.'

Luke, about to query Dave's interest in these subjects was floored by the inclusion of himself. The answer fell a long way short of satisfying his curiosity.

'Have you seen each other since?'

'Uhuh.'

'And?'

'And what? We went to the cinema. Do you want to know what I had for supper?'

'Don't clam up, Dave, just tell me if things worked out. I feel responsible.'

'Christ, Luke, I'm not into confessional mode. These things are private.'

'I always tell you mine,' he said, conveniently forgetting recent omissions.

'I know.'

Dave's mobile rang, and seeing the caller number he answered it. 'Hi, yes, he's here right now ... He's curiouser than a sackful of cats ... Well you know what happened to the cat ... OK, OK, I obey.' He pocketed the mobile. 'OK Nosey, Morris says I'm to be kind to you. You want to know if we got together? Well, I'm on a tour of the stratosphere. Come here, boyo, and give me a hug.'

Luke leant up against the familiar chest. He still struggled to comprehend that the Dave he thought he knew had gone, and been replaced by a Dave who looked and sounded the same and yet *must* be another person. All the same he felt relief that at least one thing had worked out right.

31
Blackheath: Luke & Ruth

Luke heaved his case onto a luggage rack, brushed the raindrops from his hair and slumped onto the nearest seat. Moisture clouded the windowpane on the Portsmouth to London train. The rattling cold of last night had turned itself into a soft December morning. Yesterday evening had been the last singing engagement in a trail that had taken him to Portsmouth via Keswick, Hereford and the Isle of Wight. Even in Keswick, where a flu bug had thinned out the orchestra, he had lost himself in sound, savouring the novelty, unfazed by the lack of support that undermined the other singers' performances. The Haydn Creation in Portsmouth had come off superbly. He blushed, remembering the reception afterwards. The mezzo had a voice he would be hearing again.

For the last five weeks, with mind and body at peace over Ruth, music and his own performances had filled his horizon. He had woken each morning with nothing more on his mind than the next venue and his planned repertoire. That, surely, was what happiness amounted to? Now he was free of engagements for two weeks. He sank further into his seat. Free for what? He ran his fingers over his scarred forehead; perhaps he would feel brighter after a night's rest.

Rubbing the window revealed lines of damp trees and swooping pylons. He pulled out his phone. Claudia had not phoned for ages. Two weeks? Definitely odd. Luke scrolled down his old messages. Dave had texted to say he was on his way to Manchester. So the flat would be empty when he reached London. Not that Dave was there much these days; his relationship with Morris was a time-consuming occupation. He'd talked to Barbara yesterday, but mostly about the pains of pregnancy, and to Mum the day before – about Barbara and the baby. If Ruth had a mobile, he could send her a text and turn up to see his weaving – stupid! – of course she couldn't read. Did they make Braille mobiles? He didn't fancy passing messages via Morris.

Luke dozed, the phone slack in his hand, until the buffet trolley snagged against his foot. He stared at it, repulsed by the idea of yet another instant coffee. On a whim he dialled Catford. 'Mum? Can I come home for a few days? No reason; just wanted to see you all. Can't face Dave's instant coffee. I won't be around much over Christmas itself, so now's a good time.'

He sat back with a sigh of satisfaction. He could tell Mum about the weaving Ruth had given him; maybe even take her to see it and meet Ruth and Morris. He might possibly have given Mum a poor impression of Ruth. He frowned feeling the pull of his scars. He should never have slept with Ruth. It must have been the champagne. Ever since his brain operation, alcohol seemed to have a much stronger effect. Perhaps if he saw her with Mum, that would get things onto the right footing. Luke closed his eyes and slept the rest of the journey.

'Luca, is that you? Good trip?'

'Yes, Mum.' He paused in the hall for a deep breath of home, before following her voice into the kitchen. 'Want to know about it?'

'Save it for Dad, he'll be here later. We've got Kieran coming tonight and I need to get to the market.'

'Kieran?'

'Yes, haven't you met ... oh no, you went away just before he first came over.'

'Who's he?'

'Hasn't Claudia ...? He's a friend of Claudia's.'

'Friend? You don't mean ...? That's why she's been lying low. God, is everyone pairing up, these days?'

'Why the surprise, Topo? You'll be thirty next year and Claudia is thirty-four. I'd begun to wonder ... Surely this time ...'

Luke, laughing, put his arms around his mother, as she tried to pull on her coat. 'Oh Mum, you planning the wedding already? They only just met?'

'Well, I think it's been going on for a bit.' She hesitated. 'After the explosion, when they were about to operate on you, Luca, Claudia talked to Kieran – to make sure they used the right anaesthetic.'

'Jesus, that's more than a year ago.' He held her away from him, grinning, 'You'd better have a word with Father James, Mum.'

'Don't be silly.'

That evening Luke met Kieran, an anaesthetist, who had indeed attended Luke's brain surgery. He turned out to be a lanky man, with a wide grin. He grasped Luke by the hand and held on, as he looked him over. 'They made a good job of you. I can't tell you how pleased I am to see you so well. Claudia tells me your voice is better than ever. So we didn't cause any lasting damage.'

'No, I was very lucky – in every way, really.'

'You should thank your sister. We were just heading into theatre, when she caught up with us and told us exactly what we could and couldn't do to you. Scared us all to pieces. Look at me, shaking still.' He grinned down from his six foot three into Claudia's eyes, a full foot lower, and attempted to look bashful.

Luke watched in astonishment as Gordon poured Kieran a beer without asking and Maria gazed at them, wedding anticipation written all over her face. When had all this familiarity developed? He hadn't been on the road that long. The guy was all right; he had a soft voice with a pleasing burr. But finding him already installed in the family felt a bit breathtaking. Maria and Gordon, with Barbara's baby in mind, pestered Kieran with questions about water births and caesareans. He answered them patiently, protesting that he knew less about obstetrics than Claudia. It was only after they had gone that Gordon, himself setting off to Turin the following day, asked about Luke's travels.

Four days later Luke returned to the Pimlico flat. There he found Dave, back from his oratorio in Manchester and rather blatantly walking on air. In fact everyone, Luke felt, was on some kind of a high except himself. Something of Dave's trembling excitement communicated itself over the next week, leaving Luke restless and in need of physical consolation. When Dave set off to Cardiff to sing in Britten's Noyes Fludde, Luke woke up in an empty flat. He sat in the kitchen clutching a cup of instant coffee and wondered how to fill the day. Mum had not yet made time to come and see Ruth's studio with him. He found himself phoning Greenwich.

Morris answered. 'Hi Luke. I was going to ring you. Nina's been on at me because she wanted to meet you again.' (Nina? Did Ruth want to see him too?) 'She's here before setting off to Scotland for a funeral. Why don't you come and have lunch with us?'

'Well, I was just wondering if I could bring my Mum round

one day, perhaps next week'

'Oh come on, Luke, come now, we've got something to celebrate. We've had some good news. You know probate on Dan's will was granted back in August, well maybe you didn't, but it was and yet Ruth couldn't touch the money because the lawyers were still arguing over a bequest that Ruth's Mum had made. This has finally been sorted, so now we can complete on all the sales. You can bring your Mum next week as well. It'd make Ruth happy.'

Luke, only vaguely grasping what Morris was on about, was pleased to hear him so upbeat. He also found it heartening on arrival to see Ruth with a sense of pleasure and no lingering irritation. There she sat at her loom, her body alert to his arrival, but poised to return to the task in front of her. Her voice ... well that still unsettled him, but she was easing into the role he had in mind for her – a friend: unique, admirable and with a curious take on life, but just a friend. Later, as they sat over lunch, Luke began to feel a little less certain. He wanted to talk with Ruth, but Nina, endlessly adjusting her bun to cover her shyness, asked him question after question while Ruth, her head cocked to one side and a small, enigmatic smile on her lips, contributed little.

Morris, on the other hand, exuded wild relief. He had been living in fear that his parents would lose patience and sell the house over his head. He had persuaded them to wait months longer than they had intended, while the solicitor wrestled with Ruth's finances. Now Ruth, whose house sale had been hanging in the balance, could buy the Greenwich house and save their studio.

Luke let Morris's plans for the renovation of the two upper flats flow over him, while he watched Ruth. The certainty with which her hands 'saw', as she produced coffee for the four of them, mesmerised him.

Absorbed in this, he was startled when Morris suddenly addressed him. 'Luke, there's room for two in each flat. Why don't you both come and live here? Ruth would like that too.'

'What? Oh, I don't know ...' Luke stopped; things seemed to be getting more complicated than he liked.

'Well when Dave moves into the top flat, what're you going to do?'

'I might move back home, I'm not really in London enough of the time to afford to rent a place.' Seeing all sorts of arguments in

Morris's eye, he turned to Ruth. 'What about you Ruth? You're selling your house, aren't you? If you rent out the other flats and keep the basement here as your studio, where will you live?'

'Luke, it's so exciting; I'm buying the house next door. The solicitors made some agreement with the vendors, because nobody except developers seemed to want it – it has an Order of Dilapidations or something on it -- it had to have some walls taken down, and they let me start converting it. Nina's going to stay until I am settled and can manage for myself, with just a visiting helper; then she wants to go back to Scotland. Maybe I'll have a dog.'

Nina smiled. 'A dog will be more use getting about London than I ever will.'

'But not as good at cooking.' They all laughed. 'And I don't think it will be any good at choosing clothes.'

Luke, looking at Ruth's grey, uniform-style skirt, opened and closed his mouth.

Nina shrugged. 'I'm sure you'll manage. Morris will help. Perhaps Luke will help.' Luke put up a protesting hand.

Seeing his expression, Morris said. 'Do you want Ruth to show you her new house, Luke? I'm just going to take Nina to the station, I won't be long.'

Luke jumped up, his eyes brightening.

As Nina left, she shook Luke's hand firmly then held on. Her brows registered half trouble, half question. She said, 'Ruth is better when things don't change too much, you know.'

'Sure.' As the car drove off, he turned to Ruth. 'What was that about?'

'I don't know. I suspect Nina still thinks I'm about fifteen. Come and see what we're doing next door.'

Luke took her hand. He was having trouble assimilating all the house purchase information thrown his way. He remembered the difficulty his parents experienced raising funds for a deposit to buy their Council House in Catford. Ruth couldn't be buying two terraced houses in this exclusive, if run down, part of Greenwich, surely? He must have misunderstood. Perhaps Ruth, being disabled, had some special allocation of space or funds. He became still more bewildered as he realised the scale of the work being carried out.

Eventually, after picking their way over the accessible parts of the house, Ruth listened to her watch and said, 'I must catch my bus, is Morris back?'

She could hardly be that rich if she had to catch a bus. He needed to pick up a bus too. 'I'll come with you. My Dad's back from a trip abroad, so I thought I might go home to Catford tonight.'

'We can walk if you're coming too.'

'Walk!'

'Morris and I walk whenever we can. It's only a mile or two: up the hill and across the heath. I need the exercise. It's still warm, Luke, there are leaves on the ground. I can show you my house – well it's not really mine any more, we've exchanged contracts, but delayed completion. I'm staying until the furniture goes into store. The new owners won't move in until January, so they wanted me to stay as long as possible and there's still a lot of work to do on this Greenwich house.'

Luke, never keen on walking for its own sake, and even more reluctant to do so on a darkening December afternoon, could not disappoint Ruth in her happy anticipation. She put on a hairy brown tweed coat, about three sizes too large for her. Then she tucked one hand under his elbow and set off using her white stick in the other hand to avoid obstacles in front and away from him. Luke watched her technique in some curiosity. They both remained silent, concentrating.

Luke found his role novel. Of course he had looked after girls when out with them, but in a casual manner. On the whole the women in his life had looked after him. It occurred to him that Ruth, lightly tucked into his arm, was in that moment totally dependent on him. What would it be like never to move outside unless attached to another human, or perhaps a dog? He supposed that in a completely familiar place a stick would do.

'Ruth, do you go anywhere alone or does either Morris or Nina always go with you?'

'Of course not. I walk from the bus stop in Blackheath to my house. I even went to Scotland on my own. Morris put me on the coach.' She half chuckled. 'I was fine except for using the ... the lavatory. A kind lady helped me, but I felt a bit uncomfortable.'

'Is that it? Do you never run or ... dance, or anything.'

'I run in my garden a little. I won't be able to do that when it's sold, will I?'

'No, I suppose not, but your new Greenwich house has a garden, hasn't it?'

'Yes, but it goes uphill with little walls. I'd bump into them if I ran there.'

As the last of the weak sunlight faded out of the sky, they reached the Heath. Not, on a December afternoon, the most attractive area, with its browned grass and grey paths. Still it was an open space; pedestrians didn't have to stick to a few feet of paving. An idea began to spread in Luke's mind.

'Put your stick away, Ruth. Let me guide you.'

'If you want, Luke, but I feel odd walking outside without it.'

'We're on the Heath now. There's nothing for miles except litter. I won't let you fall. I'm going to put my arm around your waist as if we were dancing. I bet you could learn to dance. This coat is a dreadful nuisance, you need something a little less enveloping. Anyway, I've got you now.'

With the stick folded away, Ruth became much more tentative. 'Isn't it dark, Luke? Are you sure you can see.'

'I can see fine. The lamps are on and there's still a little light in the sky. There's a slice of new moon up there too. Anyway I'm used to moving around backstage and not bumping into stuff *and* to keeping an eye out for my partner. Come on, relax, trust me.'

'Oh! What was that?'

'Just avoiding some dog mess. You're doing fine.'

'My hand feels lost though without my stick.'

Luke reached across and took hold of her free hand. It made walking a bit more awkward, but as soon as he held it he could feel her body resisting less. He sensed an instinctive obedience in her movements; she would make a good responsive dancer. In fact if she had a partner she could do anything, ice skating even. Why not? The heath seemed to be empty and the December air astonishingly balmy.

'OK, we're in the middle of the heath now, I think we should try and waltz.'

Ruth chuckled, and Luke's heart took a small skip. 'Luke, I can't dance.'

'You'll be able to in five minutes. Wait a mo, I'm going to undo this sack thing you're wearing, I can't hold you properly. That's better. The lining's much nicer to feel.' Luke, having undone the hefty buttons, slipped his right arm in and put his hand in the small of her back. He took her left hand and placed it on his shoulder, then grasped her right hand and pulled her chest to chest. She lifted her face, laughing again, as Luke began to hum the Skater's Waltz. He smiled, then realised she couldn't see. Having no hands spare, he dropped a light kiss on her forehead. 'Now, bend your knees a little,' he gently kicked her left foot 'and step back with this foot.' He rocked her backwards pushing her right foot outwards, 'now bring the left one to join the right. Perfect!'

It was like having a little sister, or a child of his own. She obeyed and trusted and followed him and, just as he'd promised, within five minutes she had mastered the simple back-side-together, forward-side-together of the basic waltz. 'Now we can dance. I will sing; you just do what my hand tells you. The steps will stay the same, but I'll move us about a bit.' He taught her to dip a little on the forward and backward steps, and after a few minutes had begun to ease her out of the tight square. He tried a little turn, and she lost her footing so he simply lifted her and put her down safely, but a little breathless. 'OK?'

'Oh yes! Oh Luke, can we do some more. I could do that all night.'

'I think we'll practice indoors next, we're acquiring an audience.'

'I thought I heard something.'

'Yes, never mind them, come on, let's get you home.'

The trio of teenagers drifted off as Ruth opened her stick and she and Luke walked on. Luke had not really been troubled by the youths. He had actually been taken by surprise by his own body. Just as he had been feeling all altruistic and glorying in the pleasure he had been giving Ruth, and the success of his lesson, something had changed. In the moment when he had tried to spin her and she had lost her balance, instead of tightening her muscles to save herself, she had simply surrendered to his clasp and let him take her weight. Only awareness of the potentially hostile kids had prevented him turning that moment into a passionate one.

Although, in many ways, he had the morals of a tomcat and rarely turned down a chance, Ruth's vulnerability made a difference. In fact Ruth differed in every aspect from any other girl he had spent time with. Befriending her carried a whole set of unaccustomed responsibilities. These precluded casual sex. Luke frowned as he grappled with both his instinct to seduce and his resolve to be brotherly.

'Luke, is something the matter?'

He stared down at her for a moment. 'No, nothing, what made you think that?'

'I can feel it through your arm. I like the way your body talks.'

'Christ!' Luke remembered Ruth's sensitivity too late, but to his surprise she didn't tick him off. If she started talking about bodies, he would be in trouble. 'Aren't you going to tell me not to swear?'

'No. Morris says it's normal and not meant to be blasphemous. Anyway, I was wondering why you jumped so. Did I say something I shouldn't?'

Luke sighed. 'No. I think I am just having another little confusion with Heloise. It's the dark that does it. You turn into Heloise in the dark.'

'Are you angry again?'

'No, oh no, just a bit confused. Now lead me to this house of yours with your magic wand.'

Ruth chuckled. 'I do love being with you Luke,' Luke closed his eyes, 'you're so different from Morris.'

'Hang on, Ruth, there are emergency road works – or rather pavement works – here.' He steered her round some barriers. Vandals had pushed some of them aside and Luke, replacing one, touched a still-warm workman's bucket and suddenly found a black sticky substance on his hand. He swore.

Ruth stopped dead. 'What is it, Luke?'

'I've got some muck – industrial muck – tar I think, on my hand. Ugh, I'd better not touch anything until I can wash it.'

'If it's tar, it won't wash off, but I know what to do. Butter.'

'Butter?'

'Mmm, Aunt Chloe rubbed butter on me when I got tar on my arm at the beach. It worked. What's that, Luke'

Luke laughed. His face had registered his surprised scepticism, and he had made a sound to go with it. 'Sorry, Ruth, I keep forgetting that you can't see. I never realised how much talking goes on without actual words. I was just making a face while I imagined using butter instead of detergent.'

'You wait and see.'

Ruth led him away from the shopping area of Blackheath and they walked down what he would have called a posh street then turned left into a tree-lined lane. The road was unmade up and marked private; they could have been in deepest Surrey. Ruth opened a gate and went up a drive towards a Victorian mansion. To Catford-born Luke this monstrous lump of brick and dirty stone represented a stratum of society beyond his ken. He was accustomed to travelling and visiting people, some of his Italian cousins lived in very comfortable circumstances, he had entertained at parties in large houses, he had sung in Masonic halls and small stately homes, but he had not personally known anyone for whom a large house was their own home.

He looked around, unnerved. The name Temple Lawns, formed in wrought iron, had been attached to a free-standing post beside the front door. What the hell was he doing in this weird place with this unlikely woman?

Ruth let go of his arm, 'Luke? Are you coming?'

32

Temple Lawns: Ruth & Luke

Muttering under his breath, Luke followed meekly as Ruth led up the steps to the hefty front door. He suffered a complete reversion of his earlier feelings of protectiveness and agency towards Ruth. The role he had so much enjoyed of giving her freedom of movement and releasing her bonds suddenly seemed foolish. How could he feel protective towards someone in her position? She took for granted things he had been taught to envy. Not that he would have wanted for a nanosecond to have lived in this mausoleum, but size – in building terms (especially in England) – meant money. Money, except on a day-to-day living scale, had never been part of his family's lifestyle.

In the house Ruth switched on lights. She didn't need them, but she had been taught to use them to show that she was in. Anyway, she explained, she wanted Luke to see her home. Her home appalled Luke. Large dark wooden items of furniture – he couldn't even guess their individual use – filled the hall, a *hall*, for heaven's sake, not a few feet between the bottom of the stairs and the front door. The carpets were dark, intricately patterned and surprisingly threadbare, wallpaper of a small repeated pattern covered all the walls he could see. He correctly guessed that no one had decorated or altered the furniture for over fifty years. Ruth led him through to a kitchen. This seemed to him almost as big as the whole ground floor of his own home.

'Sit here, Luke.' She said, pulling out a wooden chair from the large table in the centre of the room. 'Here, let me feel the stuff on your hand. Is it still sticky?' She took his hand in both of hers and ran her finger delicately over his palm. Then she lifted it to her nose and sniffed carefully. She answered herself. 'Mmm, sort of; it certainly smells and feels like tar.'

Luke sat passively, mesmerised as in the past by her touch. She walked over to one of the array of dark wooden glass-fronted cabinets and pulled out a silver butter dish. Using a dainty bone-handled butter knife, she cut out a large lump of butter and spread it with soft rubbing movements over the tar on the palm of Luke's hand. His hand became extremely slippery and his body began to unwind long before the tar gave in. Ruth hitched herself on to the corner of the table and pulled Luke's hand into her lap, to get a better grip on it. He leaned his swimming head until it rested against her upper arm and sat unresisting as her hands smoothed and pressed the butter in and around the tar, then her nails lightly scraped away at the resistant surface

'Are you all right, Luke? It doesn't seem to want to shift.'

'I'm fine. Don't stop, it's working.' He lifted his head to look at his hand then turned to watch her face. Odd that her face should register concentration but no self-consciousness. The blindness, he supposed, precluded awareness of others watching. She had tucked her hair behind her ear. He looked first at her eyes, those frustrating features that were most emphatically not windows to her soul. He could not stop himself from searching there for responses, tell-tale signs of feelings, inklings of hidden purposes, each time to be turned away. He tried to see if any other feature would give him a clue. Her neat but unremarkable nose said little, though she sometimes wrinkled it in an endearing way when confused. He passed on to the mouth. Her pale lips were pressed close as if her chin were involved in the pressure of her fingers on his hand. Not a bad shape to her mouth he noted. The paleness made the lips disappear into the surrounding skin. Close to, the top lip had a neat clean sweep ending in a deep dip at the corners. The bottom lip? What would that look like not compressed as it was now? What would she look like with lipstick?

'Why don't you wear lipstick, Ruth?'

She turned, with a half chuckle. 'Why would I do that, Luke? Besides, isn't it red and don't you have to paint it exactly on the lips? I would have red patches in all the wrong places, wouldn't I?'

'I suppose so. What do other people like you do?'

'I don't know.'

Luke didn't know either. He reached a finger into the butter. Her bottom lip, released from concentration, had a pleasing deep curve before rising and disappearing at the corners.

'Hold still. I am going to give you some lipstick.' He took her chin in his buttery hand. 'Open your mouth a little. There. You've got a sheen on them now, that's better.' She sat patiently, her chin

267

still in his hands, her mouth obediently half open. He kissed her lightly. At least his barely formulated intention had been light, but her first submissive non-reaction impelled him to kiss again more firmly. After a few moments, during which the kiss took over and his hands had begun to reach under her jumper, he pulled away.

'We shouldn't do this Ruth. You should stop me.'

'Why? I like it, don't you?'

'Of course, but you can't go around kissing anyone,' said Luke, sublimely ignoring his usual behaviour, 'simply because you like it.'

'I don't,' she answered reasonably, 'I only kiss you.'

Luke, nonplussed, stared down at her. A moral code, dormant until this hour, made him hesitate to take advantage of her again. On his image of Ruth, like a red sticker, lay the knowledge that she was part of a different world; she did not belong among opera singers any more than he belonged among weavers and furthermore she would not be at home among his family since she could never have children. And yet her voice, her dependency, her hands made his body sing a different tune.

Uncharacteristically hesitant, he spoke bluntly. 'Ruth, I cannot be your boyfriend ... for all sorts of reasons ... and *you* shouldn't kiss someone who ... who isn't attached to you.'

She laughed up at him. 'Luke, I think it is you who should not kiss me, then.'

Luke sighed, picked up a tea towel and wiped his buttery hands. Most of the tar had come off. 'For a religious person, you've got funny morals.'

'I don't think I am religious. Anyway, I've already committed a sin so big that nothing else makes much difference. I don't feel like a sinner about *that* – the time in the hotel – only about lying to you in the explosion.'

'Ruth, that's finished now. Forget it. I owe you my life, if you hadn't held on to me so much of the time I would have died, I think.' He shook his head, still tussling with the mixture of fear, agony and excitement induced by the memory. Ruth represented the excitement. 'Some things were good in that time, weren't they?'

'Mmm – the singing. I could listen to you singing every hour of my life. I like touching you, too, Luke. Of course I touch my weaving, but the only living things I touch are my garden and sometimes Morris's hand or shoulder. I used to touch Nina a lot when I was a child. I like skin. Yours is different.' She reached a hand up, brushed his chin, then ran her thumb softly over his lips.

Luke took a breath. 'Don't do that.'

'Sorry, does it hurt?'

Luke laughed. 'Far from it. Just not a good idea. In fact it means I will have to kiss you again.' He did, but once again stopped himself from going further. Unsettled and totally unaccustomed to self-restraint, he tried to reach back to the earlier feelings of being in charge of a vulnerable person, of being in a position to dispense help. 'Come along, I'm going to go on with the dancing lesson.'

He lifted Ruth to the ground and followed her through a passage into a large room. This had a wooden floor, set in tiny criss-cross squares, two dull leather sofas, with buttons all over, a brocaded chaise longue and unmatching armchairs. Like Smarties dropped in the playground, these barely featured in the endless space. A cavernous fireplace with a marble mantelpiece housed an inadequate three-bar electric fire. He realised suddenly that there were no radiators. Remembering Melanie's house, he wondered why the rich could not afford proper heating? Perhaps they disapproved of comfort. It made no sense. He went straight over and switched on the fire.

'Don't you have central heating? Is this the only heating in this great room?'

'No, behind the armchair near the window there's a fan heater. I'm not really allowed to use it, but I sometimes put it on for a bit if I'm planning to listen to music in here. The record player is there too. Of course I have to switch the heater off to listen, because of the noise.'

'Ruth, who doesn't allow you?'

'Oh!' She laughed. 'It was Mama, so I suppose I can now. Morris says I don't have to do the things Mama told me I had to do – or not do. He thinks she was funny in the head.'

'I'll say!'

Luke switched on the fan heater, wincing at the noise, but determined to banish the chill in the room. Then he went to a cabinet, with sliding glass doors housing ancient, 1970s LPs and leafed through looking for anything with a three-time beat. From Dan's old collection he joyfully grabbed some Lehar Waltzes and under Ruth's instruction set the record player going. The furniture was scattered inconveniently and he started to push it around to clear a space.

'Luke, are you moving things?'

'Yes, we need a clear space to dance in.'

'You mustn't do that. I'll fall over or bump into things.'

'Sorry, I didn't think.' He replaced the heavy sofa. How could people sit on that with all the hard buttoned lumps? 'I'll just have to steer you carefully. Another time, I'll bring a piece of chalk, then we can move them and put them back.'

'Another time? You're going to Glasgow next, aren't you? The new owners will be taking over in January.'

'Of course.' Shaking off a momentary twinge of disappointment, Luke took her into a dance hold and began to move in a simple square waltz formation as they had done on the heath. 'What are you doing with all this ... old furniture?'

'An auction. The button-back sofas are valuable, apparently.'

'Jesus, you'd have to pay me to sit on one of those.'

Ruth giggled.

The lesson proceeded with a certain amount of tangling with the furniture. Luke, getting into the role, became severe with missteps and demanded a high level of obedience from his pupil. At the end of the first side he turned the record over and began to relax. He had always relished the old-fashioned dance lessons, much despised by other students. Something about two bodies combining rhythms appealed to him on both musical and sensual levels. Ruth, having no other guide but his voice and his body, made fewer errors and was less inclined to be misled by her own version of the steps than other novice dancers. Holding her closer, Luke began some variations, his body delighting in her ability to follow the minimal pressures of his hand in the small of her back. He tried a half-spin and she managed it. He tried another faster, she lost her balance and he lifted her and set her down again breathless. I've taught her to dance, he thought, something she couldn't do before. Pleasure flooded him and he hugged her in exaltation.

'Luke, I'm getting hot.'

He slipped off her rugged cardigan and held her more firmly. 'One more side of the record. Come on, we'll do a fast spin before we give up.'

'All right. I'll try.'

They managed the fast spin at the third attempt.

'OK, relax now, just a last waltz. This will be very slow and gentle. He reached out and switched off the main light. You can lean on me. That's it. Put both arms round my neck.' Luke pushed her head against his shoulder and slipped both arms around her; his hands dropping naturally to rest on her behind. Lethally, his mind insisted on contemplating how the bottom would feel without the intervening unappetising cloth. He tried several times to recapture the sense of being a teacher or a helper.

At the end of the music Ruth stirred sleepily in his arms. 'I like that. Luke, you feel different. You've gone hard.'

'Ruth!' Luke sat down on the despised sofa and pulled her down beside him. 'You're not supposed to say ... you're supposed to pretend not to notice things like that.'

'Why?' She asked, genuine puzzlement in her voice. 'It's a funny thing to pretend about. I don't mind, Luke. I like the kissing best, but I don't mind.'

Luke put his head in his hands. '*I* mind. I feel bad making love to you and then going away. I might make love to someone else while I'm away. I can't be your ... your boyfriend. I can't ... Never mind. I ought to go.'

'Luke listen, I know I don't understand properly how people should behave, but I don't think I'm as stupid ... as innocent as you seem to think I am. No one else is going to kiss me. Ever.'

'Nonsense!'

'Certainly no one else is going to have sex with me.'

Luke remained silent. 'Apart from Morris, you're the only man I know who talks to me. Maybe I'll meet others, maybe I'll go back to the blind school and meet other blind people, maybe I'll get a dog and go out and meet people. I've already ordered a Braille computer. There's the Internet. I'm lucky; I've got enough money to do lots of things. I can go to concerts and opera. And of course I have my work. I am so at peace when I am weaving. If just sometimes I can listen to you sing and perhaps we can kiss or anything else you like, I will be as happy as I could be without being sighted – maybe happier than many people who can see. I'm not sure how other people feel. Anyway, I *know* I can't have you all the time.' She chuckled. 'I don't know exactly what it means, but Morris says you're a "five star stud".'

Luke blushed. 'Ruth, for heaven's sake don't repeat that.'

'Oh, is it rude?'

'Yes.'

'Well Morris just said that you could have anybody you fancied and he thinks from what Dave says, or doesn't say, that you probably do.'

'Does Morris know about ... New York.'

'N-no. I just said you were nice to me. I said we sort of kissed and made up.'

Luke took a deep breath. 'Look Ruth, Morris isn't exactly wrong. I do get about a bit. Not,' he went on dryly, 'as much as he probably imagines.' He laughed. 'Actually, there hasn't been anyone since New York, but I must admit that's just because I haven't had time for ... seductions. But there will be others, Ruth, and I don't want you to be one of several. Even I know that would be wrong. I would be taking advantage of you.'

'Luke, what if I want to be taken advantage of?'

Luke lifted his hands helplessly. He had always worked on the principle that women would look after their own best interests. He forced no one, but he had never attempted to turn down an offer he wanted to take up ... *until now*. Nor, it occurred to him, had he ever discussed the subject; things happened or they didn't. You got laid or not. Ruth wasn't any woman, and certainly hadn't her own best interests in mind. Or had she? 'Ruth, I'm useless at self-denial. If you want me to stay, I'll stay. But you ought to send me away.'

'Luke, just sing for me, please.'

'We could put on one of those old LP's. You've got some Kathleen Ferrier and Janet Baker – top notch singers.

'I like them, but I like listening to you singing just as much. Morris and I tried to record the broadcast from Rome, so that we could listen to you as we worked.'

Luke laughed, lifting her hair away from her face. 'You can have perfect recordings of Domingo or Carreras if you want music while you work.'

'I know, but I like your singing best.' The certainty in her voice shook him for a moment. Humble for the first time in his life he said, 'I've got a little way to go before I sing like either of them.'

'Oh Luke, you know what the critics say. Anyway, you didn't listen, I said, *I* like your voice best.

Boosted, Luke sang. The singing, as Ruth had instinctively known it would, calmed his unaccustomed mental turbulence. After a while they returned to the kitchen for a drink. Luke, more comfortable now in the heavy surroundings, lifted Ruth and parked her on the kitchen table, before getting them both a glass of water. There didn't seem to be anything stronger in the cupboards.

'There's still a bit of tar left on your hand, Luke, isn't there? Shall I deal with that?'

'Fine.' He sat on one of the chairs and lifted his hand.

Five minutes later, Luke took the tea towel from her, wiped the last black smears from his hand and slid his arms around her and under her clothes. 'I'm sorry, Ruth, but I have to kiss you again.'

'I like kissing, Luke.'

Luke, standing now, and with her sitting on the table, pulled her tight. Every resolution made in the last months and remade in the last hours dissolved with the butter on his palm. After several minutes of hungry kissing she pulled away and spoke wonderingly: 'Luke? This is a different kind of kissing.'

Luke remembering the tentative, leisurely, voluptuous hours in the hotel in New York, dropped his head against her chest. He spoke breathlessly. 'Yes.' His face rebelled at the unfriendly texture of her clothes and his hands made short work of the buttons until his mouth rested on warm flesh. 'Do you really not mind?' His scruples suddenly seemed of very little moment. He undid her bra strap and let the full weight of her breasts fall sweetly against his hands – of no moment at all really.

33

Greenwich: New Year 2001

Racks of grass-green skirts, peach cardigans, sea-blue trousers, all of them strung about with pink Sales notices, enveloped Luke. He had dived into Marks and Spencers to get out of the chilling rain. Now seeing the clothes he thought of Ruth. He pulled a blouse out of a rack wondering how to tell what it would look like on a real woman instead of flat on a hanger. It occurred to him that breasts, which come in such astonishing variety, must be a sartorial problem. He turned to the skirts and tried to remember how big Ruth was around the waist. Perhaps it would be better to play safe and get her music, unless...he dialled Barbara.

'Ba, I'm standing in M&S, I want to get a Christmas present for Ruth, but how do I guess her size? I mean all blouses look the same when they're on a hanger.'

'We've had Christmas, Luke, remember?'

'Well, I mean a housewarming/New year present really. She's just moved in to her new place and I'm going there tonight to see the New Year in with her and Dave and Morris. Oh, and her nanny as well. My rave New Year party.'

'Sounds a blast. Where are the others – Kes, Ange and co.?'

'Edinburgh.'

'Bit out of reach.'

'Yea, well, anyway I thought I'd get Ruth some clothes. She only has very old-fashioned stuff; but it's not that easy.'

'Mmm. Is she bigger than Claudia?'

'She's definitely bigger than Claudia, more your size I'd say. Sort of big front to back, but not side to side, if you see what I mean.'

'At a wild guess, bra size thirty-four C. Look Luke, buy a pretty top in size 14 and she can change it. Are you there? Look at the label, it should say UK 10, 12, 14 or 16. If she's got a big bosom, get a garment with deep darts, you know with lots of shape to it.'

'Jesus, Ba, this sounds like computer-speak to me.'

'OK, smile at an assistant, tell her what you told me and tell her the colour of Ruth's hair.'

Luke emerged twenty minutes later feeling flustered but warmer and with a bag in his hand.

Barbara was right though; he had half forgotten that Christmas was over. Apart from the unseasonably mild weather, there had been Claudia's defection. In the run up to Christmas Luke had been inundated with livery gigs in clubs and halls and out-of-town concerts. He had taken little notice of the family's movements and so had been quite put out to fetch up on Christmas Day itself only to find that Claudia had left for Ireland with Kieran the anaesthetist and Maria's blessing.

It had not been the first Christmas without the full family. Luke had spent a couple of Christmases in Rome. This, though, was the first one for Maria and Gordon without their elder daughter and she was much missed. Claudia's busyness tended to be the catalyst for action in the family and no one quite took over the role. Dave, who usually spent Christmas with them, defected too, going to Antigua again. He'd just got back for tonight's New Year's Eve party. Lewis, Barbara and her very large bump did what they could to fill these gaps. All the same, the dynamics of the family had shifted over the last year and not yet settled into a new pattern. Luke felt that maybe he was to blame, for having been caught up in the explosion, or alternatively that everyone else was happy about the status quo and only he felt uneasy.

He set off on New Year's Eve with low expectations. Ruth in company would probably be withdrawn. Nina, endlessly patting her bun, would look shocked almost whatever he said, yet would ask disconcertingly personal questions about his time under the building with Ruth. Had it hurt? Had Ruth told him about her dolls? Did he mind about his perfect features being scarred? Dave and Morris would look at each other just that tad too long. As if all of this were not off-putting enough, he still didn't know quite were he stood, or wanted to stand, with Ruth.

Arriving in Borrow Crescent, Luke handed over his package to Ruth. She flushed with pleasure as she tore at the tissue pulling out the glossy, deep blue blouse. Uttering sighs of delight, she felt it all over, undoing the buttons and sliding her fingers under the collar. 'Oh Luke, this is my first ever present from … from outside, you know. I mean a present not from Mama or Dad or Nina or Morris! How did you know what would fit me?'

'I didn't. Barbara and a shop assistant helped, but you can take it back and exchange it if it's the wrong size.'

'No, no, I want to keep this one.'

Luke laughed. 'It's for wearing Ruth, not to put on the mantelpiece.'

Dave arrived bringing her a pale blue silk scarf from Antigua and she sat down drawing the material through her hands in wonder. Supper, cooked by Morris in Ruth's space-age kitchen, turned out to Luke's surprise to be great fun. Morris had prepared a beef fondue. They sat at the round table with a pot of oil simmering gently on a spirit stove in the centre. Around this were dotted small pots of sauces and dips and plates of melt-in-the-mouth cubes of fillet steak. Ruth, with Luke on one side and Nina on the other, managed to spear her meat, get it into the pot and find the right dips with no more mishaps than the rest of them. Nina relaxed and stopped quizzing him; Ruth bubbled like a child at her first party.

The merriness of the supper party had been unexpected and Luke entered Ruth's new sitting room with lifting spirits. The first thing he spotted, slightly at variance with Morris's tasteful pastel décor, was the mellow walnut of an old upright piano. He had seen it before, the night he had stayed in Ruth's old house with her. He had cried out then, when she admitted that it, too, would be going to auction.

Luke crossed the room and almost groaning with envy lifted back the lid and ran his hands over the keys.

'Real ivory!'

Morris came over. 'How do you know?'

'This little seam, you can just see it here. Plastic keys are made all in one piece.' Luke sat on the stool and stretched his hands over two great chords. 'And in tune!' The keys responded instantly to his touch; the tone, warm and milky, seemed to pour out with little effort. Ignoring the others, he settled himself and began wandering though his small repertoire. Ruth curled up on a leather beanbag near his feet.

After a while he murmured, 'It would be worth returning to my old ruler-wielding piano teacher, in order to spend time on this baby. Who played in your family, Ruth?'

'No one. I did a bit when I was very little, but it stopped when my sight started to go. Mama didn't like the noise.'

Luke slewed round to stare at her. 'Noise? I've rarely come across an upright with a sweeter tone. What can you play?'

'Nothing, Luke'

'You could learn; there are several blind piano players.' He frowned. 'Why did you bring it here, if you don't play? Do you play Morris?'

'No. Ruth brought it here and restored it for you to play. Dave has fallen for it too.'

Luke gazed at her, dumbfounded. Eventually he simply let out his breath. 'Wow!'

At 1 am, having sung the New Year in, Morris, Dave and Luke started 2001 by making the freezing dash back to the studio house next door. Dave stayed with Morris in the ground floor flat and Luke had the new flat at the top of the house to himself. He looked round at the mixture of clean paint and odd bits of rubbed down wooden furniture. Why had he been so adamant in refusing to move in here with Dave next month? Of course Morris and Dave might fall out. Then where would he be? Ruth next door too? Not a good idea really. He would be committed to spending time with her, not that he wouldn't have happily spent tonight with her if Nina hadn't been in question. Ruth had hung heavy and sleepy in his arms as they had all clung together for Auld Lang Syne and it had been a wrench to let the soft weight of her go at the end. Did Nina know he had slept with her? Presumably not. He still hadn't told Dave. All the consolation he'd had during the whole evening had been one snatched kiss while Nina had gone to the bathroom and Morris and Dave had been clearing the kitchen.

Ruth had taken him to see her 'office'. Taking his hand she had led him up to the desk in the centre. 'Look, Luke, my new Braille computer. I'll be able to order wool, or Braille books or music records by myself now. I can scan in printed letters and then the voice software will read them back to me.'

Luke, treading across the plushiest carpet he could remember, duly admired the large keyboard and heavy monitor, flanked by a scanner and printer of equally gross proportions. As his lips praised the technology, his hands and mind on a totally different agenda reached around Ruth's waist and under the ubiquitous heavy cardigan. She caught her breath. 'Luke, Nina might come in, I don't think ...' She chuckled, causing his blood to race, as he pulled her towards him.

'One New Year kiss ...' he leant back against a wall feeling behind him the uneven texture of one of her hangings. For a second he worried that he might damage it, on the other hand someone might appear any moment. He pulled her close. The kiss, once begun, proved difficult to stop.

Nina called, 'Ruth? Where have you got to?'

Ruth, laughing, pushed Luke away and sang out, 'I'm just showing Luke my computer.'

By the time Nina joined them they were once more standing politely side-by-side, admiring the cyclopean hardware in the centre of the room. She must have felt something in the atmosphere, though, as she shot Luke a funny look and started patting her bun again. The kiss and the huddled dancing at the end of the evening were his ration.

He laughed, realising that he knew things about Ruth that no one else did. That snatched kiss had definitely been exciting. Perhaps Ruth was even now wishing she could be in bed with him.

Ruth, her face alight, was saying to Nina, as she dried glasses: 'I'm so happy Nina. Luke was happy too, wasn't he? Did you get to know him a bit this evening? Isn't he special?'

Hesitating and picking her words, Nina answered, 'I don't think I have ever met a more ...taking young man but ...'

'You should feel his hair. At least I suppose you can't do that, though I'm sure he wouldn't mind, but it's so soft and alive. And I told you about the dancing lesson, but it's difficult to explain, how wonderful it is to feel his muscles moving with the music.'

Growing more and more alarmed at Ruth's panegyric, Nina tried again. 'Ruth, try not to get too fond of Luke. You know so little about the world, dear, and I don't want you hurt. Luke is one of those lucky creatures who has the world at his feet. The trouble is, even if he does want to spend time with you, he won't be here very much. Morris says he's going to be famous, well you've only got to listen to the radio, to know what celebrities are like. I don't want you to be hurt, dear. It's never any good falling in love with someone like that. He's far too handsome for his own good. He'll marry and probably divorce some other famous opera singer, you'll see.' Nina, with tears in her eyes, went on, 'I don't want you to be unhappy, Ruth, and there's nothing worse than unrequited love.'

Ruth, the snatched kiss still haunting her lips, and her fingers in the silky material of the blouse Luke had given her, was in no mood to pay attention to sense. Relief filled her that she hadn't succumbed to temptation and told Nina about the sequel to the dancing when Luke took her home in December. She continued to listen, though, with her customary obedience.

34
Blackheath: Ruth's Garden

Luke, after yet another two weeks of one-night performances, returned home via Cardiff in order to sing at Melanie's wedding on the 14th of January. For this he sang Ferrando's aria *A breath of love ...* from *Cosi fan tutte*. To ease his disapproval of the union he sang as seductively as he knew how. This resulted to his satisfaction in a deal of blushing from Melanie; Bruce must have been as daft as he imagined to agree to that particular aria.

Dave, Kes and Angela were all scattered about the country. He tried ringing Ruth or Morris, but never seemed to catch them at home or in the studio. Perhaps they had an exhibition somewhere? Feeling a little left out, he tried to settle into a routine. Mornings coaching hopeful music college entrants in a poky room with a poor piano, afternoons in a room with hardly more space but at least an accompanist, being coached himself for his forthcoming role at Glyndebourne. Evenings doing the odd gig here or there.

After a week of this he came home on a freezing late January afternoon to find a message on the answerphone. It was Morris: 'Luke, if you get this message soon can you give me a call on my mobile, I've got a problem with Ruth.'

He rang immediately. 'Morris? What's happened?'

'Luke, thank God! 'Ruth's gone mad. She's in the garden of the Blackheath house. She won't come in; she's been there for hours. She'll end up with pneumonia again, I know. Nina's snowed up at the airport in Glasgow. Dave's in Hull. He said to ring you. Can you help?'

'I'm coming.'

He took a taxi. The driver deposited him in front of the bleak brickwork of Temple Lawns. He rang the doorbell and receiving no answer pushed the door open. He walked through the bare, echoing house calling out. 'Morris! Ruth!'

'Out here!' Morris yelled, then appeared and grabbed him with frantic, freezing hands, pulling him towards the French windows. 'She won't budge. She's been there for hours now. We only came for her to say goodbye to the garden. The sale's been completed ages ago, the new owners move in tomorrow. Ruth doesn't understand it's not hers any more. She signed a legal contract; she can't change her mind. It's all my fault, I wanted her to sell this place to save our studio.'

Leaving Morris, Luke walked down the garden. He found Ruth sitting on the ground at the foot of a beech tree. Tears and freezing rain streaked her hands, hair and face.

'Ruth, you fool, what on earth are you doing here in this weather?'

'Luke?' She said wonderingly.

'Yes, it's me.' He crouched down beside her and picked up her unresisting hands, 'Jesus, you're frozen.' He stripped off his long heavy leather jacket and huddled it round her. 'Ruth, come on, you've got to come in. You can die of hypothermia in weather like this. You don't want pneumonia again. What's the matter?'

'I can't leave my trees, Luke. I didn't understand. Well, I didn't think what it would be like never to come back to my garden again. This is my space, my home, out here. It's been here all my life. I can't leave it now. I want to stay here after all. Morris says I can't, but I must.'

'Ruth…Morris is right. I'm afraid it's done. There's a legal contract signed, isn't there? What about your beautiful new house? You'll get to love that in the end, and there's a garden there too.'

'But it's *this* garden I love,' she wailed, 'these trees. Nobody told me it would hurt like this. Nobody will love this garden when I go. A man came and talked about thinning out the trees for the new owners. What if he cuts down *this* tree?' She started sobbing again.

Luke bent over and held her by the shoulders, shaking her a little. 'Ruth, Ruth, stop it. Listen to me. No one is going to cut down this tree. Come inside. We'll ring someone; we'll get a preservation order put on it. There's probably one on it already.'

Morris appeared beside them, wringing his hands and shivering. 'There are no blankets or anything in the house, I don't know what to do.'

'I think we'll just have to be brutal. Come on Ruth, we're going to take you in. Take her other arm, Morris. Come on, up you come.'

The two men half carried, half walked her the length of the

garden. She resisted, protesting all the way. 'I can't leave it forever ... I can't live and never come here again ... I love this place ... I didn't realise it would hurt like this ... please let me stay ... please just leave me ... please ... oh please.'

Once inside the house, Ruth dropped to the floor. Morris locked the French windows and Luke looked round for anything to warm Ruth up with, but the house was bare and only marginally warmer than the garden. Her skin looked pearly white and bloodless. He came back and started rubbing her hands and her back as she knelt, head drooping, on the bare boards. Luke began to feel seriously alarmed. 'Morris quickly, you've got your car here? We must get her to somewhere warm.'

'Should we go to an Accident and Emergency?'

'Mmm, I suppose ... no, I know, we'll go to my sister, she's just down the road. Lewis is off duty today, I was going to visit anyway and he'll know what to do – he's a fireman. Come on.'

In the car Luke, in growing consternation, cradled Ruth, who seemed only half conscious and growing colder. He rang Barbara on his mobile to say they were coming. When they arrived, Lewis, phlegmatic and kindly, carried her in and straight up to a bed already warmed with bottles. Talking continuously, telling her what he was doing and why, he and Morris stripped off her damp outer clothes, put a thermometer under her arm, took towels off a hot radiator and wrapped them round her, including her head. Barbara, her tummy now at full stretch, puffed up the stairs with some lukewarm, sweetened tea and a straw. Morris then sat, as instructed, feeding her. Every few minutes Lewis checked the thermometer. Twenty minutes later he said, 'OK love, you'll do. It's low but not out of reach. A couple more hot bottles on top of the covers, Ba, if you've got them. Luke you fetch them, we don't want her to be giving birth just at this moment, do we?'

On his return with the bottles, Luke looked at his brother-in-law with awe. 'How d'you know all this stuff, Lewis, it's not exactly fire duty.'

'I've been doing extra training – towards becoming a paramedic – for the last year. Our boss thought it'd be a good idea to have a couple of us as First Responders on the force and I picked one of the short straws. Actually, I rather like the work. Of course this isn't the scientific way to do it, but we didn't have foil wraps to hand and I reckoned . . . ' a whimper made them both turn round. 'Ah!'

Ruth stirred in her cocoon. 'Luke?'

'Hey Ruth, how're you feeling?'

Ruth shivered. 'Sort of odd. I'm sorry. I've been a nuisance. I went out there and suddenly I couldn't bear it. I'm sorry. I can't seem to move.'

'No, you're all wrapped up like an Egyptian mummy to get you warm again.'

A couple of hours later, Ruth's temperature had risen sufficiently for her to be dressed in her warmed, dried clothes. Meanwhile Luke had had the thrill of being kicked by Barbara's baby. After that they all took turns to put a hand on the taut bulge that pushed out Barbara's jumper, including Morris and Ruth.

Ruth placed her hand on the bulging tummy. Her openmouthed awe as her hand jerked, made Luke crack up. She asked Barbara, 'Can I feel all over?'

'Sure, go ahead.'

Ruth knelt down with first her ear, then her face close to Barbara's belly, as if she were having a conversation with the hidden infant. After a while, she frowned, mystified. 'There's really a whole baby inside here? It must be packed so tight.'

They all laughed and Barbara said, 'It is. I'm going to burst if it doesn't find a way out soon. One more week – if it comes on time.'

Luke helped Ruth to stand up again. 'OK, I think we ought to get going. Lewis says we're to get you home, Ruth. He's ordered more warm bed and sleep. When's Nina coming, Morris? I don't think she ought to be left alone in case she does get ill later.'

'That's all right I stay round hers at night whenever Nina's away and there's a helper now, Christine, who comes most weekdays for a bit. Though you're beginning to manage pretty well now, aren't you, Ruth?'

The following day Nina still hadn't arrived and Morris, troubled by Ruth's continuing distress and the fact that she was coughing, once more rang Luke.

'Luke, I'm sorry to bother you again. I've got a problem; I'm supposed to be in Milton Keynes this evening. I don't know if

Ruth is ill again or just reacting to all that business yesterday. You couldn't come and sit with her could you?'

'Yup, I'm around from three onwards, in fact my gig tonight has been cancelled, so I'm available all night, if you want me to stay.'

'All night? Do you really mean that? I'm supposed to be giving a demonstration to the local guild of weavers, then going out for a meal and staying there for the night. When I booked it I thought Nina would be here and Dave would be around but Nina's on the tarmac, or rather in a snowdrift, in Glasgow. She might get back tonight, but I doubt it and Dave got that last minute engagement in Winchester. I tried Christine, but she's not available. Ruth said she'd be all right, but I worry about her. Are you sure you don't mind? The spare-room bed is made up; I slept in it last night, will that bother you? Ruth will be so pleased, she trusts you.'

Luke hadn't really expected to be taken up about staying the night, but he was not at all unwilling. He liked the idea of being trusted with Ruth. 'No problem, I'll enjoy it.'

'Phew, I hate breaking engagements. I always think no one will believe my excuse, however good it is. Thanks so much, Luke. I never meant to involve you. It's just that Ruth knows so few people. I must do something about that. I think the RNIB has a buddy group or something.'

Luke found Ruth up and dressed but curled in a heap under a duvet on the sofa, still weeping at intervals about her garden. He bent to kiss her and then, with the vague notion that music would make her feel better than anything he could say, headed for the piano like a humming bird to nectar. Ruth called him back. 'Luke, stay a minute, I need to try and explain something to you. Are you near?' Reluctantly moving back towards the sofa, Luke dropped on the beanbag. Knowing she liked contact when she talked, he put his hand over hers. The piano would wait for him.

She sighed and took his hand loosely between her own. 'Leaving my garden feels like a bit of me has been torn off. I can't explain, but it's almost as though I'm bleeding all the time. It's the last place where I really saw nature. Little things, you know, like spider's webs, and woodlice. Somehow I didn't mind so much not seeing them, because I could still be in the place where I could remember them and sense them. Now it feels as if they've gone forever. It's like going blind all over again. I know I should have realised this would happen, I mean, I haven't been to the house since Christmas. I've hardly been in the garden for a month, but it was *still there*. Now it's gone, really gone, and the new people will change it so I wouldn't find my way about it any more. You have this idea that nature is permanent, but that's stupid.' She ran her finger over the back of Luke's hand. 'This is what I miss. See, I can feel the tiny things, like the hairs just here. I feel best with my mouth.' She brushed her mouth across the back of Luke's hand. 'I used to hold leaves to my lips so I could feel the tiniest parts of the surface.' Her small chuckle surfaced. 'I did that once with a nettle. Mama was so cross, because one of those Education Inspectors came that day and my mouth looked all odd and swollen and I was so sore, but Mama was clever, she told him it had been part of a nature lesson and I had picked the nettle when she looked away for a moment.'

Luke, attending as much to the timbre of her voice as to the content, found his attention drawn to a small spider tracking slowly across one white wall. He interrupted. 'Hang on a moment, Ruth, I'm just going to catch a spider for you.'

Persuading the spider off the wall turned out to be a complex task involving a sheet of paper and a cup. He kept up a running commentary and had the satisfaction of hearing Ruth's pleasing chuckle several times. At last he captured it. 'Here we are, Ruth. I meant to give you this beastie to feel, but he's something of an escape artist, so you may not get very long. Hold out your hand. There you go. Whoops! Hang on, got him again! OK? Did you feel him this time?'

Luke and Ruth played with the amazingly robust spider for several minutes, with only one alarming moment, when Ruth unable to resist, raised her hand to her mouth with the spider in it. It skipped off her hand just in time and Luke collapsed with laughter giving the spider a chance to make good its escape. 'Ruth you're a real liability, like a toddler. I expect you'd enjoy making mud pies, too.'

Her mouth curled responsively. 'Of course. Thank you, Luke; that was fun. Nina's not too keen on spiders. I haven't handled a spider since I was a little. I like them so much.' She reached out to touch him and found his head. She stroked the hair. 'I love the feel of your hair. Go to your piano now, Luke, I know you're longing to.'

He squeezed her hand and went over to the keyboard without speaking. He felt moved by the image of the child Ruth playing with spiders until the ability to see slowly drained away from her.

He dropped his hands onto the key and smiled – *your* piano – if only!

Later he kicked off his shoes, revelling in the depth of the carpet as he led Ruth up to her bedroom. Here the peach walls and bed linen, and the spacious double bed, made a striking contrast with her old bare nursery. 'Wow, that's quite some bed, Ruth.'

'I get lost on it, Luke. I miss my old one. I could touch both sides of that. Now I feel as though I'm sleeping out in the open – in a field.'

Luke, wrapping his arms around her, murmured, 'Mmm, we'll have to do something about that.'

35
Lewisham: Baby Jake

The ringing of the phone woke Luke. Half asleep and disorientated, he could hear Ruth talking to Nina, who, it seemed, had got as far as Stansted. His muscles, all geared up for flight, had just begun to relax again when his mobile went off. Barbara thought she was in labour and Lewis was out on a call. He tore himself out of the soft luxury of Ruth's bed and threw on his clothes. Unbreakfasted, Luke took a taxi to Barbara's house and from there on to the hospital where Maria joined them. Lewis arrived an hour later and eight hours after that Barbara gave birth, without fuss, to a seven-pound, two-ounce boy, and instantly named him Jake. Only twenty-four hours after that, mother and baby, much to Maria's surprise, were allowed home. A few days after that Luke, feeling dazed by the succession of dramatic events, flew to Rome to receive a prize, take part in a gala and to help coach a local children's choir for a production of Noye's Fludde. He had not even had a chance to say goodbye to Ruth.

Jake's arrival gave Luke a new perspective on the mass of disobedient children in the San Ramone choir. He immersed himself in the work, surprised to find their excitement rubbing off on him. The two performances in the nave of the baroque chapel were a triumph and he flourished in the warmth of the reception. At first in his rare moments off he tried phoning Ruth, but invariably got Nina, who either said Ruth was in the bath, or clearly sat beside her while she talked. He gave up. March and daffodils had hit England before he returned with the voices of children still singing his head. Seeing the flower stands awash with yellow blooms, his mind turned again to Ruth and her garden. Was she sad still? He rang one Sunday afternoon and found her for once on her own.

'How are you getting on, Ruth?'

'It's going well, Luke. I think I'm going to manage. I'm still getting used to the new house. Morris or Dave stay with me at weekends and I have my helper, Christine, during the week. Nina's been with me most of the time you've been away, but now she's gone back to live in Scotland. She isn't really a London person so it's better this way. I did think of going to live in Scotland with her, but I couldn't leave Morris and the studio.'

'I should think not! How's the new garden?'

'Well, it's March, Luke, so nothing much has happened in the garden yet. I didn't move in at the right time to plant any bulbs. I'm learning to play the piano, though. Dave's teaching me. It's so easy now he's living next door.'

Dave staying the night? Teaching Ruth the piano? A stab of something (surely not jealousy) pricked him. Opening up the world for Ruth had been his idea. Dave was out of line usurping his role like that – on his piano too. These thoughts flitted in and out of Luke's mind so briefly that he could pretend not to be aware of them. 'Dave's a good teacher. I look forward to hearing you play something.'

'Well. I only play little things so far. Dave won't dance though, I asked him.' Another irrational stab. 'He said he leaves that sort of thing to you.'

'I should think so too. Anyway, would you like to come and meet Jake – Barbara's baby – today? I've got my sister's car so I could come and pick you up.'

'Yes, oh yes please.'

Luke, meeting her on the door step, noted with delight that she was wearing the blouse he had given her at New Year and with a cardigan made of some light soft material and not her usual hairy brown ones. He gave her a brief kiss and then, with an un-acknowledged need to reclaim her, pulled her close for a more comprehensive kiss. She came willingly for a moment then wriggled out saying, 'No, Luke, please.' She put her palm against his chest to hold him off.

'Why?' he asked, puzzled.

She laughed up at him, causing his heart to jump. 'Luke! How can you ask that? You told me that it was up to me to stop you kissing me, don't you remember? Nina told me as well, after Christmas, but I didn't want to listen then. Well, when Nina arrived just after you stayed last time, I was very sad because you'd gone and I talked to Nina ... '

'About us sleeping together!'

'Oh no, not that, but about you. She told me, just as you did,

Luke, to keep myself a bit separate from you. She explained that the life you lead will mean that I only see you occasionally, and you will have many women, more suited to you in your working life. She understands about sadness, Luke and I think I ought to take her advice. You did try to tell me yourself, before Christmas, but I didn't want to listen.' Luke let go of her, irritated by this sensible interference. What could he say? I rather enjoy sleeping with you, but a permanent relationship is out of the question? Can't you be like other women and just have a fling with me, then go on to someone else?

She put out her hand, suddenly uncertain. 'Are you there, Luke? Isn't that what you meant?'

Luke stepped closer again and took her hand in his. He looked down at her contracted brows and the up-tilted mouth, now effectively out of bounds. He grunted.

'Luke?'

He cleared his throat. 'Yes, absolutely right. It was good advice. You should follow it. You should make up your own mind about such things, though; you're not a child. I mean, you don't have to do what other people tell you.'

'Well, both you and Nina said the same thing.' Ruth sighed, 'I can't possibly know better than either of you, can I?'

Luke frowned and touched his scars. 'Mmm, I suppose ... The thing is, only you can choose ... ' He stopped himself. 'Still, it's good advice. You stick with it, whatever I say.'

'Does that mean no more dancing, Luke? That would be sad.'

'Of course not, we can have a dancing lesson when I bring you back from Barbara's,' he said, thinking entirely subversive thoughts.

'Oh please!'

Ruth trembled with excitement as Luke carefully placed a sleeping baby Jake in her arms. She drew a breath, her mouth open in wonder as her fingers touched the apricot-soft surface of his head, then moved round the small shoulders and on down to the miniature hand. She couldn't resist bringing him up to her face so that her mouth could get acquainted with him. Luke, glancing to check with Barbara, let her softly lip the baby's head and hands. Jake, fully fed and at-one with the world, seemed content with this new form of handling.

They stayed much longer at Barbara's house than Luke had planned, because Ruth couldn't bear to leave Jake. When eventually they returned to Borrow Crescent, Luke, grinning wickedly but unseen by Ruth, said in a brotherly tone: 'OK Ruth, dancing lesson now.' In moments he had pushed back the furniture – promising to replace it exactly, put on the Lehar waltzes (the ones she had learned to dance to in the old house) and taken Ruth into a close dance hold. The quickened rise and fall of her chest, gave him satisfaction. He lifted her slightly and picked out the beat. 'One two three, one two three.'

They had only made a couple of circuits and he could feel her beginning to swim with the movement, when the doorbell rang. Immediately afterwards, there was a grating of key in lock and Dave walked straight in. Luke let go of Ruth, who put out a hand for an armchair that was no longer where it ought to be. Dave took her hand.

'Great heavens, Luke, I didn't know you were back! Ruth, I thought you didn't like the furniture being moved.'

'No, it's all right, Luke says he can see the marks on the floor to put it back.' Ruth clutched Dave, her voice jumping with the remembered thrill. 'Dave, Luke took me to hold the baby – to hold Jake. He is so tiny and yet he breathed – like a doll come to life! And his skin under my hands felt like warm ribbons – satiny and plushy at the same time. I was afraid of squashing him, but he seemed to like being cuddled; he is sort of elasticated like a cat. He smelt of bread...don't laugh. It's true isn't it, Luke?'

'Yes. Ruth suggested it, but she's right, there is a baking smell about him.'

'And he makes little wet sounds all the time. Like a fountain, or a tap that's been left on.'

Dave hugged her. 'I'm jealous, I haven't had a proper cuddle yet.' He tilted his head, picking up the strains of Lehar. 'Ah, I get it. This is the Come Dancing lesson. OK, I shall be the judge.' He handed Ruth back to Luke and settled himself on the sofa at the side of the room.

Luke, his body roused by her voice and his spirits unsettled by the warmth of her communication with Dave, took Ruth into a close hold. He went into performance mode. Moving carefully, to give Ruth a chance to settle and murmuring his instructions, he did a couple of simple circuits. As the track came to an end, he paused, pulled her in tight and whispered, 'Now we'll show him.'

To his enormous satisfaction, Ruth, her mouth in a happy curve, followed him like a dream. After a quick glance to see that Dave was duly impressed, he forgot about him, losing himself in the complex adjustments required of the whole body as it melded sound to rhythm to muscle and to his partner. Twenty minutes later, Luke reluctantly remembered that he needed to get Barbara's car back. Dave didn't look as though he was about to leave and however compliantly she danced, Ruth clearly had nothing further in mind.

At first, as he drove the car back to Barbara's house, his body sang with the aftermath of the dancing. He cuddled Jake while Barbara sorted the laundry. She looked curiously at him. 'Ruth was funny with Jake, wasn't she? I like her and she's very ... graceful. You'd expect someone who can't see to move awkwardly, but her hands are very certain. I think she's pretty, Luke, not dull pretty, interesting pretty.'

'Yup. I was confused about her at first, but you're right. Here take your son, he's getting damper by the second. And I told Mum I'd be back tonight.'

Luke caught the bus and his mood unaccountably dropped until, nearing home, he began to feel truly forlorn. Ruth hadn't even asked him to sing for her. In spite of the dancing, he had effectively been held at a cool arm's-length for three hours by the one person he had thought his to command. Did he feel angry? Not with her, surely. With Nina or even Dave, perhaps? He felt let down, sent into the corner, shut out of the playroom, cheated. He wanted to shout, "It's unfair". He could have stayed the night too; he only had three days before he would be off again and away for most of the next three months. His relationships had never been cerebral ones and he didn't have the skills to counteract both his own and Nina's good advice. Another thought occurred; perhaps Ruth had not really enjoyed making love. Some women didn't. And yet, that night in Blackheath in that grim house, he had – they both had – finally rediscovered that new-world wonder that had made the nightmare hours trapped under the building bearable. And then, that last time in January, after she had been frozen in her old garden, they had been together, laughing – no, giggling like teenagers – in Ruth's spacious new bed – surely that was happiness? Why did she encourage him then, and send him off now?

His small bedroom, when he got to it, seemed to be overflowing with paper. Feeling thoroughly hard done by, he spent the remainder of the evening wrestling with innumerable forms from the DHSS, the Inland Revenue and random individuals and bodies who either wanted money from him or wanted a dozen forms filled in before they would pay him money that they owed him. Several correspondents sent gratifying letters begging him to come and sing for them, but failed to mention performance fees, or mentioned fees but omitted any suggestion of payment for rehearsal time. The management of finances for the self-employed ought, he felt, to be included in the college curriculum.

Dave, back in his flat and facing a pile of similar papers, thrust them aside. He felt puzzled and slightly disturbed. Luke, it seemed to him, had been having a high old time. He had clearly got over his distress about Ruth and had brought her casually into his thrall. He'd been showing off back there, putting Ruth through her paces. But what about Ruth? Perhaps Nina was right and she was at Luke's mercy. Dave had never thought of Luke as cruel in his conquests, and yet he had been aware of Luke bending her to his will, binding her with his voice. This was totally unfair, given her lack of defences. Dave threw some clothes into a bag for his journey to Scotland next day, while mulling over the complications of his current loyalties. He came downstairs to consult with Morris. Perhaps they ought to take Ruth with them to Scotland after all.

36

The North Road: Ruth, Dave & Morris

After Dave left, Ruth felt her way to the piano and tried to play. Tears dripped onto the keys. She had done as Nina suggested in order to avoid being sad and yet sadness seemed to be sitting like a malign devil on her shoulders. Sometimes she felt physically sick with it. Tonight it had been so painful; first to push Luke away, then to feel baby Jake's amazing skin and after that to dance and touch Luke, but still to keep separate from him. Why should she hold Luke off when she didn't want to and feel him resisting and bewildered? How could that be good for him or for her? Why had she left her old home and come to this house where hard edges jumped out in front of her and she had to think whenever she moved. Every corner, every doorway, each cupboard and chair had to be learned and remembered – it was all so tiring. When would she ever feel at home again?

A key grated in the lock. Morris. Ruth rubbed her hands across her cheeks and searched out the piano keys for Twinkle, Twinkle, Little Star.

'Ruth? Ah here you are. I gather you've been cuddling babies and dancing with handsome young men today. Some people get all the luck!'

'Mmm, Jake felt so ... so alive and yet so squashy.'

'I bet. Hey, what's up?' Morris took her shoulder and turned her to face the light. 'You've been crying again, haven't you? Well that settles it. You're coming with us.'

'I'm fine, Morris, really I'm fine.'

'No, I've made up my mind. If you stay here I'll worry all the way to Scotland and back.' Morris gave her a quick hug. 'You're coming to give me peace of mind, however much you hate the journey. So go and pack a bag, there's a good girl. I'll ring Christine and tell her she can have a couple of days off and then I'll come and give you a hand. Dave's cooking supper. We're picking up the van at 8.30 tomorrow morning. There are three seats in the front, so there's room for all of us.'

'What about Dave, it'll be nicer just you two. You don't want to be bothering with me. What about the bathroom problem?'

Morris put a finger across her mouth. 'Stop talking nonsense! Dave enjoys your company and we both like a challenge. There are always disabled toilets in service stations these days, so you don't need to worry about that. Come and pack.'

Later that night Ruth realised that the whole business of getting ready for the trip to Scotland had worked. She had stopped thinking about the disappointment in Luke's voice or the palm of his hand speaking to hers before a fast spin. The trouble was that as soon as she got into bed, Luke's ghost snuggled up beside her again and there was the rest of the night to get through. Still, tomorrow they would go to the warehouse, load up the old furniture and take it up to Nina and her friends in Scotland. She would be able to feel the carved ships on the backs of the old chairs, and the rippled braiding round the sofa again; it would be like seeing friends.

The next morning, waking once more in the great spaces of her Greenwich bedroom she felt, as she often did these days, queasy at the prospect of the day ahead. By the time she'd had breakfast and Morris called for her, she felt better. They set off for the warehouse. Standing in the entrance while Morris and Dave, with a certain amount of mild swearing, loaded up the van, Ruth sniffed at the mixture of cool March air, old cloth and machine oil. It smelt very different from the studio, where she half wanted to be with her current weaving. Perhaps this change in smells was what she needed.

Eventually, with a couple of bruised fingers between them, they all set off for Scotland in the hired van. It was a Saturday morning and they left London without too much difficulty. Morris drove the first leg. Just after 11 am, when they were already well on their way, Dave's phone rang. He was seated between Ruth and Morris so they could both hear the speaker clearly. It was Luke.

'Dave, where's Ruth? She's not at home nor in the studio. I called to see if she might like to sit in on some rehearsals.'

'She's with us.'

'Oh. Oh, that's all right then. Where are you?'

'Um…just passing Baldock.'

'Baldock!'

'Yup, didn't I tell you? We're taking some of Ruth's old furniture up to Nina, staying a couple of days, then back for in time for the Nelson Mass in Richmond. I'll see you there.'

'Ruth didn't say anything about Scotland last night.'

Dave grimaced, glancing first at Morris then at Ruth – who didn't of course respond. 'I don't think Ruth decided to come until late last night.'

Morris muttered, 'Tell Luke, I found Ruth moping over the piano – no doubt missing her famous dancing partner – and made her come with us for the good of her soul.'

'Tell Morris I heard that.'

Dave hearing the disappointment in Luke's voice, said placatingly, 'Well Luke, you're off again in a couple of days and we didn't like to leave Ruth on her own.'

Ruth chipped in, 'Tell Luke I would have loved to come to a rehearsal. I'm sorry I'm not there.'

'Tell Ruth I'm sorry too.'

The van with three bone-shaken travellers docked at 9.50 that night. Ruth went straight to bed, feeling a little unwell. They were staying, as on their previous visit in Hugo's sister's Bed and Breakfast. The next morning Ruth continued to feel unwell. She assured them that she would be fine and often felt funny in the mornings. This resulted in some good-natured teasing about morning sickness by their landlady. Morris squirmed, remembering the scars Nina had seen and her account of Martha arranging to sterilise Ruth. Suddenly understanding the gist of these remarks, Ruth laughed and said, 'Oh no, there won't be any babies. I've had an operation.'

Nina joined them after breakfast and they spent the day spreading Ruth's furniture around the village. Nina, on her home ground, trod briskly in and out of friend's homes, smiling continuously. 'This is so *right*, Ruth. It's as though Martha has come up and paid off all my debts of kindness to those people here who looked after me after she made me leave. Are you all right Ruth, you look a bit peaky? Are you sad to be saying goodbye to your furniture?'

Ruth, fondled each piece as it was offloaded into its new home. 'Only a little; I kept some things. It's the garden I miss. And knowing where everything is.' She perked up as the day wore on. They had a grand meal in the Bed & Breakfast that night and went to sleep early with the journey back to London in mind. Next morning Ruth was sick just as Nina appeared to see them off on their journey. Nina helped her clear up then made her lie down in the bedroom.

'Ruth, Morris says you were sick yesterday too. I thought you were a bit off-colour. How long has this been going on?'

'Since I moved into the new house. Do you think it's the paint, or something?'

'I suppose that's possible. Morris said you felt funny most days.'

'Yes, but only when I get up. I'm usually fine after breakfast. I'll be all right as soon as we get going, honestly.'

'When you get up? Ruth, do you mean you're sick every morning? You can't be...It can't be morning sickness. I mean...' Nina stared at the young woman, the inaccessible grown up version of the child she had once known so well. Ruth, her eyes closed and her teeth clenched, lay back against the pillow. Nina stroked the hair back from her face. 'Lie still, I'll be back in a minute.'

When she returned, ten minutes later with some weak tea and a biscuit, Ruth was sitting up and her skin had a tinge of colour in it. Nina took a deep breath, 'Ruth, have you had a period recently?'

'No, not for a bit anyway. Sometimes I only have them for a day or two.'

Nina took an even deeper breath. 'Ruth, I have to ask you something, have you been with someone?'

'Been with someone?'

'Yes,' Nina took her hand. 'I don't see how you can have...but I have to ask, have you been sleeping with...with anyone?'

Withdrawing her hand, Ruth opened and shut her folding white stick. 'Well I kissed Luke and...I know you think it's foolish, but I think I must love him. I did take your advice though; when he came to see me the other day, I wouldn't let him kiss me any more.'

Nina, her face puckering, pulled her into a hug. 'Dear God! Ruth, I think...was there more than kissing?' Ruth stayed silent. Nina went on, resolution in her voice, 'I'm going to tell you something. When I was sixteen. There was a boy at school. He...we... we went together and one Sunday – it was really hot – we walked

296

out of town, until we came to real fields. There were cows in the field beside the road and I wouldn't climb over the stile with Don. The cows had horns, you see. He walked down the field side of the hedge and I walked down the road. The hedge was all prickly and dusty – hawthorn – I think. The sun baked us, you could feel the heat coming off the tarmac. Don kept calling through the hedge and teasing me about the cool grass in the field. We got to a field without any cows and I went in and we lay on the grass. We only meant to cuddle and kiss a little, but the sun was so hot it practically undressed us by itself.' Nina, her arm around Ruth, stared out of the window at the two men waiting by the van. 'I think I'd better have a word with Morris.'

'But you haven't finished the story.'

'It's not a fairy story, Ruth, it's real life and it's sad and bitter. I had relations with Don just the once and then I had a baby.'

'What happened to the baby?'

'They took her away from me and then she died.'

Ruth put her arm round her old nanny. Is that why Mama...? Never mind. 'What did you call her, Nina?'

'Leila. My mother told me that they did christen her before she died.' Nina shook herself. 'Do you understand why I told you this story, Ruth?'

'I think so. But you don't have to worry about me. Mama told me I'd had an operation. I won't ever have babies.'

'Did you tell Luke you'd had an operation?'

'Yes.'

'Did you ... did Luke have any protection?' Ruth shook her head. 'Dear God, I think your mother may still be running our lives. Ruth, I think it's possible you may be pregnant.'

To her surprise Ruth laughed. 'Oh Nina, don't worry so. Look,' Ruth bared her midriff, 'feel these little lines here, they're from my operation. Mama wouldn't tell me lies.'

'Yes, but ...' Nina stopped. Perhaps the doctor had disobeyed Martha; perhaps she was completely wrong. She would get Morris to carry out a pregnancy test when he got back to London.

37
Greenwich & Colchester: Decisions

A door slammed. Dave, stirring soup, paused. A clatter on the stairs and Morris walked through the kitchen door, folded his arms, lent against the wall and glared out of the widow. Dave concentrated on the soup.

After a moment he asked, 'Is Christina with Ruth?'

'Uhuh.'

'Is Ruth worried?'

Morris transferred his glare to the floor. 'Nope.'

Dave turned to consider his friend. 'I bet we're barking up the wrong tree, you know. Luke can't keep a secret to save his life; he'd have told me if he'd got anywhere near Ruth. When he first met her he said ... he made it clear that Ruth wasn't his type. I know I moaned about him dancing with her, but that was just showing off. He's a performer. Come on, Morris. Nina's paranoid. You heard the story. She's always been funny about Luke. She thinks her little girl's been knocked up by some celebrity wide-boy.'

'Maybe.'

Dave switched off the gas, went over and draped his arm around the rigid figure. 'What is it?'

Morris shook his head then laughed without amusement. He leant into Dave's shoulder. 'You know what? I *want* her to be pregnant. I want that fucking woman's evil deeds to be wiped out. I want Ruth to be a mother, a lover. I have always wanted to undo everything that Martha did to her. *I'm afraid she might* not *be pregnant.*' He pulled himself away from Dave. 'But if she is pregnant, I'm mad at Luke.' He dropped into a chair at the table. Dave returned to the stove, his face unreadable. Morris shrugged. 'You're right, of course. I'm crazy. You say Luke would have told you. Well Ruth would have told me. Nina says she admitted sleeping with Luke, but when I asked Nina to be specific, it turns out that Ruth only admitted to kissing him. From what you've said, Luke would kiss the people in a bus queue. When I left Ruth just now she fell about laughing because I asked if she still felt sick.'

Dave spoke with deliberation. 'I don't think we should discount the possibility that it's true. It occurs to me that we've both been less ... less available than we used to be. I mean Ruth and Luke might be feeling ... Ruth depends almost entirely on your friendship and Luke ... well I've been around since our first day at school. Do you think they've been feeling left out?'

'Mmm, I suppose. Shit! No, that's not right. Ruth is glad about us. I don't know about Luke. I can't believe he'd pick on Ruth just to get at you, though.'

'No, I don't either, but I must admit, Luke's rarely celibate and there's no one else around that I know of at the moment.' He grinned at Morris. 'I guess you should still do something about that pregnancy test.'

They stared at each other. Morris, his eyes suddenly brimming with mischief, got to his feet. 'Dave, dear Dave, will you go into Brean's Pharmacy tomorrow and ask for a pregnancy testing kit?' Seeing Dave shake his head he went over and slipped his arms around him. 'C'mon, if *I* ask old George, he'll collapse with shock, it'll destroy his most deeply held prejudices.'

Dave hugged him, his own eyes full of laughter. 'Not on your life. Go to a supermarket.'

Luke eyed his accommodation in the heart of Colchester with distaste. The 1970s orange and brown décor made him long for his own small nest in Catford, or better still the spacious new bedroom with its muted colours in Ruth's house. Last night in Hungerford he'd been unable to convince his hosts that he was neither weary, after his journey from Paignton, nor concerned that his voice might suffer if he went to bed after 10 pm. Tonight his new hosts had deposited him in this uninviting Hotel room to rest until they picked him up at 5 pm for the rehearsal. He put his keys and alarm clock on the side table and lay fully dressed on the bed. More than Ruth's room, he craved her company; her delight in every new surface that her fingertips discovered; her amazement at the physical pleasure of dancing. He realised with a small shock that no one in the whole world knew this – except himself. What exactly had made her decide to exclude him? Was it reversible? Could he fit in a visit to London between this gig and the trip to Sheffield? He riffled through his diary. He could squeeze two days. That's if he'd read the multiple scribbles and post-it additions correctly. He'd better get a three-year diary next time. It was only April 2001 now and he had entries going up to August 2004.

Professionally, things could hardly be better. Personally, though, since Melanie had dumped him and Ruth had withdrawn to a safe distance, things were definitely at low ebb. Everyone that mattered seemed to be occupied with someone else. Even Angela and Kes had almost stopped phoning to see if he was in town, because he so seldom was. Only Dad, beetling back and forth across Europe, behaved as he always had, wanting to hear about every night of his last tour, how his voice had responded to different acoustics, who he had spoken to, which newspapers had interviewed him and so on.

A good thing really that the family were getting off his back at last. Time he left home properly. Maybe could move in with Dave again? And just what was Dave up to with Ruth – giving her piano lessons? Perhaps if Dave were contributing to her emancipation, she didn't need him any more. She'd cut him off without apparent distress on the advice of her nanny. Her nanny for heaven's sake!

He reached down into his bag beside the bed and shuffled through it looking for his CD player. Perhaps he should get a car; this endless interaction with smelly railway seats and chintzy Bed and Breakfasts was a recipe for depression. You ended up doing too much thinking and thinking seemed to focus exclusively on bad stuff. Luke selected a CD, shut his eyes and tried to lose himself in a recording of Handel's Theodora.

What if Dave took over the dancing lessons with Ruth as well as teaching her the piano? That would be fair enough. What could he do over the phone with Ruth that Dave could not do better on site? He looked at his watch. Perhaps he should ring Morris and take up that offer of a room in Dave's flat. He'd probably have the place to himself since Dave seemed to spend most of his life in Morris's kitchen. He could always phone Ruth; he hadn't spoken to her in a while. With Nina gone it would be easier to get through to her. There would be no harm in asking if the flat was still available.

Morris dipped the cotton bud Ruth had just given him into the tube of solution and then touched the paper with it. He felt a fool.

He stared at the blank slip of paper for thirty agonising seconds, as instructed. Nothing. He'd known it all along, he turned to call out to Ruth, but some misty shadow at the edge of his last glance made him turn back to the paper. Was that a blue stain?

Five days later Morris sat in the Blackheath practice waiting room shuffling a handful of leaflets. Ruth seemed to have been in with the doctor for hours. In that time he had been able to frighten himself by reading all about the hazards of pregnancy. Maybe when he explained all this to Ruth she would opt for a termination. After all, babies might be exciting as an event, an idea, an occurrence – but in reality? Someone had once told him that living with an infant was all puke, pee and poo. And yet, Ruth having a baby would be his only chance of taking part in the next generation.

Ruth, flushed and dishevelled, with a nurse at her elbow and yet more leaflets clutched in her hand, appeared through the door-way at last.

'Oh Ruth,' he said straightening her out, 'did they make you dress in a hurry. Tell me ... no let's get into the car first.'

In the car Morris switched on the ignition, then switched it off again. 'Tell me.'

'Well, the doctor said that she thinks I'm about three months pregnant.'

Morris frowned, it was early March now and Luke had only stayed the night in late January. Still these things, according to his recent reading, were a little difficult to calculate. 'OK, but what about your operation?'

'Luke, there's nothing in my notes about an operation. She asked me what I remembered, but of course all I can remember is going somewhere in a taxi; being put to bed; this guy with a squeaky voice telling me to breathe slowly and count to ten out loud. Then I woke up with a sore tummy. I was sick a lot. I think I stayed the night; then I came home in a taxi. The doctor did look at my scars today. She said that although they were compatible with having had my fallopian tubes tied, no doctor would have agreed to do such an operation on a child and it would have been recorded in my medical notes, anyway.'

'Jesus, Martha was a criminal!'

'Morris!'

'Well, whatever happened, she must have deliberately hidden it from your doctor and I'm dead sure that's a crime. I suppose this means we'll never know.'

'Well, I have to go for a scan and they'll be able to see if the tubes have been tied, but she said that sometimes the operation isn't fully successful.' Morris turned on the ignition again while Ruth folded her leaflets, put them into her bag and did up her seat belt. Then she sat, both hands pressed to her stomach as Morris backed out. 'You're not saying anything, Morris. Do you think it will help to know more about the operation? I can't change anything now, can I?'

'No, I suppose not. Whatever did or didn't happen, there's no going back. I'm glad that the operation didn't work, but it should *never* have happened in the first place and you shouldn't have had to find out this way.'

'No.' Suddenly exhausted, Ruth's voice trembled. 'Please don't be cross Morris.'

He squeezed her hand. 'Not with you, Sweetie.'

'I don't know what to do next. The doctor booked an appointment for me with a pregnancy advisor. I think this is a person who will help me decide whether I want to keep the baby.'

Morris stared at a red light and tried to speak neutrally. 'Do you?'

'I don't know.'

Three weeks later, on an April Fool's Day in which no one felt like joking, Ruth, Morris and Dave assembled at the kitchen table in Morris's flat. Ruth sat very still, bent over the table, clutching a glass of hot water. Dave, opposite her, pushed away his coffee mug and spread his hands out as though about to set off somewhere. Morris, in a frenzy of indecision, sat down, stood up again to retrieve his coffee then sat again. He grabbed the sugar bowl and put two spoonfuls in his coffee, then knocked the spoon sideways sending a tiny glittering shower across the table. Ruth lifted her head at the pattering sound as Morris leapt up again for a cloth.

Dave took a handful of his jumper and tugged. 'Morris, leave that and sit still for two seconds. This really is crunch time. We mustn't move from here until Ruth knows what she wants to say when she sees the doctor again this afternoon.' He turned to Ruth.

'I still think you should tell Luke, Ruth.'

Ruth's head drooped even closer to the table. 'I can't, I just can't. He will never believe that I didn't know. Mama was right, I'm useless and immoral.'

'Blast Martha. She was never right. Don't take on so. You slept with a guy, honestly thinking you could never conceive. There's nothing bad about that.'

'But he said we shouldn't do it because we had no ... protection and I said it would be all right.'

'*So?*' Morris stood up again. '*It's not your fault, Ruth!* Your mother's the real criminal. I know the scan is inconclusive about your sterilisation, but personally I think the doctor – who must have been pretty shady to have agreed to do it in the first place – had a crisis of conscience and simply did half the deed. What's that oath they take? Hippo- something?'

Hippocratic.'

'Oh yes. Either way you couldn't help it. Anyway, *of course* it's not your fault. If Luke seduces you it's his responsibility.'

Ruth tucked her hair behind her ears and took a sip of water. She spoke on a sigh. 'He didn't.'

Morris gasped and slumped into his chair. 'What! You mean it was someone else?'

'No, no. It was Luke, but he didn't seduce me.'

'Ruth, don't split hairs; if Luke decided to make love to you, he seduced you.'

'I asked him.'

Dave leant over and touched Ruth's hand as it lay on the table. 'You asked him? You mean *you seduced* Luke?'

'I asked him. I asked him to have sex with me because when we were stuck under the building he said we would one day. He promised to show me ... and I thought no one else ... ' the tears never very far away in the last few days, started flowing again, 'would ever ask me again, so ... I can't do it. I can't tell him about it, because he will think I'm a liar again, that I did it on purpose. I can't have the baby and keep it, because he would find out ... '

Morris came round and stroked her back. 'Shush, Ruth, shush. We'll find a way, perhaps someone in Scotland ... Nina ... '

'No, no, I can't bear to have his baby and give it away for adoption or anything and I don't think I *can* have an abortion; I didn't mind when I thought I would never have babies, but now there is one inside me and it's Luke's I feel differently. Having an abortion would be like killing a bit of Luke.'

'Ssh, no one's going to make you have an abortion.'

'But if I try to have it and keep it, the social services people will take it away because I'm blind. That counsellor asked me all sorts of questions about how would I stop my baby falling when I changed the nappy and how would I read labels on baby food and oh lots of things. I couldn't answer any of it. I don't have a husband either. I don't think they'll believe me if I pretend it's yours, Morris, will they?' She pushed the glass away and buried her head in her arms.

'I only wish it were, Sweetie.' Over her head Morris looked at Dave, his eyes questioning.

Dave, his face stubbornly set, repeated: 'We should tell Luke. It doesn't matter how he reacts or what he believes about Ruth's motives, it is still his baby. I think he has a right to know before any irrevocable decisions are made.'

Ruth stiffened then spoke passionately. 'It does matter! It does! I can't bear to make Luke angry or unhappy again.' She laid her head on the table, her voice breaking. 'How can I make a decision? There just isn't a right one to make.'

In the following silence, the two men stared at each other, trying to find the flaw in this statement. All three of them jumped when the fridge started churning in the background. Then Morris, still patting Ruth on the back, said, 'I wonder if we're not making too big a thing out of this. I mean Ruth has enough money to have a nanny. The Social services won't take your baby away if a qualified person is there to help, will they? You've got a decent place to live. I'm next door for emergencies. It's OK to have a baby and be a single mum nowadays; lots of people do it that way. It really was different when it all happened to Nina, besides she was only sixteen.'

Ruth pulled a tissue from her sleeve to blow her nose. 'But if I do that Luke will find out.'

Dave opened his mouth then shut it obediently as Morris raised his hand, saying, 'Hang on; let's take this in manageable chunks.' He turned to Ruth and squatted down by her chair, so that he was speaking up to her. Taking one of her hands, he said,

'Ruth, if someone asked you straight out – do you want a baby? What would you say?' Seeing her lips forming a word, Morris squeezed her hand. 'No, don't answer yet, *really* think about it. Think about the years of being tied to another person, someone totally dependent on you. Think about doing it entirely on your own; imagine that I fall under a bus or something and you really have to go solo. Think about this wet, smelly, howling bundle waking you at 2 am, 3 am *and* 4 am; think about the baby feeling hot with fever, you can't read the thermometer, you can't drive to the doctor. Think about having an idea for a weaving on Monday and not being able to get to the loom until Sunday week. What about schools and teachers; temper tantrums, teenage angst, drugs and drink.' Morris shivered. 'Think, too, about the difficulties of doing all this without being able to see and – I'm going to be brutal, Ruth, – imagine if this baby also has your genes and goes blind. There, that's the worst-case scenario. Really imagine all of this and tell me if you still want to have a baby. *A* baby, not *this* baby, not Luke's baby.'

Ruth stared down as if she could see the strange bright eyes fixed so earnestly on hers. 'Morris, do you think I haven't tried imagining all this. I never went to school, so I don't know about that. I don't know about how most children live. They watch television don't they? I've never seen television, except when I was very little with your mum, Morris. I know that I won't have the first idea how to start. I know things could go wrong and this baby could turn into a . . . a vandal or a delinquent. But it won't happen all at once, will it? It'll be more like when I started losing my sight; a little change, then another, then another one. You sort of become accustomed to one step so the next one doesn't seem such a big deal after all. I think a baby will be like that; I'll learn as I go along. Maybe if I hadn't held baby Jake, it would be different, but I did.' Ruth reached out to touch Morris. 'I don't know about *any* baby, Morris, but Luke's baby is different in a way I can't begin to explain. Will you help me to keep it? Please?'

Morris, grinning now, stood up. 'Of course, Sweetie, of course. We'll have the baby between us. I *will* be there to help. You know it'll be less like losing your sight, more like learning to weave. Remember your first piece on the frame loom? I had to help with every row of that. Now think of the business of stringing the main loom for a six-foot hanging – you can do it yourself. ' He looked up suddenly refocusing on Dave, sitting all this time motionless on the other side of the table. The triumph faded from his voice and a little apprehension set in. 'You're very quiet, Dave. D'you think we're making the wrong decision?'

'No, but I come back to Luke each time. You have to tell him. You can't conceal his baby from him. He's not daft, he'll know as soon as he finds out that Ruth is pregnant. He was definitely miffed that we had gone off to Scotland with you, Ruth, without telling him. I know you keep saying that you are not in a relationship with him, but I'm not so sure about that.'

'Well he said that he could not be my boyfriend. He said he would sleep with other people.'

Morris frowned. 'God, that's . . . He shouldn't treat you like that, Ruth.'

'You don't understand, he was telling me *not* to sleep with him, only I wanted to.'

Dave, his eyes flying to meet Morris's, laughed. 'Ruth, you really do turn the world upside down. I can't help wondering what Luke made of you. He gets about a bit, and he's rarely short of female company, but I've never know him sleep with someone unless he really wanted to.'

Morris moved away to the sink and began washing up. Ruth, digesting the words of the two men, realised that they could not understand her central dilemma. Perhaps she did have a relationship with Luke in the sense she knew what would be the effect of telling him about the baby. Was it worth trying once more to explain her fears about how he would react? She opened her mouth but at that moment Morris, laughter in his voice, spoke to Dave: 'You or I could marry Ruth and adopt the baby. I wouldn't mind being father to Luke's baby.'

Ruth heard Dave walk round the table to Morris. There was silence for a moment, then Dave's voice, very low. 'Don't be daft.'

Ruth stood abruptly. 'I'm going down to work.'

Reaching the loom, she didn't sit down but moved round it, her hands walking over the beams. First she reached for familiar working parts, then, tenderly, the surface of the work attached to it. The current weaving on the loom, with its almost sculptural additions built using satin ribbon, had been the outcome of her visit to Barbara. The tactile solidity of baby Jake's small, plush limbs had haunted her and the result had been this strange new piece of work. With a growing sense of pride, her fingers sought out the threads she was working on, this she could do, this was in her control. She paused. A weaving was one thing; it stayed in place and waited for her to attend to it. However long she took or whatever mistakes she made on her work, no person suffered, only a piece of cloth and wool. But a baby? A baby would need attention instantly; you can't repair mistakes with a real living person. How foolish of her even to think of keeping it. Perhaps she should take up Nina's offer and go and live in Scotland and then they could keep the baby and Luke need never know. What about Morris? He had Dave now and he could keep the studio house, just paying the same rent to her that he had always paid his parents. She could sell her new house and buy a place near Nina. They could bring her child up in the clean air of Scotland. Maybe holding his baby would mean that she wouldn't miss the soft weight of Luke's body and the timbre of his voice quite so much. Maybe.

Morris came clattering down the stairs. 'Ruth, I've been talking to Dave. I know none of us planned this, but he thinks we should go with the flow. We should become one family: you, me and him – and the baby. Between us we should be able to look after one baby. What do you think?'

'Oh Morris, I don't know what to think. I've just been deciding to go and hide out in Scotland. 'I can't think how else to keep it all from Luke.'

'We can't. Dave is right. Imagine telling your son or daughter one day that their father doesn't even know they exist; you can't do that, it's too cruel. You know Dave's never met his father? He knows what he's talking about.'

'But Morris you don't understand. I've done enough damage; I can't make Luke angry or unhappy again.' Morris patted her shoulder. She reached up and gripped his hand. 'Why did Mama do this?'

'Well, you know what I think of Martha, but if it helps you to come to terms with it, I reckon she genuinely believed you had been sterilised. I still think that the doctor took the money and fudged the operation on purpose to salve his conscience. I have looked through all the papers you gave me, but there's nothing at all. Martha must have destroyed them. We could go to the police, but we haven't got much to go on. I can't imagine it would do you any good either. Of course it could simply be that the operation failed. I've been doing some reading, they can, you know.'

'Yes I know now. I didn't know then, when it mattered.' Ruth set down the shuttle with a grimace. 'Luke will never believe that I didn't know. I forbid you or Dave to tell him. I won't see him much. Dave says he'll be away from now until May and then back again for another few days in June. I can wear loose dresses. After that he'll be in Chicago and then Edinburgh and he'll be in New York in September when the baby is born. Maybe I will stay here, but you must promise – and Dave too – not to tell Luke, at least not until after the baby is born. He'll forgive me then. He couldn't be angry with a tiny baby, could he?'

'Of course he won't be angry with a baby. I'll try and convince Dave, but he'll find this very difficult, you know. Luke's his best friend and he never saw him actually being mad at you. From what he says, Luke's known for his sweet temper.'

'Perhaps I could find a boyfriend and pretend that the baby is his.'

'Ruth don't be naïve, Luke can count. However promiscuous he is, he's hardly going to forget sleeping with you.'

She sighed. 'No, of course not.'

38
Colchester & Greenwich: Ruth's New Garden

Luke reached in his jacket pocket for his mobile and hit the buttons. 'Ruth?' Silence, then a couple of clunks at the other end and no voice. 'Ruth are you there, are you all right?'

'Hello Luke, you made me jump. I dropped the phone. I'm still not used to this fancy Braille one. Where are you?'

He stared at the skyline through the window. 'Colchester. I sometimes forget where I've got to. I was in Hungerford a few hours ago. I must get my agent to arrange a slightly more joined up tour next time.'

'Is that a long journey?'

He laughed. 'You haven't a notion where either of them is, have you?'

'No ... Did you want me or Morris?'

Hearing her slight breathlessness, he teased: 'Well I rang your phone, Ruth, so I must have wanted to speak to you. I'll remember why in a moment.'

'I have to go in a minute, Luke.'

'Why?'

'Well I ... well I have a doctor's appointment.'

'Are you ill? What's the matter?'

'No. No, I'm fine. It's just ...' She chuckled, 'you shouldn't ask me a question like that. It's ... it's personal.'

'I know quite a lot of personal things about you already, what's one more?'

She was silent for a moment. 'Why did you want to speak to me, Luke?'

Luke smiled to himself, imagining her tilting her head, half-indignant, half-amused. 'Well, I wanted to know ... how your garden's going and ... how well you can play that Barcarolle now ...'

'Not very well!'

' ... and I was just curious about whether Morris had managed to rent out the other room in the apartment at the top of his studio.'

There was a pause. 'So you really wanted to speak to Morris.'

Luke, about to refute her assumption, hesitated. Her voice had altered with the statement; almost it held tears. Before he could formulate his concerns, she continued, 'I don't think he's found anyone yet. Do you want me to ask? Is it ... is it for a friend?'

'No-o, I still haven't decided whether to move out of home or not.' There was silence on the other end of the phone. 'Are you all right? Ruth, are you still there?'

'I have to go. I'll get Morris to ring you. Bye!'

Luke stared at his mobile in some puzzlement. Had Ruth been breathless at the sound of his voice or was there something wrong? Perhaps she was really ill, and didn't want to tell him.

He rang Dave who sounded busy but thought that Ruth was fine. He had an idea that Morris had already promised the other room in the top floor flat to a friend. Perhaps when the flat below was finished ... Luke rang off then got up and walked the two paces between his bed and the window. A minute passed before he focused on what lay below him. He saw acres of glasshouses and rows of plants in pots. A crop? He looked around, there were also stacks of paving and pots; it must be a plant sale place – a garden centre.

On a thought, Luke grabbed his wallet and made his way out of the hotel. He walked down a street of picturebook old houses, a less attractive one of red-brick semis and finally one with a strange mixture of town houses and neglected ancient flint and brick walls, before finally coming across a gigantic arched ironwork entrance. This had advertising hoardings and plants attached to every surface. Inside, the mixture of ordered ranks of plants interspersed with chaotic piles of tubs, sacks, canes and more obscure hardware, nearly made him turn back. After some enquiry he tracked down a Beech tree, labelled, to his bafflement, *Fagus Sylvatica*. Sadly the specimens on sale were all six or more feet tall. He could neither transport them nor could he imagine them growing in Ruth's new garden. He searched out the guy who had helped in the first place and explained the problem.

Half an hour later he left, the surprised owner of a dainty cherry birch eighteen inches high. He placed it on the chair in his unattractive room, where it immediately improved things. Feeling the weight of responsibility for the life of this miniature tree, he fed it a little water and moved the chair nearer to the window.

Three days later Luke walked into Borrow Crescent. He sniffed the damp May afternoon and looked fondly down at the tree in his hands, with its triangular, serrated leaves that trembled at each step. He felt confident of delighting Ruth and needed to see her pleased after his last unsettling phone call. He pressed the intercom on Ruth's door – no answer. He went next door; no one was in. He peered down into the basement hoping to see movements or any sign of life. Then, as Ruth had no mobile, he dialled Morris.

'Hi Luke, I thought you were still in the wilds of Essex.'

'No, I got home last night. I've only got a couple of days. Morris, where's Ruth? I'm outside the house in Borrow Crescent. She's not at home or in the studio.'

'Oh sorry, no there's no one there. Ruth is ... I think she's at a ...a class, yes that's it, a Braille computer class. I'll be fetching her around five.'

'I've got a present I'd like to give her.'

'Oh ...ah ...why don't you come and have supper with us?'

Three hours later Luke, still carrying the tree, rang Ruth's doorbell again. Morris answered and Ruth hovered in the corridor behind him.

He held out the pot. 'This is for you, Ruth, it's a tree. It's a cherry birch. I didn't get a beech, because the man said it wouldn't be suitable for your garden. This one has amazing bark, not to look at, but to touch and smell. Come and feel the trunk, it's only young yet, but it'll get even silkier as it grows bigger.' To his delight, the guarded look vanished from her face as she moved forward to trace the tree's small form with her hands.

'Oh Luke, that's lovely. We haven't done much in the garden yet because ...' she gave a little gasp.

Morris spoke quickly. 'It's my fault. I haven't had a moment to help. We've got another exhibition in London in July and we're both flat out trying to get enough work together.'

Ruth smiled gratefully at Morris. 'Yes, that's why.'

Slightly puzzled, Luke inquired, 'Do you want me to plant it for you then, Ruth? I could come over tomorrow with some compost.'

'Oh please, Luke.'

The following afternoon Ruth and Luke stood on the tiny

paved area directly outside Ruth's back door. The garden, large by London standards, rose up the hillside in front of them, full of plant life but utterly neglected. Years ago someone had attempted to terrace it, now all that remained were crumbled bricks in random piles, with ivy, buddleia and the white froth of cow parsley filling all the spaces.

'Morris thinks the birch should go up at the top by the wall.'

'Where do you want it?'

'Well, if it were closer to the house I could feel it every day, couldn't I?'

'Yes, but not too close, or you'd shut out the sunlight when it gets bigger.'

They chose a spot in the first terrace so that Ruth could walk out of the back door, follow the fence until she came to the first brick wall, then reach out and touch the trunk.

Luke started digging, while Ruth with a trowel cleared a nearby patch of earth. Watching her pick up a snail and move it carefully to one side, Luke said, 'Do you like worms? I've got a terrific fellow here.'

She chuckled. 'Of course.'

Luke took her hand and put the fat, wriggling coil into it, then watched her face.

'Wow, it's so alive!' She moved it delicately with one fingertip, utterly absorbed in the sensation. She lifted it to her face and for an alarmed moment, he thought she might pop it into her mouth, but she just put it softly against her cheek. 'I love feeling living things. Gardens are good for that.'

After this Luke searched under bricks and in grassy clumps for small creatures to entertain her. One damp corner yielded the most exciting beast, a small and surprisingly agile toad. After hopping repeatedly out of reach, it suddenly gave in and sat in a pouched heap on Ruth's palm. She knelt, letting it weigh in her cupped hands, and with the tenderest of smiles hovering around her mouth.

Luke, looking down at the creamy curve of her cheek, thought in that second that he had never seen anyone more beautiful. How could he not have seen this before? She had filled out a little and it suited her. He could see that she was barely breathing in her excitement. His mind began to throw out sparks. He wanted to ignite this moment, show the world his vision, print it forever in his vulnerable memory. Ruth with Toad. How strange that sounded.

She lifted her hands very slowly until her cheek rested on the creature. Luke began to remember and to ache. 'Ruth?'

She lifted her face, head tilted in question. All her strange, almost frightened reactions of the evening before seemed to have receded. She appeared once more, the warm curious woman he had been thinking about so often on tour. Unable to resist, but moving very slowly as if *she* were the wild creature, he took the toad from her and pulled her to her feet, sliding his arms around her. 'I'm living.'

She took a quick breath then her body froze under his hands. With her mouth drooping, she pushed him away. 'No Luke, we're going to plant this tree, remember?'

The afternoon became a minuet. Luke, behaving in a brotherly way, would cause Ruth to chuckle and move towards him, then he would put his toe across the line from fraternal to lover and she would retreat to her side: sad, polite and firm. Luke would correct himself and start again. Although frustrated, Luke, enjoying the delicate balance of the interchange, delighted in recovering lost ground, making Ruth laugh again. Later he sang to her. When it was nearly time to go he thought for a moment that he had won. She came to him as he sat at the piano and put her hand on his neck.

'Luke, when you were little did you ever play with a magnet and iron filings? My insides behave like those filings when you sing.'

He turned on the stool and laid his head gently and uninvasively against her breast. For a second she stood still and his hands started to reach out, then she gasped almost in fright and moved quickly backwards. Hurt, he asked, 'What is it, Ruth?'

'Nothing!' The door latch clicked and with relief she said, 'Ah here's Morris, he's come to inspect our garden work.'

At the beginning of June, a few weeks after the tree planting, Luke managed another five days in London. He rang Ruth daily, but she and Morris were much occupied during the day preparing for an exhibition and he had performances on in the evenings.

On his last day he rang again. 'Hey Ruth, do you and Morris want to come for a dress rehearsal in the Linbury Theatre this afternoon? I've got comps. Don't say no, I'm off to Chicago and I haven't seen you since I got back. This Exhibition seems to be eating your time.'

'Well Luke it's important and you're performing every evening at the moment. When are you actually going?'

'To Chicago? Oh...ah 8/12.'

'What's that?'

'Sorry I'm speaking American already – August 12th to you.'

Ruth and Morris came to the rehearsal. They arrived just as the curtain was about to rise. Luke only had time to notice that Ruth looked strange, her face swollen and her gait stiff. At the end of act three, when the stage crew were fiddling with a sticky scene change, Morris leant over. 'Luke, I'm taking Ruth home. She's not really very well. I'm sorry we couldn't stay the course.'

'What's up Ruth? I thought you looked a bit funny.'

'Nothing,' she gasped, 'I'm fine really.'

'She's having some trouble with her stomach. The doctor's been doing various tests. She's been told to rest.'

'Ruth, you should have told me.'

'I'm fine. We must go; they're starting again.'

This was the sum of his communication with Ruth before leaving to spend most of the summer in Chicago. Luke climbed onto the plane with a vague sense of foreboding.

39
Chicago, Edinburgh, London: Losing Ruth

Escaping from the blinding heat, Luke plunged into the chill of his air-conditioned apartment. Good omen, they were going to look after him in Chicago. He dropped his luggage, found a well-supplied fridge, took a coke and lay back on the bed. What a contrast to your average British B & B! Well he wouldn't have to spend that much time in England the way things were going now. Perhaps just visit home every month or so, catch up with Dave and Ruth. Was Ruth all right? He reached a lazy arm out for the phone and dialled her number.

'Luke, I'm so glad you phoned, I wanted to ask you something. First tell me how Chicago is.'

'Excruciatingly hot, but with air-con everywhere you go. What did you want to know?'

'Well, I've joined a sort of club for blind people. We went to Kew Gardens this morning. I've been feeling and smelling plants in glasshouses. I've even been swimming and we're going to the National Gallery next week to feel some paintings – well I think they're special three-dimensional replicas or something. I'll tell you more when I've been. The head gardener at Kew gave us each a mulberry to taste. Have you ever had one, Luke? They're sensational, I'd like them every day for breakfast, but no one sells them.'

Luke beamed as he listened. 'One day, Ruth, I'll take you to Glyndebourne and we'll sit under the mulberry tree there and you can eat as many as you want and your lips will turn bright red, as if you had lipstick on.'

'Oh Luke, the woman who organises our group, Tracy, has given me some lipstick. I'm not very accurate with it yet so Christine puts it on for me, though Dave helped me yesterday. Anyway, I wanted to ask you about dancing. Yesterday Tracy asked us to think up activities for the group and I wanted to suggest ballroom dancing. What do you think?'

Luke's thoughts on the subject were tangled. That Ruth should acquire new friends and become more independent had to be a good thing, that she wanted to tell him about it meant, surely, that the relationship had arrived at the point he had originally aimed for: they had become friends – another good thing. Lately he had felt that more than good friends might be even better. Yet, were these new friends the right sort? Would she end up in a relationship with another blind person? Such a combination would not expand her world in the way that he could, rather the reverse. Where was his role in her life now? And Dave's role? Holding her chin and carefully painting her lips? Luke, recalling that there had been a question, answered randomly, 'Why not?'

When he put the phone down, he was left with a sense of irritated nostalgia. Just as he had been revelling in the good things America had to offer, Ruth had callously presented him with some of the best of England. He took out the image of home he had burned into his memory; it was insufficient. He wanted to return to the fresh smell of Ruth's garden, to sense the mild English sun, to drink in the live reality of Ruth holding her toad. He prowled round the well-designed apartment to readjust his outlook again.

An hour later he set off for his first meeting with the rest of the cast of Bohème, moving from the icy apartment to the boiling streets, then into the cool theatre. This was reality; Glyndebourne, Kew Gardens and Ruth were fading ghosts. As he walked into the rehearsal room, he almost tripped over the assistant chorusmaster, Elaine. She sprawled in a chair in a fit of laughter. Almost as if he had caught a cure from her, he felt better.

By the end of the evening, Elaine seemed to think he could do her some good too. For the run of rehearsals and performances he saw her daily and after the first couple of days, most nights too. She was lithe, quickwitted and looking for amusement. Luke wondered why he had been getting in such a sweat over Ruth's resistance when there was so much easy fun to be had in the big wide world. As August passed his phone calls to Ruth and Dave diminished. He felt well, he sang even better. Chicago made much of him and he thrived.

August the 24th, his return date, approached so fast, he revised his plan to stop off in London on his way to Edinburgh. London meant family and hassles and Ruth out of reach and other uncertainties. Here in America lay freedom from these things, not to mention uncomplicated sex on tap, it would be foolish to give it up before he had to. He re-booked straight through to Edinburgh for the 26th.

Once on the plane over the Atlantic, his thoughts disobediently returned to London and showed not the least inclination to linger over Elaine. Only hours before they parted, she had had the shrieking abdabs over a spider on the ceiling of her rather grubby apartment. As the plane droned its way above the distant glitter of the sea, Luke bent his mind to the curious phenomenon shut tight within his head: the nature of a memory. Why does the time it occupies when the event happens, have no analogue with the space it occupies thereafter? The time under the post office rubble had tentacles of memory all over his brain and they didn't seem to fade at all, yet other important events – his first solo in church – seemed to be tidy, discrete nuggets of memory.

He rang Ruth from Edinburgh at nine the next morning.

'Luke? Oh no, I can't talk now, I've got an appointment.'

'Is it the doctor again? Why?' he asked directly.

Her voice jumped. 'No Luke … the dentist.'

This was so blatantly a fib, that Luke's heart contracted. She'd been ill when he'd last seen her at the rehearsal and at the doctor the time before that. Although she'd sounded happy in most of their phone conversations, he had sometimes heard an undercurrent of anxiety. Perhaps she had some serious long-term illness. Dave had been evasive last time he had asked if Ruth was all right. Jesus, why couldn't they tell him the truth? Suddenly angry, he spoke roughly. 'Don't lie to me, Ruth. You ought to know better by now.' He thought quickly, he had no performance tonight and had only half promised to rehearse with someone this evening; there was no early rehearsal tomorrow, just the technical in the evening. He had enough hours to get to London and back. 'I'm coming to see you. I'll be there late tonight or first thing tomorrow.'

Ruth put down the phone, and pressed her hands together to try and stop the trembling. She blundered into the garden and stood stroking the tree Luke had given her, but the panic inside refused to be calmed. There was no hiding her pregnancy now. The baby: neat, tight and energetic, bulged out in front as she walked. She had to find somewhere safe to think, somewhere to work out what to do next. She returned to the sitting room to grab her stick and headed for the front door, then stopped. How could she get to Blackheath? Her first instinct had been to walk, but even if she could have found her way there, her body, heavy now with it's burden, would struggle over that distance. There was the bus, of course, but she had never walked to the bus stop at the studio end by herself. A taxi! She went to her Braille phone and stood over it, then her face crumpled, she didn't know a number for a taxi. She cried for a few moments, but so great was her need that her brain seemed to be responding for once. She remembered the number for the blind helpline and rang that. Not only were they happy to assist, but they asked how far she was going and told her what level of fare to expect. Within quarter of an hour a taxi had appeared on the doorstep and another fifteen minutes later she paid and dismissed the driver and trod up the steps to her old home.

She could hear the familiar bell clanging through the house. She waited. Another fifteen minutes later, after repeatedly ringing the doorbell, she realised that the new owners must be out. She sat down on the doorstep to wait. After an hour, with the demands of her bladder growing, she began to despair. She walked out of the drive and along the little path than ran outside the garden fence, feeling the wooden palings at intervals. Somewhere down this side there had once been a small gate. No one ever used it, and shrubs hid it on the inside. Eventually she found an anomaly in the smooth boarding of the fence and felt around. There seemed to be no latch so she simply pushed. It gave a little. She found that if she pushed it rhythmically she gained an inch or so each time. There was a lot of her to get through the gap, now that she had the bump on her front. After fifteen minutes of shoving, she squeezed through and found herself inside an overgrown Garrya bush. She knew exactly where she was. Straining a little, she pushed the door shut behind her and crawled out through the tangled branches.

She sat for some time on the grass, her breathing short and ragged. As it eased, she began to feel desperate about her bladder. After trying the back door, she found a corner of the garden and relieved herself. Feeling like a naughty girl but also much comfier, she began tentatively at first and then with increasing freedom and joy, to reacquaint herself with her garden. Nothing had changed. Even the bench sat in exactly the same spot. The grass felt very long. No one had mowed for several weeks. Feeling peaceful and safe she lay down under the beech tree and fell asleep.

When she woke it was after 3 pm with nothing decided though much of her panic had faded. The sun had moved away and she felt hungry. She went up to the back door of the house and knocked and called, but no one answered. It was at this moment that Ruth realised that she had no way of getting home. Her plan, in as much as she had ever planned this visit, had been to ring for another taxi from her old home. She would have to get out of the garden the way she got in and ask a stranger for help. The peace she had achieved began to dissolve.

She made her way over to the Garrya and struggled back underneath it. Bending had become increasingly difficult in the last few weeks. The bush seemed less welcoming on this reverse route and her arms were scratched. A branch whipping back struck her jaw. Eventually her groping hands encountered the dry surface of the fence door. This time she needed to pull the door to open it, but although she worked at the edges with increasing frenzy, she could not get her fingers into the gap; it had shut too neatly. There was a little hole where a handle had once been but she could not even get her little finger in it enough to get a purchase. By 5 o'clock, with a light drizzle starting to penetrate the greenery above her, she realised that she was totally stuck.

Dave trod up the steps to his front door. The pleasure of walking into the house in Borrow Crescent never failed. He must, he felt, be a domestic animal at heart. He knocked at Morris's door, but knew instantly that the downstairs flat was empty. Morris would probably be setting up at the Gallery and Ruth resting at home. It occurred to him, not for the first time, that a life of coaching and coming home most nights might suit him. Perhaps he should opt for the more stable, if less exciting musical route. Especially now that Morris would need him as back up once the baby was born. Leave the big stuff to Luke, who had clearly been on top of the world out there in Chicago. He had as usual landed a chick and seemed to want for nothing. Perhaps Ruth's instinct had been right.

Dave passed the still half-decorated middle flat and climbed onwards to his own well-ordered space at the top of the house. Ruth was his landlady now, a change in his fortunes so beneficial and astonishing that he thanked providence daily. He wished he could give her more in return for the freedom and peace of mind she had given him. The daily battle over broken furniture and machines and the smelly climb up the concrete stairwell were fading memories. His mobile rang.

'Dave, where's Ruth?'

'Luke? What's the matter? She's at home, why?'

'I don't think she is. I'm on my way back from Edinburgh to see her, I spoke to her earlier and I know she was telling me fibs. I may have spoken a bit fiercely to her and now she won't answer the phone. I've rung ten or more times since this morning. I just want you to make sure she's all right.'

'Jesus Luke, you should treat Ruth with more . . . respect. I'll go see.'

'Thanks. Ring me back.'

An hour later still not having heard from Dave and being about to board the plane, he rang again. Dave cut him off. He rang Morris.

'Who is it? Luke! Jesus I can't talk now, I'm expecting a call.'

Morris, too, cut him off. Seriously alarmed, Luke made one last call before he boarded the plane, but Barbara did not answer. Reaching Stansted, he rang Dave again. He had never heard his friend so curt.

'She's gone. We can't find her anywhere. What the hell did you say? You must have scared the living daylights out of her.'

'Gone? What do you mean? She can't go anywhere . . . can she? I just said I was coming to see her. I was afraid she was ill and not telling me.'

'She's vanished. She's taken her purse but no coat and it's raining.'

'Where have you looked? What about the police? She can't have gone far, surely.'

'The police are searching. She could have got on a bus, she could be anywhere in London.'

'What about her old house? She has a thing about the garden.'

'We tried that; the new owners are in Barbados. It's all locked up.'

'Oh my god, I'll be there in an hour. I can't believe she would run away from me. She . . . we . . .'

320

'*Don't come here!* Go home to Catford. I'll call you there when I get some news. I've got to go, Morris wants me.'

Luke, moving automatically, got on a train to London. Rain dotted the windows. What if Ruth were outside somewhere and lost? He tried to activate his brain to address the problem. All that came into his mind were images of Ruth walking out into traffic or lost in Greenwich Park or being hassled by teenagers or dripping wet in some back alley in Deptford. All these images came and went, but the most obtrusive one showed her sitting under the beech in her old garden. He sent Morris a begging text message "please, please try her old garden again". Reaching Catford at 10.30 that night, he hugged his mother convulsively.

'Ruth is lost, Mum. She ran away because I was coming home.'

Maria, hearing his distress, but uncertain of the implications of Ruth's disappearance, murmured soft nothings as if he were still a child, while he poured out his worries.

'Sit, Luca, I'll make you coffee.'

Without taking off his coat, he dropped into a chair at the kitchen table. 'She's lost in London, Mum. She can't see at all. Anything could happen to her. She could get run over or fall into some goddam hole or be mugged or raped even.'

'Shhh, Topo, the police will find her.'

'But if something happens to her, it will be my fault.'

'How Luca? You were not here.'

'I frightened her and I should know better. I understand her, Mum. She reacts to voice not movement. She knew I was angry. I wasn't really, more worried that she might be ill and lying to me about it. Oh Mum, what am I going to do?'

'*Calmati*, Topo, it will be all right. Here drink this.' She put the mug of coffee by his restless hands and sat down opposite.

Luke shook himself, reached out and grasped the mug. He took a sip and managed a quick smile. He would not help Ruth, by reverting to infancy. Anger shook him as he thought of Dave forbidding him to come near her. Dave couldn't know Ruth as well than he did. Surely Ruth knew that he would not hurt her? She did know. Another problem must be confusing her. She must be seriously ill and unwilling to tell him.

Luke took another sip of coffee, recognising that his thoughts had covered a familiar circuit. He interrupted Maria's gentle monologue on Gordon's travel plans. 'Mum, if...when they find Ruth, I think I might move in with Dave again – to be near her. You see she needs people who understand her, who can interpret the world for her. I've started to teach her to dance. She's really good. There are masses of new things she could do with me as a partner. When I'm not there, there's the weaving. She's got Morris for that. But Morris is gay so...' His mobile rang. Luke tensed, listened for a moment then his shoulders drooped. 'That was Morris, Mum, to say the police think Ruth might have taken a taxi. That's good news, I think. They're ringing round and hoping to discover where she went. They should be able to track that down within the hour. They should know, apparently. Let's hope.' Luke got up and took his coat off. 'You know Morris and Dave are together now, Mum?'

'Yes, Dave came to see me a while back. He seems very happy with this young man.'

'He is. I still haven't got used to it.'

Maria's brow wrinkled. 'Luca, I don't really understand. You want to move in with Dave, but isn't he with Morris in his house? That's not the same as Ruth's house is it?'

'No, Ruth owns two houses; the one with the studio and Morris and Dave's flat, and also the house next door. She lives alone there, but a carer comes in regularly. Sometimes her old nanny stays with her. It's a beautiful place now they've finished doing it up – seriously upmarket though. There's a piano to die for. She'd let me practice on that any time, I know, if...when she comes back. If she took a taxi, she must have been going somewhere in particular, don't you think?'

'I think so. Will you bring Ruth here to meet me, Luca?'

'Of course. I should have done that ages ago. I wish Dave would ring. I've got to be back at Stansted by 1.15 tomorrow...' he checked his watch...Oh god, it's almost today. I ought to sleep, but I can't. I'll take my bag up.'

40

London: Storm

To Luke, still jet-lagged after his return from Chicago and his switchback route via Edinburgh, the staircase up to his room that night felt like the ascent of the Matterhorn. He dropped his bag on the bed and his coat over the back of his chair. He went over and pulled the curtains against the gusting rain; then he stood quite still staring at the mobile in his hand, willing it to ring. When it did; he jerked with shock.

'Dave?'

'We've found her.'

'Is she all right?'

'We think so, but I'm in Accident and Emergency at the moment. They need to check her over because of the baby. You were right. She'd got into the old garden through a side gate. The police traced the taxi driver ... Damn!'

'What d'you mean, *because of the baby?* Not Jake?'

'No, no. Jesus, I've really done it now! You'd better sit down Luke. I'm going to commit every crime in the book and tell you what I promised not to. I always thought you should know anyway, but Ruth is too frightened to tell you.'

'*Too frightened?* What do you mean? I don't believe you.'

'Yes, well . . . Ruth is pregnant with your baby, Luke. And before you hit the roof ...'

'Hit the roof?'

' ...you should know that she genuinely thought she was sterilised.' Dave paused but no sound emerged from Luke. 'Are you there, Luke?'

'Uhuh.'

'We don't know if Ruth's mother lied to her, or the doctor lied to Ruth's mother or whether the operation simply didn't work. Whatever. It's not Ruth's fault. Are you listening, Luke?'

'Yes.'

'Are you mad with her?'

'No. I ...no.'

'Ruth was convinced you would think she'd lied to you again

and she wanted to disappear and never tell you. We persuaded her not to, but we couldn't persuade her to let us tell you ... Are you all right, Luke?'

'What do you think? I can't believe after all we ... that she didn't trust me; that she didn't tell me. But she was so sure; her mother had told her about the operation. I mean she remembered being given the anaesthetic. I even saw the scars ... I mean what if it's something else, something bad inside her. Are they sure?'

'Luke what *are* you on about? I've seen the scans, I've felt the baby kick ... Is that you?'

Luke, trembling now, put the phone down and groped for a handkerchief. He picked it up again. 'Hello? Dave? She really is all right, isn't she? I thought ... I don't know, I thought she was hiding something ghastly like ... cancer? I'm just getting used to the idea of a baby. It's a bit of a shock. You mean my baby is inside Ruth?'

Dave laughed. 'Oh Luke, that's the first time I've felt like laughing for hours. You daft bugger, that's usually how it works. You put it there; it doesn't happen by magic.'

'So I did.' Luke blew his nose. 'God it takes a bit of getting used to. Are you sure she's OK now. Has she been in the Black-heath garden all day?'

'Yes, she got in through this old side door and then couldn't open it from the inside to get out. She's cold, wet and hungry but otherwise fine, we think. The question is, what are you going to do about it?'

'Do I have a choice?'

'Jesus is that all you can say? You could at least give her some support. Stop getting mad at her.'

'I didn't mean it like that, of course I will. Of *course* I will. And I'm not mad at her. I'm mad at you two for not telling me. What the hell were you playing at, Dave? I can't believe you've both been lying to me all this time. Chrissake I'm an adult, I'm about to be a father even, and you and everyone else – except Ruth – treat me as though I'm a kid. Tell her I'm on my way. And don't make funny noises at me; do you think I'd hurt a hair of her head?

'I'm sorry, Luke, I'm sorry. I did want to tell you but ... Please don't come tonight. She needs quiet and sleep and they may keep her in anyway. Besides I need to confess what I've done. Please. I'll tell her it's all right, you're not mad, you're ...'

'Why can't I come and see her now? You *sure* she's OK?'

'Luke, she's absolutely fine. It's after midnight and she should sleep.'

'But ...'

'Look I'll ring you if there's any kind of problem, but leave her in peace now.'

'OK, OK, but give her my love and ...' Quite suddenly Luke laughed. 'Jesus, a baby – my baby! I can't get my head round that at all.'

'Well, digest it well because it's going to happen. I must go.'

'No don't; hang on a minute. When is it due?'

'I'd have thought you could work that one out.'

'Well, how am I supposed to know which ...?'

'Luke! You mean there's been more than one time? And you had the gall to call me secretive.'

'Yes, well, I was confused. It wasn't like an ordinary relationship. I didn't know where ... Never mind that now.'

'Well the doctor originally estimated the first week in October, but they've been bringing the date forward recently and they're talking end September now.'

Luke fished around for his diary. 'Well I go out to New York on the 7th of September, Jesus that's in ten days time! I only finish in Edinburgh on the 2nd. Then I'll be rehearsing or performing from the 11th to the 23rd. I could probably fly back on the 24th September. God, it's complicated.' Suddenly exhausted, Luke leaned on his desk, scattering papers. 'Dave, were you really going to let Ruth have our baby and not to tell me?'

'I don't know, Luke. I wanted to tell you and I knew you'd find out in the end, but Ruth panicked every time I suggested it. Talk about stress!'

Luke looked at the letter under his hand: an offer of work in Stockholm in 2002. 'Dave, what am I going to do? I've got engagements for the next few years; I couldn't just chuck them and stay at home with Ruth and the baby.'

'I know. I don't think you'll persuade Ruth to give it up for adoption, though.'

'Jesus, no! I wouldn't want to hand over my child to some stranger, but how can Ruth manage without someone to help?'

'Well Morris is next door and so am I half the time. Of course she'll have to have a nanny, but she can afford that.'

'Look, my head isn't working. I'll come over first thing tomorrow, just...just give her my love and tell her not to worry. I think I'll go and tell Mum, if she's still up.'

'OK. Luke, there's one thing you need to think about. It is always possible that the baby may have the same condition. It may go blind. The early tests were inconclusive and Ruth refused the late tests, because of the risk to the baby.'

'It's no good, I can't get my head around anything more now. I'll worry about that later. I'm still grappling with the whole father idea. See you in the morning.'

'Wait, Luke, just tell me something.'

Luke slumped on his bed and waited. 'Well what?'

Dave laughed. 'I don't know how to put this nicely. I want to understand. What's in it for you – for you and Ruth together? I mean why, after all that she's-not-in-my-zone stuff, did you sleep with her – and not just once, apparently? Were you being totally irresponsible? Have I missed something? Why the secrecy?'

'Jesus, you don't want much, just an existential essay before I go to sleep.'

'I need to understand.'

Luke covered his eyes, then got up and put out the main light and lay down again.

'OK. Well it's complicated. First, I never planned to sleep with her.'

'Tell me something new.'

'No, I mean it was her idea. I know, I know, it's still my responsibility. What I'm trying to say is that she knows her own mind. Of course she's naive, but she's not a child. She thinks things through, you know.'

'You're not answering my question. You can find an easy lay any time. Why Ruth?'

'You want the big I-Love-You, don't you?'

'No, Luke, I want the little stuff. Why Ruth? Why not Ange, or Melanie or any number of others?'

'She's the only woman I've met who needs me as a person – a man, not as some cute kid with a voice to sell, OK? The celebrity stuff means zilch to her. I'm still the guy with the bleeding head under the post office. Sure she likes that I can sing, but I can do things for her *other* than singing, like giving her the visible world and boy is she ready to receive it. Her work is amazing – real quality. She's smart, she's open in a way I've never known in another woman. Her voice is the sexiest and her hands are amazing. You should see her with a toad in her hand. I should be with her now. Is that enough? I'm going to sleep. I'm performing in Edinburgh tomorrow. I'll be with you by nine tomorrow. Goodnight.'

As Morris opened the door, another roll of thunder shook the house, propelling Luke across the threshold. The two men stood face to face, Luke dripping, as they waited for the reverberations to die down to speech level, then both spoke.

'Fearsome...

'Where is she?'

'In the workroom. Hey, Luke, hang on; you're trekking mud, get those shoes off, man.'

Barely pausing, Luke tore off his shoes and handed them to Morris. Morris started speaking but another mighty cracking of the skies rocked the house. Luke pulled away from Morris's restraining arm, went through the door to the basement and shut it firmly behind him. He leapt down the steps. In the doorway he stopped dead. Ruth sat at the loom, her face towards the window. The window, in Wagnerian mode, first sent light slicing across the room then rattled with the force of the immediate blast. Seeing Ruth ignore the lightning, but flinch at the thunder, Luke understood, really for the first time, that she could see nothing at all. In all their hours together, she had been so competent that he assumed some glimmer of sight to be remaining. As she sat there in the storm's limelight, he found it hard to remember that he had ever thought her unattractive. Between the blasts, he could hear her talking soft nonsense as she held both hands to the bulge of her stomach.

'It's all right. You're safe inside. It's just the cymbals in the sky. God has a giant orchestra up there and sometimes we make such a mess of things he has to let fly. He's not cross with you. I don't think he's cross with me either. There are bigger things to trouble him than you and me. We'll just get on with our lives. Maybe I'll get you a drum set one day and you can rock the skies too; would you like that?' Her hand moved rhythmically up and over the invisible inhabitant of her womb. Luke winced as light sliced across the room again, burning the figure in the chair onto his retina. An instant later he saw Ruth jump, as the thunder hit her without warning.

Like a swimmer folded into a wave, he launched himself at last into the flow. Here, in this room, this dry hollow, lay the core of matter, Ruth, and within her, pulsing under her fingers, a particle of himself. The thin thread linking Luke and Heloise all those months ago in that concrete jungle, had thickened into a web. Heloise owned territory in his mind that he could never reclaim. Ruth now also inhabited a space there. Why had he ever shut the door between Heloise and Ruth? The simplicity of joining these elements together left him with his mouth open and a surge of energy lifting his muscles.

'Morris?'

'Ruth, it's me.'

'Luke! Oh, you're wet!'

Luke, kneeling with his arms around her and his head on her stomach, did not speak or move. He still inhabited some ethereal realm in which no explanations could possibly be needed. With a little sigh, she smoothed back his wet hair. Several minutes passed and the spaces between thunder blasts grew. Luke's tightened arms warned her of each crack before it came, so that she no longer jumped. After a while, feeling him flinch again, she started counting softly. She reached ten.

'I think the storm is further off now.' She moved slightly, then laughed as the baby moved too. 'Did you feel that?

Luke lifted his head. 'Yes, he kicked me in the ear.'

'Or she.'

'Yes, or she. I tend to think of a tiny Jake. They'll be cousins, you know.'

'You're not angry, Luke?'

'No. Only with Dave and Morris for not telling me. I've missed all this.' He turned and kissed her bump.

'I wouldn't let them.'

'Oh Ruth, you dear fool.'

Luke settled on the floor beside Ruth, leaning against her with one hand resting on her stomach. Neither spoke much; the important thing seemed to be to absorb the minimal shiftings from within. Luke had a bare half hour to catch up with eight months of silent acquaintance.

'She or he may lose their sight, Luke, like me.'

'I know.'

'Sing to us.'

Luke, his head full of the Bohème he had performed in Chicago and would be performing with a different cast in Edinburgh, launched softly into the highlights. The storm acted as orchestra. *'Chi son? Sono un poeta. Che cosa faccio? Scrivo. E come vivo? Vivo...(Who am I. A poet. What do I do? I write. How do I live? I live...)/ O soave fanciulla, O dolce viso di mite circonfuso di alba lunar...(Oh lovely girl, oh sweet face bathed in the light of the moon).'*

Eventually, he rose. 'I have to go now. I have to get back to Edinburgh, Ruth. I'm singing tonight. I'll phone you. You'll be careful now, won't you? Mum wants to meet you.'

She reached out and found his hand. 'Does she mind? Is she cross?'

'She's crazy with happiness for us. So will Dad be when I tell him. Give me a kiss.'

He lifted her from the chair and, laughing as he accommodated his body to hers, kissed her tentatively at first and then with increasing hunger. Breaking off, he sighed, 'I've been wanting to do that for months. I must go now. Listen a moment, Ruth, I mean this. Whatever I say, you must never be afraid to tell me things. Ever. OK?'

Luke left as hurriedly as he had arrived, flinging a final instruction at Dave to take Ruth to see Maria. As the door slammed behind him Morris and Dave converged on Ruth.

'What did he say?'

'What are you planning to do?'

Ruth smiled serenely towards them. 'Oh, I don't know. We didn't really talk. But it's all right.'

The two men exchanged glances. Morris said, 'Jesus, you've had nearly an hour together with a guy whose timetable rivals Waterloo Station's and nothing's settled.'

'I'm sorry, Morris, I think Luke just needed to get close to his baby. It's going to be all right, though.'

Dave put an arm around Morris. 'Relax, she's right, we'll get Maria in on this. Once the family is involved it'll work out somehow.'

Seeing Ruth at peace and preparing to work, the two men retreated to the kitchen.

Morris moved around restlessly. 'I'm worried, Dave. Will Luke be all right with a baby? I mean, he's a bit fly-by-night. You said he shacked up with some girl in Chicago. Will he stay with Ruth for a while and then abandon her just as she gets to rely on him? I think the baby needs a father.'

'You're disappointed not to be in *loco parentis*, aren't you?' Dave teased.

Morris grinned. 'I suppose.'

'Well I don't think you need to worry on either front. Luke's basically a family man. Look at the way he's stayed happily at home all these years. They look out for each other constantly, that lot, and that includes add-ons like me. I think he'll take his duties as a father seriously enough. Whether he'll remain entirely faithful is a different matter. I can't tell, to be honest. He's changed, I thought he was transparent and that I knew him backwards, but he never gave a hint about sleeping with Ruth.' Dave busied himself with the kettle. 'Cheer up. I think too, that because he will be abroad so much of the time, we'll get to be changing nappies and playing with ducks in the bath after all.' He turned around a mug with a butterfly painted on it. 'Damn! We never asked about the toad.'

41

New York: September 2001

On the 7th of September Luke arrived in New York four hours later than planned. He threw everything into his hotel room and picked up the phone. The cast get-together must have already started. He consulted his watch and did a rough calculation. New York was 6 hours behind and it would be late evening at home. He needed to know about Ruth's antenatal visit that day. He rang her.

'Luke? Is everything all right.'

'I'm fine, what about you? Did you see the doctor?

'I had to have another scan today. They said there's nothing wrong with the baby, but because my blood pressure is rising and the baby's bigger than expected, they want me to stay in hospital. Morris is taking me in tomorrow. Your Mum is lovely; she's going to come in while Morris is at the gallery. They may induce the baby.'

'What does that mean?'

'Starting it artificially. Making it come a little early. They say it's old enough. It will be all right.'

'When will this happen?'

'Well that seems to depend on my blood pressure.'

'Christ, why did I come to New York? I should never have left you. I think I'm coming back.'

'But Luke, they may keep me in for two days and then send me home again.'

'And if they don't, I'll miss the birth.'

'If you come home you'll be in trouble with the opera house and the baby might not arrive until the end of September. Dave explained it to me; you must honour your contract.'

'I know, I know. I just ...I don't want to get it wrong again and there are an awful lot of hours between here and there. I'll talk to Claudia. Love you, bye.'

'Claudia, it's me Luke, can you give me a ring when you get this message. Ruth is being taken into hospital – something to do with blood pressure. I don't know whether to come home and risk making my name mud here. I really want to be there when our baby's born. I've missed so much already.'

Claudia did not answer that night. Luke attended rehearsals the next day in a growing state of uneasiness. He phoned his family whenever there was a break and finally got through to Claudia late afternoon. 'Where's Ruth, I can't get her on the phone?'

'She's in Greenwich District Hospital. They're just monitoring her, but her blood pressure is erratic. She may be pre-eclampsic and I don't think they'll hang about for very long. What are you going to do, Luca? Mum and I can be with her, you don't need to be back for the birth.'

'I think I do, but I don't know, I really don't know. What the hell's pre-eclam-whatever?'

'It's a problem they watch out for when the blood pressure starts rising. She's in good hands.'

'And I'm rehearsing all day tomorrow and for the next week. I think ... Claudia, I can't explain, but I need to be with Ruth when she gives birth. She was there for me when it really mattered. I ... we ... no one, except perhaps Morris, really understands her. They don't think about what she needs to see, what she isn't aware of. I can do that. I must do that. I'm going to look at plane times. I'll ring you back.'

An hour later Luke rang Claudia again. 'I've got a ticket for tomorrow night, I'll get into Heathrow about 12 am your time on Tuesday, that's the 11th. Claudia, will you do something for me? Tell Ruth I'm coming and tell them – the doctors – to wait, if possible, until I can be with her. I've probably got it all wrong and I'll miss the birth *and* get pasted at this end. They'll eat me alive when I tell them. But Claudia I must be there. I mean, what if something goes wrong? It does still happen doesn't it? Ruth – saved my life under that building. I have a feeling she will need me now.'

'All right, Topo. You must do what you think best. I think it'll be fine, but the blood pressure is a worry.'

'Ring me if anything changes?'

Jet-lagged and wondering if he had made the most colossal error in flying halfway across the world for an event that might not happen for another three weeks, Luke climbed out of the bus. In the foyer of the hospital he stood for a moment to get his bearings and met Morris heading towards the exit.

'That's fantastic timing, Luke. They put Ruth on a drip to start the labour about half an hour ago. I was just coming out of the hospital to give you a ring. You can't use mobiles in here.'

'How is she?'

'Fine, everyone seems calm. It'll take hours even now, apparently, unless they decide to do a Caesarean. You OK to take over?'

Luke, pausing only to phone Maria, made his way to the maternity ward. As he passed a patients' sitting room a crowd of nurses, doctors and women in dressing gowns stood around the wall-hung television. Like extras on a film set, they all had their hands to their open mouths in a parody of shock. A disaster movie was unrolling on the screen. Something about the watchers made Luke pause. Then he, too, lifted his hands to his open mouth as one of the twin towers he had been standing underneath forty-eight hours ago imploded and crumbled belching a great balloon of dust into the eye of the camera. People around him made strange whimpering noises. One man stood repeating endlessly, 'No, no, no, no, no, no, no ...'

Luke dragged himself away. His legs were shaking; his hands wet. When he reached the ward, he found Ruth surrounded by people in varied uniforms. In his present state of panic he assumed a problem had arisen. He shoved his way through, trying to compose his face, while his body ached with a sense of doom as it remembered his hours under a crumbled building. 'What's happening?'

'And you are?' asked a doctor, looking from him to Ruth.

'I'm Luke. I'm Ruth's partner.'

'Luke, is that really you?'

He reached out for Ruth's hand. 'Yes, I'm here now.' The doctor, unconvinced, moved as if to eject him. 'I'm the father.' Seeing faint surprise on the doctor's face he added, 'That was Ruth's cousin here earlier. I've just got back from America.'

The doctor nodded. 'Fine. You can stay.' He took another look at Luke's face. 'Though if you are planning to faint, I should warn you that we will leave you on the floor. Ruth is having the baby, not you.'

Luke grinned weakly and tried to concentrate. He could feel

the dust of the falling twin tower billowing out behind him. Surely he could taste it. The need to run, to get out of the building was almost irresistible. The doctor was speaking again.

'We've started Ruth on some dinoprostone, but as she appears to be in natural labour, we are using a minimal dose. She is over two centimetres dilated now, that is, she is in full labour. She's only two and a half weeks off full term and her blood pressure has stabilized and the baby's heartbeat – you can see it there on the screen – is fine, so we plan to let nature take its course from now on. Jennifer here will be your midwife, she will monitor Ruth's progress and call me ... Are you unwell?'

'No,' Luke sat down quickly. 'I'm a bit jet-lagged, that's all.' He shuddered and tried to concentrate on the dot pinging up and down on the screen at Ruth's feet. 'The heartbeat ... yes, I see it. Is that a good heartbeat? It's very fast.'

'Yes, it's just right for a baby. I should rest now, if I were you, this may take many hours.'

Someone appeared in the doorway and signalled to the three people by the bedside with a jerk of the head. They all left swiftly. They're going to hear about New York, thought Luke. No one will be left to help; we'll be having this baby alone.

Ruth's grip on his hand tightened. 'Luke? There's another pain coming.'

'I'm here. Start your breathing. I wish I'd gone to the lessons too.'

'I didn't know it would hurt like this.'

Luke looked round. 'The midwife will give you painkillers, but she's not here at the moment. Breathe sweetheart – in, out, in – that's it.'

Fifteen minutes later, the midwife appeared again. Luke caught her eye and knew that she knew, but she maintained a professional manner. 'How are you feeling Ruth? Have you been timing the pains, Luke?'

'I'm sorry, I didn't think about the timing. Ruth is finding the pains hard.'

'Are you doing your breathing, Ruth?'

'Yes, I'm trying. It doesn't stop it hurting though.'

'Good girl. I'll give you something for the pain soon, before it gets too bad. Ah here we go. Luke, note the time. Come on

Ruth, in – one, two, three, four, out – one two, three, four. Good girl! Keep it going. As the contraction eased she looked at her watch then tried to chat lightly as she waited for the next one. She flinched when Luke said that he had just returned from New York. They exchanged glances and Luke looking towards Ruth shook his head at the nurse. She nodded.

The next contraction followed after eleven minutes. When it had subsided, Luke said, 'Ruth, I'm going to get a coffee? I'll be back before it starts again.'

Ruth nodded but the midwife answered, 'OK but don't...well just don't do anything else. Ruth is progressing well and I need to check the delivery room in a moment. You'll need to wash and put a gown on if you are going to be there for the birth too.'

'Back in a minute, Ruth, hold tight.'

In the corridor, instead of heading for the coffee machine, Luke leant against the wall fighting giddiness. Unlike those grouped in horror round the television set, he had a genuine grasp of the scale of the disaster. He had stood, head tipped back, beneath one of the towers so recently that his muscles remembered the drag. His body recalled in painful flashback the dust, metal, glass and concrete of a pulverised building. Why today, why on his baby's birthday? He bent over and pressed his hands against his knees to stiffen them. Then he stood and walked towards the coffee machine. At least Ruth would never see what he had seen on that screen. He was free, alive and Ruth needed him. His about-to-be-born baby needed him. This oblivious infant had not chosen the day of its birth and should not suffer for its father's traumas. Grasping the hot paper cup and forcing his steps back to the ward, Luke tried to stretch his comprehension around this moment. In New York people were dying, deliberately killed by other people, yet here in this hospital – in homes and hospitals in every country on earth – millions of infants, untouched by hate or prejudice, were being born.

He let go of these vast concepts over which he had no control, to re-enter the tiny world where he could make a difference. Ruth lay enclosed in her bubble of pain and sightlessness and blessed ignorance. Resisting the desire to simply climb in there with her, he willed himself into his new role, his role for life. 'Ruth I'm here.'

'It hurts, Luke, I didn't know...It's coming again...'

'I'm here. Squeeze my arm, sweetheart.' He took a wet cloth from a stand and wiped the damp hair away from her face. 'Well done. Keep the breathing going until it's passed.'

She relaxed against him. 'I'm so glad you're here. Would it be wrong if you sang a little? Just quietly. Something ... something to make me stronger, braver.'

'You're being very brave already.' He and the midwife spoke together.

Luke bent and whispered, 'You're so brave you're giving me courage. Of course I'll sing if that will help.' He hummed a brief arpeggio then, with his mouth in her hair he began sotto voce: *'Celeste Aida, forma divina ... '*

Her chuckle broke through. 'Hardly ... ' He stopped to kiss her. ' ... no, no, go on.'

'Del mio pensiero tu sei regina, Tu di mia vita sei lo splendor (queen of my thoughts, light of my life).

As the labour progressed a stunned doctor appeared and stood briefly in the room. The midwife, to Luke's relief, ignored him and continued to issue encouragement and instruction to Ruth alone. There were several similar visitations; glances were exchanged, but no one spoke.

Four and a half hours later, his mind wiped clean of world disasters by the drama in his own life, Luke reached out to lift his new daughter off Ruth's chest.

'It's all right, I'm just holding her until they've tidied you up, then you'll get taken to the ward.'

The baby was loosely wrapped in a sheet of green cloth, which seemed to have no staying power on the damp, pinkish purple limbs. She opened her mouth and emitted a noise like a squeaky hinge, then shut it as he took a firmer hold.

'What does she look like Luke?'

'That's tricky. Everything looks about right to me, but you know, I thought I'd recognise her. I don't, she's a stranger, a new person. She doesn't look like Jake. Her skin is almost furry and a rather darkish red, but that's good apparently – all the blood flowing nicely. She hasn't really got a nose yet. Could we call her Heloise, do you think?'

'I wondered if we couldn't call her Maria, after your mother. She's been so kind. What colour are her eyes.'

'They're closed, but she has lashes. I don't remember babies having lashes.' He shifted his daughter towards the light. 'Wait a moment. They're opening now. She has ... well they're just very dark and bluish.' Luke laughed. 'She's looking at me as if I were a mathematical equation or something the cat brought in. She has a miniature frown. You wouldn't think anything this small could frown. She is being wrapped up now in a blanket. Here you are Ruth. I need to go and sign something. Don't worry, I'm not going anywhere.'

He laid the baby against Ruth's breast, placing one hand carefully on the fragile head.

A nurse stood with pen poised above some forms. 'Do you have a name?'

'Maria Heloise.'

'Maria Heloise Gardiner?'

'Danford.'

The nurse, breathing heavily, murmured as she wrote. 'Maria Heloise Gardiner Danford, six thirty pm, September the eleventh, two thousand and one, Apgar 10. She wrote out a label and attached it to the baby's ankle.

Luke returned to sit on the edge of the delivery bed, one arm round Ruth's shoulders, the other resting on the softly pulsing body of his daughter. In a minute they would take Ruth to the ward and he would ring Mum and Morris and Dave with the *good* news for today. In a minute. The world and its disasters lay outside this door. Tomorrow he would move his life into Ruth's house, then think about returning to the nightmare of New York and singing there. Today belonged to Ruth and Maria Heloise. The post office explosion? He shook his head in amazement, a speck on yesterday's horizon – history. For baby Maria, growing up, the unimaginable would happen; today would also condense into history.